Three Junes

Three Junes

JULIA GLASS

PANTHEON BOOKS, NEW YORK

All rights reserved under International and Pan-American Copyright Conventions. Published in the United States by Pantheon Books, a division of Random House, Inc., New York, and simultaneously in Canada by Random House of Canada Limited, Toronto.

Pantheon Books and colophon are registered trademarks of Random House, Inc.

Grateful acknowledgment is made to Michael Goldsen, Inc. for permission to reprint song lyrics from "If I Had a Boat" by Lyle Lovett. Copyright © 1987 by Michael Goldsen, Inc./Lyle Lovett (ASCAP). All rights reserved. International copyright secured. Reprinted by permission of Michael Goldsen, Inc.

Library of Congress Cataloging-in-Publication Data

Glass, Julia, 1956–
Three Junes / Julia Glass.
ISBN 0-375-42144-0
1. Scots—United States—Fiction.   2. Long Island (N.Y.)—Fiction.   3. Fathers and sons—Fiction.   4. Scotland—Fiction.   5. Gay men—Fiction.   I. Title.

PS3607.L37 T48 2002   813'.6—dc21   2001055448

www.pantheonbooks.com

Printed in the United States of America
First Edition
2 4 6 8 9 7 5 3 1

For
Alec and Oliver,
my extraordinary sons

Assuming that our energies are sufficient,
love is interminable.

—JIM HARRISON, *The Road Home*

Collies

1989

ONE

PAUL CHOSE GREECE for its predictable whiteness: the blanching heat by day, the rush of stars at night, the glint of the lime-washed houses crowding its coast. Blinding, searing, somnolent, fossilized Greece.

Joining a tour—that was the gamble, because Paul is not a gregarious sort. He dreads fund-raisers and drinks parties, all occasions at which he must give an account of himself to people he will never see again. Yet there are advantages to the company of strangers. You can tell them whatever you please: no lies perhaps, but no affecting truths. Paul does not fabricate well (though once, foolishly, he believed that he could), and the single truth he's offered these random companions—that recently he lost his wife—brought down a flurry of theatrical condolence. (A hand on his at the breakfast table in Athens, the very first day: "Time, time, and more time. Let Monsignor Time do his tedious, devious work." Marjorie, a breathy schoolmistress from Devon.)

Not counting Jack, they are ten. Paul is one of three men; the other two, Ray and Solly, are appended to wives. And then, besides Marjorie, there are two pairs of women traveling together, in their seventies at least: a surprisingly spry quartet who carry oversize binoculars with which they ogle everything and everyone, at appallingly close range. Seeing the sights, they wear identical, brand-new hiking boots; to the group's communal dinners, cork-soled sandals with white crocheted tops. Paul thinks of them as the quadruplets.

In the beginning, there was an all-around well-mannered effort to mingle, but then, sure as sedimentation, the two married couples fell together and the quadruplets reverted more or less to themselves. Only Marjorie, trained by profession to dole out affection equally, continues to treat everyone like a new friend, and with her as their muse, the women coddle Paul like an infant. His room always has the best view, his seat on the boat is always in shade; the women always insist. The

3

husbands treat him as though he were vaguely leprous. Jack finds the whole thing amusing: "Delightful, watching you cringe." Jack is their guide: young and irreverent, thank God. Reverence would send Paul over the edge.

Even this far from home there are reminders, like camera flashes or shooting pains. On the streets, in the plazas, on the open-decked ferries, he is constantly sighting Maureen: any tall lively blonde, any sun-struck girl with a touch of the brazen. German or Swedish or Dutch, there she is, again and again. Today she happens to be an American, one of two girls at a nearby table. Jack has noticed them too, Paul can tell, though both men pretend to read their shared paper—day before yesterday's *Times*. By no means beautiful, this girl, but she has a garish spirit, a laugh she makes no effort to stifle. She wears an eccentrically wide-brimmed hat, tied under her chin with a feathery scarf. ("Miss Forties Nostalgic," Maureen would have pegged her. "These gals think they missed some grand swinging party.") Little good the hat seems to have done her, though: she is sunburnt geranium pink, her arms crazed with freckles. The second girl is the beauty, with perfect pale skin and thick cocoa-colored hair; Jack will have an eye on that one.

The girls talk too loudly, but Paul enjoys listening. In their mid-twenties, he guesses, ten years younger than his sons. "Heaven. I am telling you exquisite," says the dark-haired girl in a husky, all-knowing voice. "A sensual sort of *coup de foudre*."

"You go up on donkeys? Where?" the blonde answers eagerly.

"This dishy farmer rents them. He looks like Giancarlo Giannini. Those soulful sad-dog eyes alone are worth the price of admission. He rides alongside and whacks them with a stick when they get ornery."

"Whacks them?"

"Oh just prods them a little, for God's sake. Nothing inhumane. Listen—I'm sure the ones that hump olives all day really get whacked. By donkey standards, these guys live like royalty." She rattles through a large canvas satchel and pulls out a map, which she opens across the table. The girls lean together.

"Valley of the Butterflies!" The blonde points.

Jack snorts quietly from behind his section of the *Times*. "Don't tell the dears, but it's moths."

Paul folds his section and lays it on the table. He is the owner and publisher of the *Yeoman,* the Dumfries-Galloway paper. When he left, he promised to call in every other day. He has called once in ten and felt grateful not to be needed. Paging through the news from afar, he finds himself tired of it all. Tired of Maggie Thatcher, her hedgehog eyes, her vacuous hair, her cotton-mouthed edicts on jobs, on taxes, on terrorist acts. Tired of bickering over the Chunnel, over untapped oil off the Isle of Mull. Tired of rainy foggy pewtered skies. Here, too, there are clouds, but they are inconsequential, each one benign as a bridal veil. And wind, but the wind is warm, making a cheerful fuss of the awning over the tables, carrying loose napkins like birds to the edge of the harbor, slapping waves hard against the hulls of fishing boats.

Paul closes his eyes and sips his ice coffee, a new pleasure. He hasn't caught the name for it yet; Jack, who is fluent, orders it for him. Greek is elusive, maddening. In ten days, Paul can say three words. He can say yes, the thoroughly counterintuitive *neh.* He can wish passersby in the evening—as everyone here does him—*kalespera.* And he can stumble over "if you please," something like *paricolo* (ought to be a musical term, he decides, meaning "joyfully, but with caution"). Greek seems to Paul, more than French or Italian, the language of love: watery, reflective, steeped in thespian whispers. A language of words without barbs, without corners.

When he opens his eyes, he is shocked to see her staring at him. She smiles at his alarm. "You don't mind, I hope."

"Mind?" He blushes, but then sees that she is holding a pencil in one hand and, with the other, bracing a large book on the edge of her table. Her beautiful companion is gone.

Paul straightens his spine, aware how crumpled and slouched he must look.

"Oh no. Down the way you were. Please."

"Sorry. How was I?" Paul laughs. "A little more like this?" He sinks in the chair and crosses his arms.

"That's it." She resumes her drawing. "You're Scottish, am I right?"

"Well thank God she hasn't mistook us for a pair of Huns," says Jack.

"Not you. You're English. But you," she says to Paul. "I can tell, the way you said *little,* the particular way your *t*'s disappeared. I'm wild about Scotland. Last year I went to the festival. I biked around one of the lochs. . . . Also, I shouldn't say this, you'll think I'm so typically rudely American, but you look, you know, like you marched right out of that Dewars ad. The one, you know, with the collies?"

"Collies?" Paul sits up again.

"Oh, sorry—Madison Avenue nonsense. They show this shepherd, I mean a modern one, very tweedy, rugged, kind of motley but dashing, on the moors with his Border collies. Probably a studio setup out in L.A. But I like to think it's real. The shepherd. The heather. The red phone booth—call box, right? . . . *Inverness*." She draws the name out like a tail of mist, evoking a Brigadoon sort of Scotland. "I'd love to have one of those collies, I've heard they're the smartest dogs."

"Would you?" says Paul, but leaves it at that. Not long ago he would have said, My wife raises collies—national champions, shipped clear to New Zealand. And yes, they are the smartest. The most cunning, the most watchful.

"Hello *here* you are, you truants you." Marjorie, who's marched up behind Jack, bats his arm with her guidebook. "We're off to maraud some poor unsuspecting shopkeepers. Lunch, say, at half past one, convene in the hotel lobby?" Paul waves to the others, who wait beyond the café awning. They look like a lost platoon in their knife-pleated khakis and sensible hats, bent over maps, gazing and pointing in all directions.

"Tally ho, Marj!" says Jack. "Half one in the hotel lobby. Half two, a little siesta; half three, a little . . . adventure. Pass muster with you?"

"Right-oh," she says, saluting. She winks, accepting his tease.

This has become their routine: The first full day of each new place, Marjorie directs an expedition for souvenirs—as if to gather up the memories before the experience. While the others trail happily behind her, Jack and Paul read in a taverna, hike the streets, or wander through nondescript local ruins and talk about bland things, picking up odd stones to examine and discard. Paul buys no souvenirs. He should send cards to the boys—he did when they were in fact boys—but the kinds of messages adults send one another on postcards remind him precisely of the chatter he dislikes so much at drinks parties or sitting on a plane beside yet another, more alarming breed of strangers: those from whom you have no escape but the loo.

There's one on every tour, Jack says of Marjorie: a den mother, someone who likes to do his job for him. And Marj is a good sport, he says, not a bad traveler. He likes her. But she exasperates Paul. She is a heroine out of a Barbara Pym novel: bookish, dependable, magnanimously stubborn, and no doubt beneath it all profoundly disappointed. At an age when she might do well to tint her hair, she's taken up pride in her plainness as if it were a charitable cause. She dresses and walks like a soldier, keeps her hair cropped blunt at the earlobes. She proclaims herself a romantic but seems desperately earthbound, a stickler for schedules. Jack tells her again and again how un-Greek this attitude is, but she is not a when-in-Rome type of tourist. ("Right then: three on the dot at the Oracle, tea time!" Marjorie, sizing up Delphi.)

She turns now and waves to her regiment, strutting through the maze of tables. Jack smiles fondly. "O gird up thy loins, ye salesmen of Minotaur tea towels!" The American girl laughs loudly, a laugh of unblemished joy.

WHEN THE WAR ENDED, when Paul shipped back to Dumfries from Verona, he found out, along with his mates, that half the girls they'd known in school had promised themselves to Americans—even, God forbid, to Canadians. Many were already married, awaiting their journey across the Atlantic with the restless thrill of birds preparing to migrate. Among them were some of the prettiest, cleverest, most accomplished and winning of the girls Paul remembered.

Maureen might have been one of those brides, if she'd chosen to be. But Maureen, pretty, outspoken, intrepid, knew what she wanted. She did not intend to wager away her future. "Those gals haven't a clue what they're in for, no sir. The man may be a prince, sure, but what's he hauling you home to? You haven't a clue, not a blistering clue." She said this to Paul when she hardly knew him. Paul admired her frankness—that and her curly pinkish blond hair, her muscular arms, her Adriatic eyes.

When Paul came back, he was depressed. Not because he missed the war; what idiot would? Not because he lacked direction, some sort of career; how thoroughly *that* was mapped out. Not even because he longed for a girl; for someone like Paul, there were plenty of prospects. He was sad because the war had not made him into what he had hoped it would—worse, he came to realize, what so many similar fools hoped it would. He supposed he could assume it had made him a man, whatever that meant, but it had not given him the dark, pitiless eye of an artist. All that posturing courage (all that aiming, killing, closing your eyes and haplessly pretending to kill but rarely knowing if you had); the simultaneous endurance and fear of death—the dying itself heard in keening rifts between gunfire or in continuous horrific pleadings— all those dire things, Paul had thought when he shipped out, might plant in him the indelible passion of a survivor, a taut inner coil like the workings of an heirloom watch. He had told this rubbish to no one and was grateful to himself for that much. Of the virtues his father preached, discretion began to seem the most rewarding: it kept people guessing and sometimes, by default, admiring.

Mornings he spent at the paper: proofing galleys, answering telephones, cataloguing local events. He learned the ropes as his father expected. But after a late lunch at the Globe, often alone, he might wander into the bar, lose all sense of time and obligation. At night he sat in a neglected room of his parents' large cold house and tried to write short stories. Paul was a good reporter—later he would win awards—but everything he tried to conjure from his heart sounded mealy and frail when he took it out to read in the morning.

The first year after the war was a time of modest anticipation. There was immense relief, drunken cheer, a stalwart sense of vindication. But the people he knew were careful not to voice grand expectations. When Paul stood back to consider the girls he courted, their dreams seemed to him self-consciously stunted; to be fair, so was his enthusiasm for courtship.

Maureen was not one of the girls from school. She worked at the Globe, sometimes as cook or barkeep, sometimes as a maid for the upstairs rooms. Always variety, she said. Always good company. Maureen flowered in the company of men. On nights she took the bar, she'd smoke, pour tall whiskeys, and hold her own on politics and farming. She told Paul without hesitation exactly what she thought of his father's editorial opinions. ("Ah, the specially elegant ignorance of gentlemen!" she crooned—a remark that made him smile for days.)

One winter night after dinner, when his sisters had a dance show turned up so loud that it made his work more discouraging than usual,

Paul took his father's Humber and aimlessly cruised the town, stopping at last in the High Street.

The night crowd at the Globe was rural, more working-class than the customers at lunch. Feeling sorry for himself, despising his unshakable sense of superiority, Paul drank too much and argued too sharply. He knew now that it was just a matter of time before he'd give it up: "the fiction of the fiction," he'd come to call it. At closing time he was the last man in the bar. He had no desire to face the cold, to be hit by the disappointment of no one's company but his own. He watched Maureen wipe the snifters, lock the till, polish the bar to a glassy sheen.

"Collided with the ghost," she said abruptly. "I finally did."

Paul laughed. "You don't believe that rot."

Maureen looked at him with cold sincerity. "Sure I do." She'd been sweeping the stairs, she told him, when she stepped into a sharp chill on the landing. "Like falling through the ice. Ten degrees' drop, I'd swear. And Marcus, y'know, he always balks at following me up those stairs." Marcus was her dog, an arthritic old black and white collie.

Paul ran through all the rational explanations: obscure drafts, trapped pockets of air . . . a wild imagination. Maureen shook her head at each one.

"Poor gal," she said. "I'da steered cleara *that* man, no mystery there." The ghost, said believers, was the roaming soul of a susceptible lass seduced by Bobbie Burns, who broke as many hearts as he wrote poems. The Globe had been his lair, and his upstairs rooms were hallowed, their unremarkable knickknacks like relics in a chapel. How predictable, Paul had always thought, that someone would invent a ghost. Another cheap lure for tourists. Maybe he'd write an article on the ghost and its role in commerce.

"Well then, Miss, I wouldn't want to see you spooked. Shall I run you home?"

"If you don't mind Marcus along." She put on her coat without waiting for Paul's assistance and went behind the bar again. Looking in the mirror behind the bottles of whiskey, she ran her fingers quickly through her hair and smoothed it back over her collar. Then she pulled a lipstick from her pocket and, so deftly he hardly saw her do it, colored her lips. When she turned around, her mouth was a deep, startling red.

While she helped the dog onto the front seat of the car, between them, Paul warmed up the motor. It was a harsh, snowless night, and the streets were empty. "Pity," said Maureen. "No one'll half believe I was on the town with Mr. Paul McLeod. Pardon me; *Lieutenant* McLeod, town hero, resident intellect. Lieutenant McLeod the *eligible*." By enunciating the word, she let him know that she knew she was not in the running.

In front of the house Maureen shared with her mother, Paul turned off the motor and listened to her gossip, never meanly but with relish. He was surprised at how much he enjoyed listening. The car was warm now, and the windows had shed their crystalline frost. Softened by heat, the leather of the seat felt luxurious, as if the two of them sat in a dim after-hours club. The old dog slept happily between them, like a child.

They came to talk about war brides when Maureen mentioned how a girl she'd been friends with forever had gone off to a place called Quaqtaq. She removed a glove and, in careful block letters, spelled out the name in the condensation of her breath on the windscreen. The girl had since written Maureen to tell her what a shock it had been to arrive there. "A name like that, some garbled croak of a place you can't even pronounce, what would you expect? Every whichway, she says, the land is what's called 'tundra.'" Maureen shivered for emphasis. "Snow and blinking ice from September to May. All the creatures white. White bears, white rabbits, white foxes, white owls, white everything you could dream of. As if it was all scared bloodless. Half the year, your eyes just pine for green." She laughed at her pun. "Well no thank you sir, that would've been my RSVP to that invitation."

Paul watched Maureen extinguish her cigarette on the sole of a shoe and tuck the end into the cuff of a coatsleeve. She was looking out the windscreen when she said, "I for one would never want a military man—the kind, I mean, who lives for that life. Not if he was the Second Coming incarnate."

"A fierce opinion," said Paul.

"I'm twenty-six. An old maid, Mum drones on. A cloudy marble. Too set in my ways, she says—that dirge." She laughed, a sharp summery laugh.

"And what would you trade it for, this independence you so clearly prize?" Paul was twenty-five. He was likely, in a year or so, to marry one of two girls he knew, both daughters of friends of his father, both lovely and suspiciously compliant.

Maureen laughed again and leaned into her seat. She accepted another cigarette from Paul and let him light it. She stroked her dog, her affection absentminded—second nature, guessed Paul. "Leave aside the deserving man? For a big old house in the country. I'd trade for that. For a brood of sons, that too." She paused. "Five—four would do, four sons. Daughters turn against you faster, that's what I hear. Boys adore their mothers. . . . And, you'll laugh, but collies. Not the sheep—or maybe a few, for training the dogs—but just the collies, for themselves. I'd have a kennel, a dozen at least. Grandfather had them on his farm, out by Hawick. Marcus here's the end of that line. I remember watching those dogs work the herd, back and forth, back and forth, like shuttles on a loom. . . ." Her hands darted to and fro, the cigarette glow a snake in the dark. "But to raise 'em purely for trials, for the competition alone, that takes money."

"Collies," he said, to fill the silence. The word sounded as foreign as the name of the Canadian outpost now melting away on the windscreen.

"Well, first ghosts, now collies. Daft, what? My wild imagination again," said Maureen. "Better commit me, Lieutenant." She squeezed his arm quickly, opened the door, and dropped her cigarette in the gutter. After stepping out, she leaned down to thank him. Patient and coaxing, she wrapped her long arms around Marcus and eased him down onto his feet.

"RALLY UP, CREW. Refreshments around the bend," calls Jack, dismounting from his donkey. He beckons energetically to the stragglers. They have reached the grove after a hot, wracking ride up the mountainside, and even Marjorie, coming in close behind Paul, looks beaten. "You're a wicked, wicked man," she says to Jack when she is on her feet. Her white blouse is dusty, with drooping oval stains beneath her arms.

"Said you were a horsewoman, Marj."

"I believe that means I ride *horses,* young man."

Jack laughs and puts an arm around her. "No pain, no terrain." He helps Irene off her saddle, then Jocelyn. Their husbands, Ray and Solly, are halfway to the rest hut. The quadruplets stayed behind to loll about at the beach. "No beer!" Jack shouts after the men. "I want no casualties on the way down!" Paul waits while Jack tethers the donkeys. The grove is smaller than he expected, a cluster of cowering, wind-battered trees. A sad, dessicated little place, hardly worth the climb. Except for two other donkeys drowsing nearby, there is no sign that anyone else has made this ridiculous trek.

"Don't look now," says Jack, "but it's the Andrews Sisters."

Paul follows his glance, past the table where their group is seated. He sees her hat first, that extravagant hat. The friend, who leads her toward the entrance to the grove, gesticulates wildly. He can just hear the lilt of her voice. "Extraordinary kimonos!" he hears, ". . . inconsolable weeping!"

"Not much of a 'valley,'" says Paul.

"No, but wait, bucko." Jack takes a bottle of water from his shoulder bag. He drinks half, then hands it to Paul, who drinks the rest.

Paul follows the flagstone path to the grove, overtaking his companions. As he steps through the gate, he feels instantly cooled. Here is the first small breeze, the first shade in hours: an acute and unexpected pleasure. Where the trees begin, the ground dips down—a modest crater more than a valley—and the brownish leaves make a rattling noise, like wind in a field of maize. He follows a dirt path, turns a corner, and gasps. The rattling comes from a stick with which a short man is beating the branches. Abruptly, the air fills with a scarlet haze, like a cyclone of vermilion confetti, the rain of petals tossed at the end of a wedding.

He thinks of the jungle and its sudden surprises. Years ago, in Guatemala, he stood with his son and a group of journalists, admiring a ruined temple, when someone laughed or raised his voice. Out of nowhere, all around them rose a funnel of color—red, orange, turquoise, violet—a startled swarm of parrots.

Through the red blur, there are flashes of the one girl's hat, the other girl's shirt, the man's arm as he thrashes the trees. Infinitesimal wings touch Paul's face, the air is alive, but the only sound in all this commotion is the rattling stick. He would have expected noise, the applause of birds rising in flight, but the moths are stone silent. Their color is noise enough. And then, gradually, they settle back onto the branches and vanish. Closed up, like twigs or buds, they are invisible. Again, the place is parched and brown, nowhere special. The short man stands close to Paul, probably hoping he'll pay for another go-round. At the opposite edge of the clearing, both girls are still immersed in their ecstasy, eyes half closed, faces lifted solemnly, glowing.

———

HE WAITED, and Maureen agreed it was only proper, until his father had died. His sisters, both married and settled in Edinburgh, were unhappy—and shocked, they told Paul, at how callously he could dispose of their legacy—but neither was in a position to stake any claim. Their mother, her reticent self, took no one's side. Within two months the family house was sold, furniture divided, and Paul had found a place for his own family out in the country, half an hour from town. The house was called Tealing. It was skirted on one side by a burn and an overgrown meadow; on the other by a tall hedgerow, shielding another large house, the only one within sight of theirs—occupied, the agent said, by a widow who looked after herself.

Fenno was eight, and the twins, Dennis and David, were six. The three of them roared and clattered through the wide halls and across the lawn playing bomber planes or Panzer tanks—denting banisters, felling chairs, maiming shrubs. They couldn't wait till they were old enough to fight in a war, like Daddy, to have real-life enemies to vanquish.

Maureen hired a part-time nanny to stay with the boys while she trekked off to Aberdeen, Oban, Peebles—wherever there were sheepdog trials to watch or farmers to meet. Within a year, she bought four bitches, three dogs, and half a dozen ewes. Paul hired a joiner to build the kennel on the lawn out back, behind it a shed for the sheep.

The paper was thriving, so Paul, too, traveled a good deal. He gave lectures at universities, awards to authors, advice to younger editors. The hectic separations and reunions were often renewing for the family, romantic for Paul and Maureen. He was generous with the boys, patient with their wildness. He loved the rare evening together at home, a birch fire in the timber-striped parlor: Paul going over the ledgers, Maureen telling stories to the twins while she brushed out one of the dogs, Fenno assembling a model ship or spreading his arms and careening in circles, quietly strafing the carpet.

Sunday mornings Paul rose early, before church, and took a long walk. Spread out behind them lay woods and fields, partitioned by mossy stone walls. In some of the fields sheep and cattle grazed, but most were vacant, tall with timothy waiting to be hayed.

Along one wall, a dirt path led away from their lawn. Half a mile out it diverged, the left way leading to a farm, the right way to Conkers, the manor house adjoining the farm. Beyond the fork, other trails and tractor lanes crisscrossed the land, and often Paul saw the prints of horseshoes. In autumn and spring, the foxhunt came through. Some Saturdays, from the house, Paul heard the huntsman's horn in the distance, its monotonous bittersweet warbling; in November, through the leafless trees, he'd glimpse splinters of red as the riders sped past in their vivid coats. If the hounds were on a fresh line, giving tongue, Maureen's collies would gather against the fence of their kennel and yowl with longing.

The only trouble came from their neighbor. Mrs. Ramage spent a great deal of time maintaining a colorful, highly regimented garden, and as she worked, she would peer through the hedgerow. The Lurker, Maureen called her, amused at the outset. But not six months after they arrived, Mrs. Ramage voiced her dismay as to how they'd destroyed their flowerbeds. Maureen kept up the roses in front, the lupines by the kitchen, but to make room for the kennel she had flattened two plots of peonies, lilies, and hardy, deep-rooted lilacs. The rest of the beds had seeded over with mustard and loosestrife. When Mrs. Ramage pointed a garden glove at the lush purple flowers and told Maureen how their roots would slowly suck all moisture away from the rest of her lawn, killing off the flora one species after another, Maureen answered, "Actually, I've always thought them rather gorgeous," and walked around the house, out of sight.

Nor did Mrs. Ramage approve of the way they were raising their boys. Every so often, she would lean through a break in the hedgerow and ask if the children could please calm their racket. Her own children were grown and gone, so Paul chose to see her meddling as a kind of nostalgic envy. He indulged her with confessions that yes indeed, these lads were spoiled something fearful and there'd be hell to pay down the road if he and Mrs. McLeod didn't crack the whip a bit more. It was Paul who apologized, herded the boys indoors and hushed them. Maureen could barely contain her rage. After enduring months of complaints, she refused any longer to acknowledge their neighbor with the slightest nod. Following Paul into the house, she would storm, "'Seen and not heard, seen and not heard'! If I hear that fascist platitude cross her lips one more time, no one'll see or hear a thing more from *her!*"

But if Maureen went easy on the boys, she was strict with her dogs. The pups were whelped in the scullery off the kitchen and slept in the house, with their mother, for the first two months. Every day, Maureen took them outside for supervised play. She let the boys fool with them, chase them, roll them over, tickle their spotted pink bellies. But then the pups were sent away to nearby farms for another few months. When they returned, they lived in the kennel and training began. They became obedient yet willful, commanding yet stealthy. Their attention to Maureen, her voice, her hands, was unwavering and intense; Paul wondered sometimes if this was a standard against which his own attention might be secretly held—and found wanting.

She never struck a dog, but her voice when she was displeased became deep and rough, a tone that Paul had never heard in any other context. "I'm a wolf. Ruthless. Unyielding," she told him. "That's what they learn." From his library, upstairs, he could see her on the lawn, putting them through drills, often out there till twilight. Without seeing her face, he might hear her scold a disobedient dog. He would see the dog, even from that distance, looking at her in apparent fear, crouching low to the grass. She commanded this fear through words and gestures alone.

One Sunday they were out on the lawn: Paul resting on a chaise, Maureen hosing down the pens, and the boys playing quietly for a change, each on his own. Betsey, Maureen's favorite bitch, hunted insects among the wildflowers. David had a new toy, a red ball, which caught Betsey's eye. He threw it to her and shouted rudely, "Fetch!" But Betsey carried it off, and when David followed and tried to take back his ball, she growled. In an instant, Maureen had lifted the dog off her feet by the loose skin on her chest. She shook Betsey so hard she yelped. "Do that again, anything like it, and I will have you shot." Maureen spoke, literally, in a growl. This time, lying nearby, Paul saw her face up close. Her eyes were so wide she looked crazed. After she let the dog go, her hands shook. Betsey looked up at Maureen with the most bereaved expression Paul had ever seen in a dog. "That's a promise," Maureen told her, quietly but unrelenting.

That was their second summer at Tealing. A year later, Paul took a call at his office from one of the county aldermen. Mrs. Ramage had filed a complaint. The alderman was delicate, apologetic, but there was no getting around it. The sheep smelled, Mrs. Ramage claimed, and the dogs barked up a row. The kennel, visible from her bedroom, was a "blemish upon the landscape." Paul was glad she had not come directly to them. For all her insolence, Mrs. Ramage was afraid of Maureen, perhaps with some justification. Paul told the alderman that he would not challenge the complaint but asked for two months' grace. He had a compromise in mind.

He was thinking of the long meadow on the opposite side of their property, the one beyond the burn. It belonged to Colin Swift, the man who had recently bought Conkers and the adjoining farm. A sea of weeds, the field lay unused, since its back half tended to flood in the spring when the burn spilled over its banks.

"SHE WAS TELLING ME," says Fern, "about a production of *Madame Butterfly*—she saw it at the Met. Amazing set decoration, she was telling me, with a full-grown actual live tree onstage, light through the branches, purple kimonos with gold butterfly medallions, hung like ghosts on the walls of the house. The butterflies up there made her think of it. . . . I've never been to the opera. I used to think it was silly, I never thought I'd change my mind, but . . . you get older, you know? See things differently? Anna, though: Anna was *born* a woman of the world." She smiles at her friend, who's talking to Jack.

Fern is prettier without the hat. Her wet hair is contained in a flat coil against her skull. She has a long studious face, a small chin. She tells Paul she's a painter traveling on a fellowship. She finished university a year before and has been in Europe since then—mostly in Paris, where she rents a small flat. Anna, a college friend, is living on Paros all summer, working on a dig.

At a nearby table sit Irene and Ray. They glance over now and then, their suspicions undisguised. Well fine, thinks Paul, let me take a nose-dive from the widower's pedestal. He has drunk too much retsina already; the heat in his skin and the ache in his legs from that torture rack of a saddle have given him a vicious thirst. And he drinks out of restlessness. In the grove, after small talk, introductions—what had possessed him?—he invited the girls to join their group for a drink before dinner. But dinner is not until nine, an hour away, and most of the others won't show up till then. For now, the low sun seems to linger indefinitely, a party guest reluctant to leave.

"Absurd the things people say. I mean, people think we don't have a single *tree* in the entire city, for God's sake, that you have to carry an *Uzi* to feel safe, that sadistic black boys roam the streets in search of white *prey*. Look, you could be raped and murdered in . . . well certainly London, but anywhere. Dangers lurk *everywhere*." Anna is from Manhattan and seems to see the rest of the world as woefully benighted. She is defending the city's virtues to Jack, who nods and smiles, unusually quiet. Aggressive and passionate by turns, the girls have talked for nearly an hour. Once, Jack turned briefly to Paul and cocked an eyebrow. Mockery; desire; conspiracy: it could have meant just about anything.

"Yes, Anna, but you can't tell me honestly you wouldn't really rather live somewhere like . . ." Fern smiles at Paul. "Scotland. In the long run, I mean."

"Oh, no offense to Paul here, but never," Anna says. "Too homogeneous." She draws out the middle syllables, as if the word itself contains a genie. Paul has heard his son Fenno refer to this woman or that as a "drama queen," and now he's sure he knows exactly what it means. Fenno, like Anna, lives in Manhattan, but Paul decides against mentioning this. To do so would hand the conversation entirely to Anna— and place Fenno's vital statistics under her dissecting eye. Paul's oldest son, who has ventured the farthest from home, is the most independent and ought to worry Paul the least, but the distance in itself has always been a source of worry—as if, were something to go wrong, Fenno couldn't be reeled in fast enough. And the twins, Paul can't help feeling, will always have each other to lean on, collapse against, push each other upright if it comes to that.

Fern sighs and turns her chair slightly aside, facing the sea. She closes her eyes and tilts her face upward, the same yearning, pious expression Paul saw in the grove after the butterflies—the moths. He continues to drink his retsina but tries to step outside its field of distortion. What could he want from her? She likes him, but she isn't flirting. He watches Jack, the way Jack looks at Anna as she talks on and on.

Fern says suddenly, "Pink sky at night, sailors delight."

Anna pauses, and Jack turns slowly toward Fern. "So then, must be a bloody lot of delighted sailors out there tonight, would you say?"

"All right, all right," says Fern, laughing self-consciously. "It's something silly my mother recites whenever she sees a beautiful sunset. It just popped out."

"'Just popped out!'" Jack warbles in falsetto, batting his eyes at the sun. "Ah, like a wanton champagne cork." Fern continues to laugh, but Paul feels as if he is looking at Jack through the backside of a telescope. For that moment, he does not like the young man's wit, its facile malice.

At nine (promptly, since Marjorie's in the lead), the rest of the group arrives, and there is a complicated move to a larger, more sheltered table.

Anna takes Fern by the elbow. "Well, boys, we have crispier fish to fry."

"So . . . well," says Fern. When she stands, she is clearly dizzy and leans for a moment on her friend. Paul murmurs a polite good-bye. For the third time in a day, he tries to memorize her features, sure it's the last he will see of this awkward, inexplicably appealing girl.

In the hotel bar after dinner, after the others have gone upstairs, Jack puts on an American drawl and impersonates the two girls. "'Why these donkeys lead the life o' Riley! Why, compared with the steeds of the New York mounted bobbies—no picnic that, keeping all those bumpkin tourists in line!'" He unfolds a napkin, drapes it on his head, and raises his voice an octave. "'Oh but if the poor things lived in heavenly Scott-land . . .'" He drops the napkin and his voice. "'Land of warm beer, boiled sheep guts, and men showing off their ugly knees, you mean!'"

Paul laughs, too drunk to feel guilty. Jack leans toward him and says, "So which one, Paulie, which one would you have? Just supposing."

"Me?" Paul is so stiff that he longs to lie down then and there, on the grimy tiled floor. "I'm too decrepit for shenanigans of that sort."

"Oh rot. Bull, as those Americans would say. Look at you."

Paul looks down at himself, as if he will make an invigorating discovery. He pretends that pondering the choice is an effort. "The blonde, I suppose. I like her wild hat. Her pink skin."

"Her wild *hat*. Her *pink skin*. Oh Paulie." Jack laughs hard, leaning on the bar, shaking his head. "Bucko, that hat would be the first thing to go." He picks up the napkin he wore as the hat and lets it drift to the floor.

MAUREEN BECAME SICK—or her sickness chose to show itself—almost a year ago, in the summer. Despite her jesting about the surgery ("Just a long-overdue rearrangement of my soul!"), her sons all came home: Fenno from New York, Dennis from Paris, David from two counties north. Fenno's homecoming was the most momentous, because he had traveled the greatest distance and came home least often, but it was marred for Paul by Fenno's unexpected traveling companion, a young American named Mal.

Mal was a perfectly easy, considerate houseguest, but his flawless courtesy seemed like a screen. Sometimes when Mal and Fenno were upstairs in the room they shared, Paul could hear waves of sardonic laughter. Clearly Mal, yet he never laughed that way in Paul's presence.

Handsome but frail, Mal looked as if someone had carefully slipped the muscles and tendons out of his arms and legs, like stays from a dress, leaving him only brittle bones and sallow, translucent flesh. Perhaps he wasn't ill, Paul argued with himself—or wasn't ill with what it seemed the obvious and hence shameful conclusion to draw. Perhaps he was simply one of those ascetic young people who, having never been shortchanged on sustenance, used self-deprivation as a means of expressing scorn at what they saw as their parents' myopic pleasures. Every time he heard Mal's name, Paul could not help thinking of its French significance. Mal wore cologne, a grassy scent that was strongest in the mornings. *Les fleurs du mal,* thought Paul the first time he smelled it. His fears left him helplessly petty.

When Paul was finally alone with Fenno, the third day of the visit, he asked if the boy's name was Malcolm (perhaps Paul could address him that way).

"Malachy. But God, no one ever calls him that." They had taken the collies out for a run in the field across the burn. It was Maureen's first overnight in hospital. Mal was taking a nap. "You don't like him, do you," said Fenno. "You're so uptight."

Paul sighed. "Do you want me not to like him? I've spent the sum of a few hours in his company. And if I'm 'up tight,' it's probably because your mother's having her chest sliced open first thing tomorrow." Fenno's proliferating Americanisms depressed Paul, as if they were proof that he had chosen, literally, new patronage. (Of Paul's three sons,

the oldest was, ironically, the one who made him feel the most outmoded.)

"You're free to like him or not, Dad."

The collies ran helter skelter in widening, playful circles, but they
never barked. Paul did not worry that they might bolt. They wouldn't
leave the circle of Maureen's influence, even if she was not physically
present.

Fenno approached his father and put a hand on his back. Paul welcomed the physical warmth of the gesture and wondered if it was
meant to be consoling or conciliatory. "Mal is a good friend," said
Fenno. "So could you just be less of a Brit and act like you care about
knowing him, just a little? Do more than give him tours of the manor
and speeches on why we Scots are anything but English?" Fenno
laughed and pulled his hand away, reaching down to stroke one of the
dogs. "Do you know one of the first things I loved about New York?
People don't waste any time telling you what they aren't. Nobody has
that strict an identity, never mind nonidentity."

"I've given speeches? What speeches?" Paul said.

"Dad, you know what I mean. All that if-we-had-our-own-leadership
crap; God save the Queen, but keep her the hell down below. It's de
rigueur when Americans visit, I know. Just get past it."

Get past it. A piece of advice Paul had never heard in so few words.
Perhaps it was a motto he ought to have stitched or tattooed somewhere, to snap him out of his retentive ways.

"So give me the truth," Fenno said. "About Mum."

Back then, her prognosis looked hopeful, though the cancer had
begun its campaign abroad. As Paul told Fenno what the doctors had
said, as he talked about chemotherapy schedules and surgeries, he felt
himself levitating over the field, above his own head, and one of the
many voices in his incessantly verbal self told him that on this already
fateful piece of land, on this beautiful summer afternoon, a few simple
observations about his own son had finally crossed the blood-brain bar-
rier and were shooting toward his heart: Fenno would never move back
from his expatriate life, he knew his own mind more surely than Paul
knew his, and he was a homosexual. The third acknowledgment was
more oblique than the others, but of course it stood out the largest
(though it shouldn't, Paul knew). It stood out as both a relief and a terror. A relief because for several years he had only pretended to know. A

terror because if his son was ill, too—though Fenno looked healthy in
an offhand way, in the most reassuring way—Paul would not bear it.
He would crumble and disintegrate, like dead leaves underfoot.

The inevitably childish bargain crossed his mind: If I have to lose
one of them, take her. "Biology speaking," Maureen would have said;
she would have applauded. But Paul did not want to give so much credence to the grandiosity of genes.

Within a few days, Mal left for London, but from that moment in the
field until Fenno's departure a fortnight later, Paul could not speak to
his son without the fear that his panic would puddle brightly around
him, like milk from a bottle dropped on slate. He could not make his
voice sound anything other than phlegmy and distant, his turns of
phrase stilted and prim. Fenno's contempt was quietly apparent, but he
did not criticize his father again. Paul lay awake for hours each night
trying to think of a way to find out what he needed to know. There
might be a way to ask, but he couldn't imagine waiting for the answer
without knowing it first.

One morning, from the library, Paul had watched the two men head
back into the fields, Fenno pointing out trees and birds. Fenno loved
birds; when he was a child, they kept a small piece of paper taped to one
window in each room of the house so that anyone who spotted a new
species could write it down then and there. Paul had left the lists up
even after Fenno moved to New York. Gradually, the sunlight had
faded the names of the birds, first on the windows facing south and last
of all the north, until they had vanished altogether, leaving no record.
Maureen, always less sentimental than Paul, took them all down while
he was away on a trip.

Spying on Fenno and Mal, Paul never saw them hold hands or embrace, though he assumed they must, and he thought how, all of a sudden, that might not be so awful. Just weeks ago, it would have upset
him tremendously. Paul remembered his own father's reaction when he
announced his engagement to Maureen, the disappointment muted but
clear. Paul harbored a disappointment in Fenno, but it was not about
his choices in love or because he might not produce heirs.

Fenno ran a bookstore—a logical enterprise for the son who, in Paul's
memory as a child of five or nine or twelve, was always reading. But
Fenno was the one Paul had hoped would take over the paper—even
after Fenno went overseas to get an American doctorate. Neither of the

twins had shown much interest in anything to do with the veneration of language. David was a veterinary surgeon, his mother's son; Dennis, a romantic like his father but without intellectual cravings, was (after years of meandering) studying to be a chef. When these two came of age and, simultaneously, emptied the small trusts left by their grandfather to follow their respective curiosities, Paul looked on happily. He loved their separateness and, when they shared their enthusiasms, felt the privilege of being admitted to different worlds. But when Fenno took some (only a prudent fraction) of his inheritance and invested it in his own business, Paul felt instinctively, illogically betrayed. Again and again, he reminded himself how enslaved he'd felt to his father's desires (though he could have denied them without any dire consequence); still, he came away feeling wounded.

Maureen came home for good in mid-December. As Paul pointed out their house to the ambulance driver, he saw against the hedgerow an obscenely white car that he knew must be Fenno's, the one he'd have hired at the airport. Fenno he found standing before a fire in the living room. "*There* you are," said Fenno, as if Paul were the child, hiding out from a scolding. Fenno's coldness was painful, but it was not a surprise, not since Paul had bungled his visit five months before.

Beside Fenno, Mal rose quickly from Paul's reading chair. Greeting him, Paul struggled against the same revulsion he'd felt in the summer. (Was the young man frailer? He was certainly paler, but this was winter.)

So now, as Maureen was being carried across the snow into their house, as Paul wanted so much to feel his sons hold him together, secure him like a seaworthy knot, Fenno seemed lost to him entirely. He remained between Paul and the fireplace, so miraculously close, but he might as well have been back at his home in New York, a home Paul had never seen and now supposed he never would. His oldest son, after the funeral—which would be soon—might become little more than an address on the flimsy blue tissue of an airborne letter. If that.

Paul instructed the orderlies to take the bed and the equipment upstairs to the library. There, Maureen could look out at the kennel. Her three favorite dogs were given free roam of the house. Most of the time they lay on the floor near Maureen's bed, but once Paul caught them chasing one another up the front stairs, skidding on the hallway runners. He thought of the boys when they were small, their never-ending war games. He thought of Fenno, making an imaginary conflagration of the house and everything in it. Cupping both hands around his mouth, Fenno had been able to broadcast a near-perfect air-raid siren; every time, for an instant, the wail made his father's chest throb with fear.

"LUNG CANCER," he told Jack. "A terribly ordinary death, you might say. Or an ordinary terrible death. But she died at home. All of us there. The children—our sons, not children anymore by a long stretch, in fact. A bright day. How we'd all like to go." It sounded as if he were composing a telegram.

They were sitting together on the airplane from London to Athens. Jack, who seemed to use teasing as a way of forcing acquaintance with people he liked (and it worked), had asked how an obviously attractive, apparently independent chap like Paul could wind up alone on a guided tour. "Not your usual follower," Jack had said. "Or should I say not one of mine."

"Christ, sorry," he said now. "Christ, that's a trial."

Paul held his hands up and shook his head. "Please. I came to escape how sorry everyone feels for me every bloody minute of my life these past six months. My sons fuss at me as if I'm an invalid, one foot in the grave myself. At the office they fuss. My old friends fuss."

"Bet your old friends' wives make another kind of fuss."

They laughed together. Paul looked out the window and saw the Alps. Maureen had loved flying, loved seeing everything pressed below her like a map. She liked the thrill of vertigo when the plane banked to turn, when the earth tipped up alongside you—mountains and rivers reaching inside you and seizing your heart.

Below him now, horizon to horizon, June was spreading its green, abundant promise, disputing the few peaks that guarded their snow. Up close, there would be flowers, wildflowers, yellow and purple and white. One long-ago June, Paul and Maureen had driven somewhere along these slopes, tiny Fenno asleep in a crib they'd wedged into the car (there was none of this safety gear back then; most parents were too young to fret about dangers unseen). They had pulled into a field of flowers to eat their lunch. After the food, they made love until Fenno's crying interrupted them. As she changed the wet nappy (Paul wistfully stroking the small of her back), Maureen had said, "Well then, we shall just have to find this place again when our children are grown." The multiple expectations in her simple remark had thrilled Paul; he was so naive.

When he turned away from the window, he told Jack that he had traveled a great deal, but never on a tour. "But now . . . now I like the idea of everything planned. No surprises."

"Ah, but I can't promise you no surprises," said Jack.

Jack was thirty-six, Fenno's age. There, all similarity ended. Jack was not willowy, not soft-featured, not articulate in a well-schooled way. He was compact, muscular, ruddy. He had the body of a swimmer and the coloring of the fair-haired Italians Paul remembered from Verona and Venice. Like a fox, he had shrewd glassy eyes, very blue, and a long sharp nose. He spoke with a trace of Yorkshire farmhand. Jack reminded Paul of fleeting friendships he'd made in the war, with men from a different but parallel world. He felt a quick, irrational trust and warmth—nothing of the distance he kept these days, without wanting to, from his sons.

Jack had been married once, briefly and much too young. Took the taste for it out of his mouth. He had managed a pub; after the marriage ended, he took his savings and went to Greece for a year, hitched around, lived here and there. He made good money now, running these tours. Exhausting at first—twelve tours back to back—but he had learned how to relax. And then, five months off. A good life. No complaints. He had a girl in London, but she was easy. An actress in her late twenties: too ambitious to settle down, and the mere thought of children made her shudder.

PAUL HAD ALWAYS ASSUMED that at the end, whenever it might be, he and Maureen would have great stretches of time together, alone. They would talk about everything. But why should this have been so? Even while Maureen was in hospital, there was still the paper to print, the dogs to feed and exercise, the friends to reassure: more occupations than ever. And his sons' presence in the last weeks, however welcome, created yet more tasks, more diversions. At times, they seemed to move about the house—fondling objects, appraising pictures—as if they were about to divide its possessions and take them all away. Though Paul knew they were only drawing memories from their surroundings, he sometimes wanted to shout, "*I* am still very much alive! You're not about to be orphaned!"

A week before Maureen died, the jetliner with the bomb on board shattered in the air over Lockerbie. When the news came, Paul was sitting beside her, reading aloud from *My Dog Tulip*. By then, Maureen rarely spared the breath it took to speak, but as Paul crossed the room to take the call, he heard her say hoarsely, "Rodgie boy, my little king." She was looking past Paul to where the dog stood, returning her look. She touched an ear, one of so many signals whose precise meanings Paul had never summoned the interest to learn, and Rodgie shot past him and jumped up beside her. When Paul rang off, she did not ask what the call was about. Her hands were buried in the dog's coat, teasing out a burr. Paul knew then that they would not really talk to each other, not intimately, not even idly, ever again.

Seen from every angle, the week was a tragedy, a crippling chaos. Divine vengeance, thought Paul, worse than anything he had seen or felt in the war. The morning after the crash was the only day he left Maureen, driving to Lockerbie with a detective whose daughter had long ago, for a summer, captivated Dennis. Together, the two men pressed through crowds and crossed barricades to walk through scatterings of oily, singed debris. In many places there was little to see but fragments—their smallness a horror in itself—and they looked so consistently obscure to Paul that he saw a kind of visual frolic in the wreckage: a sonata of quirky shapes, dark against the newly frosted ground, like a painting by Miró. As the detective stopped to speak with one of the men collecting the pieces and placing them in numbered, zippered plastic bags, the toe of Paul's boot uncovered a glint of gold. Turning his back to the policemen, he squatted, shielding the object from their view. Slowly, he lifted a shiny cylinder and held it in his gloved palm. It was a bright gold tube of lipstick, fallen intact from the sky. Without hesitating, he slipped it in a pocket. Walking alongside the detective again, he focused on the fog of his own breath, reminding himself to inhale, exhale, inhale, exhale. When he got home, he went straight to the scullery sink and vomited.

For five days he did not sleep. He forbade everyone who entered the house to mention the crash in front of Maureen. She no longer read the paper. From a mask, and then from plastic tendrils that snaked up her nostrils, she drank oxygen like an elixir whose magic was fading.

TWO

"THIS SEEMS TO BE A VERY SMALL ISLAND," he says when there she is, yet again, on the boat from Paros to Delos.

"Only so much to do, I guess." Fern seems embarrassed but pleased.

Jack passes them with a fast grin. "You tailing us, girl?"

Paul sits beside her. "How fortunate for us, then."

Jack is on the foredeck with the captain. Old familiars, they laugh and joke in Greek. Jack wears dark spectacles that flash back the sun as he talks. Most of the others have gone below, nervous about the swells. For a sunny day, the sea is oddly rough, and the boat, a graceless trawler, bucks and creaks against the wharf. Jack has assured everyone that once they're moving, the water will seem a lot smoother.

"I'm guessing there's a storm out there," says Fern.

"If there is, it's a ways off. Nothing to worry about," says Paul.

Marjorie comes up from below. When she sits beside them, she is breathing heavily from climbing the ladder. "Go down there," she says, pointing at her feet, "instant scurvy." She leans across Paul. "Hello, dear. Did I see you yesterday, in the taverna, sketching the local color?"

Fern smiles at Paul. "Small island," she says to Marjorie, and introduces herself.

Marjorie pats the bulky rucksack in her lap. "Paul dear, I packed extra biscuits and cheese for you boys. About an hour from now, we'll be awfully glad to have them. Salt air makes you ravenous." She pats her rucksack again. "Though what kind of cheese this *is,* I have to confess I'm not sure."

The motor starts up with a grinding roar and chokes forth a cloud of black smoke. Marjorie frowns and waves an arm, shooing at the exhaust as if it were a swarm of mosquitoes. "*Not* auspicious. A lovely day, but looks are deceiving!"

Paul and Fern smile and nod in unison. Paul turns his head slightly toward Fern and winks. Her smile tightens and trembles. Paul feels quite unlike himself: boyishly cruel and happier than he has been in months.

Jack comes up to them and holds out a plastic sack. "Be a sport, Marj, and hand these round below, will you?"

Marjorie looks inside the sack. "What did I say?" She holds it open toward Paul. Inside are brown wax-paper bags, a cheap version of the sickbags on airplanes. After Marjorie climbs below, Jack takes her place. Fern laughs. Jack says, "What's so funny, girl?"

"You," she says. "The way you run people around. I mean, you know, these people *pay* you."

"Paul," says Jack, "how do I take that?"

"As flattery."

Jack lifts his sunglasses and stares at Fern. "So. Where's Madama Butterfly?"

"In the trenches. She's here to work. I'm here to play."

"Archaeology?" Jack says. "Christ, a lot of sunbathing. Mucking about in the dust. I don't call that work."

"Trailing a lot of happy tourists around, swilling beer every chance, wolfing moussaka . . . well, I don't call *that* work."

Jack laughs. "Touché, girl."

The trip takes an arduous two hours, the boat pitching through the high waves and deep troughs between them. Some of the other two dozen passengers emerge from below, grip the rail and lean out, looking mournful and blanched. Fern and Paul—along with Jack, Marjorie, and a few others—know how to roll with the boat, to keep their stomachs from seizing. It's something you can't explain, they agree. Your body knows or it doesn't. "Like lust," says Jack. Marjorie giggles, pretending shock.

Jack spends most of the time below, trying to distract the more nervous members of the group with his jokes. Marjorie takes photographs of the open sea with its canted horizon, the distant islands, the crew, the boat. Fern tells Paul about studying art, about her paintings, about her hometown—Cornwall, Connecticut. He persuades her to let him look through her sketchbook.

There are watercolors and pencil drawings. Most are pictures of people, but there is a handful of landscapes. When Paul reaches the first one, a twisted olive tree, she says, "I'm no good at nature, but it's sort of required when you're traveling. I mean, people expect you to paint the scenery, like they expect you to carry a camera, put together a slide show. As if your memory doesn't count or can't be trusted, right?" Paul has begun to notice a habit Fern has of asking for reassurance she shouldn't need. She isn't much like Maureen after all.

The tree is drawn gracefully yet somewhat timidly. "I feel as if I can see the wind," says Paul. "In the tension of the branches." But already she's turned the page; on the overleaf is a young woman in a bathing suit, with a little boy asleep in her lap. Fern has captured well the little boy's hands around his mother's neck, holding fast even in sleep. The mother's gaze is fixed elsewhere, perhaps on a beautiful sunset. "That's marvellous. I love how you've painted her hair."

"I like to draw people on the ferries. Portraits—that's what I like doing best. I refuse to believe the portrait's finished as something vital, something, I don't know . . . provocative. I think there must be new ways of getting inside a person and sort of . . . eviscerating the self. Art-wise, I mean." She looks up. "Listen to me: 'artwise.' Like I'm still in school."

Fern's portraits are sure, not timid. Many are self-portraits. At one place, she reaches over and turns the page before Paul can look at it fully. "I forgot about that one," she says. It was, he saw briefly, a picture of Fern sitting naked on a bed, reflected in a mirror beside a window with a view of hills. Hibiscus pinks, cobalt blues, pungent coppery greens. On the next page, Paul sees himself. He gasps.

"You did this in, what, ten minutes?"

"It's not finished. We were interrupted," she says. But there he is, in three-quarter profile, recognizable at once: shaggy hair blown over one ear, big jaw, bristled eyebrows. The near eye is dark, a white liquid glint in a scribble of shadow. "What were you thinking? You looked so . . . I don't know, tragic."

"I was thinking how little time I have here, on this trip. I'd like just to roam around for years, live on every island," he invents. "Or choose just one and make it an actual home. Wouldn't you? Wouldn't—" He falters at his eagerness. He feels as if he's issued an invitation.

"If only life were so generous," says Fern. She ducks her head and pulls back her hair, coiling it nervously around one hand. She points out to sea. "Look—is that it? Where we're going?"

MAUREEN WAS IN THE KITCHEN, putting together their tea. From the living room, Paul heard what sounded like hooves. He heard the kitchen door close, followed by indecipherable chatter, then Maureen's voice, raised: "How does Juno take hers? Or does she fancy a sherry?"

A man's vibrant laugh. "A cup of plain sugar would suit her. Bust her girth, too."

Then Paul heard Maureen calling his name, footsteps heading rapidly through the dining room toward the front of the house.

"You don't mind, I hope?" said Colin Swift as he entered the room after Maureen. "My dropping by so boldly? My interrupting your tea?" He extended his hand. When Paul stood, a book fell from his lap. Paul had met Colin Swift, but only in passing: at a retirement party for Paul's deputy publisher; at a political reception. He was a man whom everyone watched but few people seemed to know.

After tea, they walked the borders of the meadow. He would sell the meadow—the mall, he called it—but only with a right of way during hunt season, across the back half. "You see, riders jump the wall here, then they're away through the glen. Not likely, though, we'd barge through more than twice a season—if that." He wore, Paul noticed, a white stock tie—absurdly formal for a solitary hack in the woods, but it had the dignifying effect of a ruff in an old Dutch portrait.

Maureen stood in the center of the meadow. The kennel would still be within easy sight of the house if she built it in front, she said, pacing out the length. She could plant a screen of shrubbery to hide the back (or fence it; would he mind?) and, behind it, shelter and graze the sheep.

Colin Swift was the master of Swallow Run, the foxhunt. He was also the owner of Conkers, of the adjoining farm, and of a thousand handsome acres—hills, hayfields, forests, streams. He was a newcomer, a transplanted Englishman who'd bought the estate only the year before. It was well known, because he made it no secret, that he had left behind in Cornwall another estate and a hostile wife. People in the village called him The Major, with a mixture of worship and chiding. In his late fifties, he was tall and fit—handsome, with a storklike grace—and would appear at formal events in dress uniform, his medals bright as confetti. At Tobruk, he had lost his left hand and most of the arm to the elbow.

Before leaving, he asked Maureen for a pail of water. While the horse drank, he inquired about the collies, who had lined up along their fence to watch him. "I'm buying a flock of Shrops in the autumn. Just twenty head to begin," he said. "Would you have pups then? I like to do things the old-fashioned way." Maureen took him back to the kennel. Paul made his excuses and returned indoors, to his book.

When Maureen came in, she was laughing and shaking her head. "The 'mall.' The 'glen.' The 'linden wood.' La-dee-da."

"Will you sell him a dog?"

"Of course. He'll let me work his new flock—the 'Shrops,'" she drawled in shrewd imitation. "As if he's so fluent in sheep that Shropshires, Cheviots, and Oxfords are just other currencies to him. . . . But laugh too hard and I'll jinx this bit of luck."

"But that's you, Maureen—lucky. Charmed," Paul said. He reached out to touch her waist. "And charming." She put a hand on his, but the affection seemed to surprise her.

"I do get just about everything I wish for," she said as she stacked cups and saucers. She had left the room by the time Paul thought to ask what wish she hadn't got.

TONIGHT, WHEN THEY RETURN, he will ask her to dinner. They will go to the opposite side of the island, to Naoussa, the smaller village. (Jack will know exactly where he should take her, where to find a car.)

He keeps his distance for the moment but watches her. She disappears behind a wall, reappears next to a decapitated column. She meanders deliberately, enjoying whatever she looks at or touches. The day is still bright, but windier and slightly cool. Paul offered her the wool jumper he brought along; she wears it now as she sits on the ground, opens her book, and begins to draw. Paul's stomach feels like it's made of glass. His hands sting, as if they were dipped in ice.

They have two hours in which to explore the ruins, and then they will head for Mykonos. Paul lets Marjorie and the two wives lead him to and fro, Marjorie reading aloud from her guidebook about the birth of Apollo and Artemis. Delos is a place of rooms without ceilings, rooms that let the sun stream over everything: cratered mosaics, fallen lintels, crumbling walls. In one room, Paul stares down at the image in the broken tiles beneath his feet: an octopus. He listens contentedly to Marjorie's didactic singsong.

Out in the open again, the wives find their husbands conferring. Ray squints and holds his arms in front of him at odd stiff angles. An engineer, Ray will have found a way to measure the place. Perhaps that's how he remembers the sights he's seen, by their dimensions.

Looking in one direction, Paul sees the quadruplets at the postcard kiosk. In another, he sees Fern, absorbed in a drawing; behind her, Jack sneaks up and tilts her hat over her face. She turns accusingly; Jack says something that makes her laugh. She stands and dusts off the back of her legs, puts her book away. Jack points toward the room with the octopus floor.

"Now does that sea look wine-dark to you? I'd call it peacock, or indigo, or navy gabardine, but that is resoundingly blue, and no wine I know is *blue*." Marjorie, still beside him, scans the water with a hand tenting her eyes.

"I don't believe this is the sea in question," says Paul. "Homer was writing about the Ionian Sea, I think. The sea around Ithaka."

"No, there you're wrong. Shame on you. That renowned metaphor is from the *Iliad*. The allusion speaks of the soldiers' sacrifice, of course, wine as a stand-in for blood. I do get quite literal about these things, I confess, but good art is never flabby."

Paul smiles. Marjorie's conviction would have swayed even Homer.

Without taking her eyes off the sea, as if willing it to become less blue, she says, "So are you liking it here? Are you finding your sea legs again—ha, so to speak?"

"My sea legs?" Paul laughs. "Today, hard ground seems quite secure."

"Oh, I mean back in the saddle, living life, all that."

"I'm having a good time."

"I'm glad," says Marjorie. "A friend forced me to take a trip like this after I had a loss of my own. Spain. I was just in my thirties then, but I became an addict. Personally, I credit El Greco. Hard to stay maudlin in a place like Toledo. Since then, I've never stopped."

"Taking trips?" Paul says.

"Collecting worlds, that's how I think of it. Different views, each representing a new window. Take stock—architecturally, so to speak—and I've built myself quite the mansion."

Before Paul can answer, she's looking away again and waving. "Halloo, fellow wanderers, isn't this place magnificent?" she calls. The rest of the group, approaching them, wave back almost collectively. No one, in the end, can resist Marjorie's bullying charms.

"HELLO, HELLO! Did we make a rousing sight?" Colin Swift noticed Paul and Maureen among the spectators as he walked past leading his mare, the reins looped around his left elbow, the arm with the sleeve doubled back. The horse was striped in a lather of sweat, and his hounds, muddied but still lively, trotted in tight formation close to his legs and the mare's. With his one hand, he'd wave to someone, then reach down to stroke a hound. His royal air—the way he wore that clownish red coat like just another layer of skin—irritated Paul, but you couldn't help envying the nimble satisfaction in everything he did.

When Colin reached the house at the end of the field, he passed his horse and hat to a waiting boy and knelt on the grass. The hounds engulfed him like a mob of zealous disciples. They licked his ears, shoved one another to reach his asymmetrical embrace. There was yipping and whining—some of it, Paul would have sworn, from the man. When he stood, he called out, "Enough gossip, ladies and gents! Git, git, board up," and urged the hounds toward a van, where the kennelman herded them in.

"I've never seen anything like it. There must be *fifty,*" Maureen said to Paul. "Rivals anything I could do." Her face was bright from the cold air.

Colin came up and shook Paul's hand, then Maureen's. "See you later, over at the house?"

Paul had hoped they could skip the party, but Maureen was thrilled by the invitation to a hunt breakfast at Conkers. At least there had not been a blooding; the hounds had lost the line in a marsh. This meant there would be no "trophies," no bits and pieces of the torn-apart quarry to award over watercress and crumpets.

On the way to his car, Colin turned. "Like a look at my kennels? I can give you a lift back." Maureen let go of Paul's hand and ran ahead.

The kennel was a refashioned armory, a small fortress complete with ramparts. Outside, the hounds roamed a grassy enclosure. As the car drove alongside, they leaped at the fence in a wave, howling and barking. Colin leaned out his window and howled right back. Maureen giggled. "Got to speak their language," he said.

"I know about that," she answered. Sitting behind her, Paul saw a tendon distend at the side of her neck: pride and irritation.

"Oh, you and your renowned collies. I could probably learn a thing or two," said Colin as he opened her door.

He gave them each a white coat, like a doctor's smock, to protect their clothing. "Wait here," he said. He left them alone in a great stone room with a wooden berth along one side and a gate, a sort of portcullis, on the other. "Medieval," Paul whispered. "The whole thing's barbaric."

"You're such an old crosspatch," Maureen whispered back.

The door behind them opened. Instantly, hounds swarmed around them. Paul cringed, but Maureen stood straight, laughing as they ran circles around their guests. The hounds did not jump up or growl but greeted Maureen and Paul with an amicable din of yipping and whining. On all fours, they stood nearly as high as Paul's hip.

"All right you devils!" Colin called out. He clapped the back of the door with his hand. Right away, the animals were silent, noses pointed toward him. Only when they were all still did he walk among them, handing out treats from his pocket—scraps of meat, not the biscuits Maureen gave—and praising each one by name. Nimrod, Aria, Faultless and Faithful; Piccolo, Gallant, Delilah, Intrepid. Hannibal. Harmony. Diva. Orion. Their names ran off his tongue like a poem, a stream of mythical consciousness.

"Permit me a bit of showing off," he said. "Bench, gentlemen!" Half the hounds, thirty or more, scrambled onto the wooden berth. They sat in a row, tense but quiet, facing the door in the opposite wall. The rest sat in front of them, lined up along the floor.

"Tom!" Colin shouted, and the kennelman, standing on the other side, hauled the door up on its winch. In the next room was a long trough. Still patient, the two rows of hounds looked back and forth from the trough to their master. Colin waited a long moment. "Ladies," he said at last. The hounds in front, the bitches, bolted through the door. Those on the bench continued to wait, the only motion their quivering tails. Colin watched them for several seconds; they watched him back. "Gentlemen," he said, and they leaped off the bench in unison, as if released by a latch.

Maureen applauded; Colin bowed slightly. "Utterly frivolous," he said. "You see how I long for the army. Order for its own sake."

He showed them the feed room, the heat pens, the whelping stall, the butcher's table where the kennelman prepared the hounds' meals. With his one hand, he helped Maureen and Paul out of the white coats and hung them neatly in a closet. He did everything, thought Paul, as perfectly as a dancer. On the lane back to the house, an incoming lorry pulled into a lay-by to make room; its driver waved to Colin. Paul looked back and saw its cargo—two dead cows. Meat from Colin's own farm, he supposed, and he waited (unkindly, he knew) for their host to praise the economy of his little fiefdom.

Conkers was a square stone house, softened by thickets of yellow roses clambering to its eaves. Six full chestnut trees stood out front, and the sun through their changing leaves amplified the glow of the roses. Mobbing the downstairs rooms were boisterous riders who'd already drunk too much, unchecked small children pilfering cakes, and half a dozen barking terriers careening over the furniture. Colin led Paul and Maureen through the throngs—more at home, Paul suspected, than he would have been in a house without guests. He stood on one of his dining-room chairs and blew his hunting horn. Confined, the sound was uncomfortably shrill. It silenced even the terriers. "Hunters and civilians!" Colin announced. "We are here to inaugurate a splendid season of sport!" He raised a glass. Everyone cheered.

Maureen leaned toward Paul. "That's 'Gone Away,' what he just played. It's when the hounds have caught the line and taken off full tilt."

"How do you know that?" Paul said.

She shrugged. "Grow up in the country, you learn a few things."

BY THE TIME they reach Mykonos, the sky has curdled, and the captain of the boat tells the passengers that he will want to leave an hour earlier than planned. Marjorie rallies a shopping group in record time.

Jack, Paul, and Fern walk through the streets until they reach a taverna that juts on stilts toward the water. As the waiter serves their lunch, the rain begins: large, ominous drops like the crystals that dangle from chandeliers. Jack winks at Fern and says, "So much for your delighted sailors, love."

"Sailors in Greece," she says, "probably go by different rules."

Jack nods. "All the rules are different. It's a turned-around place."

"Widdershins," says Fern. "Like in the fairy tales."

Briefly, Jack sets a hand on top of her head. "Girl, if you aren't a stitch."

They eat quickly, without much talk. Jack looks repeatedly at the sky. Fern pushes away her plate after just a few bites of lamb. She takes out her book and a pencil, begins a sketch of the tossing boats.

When the rain lets up, Jack stands and gives Paul some money. "I'll head over now, round up the souvenir hounds."

As Paul counts out drachmas, Fern continues to draw. Only after they have left and are walking along the water does he speak. All that comes into his head is "You must love Paris."

Fern doesn't seem to find this pathetic. She says, "Oh, well, *love* is a tricky word, even in that context. But yes, I love it. At least, in all the ways you're supposed to. As anyone would, right?"

"But in others . . ."

She looks at Paul, puzzled.

"In other ways, you're not so sure?"

"All I meant was that people take their same old lives wherever they go. No place is perfect enough to strip you of that. And some places have a way of magnifying your demons, or of, I don't know, giving them pep pills. And *there* I'd better stop." She laughs, but the humor is forced.

What, Paul wonders, is a "same old life" to Fern? What could even be "old" to someone so young? When Fenno left for New York at her age, was he out to strip himself of some life he perceived as too same, too old?

"But you're happy to be there."

"To be somewhere that lives up so exactly to its reputation, it's so outrageously beautiful—it's fabulous and paralyzing all at once. Anna says the paralyzing's self-inflicted, my fault entirely. But right now, I doubt I could be happier anywhere else. Or luckier. Most of my friends back home are in punch-the-clock jobs. I guess that's the fate I'm just putting off, right?" She laughs awkwardly again. "So what do *you* go back to, after this trip?"

"Quiet. Domestic peace and quiet. *My* same old life." They are almost at the quay, and Marjorie has spotted them. Paul stops. "Listen. I'm thinking of going over to Naoussa for dinner tonight, on my own. But I wouldn't mind a companion." She does not look up in response, and he adds, "Tomorrow we leave for Santorini."

"Tomorrow? That's quick." She looks up now. She looks alarmed.

"Tours," says Paul. "That's tours for you. No stopping to savor anything, just a taste here and there, a sampling . . ."

"Antipasto," says Fern, her nervous young way of deflecting unwanted silence, just as Marjorie pulls them both toward the queue at the gangway.

THE SAME AUTUMN they were invited to Conkers, Betsey had her second litter. The night she whelped, Paul sat in bed reading. Downstairs, he could hear Maureen coaxing the bitch. Now and then he heard whining. He had been through a dozen such nights and still could not sleep when a bitch was whelping. He'd think of Maureen when she had Fenno: the long labor; Maureen's gasping—more like a prolonged seething of air between her teeth, over and over—from the other side of the bedroom door. He was sure that if she were dying, no one would tell him. All he'd been told was that Fenno had turned around in the womb (as if, at the last minute, he'd decided to run for the hills) and was entering life backwards. "A nonconformist, just you wait," the doctor joked once the baby was cleaned and swaddled.

Sometimes now, while Maureen sat with a bitch giving birth, Paul would go down and make tea. She'd scold him for losing a good night's sleep. He'd lose it no matter what, he told her.

He waited this time until he could no longer stand it, till he'd read the same unturned page in his book half a dozen times. He had heard nothing for a while, then running water.

Maureen stood at the scullery sink. She jumped when he said her name. "Paul! It's past two." She looked at him over her shoulder but did not turn around.

He could see the red glow of the heat lamp over the whelping box, where Betsey nosed among the indistinct creatures that shivered and writhed between her legs. "Good girl there, Bets," he said. Betsey did not thrash her tail to greet him as usual but stiffened and warned him away with her eyes.

"Let her be," whispered Maureen. "She's had a hard time. Thirteen all together."

Paul came up behind her. Under his hands, her body felt like a barricade of muscle. There was a pail of pinkish water in the sink; she held her hands under the surface and did not move when Paul touched her.

He stepped back when she pulled her hands out of the pail. He'd thought she was washing them, but she held in each one a newborn black puppy. She laid their bodies on the drainboard. "A mongol," she said as she emptied the pail down the drain. "And this little one, no tail."

"No tail? Why kill that one? You could have found it a home."

"Paul. Paul." She spoke soothingly, as if he were one of the boys, acting up over a lost toy. "Something else is bound to be wrong with it, you can't be soft." She faced him. "Go back to your book, Paul." She might as well have said, Go back to your cave.

Maureen wrapped the drowned puppies in sheaves of yesterday's *Yeoman*. She went about cleaning up as she always did after a whelping, as if Paul were not there. Without offering to make tea, he went upstairs. In an hour, she lay down beside him and fell fast asleep.

The rest of the puppies were healthy and bright. When they were eight weeks old, they were let out to play with the older dogs. Colin Swift rode over from Conkers to see them. Working upstairs, Paul watched the dogs race loops around the lawn, leaving behind them a maze in the snow. When they were put away, he joined Maureen and Colin in the kitchen. She toweled the pups dry while Paul made the tea. Colin chose a small bitch with a white blaze, the one he claimed had chosen him.

"Her name's Flora," said Maureen. "None of your swish foxhound names. No crown princes or movie starlets bred here."

Colin laughed and saluted her.

At the beginning of January, Paul was scheduled to go on a trip to Mexico and Guatemala with a group of editors, most of them from America. He'd accepted two tickets, but Maureen told him that now, with puppies to watch, there was no way she could go. Why not take Fenno? It was his first year away at school. He was doing well, and his masters liked him, but Maureen thought he needed a little adventure. He seemed so awfully serious, she said, not at all his old bombardier self. If he went with Paul, he would miss just a few days of school after the Christmas holiday.

Fenno was the only child on the trip, but he did not need playmates. He replied politely, even learnedly, to everything he was asked, and he never complained when Paul sent him to bed by himself after dinner. Later, when Paul retired, he would often find Fenno doubled over, asleep on the pages of a notebook. After unfurling his son's body back onto the pillows, Paul would close the book and set it on a table, resisting the urge to read it. Not because he was so discreet but because he was afraid of the imagination he might uncover—one he might wish had been his.

The other editors and their husbands and wives told Paul to count his lucky stars for having such a son. They took Fenno's presence as an invitation to complain and then boast about their own children.

In his few months away from home, Fenno had become assertively self-sufficient; this must be what Maureen saw as so "awfully serious." But when Paul looked at Fenno, he saw a fledgling intellectual with interests all his own. He loved the jungle, especially the parrots and the monstrous insects; in Mexico City, Paul bought him a pair of high-powered binoculars. Paul was genuinely proud, but he was sad, too, when he noticed a new habit in Fenno, a habit of maintaining a solitary distance even in company—quietly, not belligerently—for half an hour or more. Paul felt his own presence erased at such times. At Tikal, when they emerged together behind the guide from the hot green tangle into the clearing around the pyramid, Paul realized how much he missed Maureen, how much he wished that she were here to share his amazements; Maureen with her quick eye and tongue, her capering passions. She would lower her voice to a whisper in awe but probably never stop talking. He knew that she embroidered silences for both of them, but not till he spent so much time alone with Fenno did he feel what it must be like for someone to be alone with him, with Paul.

Returning home, Paul saw Maureen as livelier, younger than ever. This was the way he felt about her when he returned from any trip, but now the extreme distance he had traveled made the illusion that much more acute. That winter and spring, he noticed for the first time how frequently she was away from home. If she wasn't driving the twins to some sporting event or lesson, she was over at the farm. Colin Swift's foreman had chosen a second pup, Rodney, to keep for himself and train with Flora.

In the evenings, Maureen spoke effusively about her new arrangement, how the collies were progressing. She spoke about them respectfully, each as an individual with, already, full-blown talents, tics, unique ways of thinking. A breeder of Australian shepherds had written to say he'd like to visit in May; he'd like to watch her work the dogs. A farmer up north had called to ask the stud fee for Roy, who'd placed well at the nationals last summer. Colin, she said, was working hard with his flock. She had misjudged him; he was anything but a snob. "Nauseatingly posh exterior, I'll give you that. But under all that varnish a heart of gold. And entertaining. He tells the most extraordinary stories—mostly about the war. In Africa . . . just imagine." She stared pointedly at Paul. "You never do, you know. I hadn't realized, but you never talk about the war—tell stories."

"Maybe I haven't got stories."

Maureen looked at him as she would look at one of the boys when he made a flimsy excuse to get out of a chore. "Paul, everyone with a mouth and a memory has stories."

"Colin Swift wears the war by not replacing his arm. You see the wound a mile away. Make that choice and you're compelling the world to ask, 'Dunkirk? Sicily?' Compelling them to hear your stories."

"I'm talking about you," said Maureen angrily. "It's almost like you were never there."

Paul looked into the fire. "Maybe I wasn't dismembered, Maureen, but I believe I was there."

"That was rude, I'm sorry." She took their plates to the kitchen. He listened to her rinse them in the sink, listened to her, slowly, take out new plates for the pudding. When she brought it out, she said, as if they'd never mentioned the war, "Colin's a good student. I have to say I'm surprised. But then Flora's a keen little bitch. We're working her on the get-by, with her dad of course, and Rodney. But Flora—she's caught on like it's in her blood. Well it is, of course . . . but for a pup she's so sure: she trusts you completely, she looks at you as if she reads your mind, she *knows*. You can see it in her ears . . . I had Roy part a ewe, and the way that girl watched, *listened* . . ." Maureen talked quickly, on and on, without touching her cake.

"Colin's good to her?" asked Paul, thinking of the foxhounds lined up in Napoleonic ranks. If the collies were Paul's, they'd live a fat, indolent life of lolling about by the fire, eating biscuits under the table, spending their nights at the foot of a bed. Paul's childhood dogs had been nothing more than freeloading eager-to-please companions.

"For now he spoils her—keeps her in the house with those deranged terriers. But once it's warm, she'll go to the farm with her brother."

When Maureen retreated to the kitchen again, Paul realized that they had passed an entire evening without speaking once of their children; most of her maternal instincts seemed to have turned toward the collies since his return, toward Betsey's pups. Perhaps this was just because the boys were so seldom at home now; sometimes it felt as if David and Dennis came back to the house only to sleep. And it seemed truer than ever, as they grew older, that having each other rendered their parents obsolete except as providers.

It was not unusual for Paul to come home each evening to an empty house. If he walked out behind, he would see Maureen's footprints, mingled with the dogs', pointing left toward the farm or right toward Conkers. If he was home early, he might hear her whistle in the distance. Later, sometimes not until after dark, he'd see her returning along the path by the wall. She would come in exhausted, and Paul would rub her feet by the fire. Then the twins would come home and gallop around like ponies, fired up from football or cricket.

THE CAPTAIN ORDERS THEM BELOW, where the air is hot, rancid, and smells of burning petrol. An hour out, they hear the rain turn to hail: the clattering overhead becomes a roar that drowns out all attempts at conversation. Now, except for the boat's crew and Jack, everyone is sick. Even Jack looks gray. He sits on the other side of Fern, who leans down between her knees. The reeling of the boat throws her back and forth between the two men. Paul feels the heat of her legs through her skirt and wishes desperately for sun and calm. His lunch is long gone; to steady himself, he focuses on one of Fern's white sneakers and her bare ankle above it.

There is something so girlish, so ingenuous, about her simple sneaker;

without daughters, Paul has no idea what other shoes might seem more her age, but these do not. He saw shoes of various kinds, six months ago, at the Lockerbie crash site; shoes are so ubiquitous at catastrophic accidents that their image has become a cliché of pathos. That week, Paul vetoed at least half a dozen photographs of shoes. In the same week, he was asked to choose shoes for his wife to wear in her coffin (David's wife did the actual choosing: something formal and black is all Paul remembers).

How often do Fern's parents back in the reportedly pastoral Cornwall, Connecticut, stop to worry about her, consciously? When Fenno first went overseas—not the same as going to boarding school, where other parental people watched him, or to university, where hard studies were expected to keep him from harm—Paul would habitually subtract six or seven hours when he was going to bed each night and wonder what Fenno was doing in that foreign late afternoon. Would he, exactly now, be in the library (a good, safe place), or out on the streets marketing for dinner, or choosing a shirt to please a lover? And if Paul woke in the middle of the night, what he hated was imagining Fenno anywhere but dully in bed like his father.

In Connecticut, where it is now midmorning on a Saturday, whatever those other parents are doing, they couldn't possibly be thinking that a man probably ten years their senior longs to spirit their daughter away, alone, take off her clothes, lie down beside her equally naked and forget every other need but this one. "Take advantage of her"? "Seduce her"? How would they think of it? When he pictures it that way, his desire for Fern becomes ridiculous. But her company, he argues with himself—that's reasonable to want, simply that. He will start with that.

Abruptly, the hail stops. Gradually, the boat slows its feverish tilting. Jack climbs to the deck. He comes back down in a moment and stands over Paul and Fern, grinning. "You still alive there, girl?"

She gives him an impatient look. "I'm going up. I don't care what the captain says."

"All clear is what he says," says Jack, and follows her up the steep stairs.

Paul sits alone a long time, perhaps fifteen minutes. He waits for his stomach to settle. He breathes deeply. He takes out a comb and runs it through his salt-stiffened hair.

When at last he goes up, he is surprised by the brightness. He shades his eyes and sighs with relief. The air is like a drug, fresh as new leaves. The deck shines, and a few unmelted hailstones lie about like jewels from a broken necklace. Several passengers, none from Paul's group, are gathered at the bow, taking pictures of Paros against the retreating storm. One by one, they take turns standing in front of this view, posing. Paul does not see Fern. Heading back toward the captain's cabin, he recognizes her laughter. He hears her say, "You're an octopus," and then sees her, behind the cabin, kissing Jack like a prodigal lover she thought she had lost for all time.

THE YEAR THE TWINS followed their brother to boarding school, Flora placed first at an important trial in Ayrshire. Colin Swift's foreman was her handler. Maureen took a younger dog to show, and Colin drove her up. They left at dawn and did not return until midnight. Maureen woke Paul to come downstairs and drink brandy. She and Colin had been celebrating already, out with their competitors. Paul could smell the cigarettes and whisky on her breath; in the mossy dark, he saw the shape of her lips after she kissed him and tasted fresh lipstick, its familiar mixture of talcum and fruit.

In the kitchen, they were heady with conceit, tripping over each other's words to tell how the day had gone.

"The outrun was wretched, wretched—"

"A crooked course like a closed elbow, with two steep dips—"

"She came around fast as a cheetah." Colin lifted his glass.

"But then the sheep closed up in a blinking knot." Maureen squeezed one hand into a fist and brought it in toward her chest like a punch. "Made for the gate like they could taste it."

"Taste it!" Colin exclaimed; the two of them laughed at this absurdity.

Maureen brought out another cigarette, to which Colin instantly offered a light. "A sight you can't describe."

Paul listened to the deft volley of their narrative—brilliant to them, silly and hopelessly confusing to him. He was glad for Maureen, proud of her. But he also saw, with the distance of his confusion, something new in her, new but old, something he might have seen years before had he chosen to see it. He saw her as he had first noticed her, tending bar at the Globe, so at home among all those men: men's work, men's words, men's vanities like a sea she could navigate in any vessel, any season.

All that summer, the house was filled with noise and activity. There were more sheepdog trials, and the boys were underfoot again. Fenno was to start his first year at Cambridge. He read obsessively, huddled in corners, or brooded from room to room, complaining when his brothers invaded the house with their friends, raiding the larder before they went out to find whatever bathing hole or playing field they'd chosen as that day's destination. When Fenno could no longer stand the close quarters with others, he would walk to the village, taking a book and one of the dogs. On a scorching afternoon late in August, Fenno went down with Silas. Silas, bounding ahead, found Flora, and with her the foreman from Conkers. Casually, in the kitchen as Maureen served dinner, Fenno mentioned the news from town. Colin Swift—wasn't he master of Swallow Run, that character out of Fielding who seemed to change from one outlandish costume to another?—had been killed in his car in the morning fog, overtaking a lorry.

Colin's funeral, a populous military affair, was on the front page of the *Yeoman* not far below a story on a series of IRA arrests. That week, the boys had to be packed up again. After their departure—never a smooth or easy parting—Paul went around the house retrieving bats and balls and shoes from under the furniture; picking up books where Fenno had left them, cast off in restless, open-faced tumbles, on windowseats, staircases, dining room chairs. As he set everything back in the proper shelves, he saw himself as the one in charge of restoring order, the one who comes after but never the first.

The next Saturday morning, so early the sun was still below the privet, Paul awoke to the hunting horn. No sound of hounds, which was odd—just the horn playing "Gone Away." It was still summer, too early for opening meet. He realized that it must be a ritual, a requiem to the departed master. The horn changed melodies then—if melodies they could be called, all variations on the same inharmonious drone, much like the wail of bagpipes. This one was urgent: first steady, then quivering—a sob—then trailing away. Then came the huntsman's voice, a long desperate wail like a war cry.

Maureen was not beside him in bed. This was not unusual, but Paul rose and went to the window, to see if she was out by the kennel.

She stood barefoot in the middle of the lawn, facing the fields, listening. The sun, as it cleared the top of the hedgerow, flashed on her still figure, showing her legs through her white cotton nightdress. Paul turned away from the window and went to the cupboard to find a clean shirt, moving slowly, with deliberate indecision.

In the kitchen, he saw Maureen at the scullery sink. She might have been preparing the dogs' food, but she just stood there idly, staring out the window. Paul thought of the time he had found her there, equally motionless, drowning two of Betsey's pups. But this time, when he put his hands on her shoulders and leaned around to see her face, it was clear that she had been crying. Paul stepped away from her, took the kettle from the cooker and filled it. He carried it back and lit the gas. He took two cups from their hooks. He willed himself not to speak first.

She said, without turning around, "I've been . . . "

Paul saw how the dew had seeped up her nightdress all the way to her thighs. He saw blades of grass slicked to the backs of her heels, the wet haloes on the slate floor around her feet. He waited for her to say *unfaithful* or *deceiving you,* but of course she did not. She said, " . . . out to check on the dogs. I thought I heard Betsey whining."

"You were listening to the horn."

"Yes. 'Gone to Ground.'" She had turned around and was rubbing her eyes. She went to the cooker and cupped her hands over the kettle. "I'm dead tired. Do you mind if I go up and sleep just another hour?"

"I thought we might talk."

"Please, Paul." She looked him straight in the eye, plaintively. "Another time, whatever it is, I promise we will."

Paul stepped aside and let her go up the back stairs. His heart felt like a flock of sheep outrun yet again by a good cunning dog, forced neatly into a cramped square pen.

THREE

ALTHOUGH THE FERRY IS NOT SCHEDULED to leave until eleven—and will almost certainly leave a good deal later—Paul's suitcase is down in the lobby, his room key turned in, by eight o'clock. He wears a blue shirt which he washed by hand the night before and hung in an open window to dry. The sea spray and sun on the boat will smooth out the wrinkles acceptably. Such are my tiny preoccupations, Paul thinks grimly as he leaves the hotel: that I look as unwrinkled as possible.

He takes the more circuitous route to the harbor, choosing the lanes too narrow for cars, where an occasional donkey saunters by and the same interchangeable old women sit at their spinning wheels each morning, wearing black but spinning white. They grin at the tourists who take their pictures and wish everyone a good day. Today one of them waves at Paul as if she knows him. He waves back.

THE MORNING AFTER Maureen's funeral, when Paul opened the door to the library, Fenno looked up from Paul's desk. Without betraying the slightest surprise or guilt, he held up the deed to the house. "Are you selling it?" Fenno's voice was neutral, almost bemused.

"I don't know." Along with other papers, the deed had been in a folder tucked into the side of the blotter.

"Davey and Dennis would be crushed."

"I know that. I'm not ignoring their sentiments. And you?"

Fenno laughed. "Do I have a say? I live across an ocean."

"If you told me that coming here just once a year made a difference in your life, that would matter. It's not that I can't afford to stay." Paul crossed the room to stand between the desk and the windows. Snow, falling swiftly, filled the room with a crisp even light. In it, Fenno looked pale and tired, and though Paul knew that he and his brothers had been up until dawn, talking and drinking, he couldn't help trying to assess Fenno's well-being. Would he be doing this constantly now? The thought exhausted him deeply.

As if guessing at the scrutiny, Fenno swiveled the chair and stood. The wall he now faced was covered with newspaper cuttings, award-winning stories in staggered states of acidic decay. The oldest, written when Paul was in his twenties, would have crumbled to dust if removed from their frames.

Fenno leaned close to one of the cuttings. "'Mill Saw Tragedy Reversed.'" He read to himself for a moment, then turned to his father. "Dad, this is gruesome stuff."

"It's medical reporting, Fenno. It's not sensationalism." Paul smiled. He knew that Fenno was looking at a grainy photograph of an arm which, once severed, had been successfully reattached. The article had been one in a series on the kind of plastic surgery that had nothing to do with vanity. Paul remembered watching a seven-hour surgery in which a young girl's fingers were meticulously re-fused to her hand, one spidery vein at a time. The surgeon's talent made him think of the patient rigor of Old World embroidery.

Fenno turned to other articles, here and there smiling or raising an eyebrow. Paul knew that his chance to speak honestly was now or probably never.

Fenno walked back to the desk and picked up a packet of letters that had been in the folder with the deed. "What you do with the house is up to you, but you're not getting rid of the collies."

Two months ago, Maureen had given away three yearling puppies, but that left six dogs to care for. Two were trial champions; the others shared their bloodlines. The letters Fenno held were from Maureen's files and contained the addresses of local farmers she had sold to in the past and other breeders she trusted. Paul had planned to invite them by, to take the dogs off his hands.

Paul lost his patience. "Oh, all right, so you, I suppose, you plan to take them back to New York and keep them in your city flat. Run them in some car park every day. Take them along to the shop so they don't destroy your armchairs out of boredom."

Fenno ignored his anger. "David can take two. We talked about it last night. And yes, Dad, I can take one; I'll take Rodgie because he's

the youngest; he'll do best on the flight. And the others . . . you have
the space if you stay."

"Well, I might want to travel. I might want to . . ."

"You can find someone to look after them when you're gone. Pay that
farm foreman over at Conkers to take them."

"What if I've never cared for these dogs?"

"As likely as your never caring for Mum."

Paul leaned into the window bay. Directly below, he could just see
one of the birdfeeders they kept filled, even since Fenno's absence. It
hung like a pendulum from a dogwood tree, stilled by the weight of
the snowfall. Across the burn, the kennel fence resembled lace. The
dogs, nowhere to be seen, were probably hunkered away in their house,
filling it with their feral warmth. "Fenno, this isn't your business,
really."

"I think it is. I think anything you plan to do with something as
much a part of Mum as her legs or her hands is very much my fucking
business."

"Well then, perhaps the dogs should be buried with her, Egyptian
style." Despite the cold radiating from the pane against his forehead,
Paul's face and neck burned. He thought about the potential vengeance
he held in that packet of letters. He should be relieved Fenno hadn't
guessed at that. "Fenno, I hate it when you curse. For one thing, it's
affected."

"I'm sorry. I'm worked up about this." Fenno's voice, softened, came
from directly behind Paul's back; its sudden proximity unnerved him.

Paul said, without turning around, "I just don't want you, any of
you, to expect me not to change anything. I don't want you to treat me
like the curator of your mother's memory."

"And I just don't want you to do anything on impulse."

"Maybe a little impulse would do me good," said Paul, and it was
right then, looking into the snowflakes, deliberately blinding himself
with their brightness, that he thought of Greece. A fleeting notion, but
one he grasped like a root reaching toward a swimmer tumbled over
and over by a fierce rogue current.

"What would do you good, Dad, is a little self-pity. Suffer and whine
a bit, would you please? I'm not joking. And then, I don't know, start
going to parties. Make the small talk you hate or roll up your sleeves

and pry into other people's lives. Stop standing back all the time. Stop being so . . . sober."

Paul smiled at the withheld obscenity. "The American approach to bereavement: martini therapy."

"Right now, you could use American anything," Fenno said tartly. "Why don't you come for a visit? You've never come for a visit."

Paul heard the packet of letters fall back on the desk. When Fenno next spoke, Paul could tell he was standing in the doorway. "This is just me speaking, you know. Me blowing off steam. I'm not some kind of . . . delegate. Just so you know, so you don't feel . . ."

Paul turned around. "Ganged up on?"

Fenno's smile erased the fragility Paul had read into his face. "I'm going downstairs to make coffee for Mal. He claims to hate the colonial implications of tea."

Paul looked down at the birdfeeder, trying to gauge from the snow on its miniature roof how much had fallen. Fenno and his friend were to fly to New York late that night—though in the wake of Lockerbie (which would hold the headlines, Paul knew, for weeks to come), bad weather seemed the least of a traveler's worries.

Fenno had always been conscientious; in that way, he was very much an oldest child. Impulse, Paul thought, was even more foreign to his son's constitution than it was to his own. He thought everything through to its every consequence, trivial or major. He saw the details others neglected to see (what he had seen between his parents, Paul did not want to know). Just now, Fenno had said he would take the youngest dog. Rodgie was two; if he lived a good, hardy collie's life, he'd depend on Fenno another ten years. Fenno would have thought that out.

"WELL HALLOO THERE, if it isn't *you*—and where's our peerless leader?" Marjorie emerges from a wide straight road that intersects Paul's rugged lane. She carries a large cardboard box awkwardly fitted with a twine handle. "On your way to breakfast? I could eat a Trojan horse—ha, so to speak."

"Let me take that," says Paul, and she gladly hands over her box. He has no choice but to join her.

"I thought I'd never get this picked up," she says. "It would have been an absolute tragedy! The hours these merchants keep—or don't keep—are jolly scandalous. I applaud their sense of leisure, but to a *point*." Marjorie does not wait to be seated by the waiter who greets them but chooses a table right by the water, one which would almost certainly have gone to a local. "One—no, two, *dio*—of those wonderful ice coffees—*kafess tou pahgoo* . . . oh dear, I've probably asked for a pair of cold flannels. . . ." She then names, or tries to name, something else. The waiter smiles at her Greek, but kindly, and points to some pastries on a nearby table. "Yes, those, exactly. Thank you," Marjorie says, nodding vigorously. She turns to Paul. "There. These boys are jolly nice, so long as you have a go at their language. However mangled your going at it may be!"

They talk about the remainder of their trip: Santorini, Crete, a last night at some deluxe hotel in Athens. Marjorie can't wait for Knossos; this, she thinks, will be the apotheosis of their journey. She hopes they'll see dolphins on the ferry this time; so far, they haven't. She wonders if this is a sign that the Aegean is hopelessly polluted. No one would tell them, of course, if it was. She talks on and on, and Paul listens.

"I've bought so many beautiful things, but this is the pièce de résistance. Let me show you." She wrenches the twine from her box and opens it. Out of the raffia she pulls a brightly painted ceramic bowl, crisscrossed with orange, green, and purple patterns, an octopus painted inside. "Eight of these, and a big one to match—each one has a different pattern, they're so whimsical," she says, insisting that Paul take the bowl and examine it. "Isn't that a pleasing shape?"

"Yes, very pleasing." He hands it back.

"And you, what are you taking back?"

Paul sighs. "I'm not much of a collector." More truthfully, he might have said that he had come here not to take memories away but to leave them behind, to bring some of the ones he already has and drop them like stones, one by one, in the sea.

"A shame. You should see the marvellous things I've collected; I always take an extra suitcase for my loot. When I go back, I make exhibits in school for the children. Gives me a little tax write-off too."

Paul watches the boats tug their moorings and thinks of his fantasy on the way to Delos: setting himself adrift from island to island. Or choosing one and staying indefinitely. He remembers how he mentioned this to Fern and wonders if that's when he made a fool of himself, if that's when he suddenly looked his age to her. On the other hand, what a youthful, unlikely thing it would be for Paul to abandon the tour. He would be a deserter. He has never, after all, deserted anyone or anything. He has been a good lieutenant, a more-or-less obedient heir (at the very least producing three more), a patient husband; in all eyes but Fenno's, perhaps, a dependable father. A shepherd, just as Fern suggested.

Paul has acted, always, as if life must predict itself step by step or all hell will break loose. Is the wild dream so unreasonable—jolly scandalous, as Marjorie might righteously say? What if, after all these years, it's circled back into reach?

He remembers dinner last night: the looks on everyone's faces when Jack bolted his food and left, claiming he had errands to run—errands at ten o'clock in a town where only the one discotheque and a few bars would be open for business. There were whispers of *scandalous* then. The quadruplets huddled and giggled and nudged one another with their sandaled feet. Ray said that he would complain to the tour company back in London. But Jack is Jack: he has probably got away with worse crimes than running off for a night to sleep with a girl. Some people have an inborn buoyancy, an immunity to being held accountable.

Too easily, Paul sees Jack's brown hand like a starfish on Fern's rosy, freckled back, his mustache chafing her neck. To supplant this vision, he looks at the harbor, concentrates on a sloop, its sails furled, gliding straight toward him. So what if he were to retire from the paper, even sell it; what if he were to travel alone for a year? What if he were to say to Fenno, All right, the house and the dogs will stay, but *you* take them on.

Paul recognizes this immediately for the false wish it is: not just to call Fenno home but to make him see his father's life from within. The house could simply be closed for a time, or let; the dogs, as Fenno suggested, sent over to board at the farm.

"Yoohoo in there," says Marjorie, her face a few inches from his.

"What?" he says, embarrassed at his absence.

She touches his arm, the way she did the first morning in Athens, extolling the benefits of time. "Oh listen, you do deserve to drift. I understand completely about the drifting; back then I called it the suppositions. You know: supposing this; supposing that. I did a lot of it back then."

"When?" Paul is startled by how much she knows. He's only beginning to realize what a good traveler she is.

"When my farm burned down. Before I taught real school, I had a horse farm, a riding school, and the whole thing burned to the ground, not a single animal saved. I could probably have replaced it—insurance, I'm good about those things—but each horse . . . no, I couldn't possibly. So that's how I started on my rovings. Next winter, I'll see the Yucatán." As she delivers this oddly cheerful speech, Marjorie repacks her box of bowls. When she's finished, she sits back to enjoy the sun, which has moved just high enough to touch their table. "I *was* a crack hand at dressage."

This thought seems to leave her more satisfied than wistful. And then she changes course again, suddenly raising her hands above her head and exclaiming, "Oh it is not for me, it seems, to touch the sky with my two arms!"

"What?" says Paul again, but now he's laughing. "Marjorie, you're losing me at every turn."

"Sappho. One of her curious, lovely fragments. And here you are, snapping out of it; I see a start anyway. But honestly, will you look at those majestic clouds? The quintessential June sky—and such an everyday thing in these parts! I don't know about yours, but my eyes were jolly famished for a sky like that." She checks her watch, makes noises of polite alarm, and hastily begins counting coins. Paul stills her hand.

"Gentlemen are too rare," she says as she stands and hoists her box to her hip. "And no, you may not carry this back to the hotel." She waves down their waiter. "Taxi, *paricolo?*"

Paul orders another coffee. He looks around, hoping to find an abandoned newspaper in a language he can read even badly. Sitting up to scan the tables, he sees, under the far side of the awning, Fern and Jack. Jack is eating a souvlaki. He eats greedily, radiant with energy and carnivorous content. Shaded by her hat, Fern sits very close to Jack, touching him often. She is trying hard to look carelessly affectionate, but her face refuses to conceal her panic. She looks bereft already. She has fallen hard for Jack, though of course she doesn't know him. Paul doesn't know him either.

Fern lays her head on Jack's shoulder. Jack is licking his fingers and constantly talking. He kisses the top of her head, but his eyes are on the harbor. He must know, from experience, just how to tell her good-bye: Wasn't that a lark; enjoy the rest of your travels, love. Give 'em hell back in Paris.

Turning his back to them, Paul stands up and leaves. Fifteen minutes later, reading in the hotel lobby, he sees Jack rush past without noticing him, up the stairs two at a time. Irene, buying postcards at the desk, glares after Jack, then looks at Paul as if he is some kind of playboy accomplice. Come Santorini, he will no longer have the room with the coveted view; what a relief it will be to unburden that debt.

TWO DAYS AFTER Maureen's funeral, Paul removed the lipstick from his overcoat pocket. He had carried it there for a week, like a sputtering coal, waiting for the first moment when he would have Tealing all to himself (not counting the collies). Hands trembling, he locked himself in the bedroom.

It was an ovoid tube, expensively made, with four subtle furrows at the base where the kind of woman who could afford it would press her manicured fingertips. The hue of the lipstick itself was gratifyingly bright, the waxy scarlet of tulips, a color someone had christened Ingénue. It had yet to be used. Paul wondered if this had been the "signature color" of the woman who would have worn it—a term he had recently learned from the paper's new fashion editor (its first), a young woman from London who wore only green. In various loos in various houses he's visited, Paul has seen baskets or shelves holding six or seven perfumes, half a dozen lipsticks. But Maureen, on the occasions she wore lipstick, wore only one color, that same dark red which in certain light looked nearly purple. She had worn it for as long as he knew her; it had startled him that first night they spoke, the night he had driven her home from the Globe.

Funny, he thought when he turned the pirated lipstick over and saw its name, how he had never known a detail like that: the name of his wife's lipstick. He had bought her many things, but never cosmetics.

Immediately, he went to Maureen's bureau and opened the top drawer, from which he had seen her, hundreds and hundreds of times, remove her makeup.

The drawer was spotlessly empty. Even the lining paper had been removed. His blood seemed to pause in his veins, he was so stunned: someone had ransacked the house. He started toward the telephone and then stopped. He sat on the foot of the bed. David's wife, in a too-efficient but well-meaning gesture, had asked him just the day before if he would like her to clear out Maureen's things while he drove Fenno and Mal to their plane.

He saw himself in Maureen's mirror; so many conversations had taken place like this. Paul, ready to leave or ready to sleep, would sit on the end of their bed and listen or talk to her reflection as she combed her hair or put away her bracelets. One conversation which would always stand out took place on another night after Fenno had left, the night they returned from sending him off to New York to begin his studies.

Sitting in his pajamas, Paul had said, "I suppose he'll meet some charming American girl, fall head over heels and marry her. Our luck, she'll be from California, and she'll lure him away to San Diego or Rancho Mirage." He pronounced these place names as if they were colonies on other planets; he'd never been to either. "We'll see him every third Christmas."

Maureen was wiping off her lipstick, which she did in one clean, assertive motion. Her mouth was left with a slight magenta stain, and her face looked wholly different. It always took Paul a moment to adjust to her eyes, suddenly so prominent.

That night, she looked at him in the mirror at the exact moment her face seemed to change. At first she said nothing, then *"That* he won't do." She busied herself putting things away: a compact, a locket, a dog collar which she had pulled from the pocket of a jumper.

Paul laughed. "You know your son that well."

"I know he won't marry. Or, well, won't settle down with a woman."

"You mean you can't picture it."

"You know it, too, don't you?" She looked at Paul again. He did not understand the strictness in her glance, the hint of arrogance or impatience. "You do know Fenno doesn't like women."

"Doesn't like women?" Paul wished that Maureen would turn around. She was occupied with nothing now but sat with her arms crossed and continued to address him only in the mirror.

"Oh, he *likes* women," she said. "Of course he likes women. In a way, I suppose, he may like women better than most blinking men do!"

"Maureen, you're speaking in riddles."

"I am not." She laughed, and at last she turned around. "Paul, you're being dense. For the benefit of wordsmiths here, I meant *like* as in 'fancy.' What did you suppose about that boy he brought here from Cambridge last summer? Did you think they were nothing more than literary pals?"

"Did he tell you something?"

"Of course not. Oh, Paul." She sat beside him on the bed, but she was still laughing when she put her arms around his neck.

"This isn't something to laugh about," he said.

When she said, "Is it something to cry about?" Paul supposed she meant to reassure him, but he felt mocked. She had called him dense; whether or not he was, this was how she saw him: opaque and obstructive as fog. And in a secret rage, he refused to believe that there was one thing, significant or not, she could claim to hold over him when it came to knowing his son.

He thought of the five years that passed after their marriage before she was willing to start having children. Maureen told him how important it was they take the time to enjoy each other alone before children; she said she would know when the time was right. In their third or fourth year together, he began to fear that she had deceived him when she expressed the desire for those four hypothetical boys. By then both his sisters had babies, and though Paul's father never said anything explicit, there were unmistakable piercing looks across the table at Christmas and other holidays which brought the larger family together. Paul imagined that his father was telling him he had made *two* grave mistakes in his marriage: not just the mistake of marrying down but the mistake (or bad luck) of choosing a barren wife. Paul's father would never have dreamed that his son, still loving his wife's very willfulness, its comforting power, would have let the issue of heirs be a *decision,* least of all hers.

And then, of course, just as Paul knew he would have to force the question, Maureen quite happily announced that she was pregnant.

The pregnancy, she claimed, had surprised her as much as it did Paul. Not a doubt crossed his mind at the time, but Paul has long since realized how unlikely such a "slip" would be for a planner like Maureen. And back then it would hardly have mattered: All his festering resentment dissolved (as did his father's, especially once he learned it was a boy). Still, as he saw her attention turn inward, if rightfully so, he had a moment of panic: In those years alone together, how much had they actually stopped to *enjoy* each other, as Maureen had insisted they must? They had laughed a great deal, fought little, made love often and in a fever; but why had Paul felt such a constant undercurrent of worry? He wondered if this tension had always been a part of his nature; the more understandable tensions he had felt in the army stood like a wall against the penetration of memory beyond them. Perhaps those tensions themselves had simply become a habit. Small price to pay for remaining alive.

THE SEA IS CALM, as if to repent yesterday's misbehavior. The sky is lavender blue. Paul stands with Jack at the bow, looking toward Naxos, its tall peaked silhouette. It is an exceptionally green island—a burnt, wry green. Jack is telling Paul how Naxos is an island for hikers, not for lazy middle-aged tourists the likes of Solly and Ray. The men have been acting chilly toward Jack. Once on the boat, they made a show of leading their wives to the opposite end of the deck.

"But you, Paul. You have the spirit. You'd like it."

Paul thinks, Perhaps I will. Perhaps, after Crete, he will not head back to Athens. But he keeps this thought to himself, so the two men stand together silently, watching this island slip away. As it does, another looms ahead, demanding attention.

"That girl," Jack says suddenly, "those Americans. They watch too many movies, get too many notions."

"Notions?" says Paul.

"She asked, this morning, if she could come along with us. Can you imagine? I had a devil of a time explaining . . ." He seems to expect Paul to pick up the slack, agree with him. When Paul says nothing, he says, "I suppose she's too young to know that these things don't matter so much."

"I'd say she's still young enough," says Paul, "to know that they should."

Jack looks surprised but not caught out. "Well touché, Bucko. I forgot your horse is white." Simultaneously, Paul hears Maureen's teasing voice strike the very same note, calling him an old crosspatch. All along, Jack's voice has been mirroring hers.

Jack sits by the rail and reaches into his rucksack. "She gave me a couple things to give you. This"—he hands Paul the jumper she borrowed on Delos—"and this, I'm not sure why."

Paul takes the sketch. "Oh I have a notion. Notions are a weakness of mine as well." But his scorn, this late, is wasted on Jack, who winks at Paul and heads off to check on the rest of his flock.

It's the watercolor of the woman and her little boy, carefully torn from Fern's book. On its obverse is the olive tree, the one where Paul said he could see the wind in the branches. Entanglements of family, solace of nature. Or comforts of family, isolation of nature. In the little boy he sees something of Fenno, the determined hold. It dawns on Paul that Fenno has always been caught in the middle between two pairs: his differently fixated parents (Paul on Maureen, Maureen on her dogs), the happy self-occupied twins. And milling around them all, like lurking base instincts kept under control, the collies; everywhere, always, the flawlessly disciplined collies, both clever and cruel.

Paul thinks of the responsibility with which he would love to saddle his son. He likes to think this is exactly what Fenno would love too, what would gratify him, at least for a while. Paul sees him setting up house with Mal (friend? lover? surrogate twin?). The two of them live however they wish to live: reading and walking the countryside or, who knows, giving clamorous dinner parties and dancing on a lawn gone entirely to brazen purple loosestrife. He likes the small mean thought of Mrs. Ramage—now bedridden after a stroke—still able to spy and feel offended but no longer able to complain. Outraged but speechless as young men and women carouse through the hedgerow after midnight, storming her flowerbeds, singing, kissing, misbehaving in ways she never imagined in her greatest indignation.

Years ago in the Guatemalan jungle, there was that moment when he wished he could put Maureen in Fenno's place. Replace simplifying silence with elaborating wit. Now here he is wishing, with even more futility, the opposite. After all, Fenno is happy where he is. Paul is as certain of this as a father can be.

He folds the jumper and unzips his bag to put it away. He slips the sketch into the folds of his newspaper, until he can find a safer place. He looks backward, at the boat's wake, the foam folding crisply down under itself, twisting broad ropes into Marjorie's gabardine blue. The flanking waves close in behind, smoothing over the surface, leaving the sea just as it was, no trace of the boat's recent passing. Satisfying, he thinks, the way the sea is stirred up, churned so briskly, then returns to its original calm—though not quite: for a moment, if you look hard, the water sparkles there with a little more brilliance. Ahead and behind, always islands, more islands; one fades away, another draws near. Turning full circle to take them all in, Paul sees each one as a welcome mystery, a choice to be weighed without prophecy or speculation.

Upright

1995

FOUR

MY FATHER'S FUNERAL will be the first one I've been to in a long while—the first since my mother's—where most of the mourners and grief junkies will not be my age or younger. My father died swiftly and in the punctilious order of things: he was seventy-four years old and had a heart attack on Naxos, in a small house on a hillside with a view of tiered olive trees and the Aegean Sea. It was a house he had leased several years running, to which he'd retreat for the hottest months of the year. He was alone and suffered whatever pain there was to suffer without the so-called solace of family or friends. His solitude notwithstanding, most of the people whose funerals I've attended in the past several years would have killed to die that way, that late. (A death to die for, is that what I've just said?)

David and Lillian meet me at Prestwick. I haven't seen them in a year and a half, and the first words out of my brother's mouth are "Excellent timing, Fen. Dad's just in from Athens; you've saved us an extra trip."

Lil gives me a close hug and one of her sweetly conspiratorial smiles. "Speaking of trips, how was yours?"

"Predictably dreary—or let me amend that: fabulous. No one blew us out of the sky, no engines caught fire, no drunks urinated on the beverage cart." I put down my bags to hug her back, intentionally harder.

Lillian always smells to me like honeydew melon; I like to imagine it's not a perfume—perhaps it isn't—but the irrepressible succulence of a good heart, the fragrance of her innate generosity. I find it slightly exasperating, disorienting, that my favorite sister-in-law is married to my least favorite brother. I'm always secretly wishing they'd swap. Once I stopped to muse what preternaturally sweet offspring, good to their primal reptilian core, would have to result (to be thrown off, my mother the breeder would correct me) were Lil married to Dennis. I should add that I don't dislike David—we had fun when we were boys—but somehow that final surge of testosterone left him workaday in his sensibilities and strikingly devoid of wit. I probably stiffen him up (figuratively, of course), but if so, isn't that in itself dislikable?

David looks at his watch (a large, multigadgeted thing that belongs on the wrist of Jacques Cousteau). "We have to take some shuttlebus to some godforsaken freight depot to fetch him. What do you wager there'll be reams of bureaucratic rubbish to fill out before they'll let us take him home?"

Lil tucks an arm through mine, though we are still standing just outside customs, yet to head anywhere constructive. "Davey, why put Fenno through it? He's probably been awake all night; let me help him fetch his bags, stop for tea, and we'll bring the car round to the freight place and wait."

"Lillian, in this day and age you can hardly just cruise about an airport as you please," says David. "You could have a kilo of Semtex in the boot or bazookas sewn into the seats."

"I did sleep, and these are my bags," I say, lifting my carry-on and my bagged funeral suit. "And I'm mildly talented at bureaucratic nonsense. So head me toward this bus and I'll meet you back here." I hand my bags to David and point to a cocktail lounge (an Americanism I lovingly own, for its aura of odalisques). With any luck, he'll soften up after a beer.

"But you're on holiday, a guest!" says Lil.

"What makes him a guest?" says David.

"The distance he's traveled."

"He's right," I say. "Funerals are business, not pleasure, except for those who arrange the flowers." Ten to one, the sister-in-law I very much don't like has that job. ("Ah, so the little skunk does flowers," Mal whispered to me the afternoon he met her. "Sometimes God *is* in the details, isn't She?")

"Well then, long as you're offering," says David, and hands me three fifty-pound notes. "In case there are Greeks on this end too." His wife gives him a fondly disapproving look. He doesn't notice. They are halfway to the lounge when he turns and calls out to me, over the heads of several strangers, "But hang on—Dad's addressed to me!"

OFF AND ON FOR YEARS, you wonder where you'll be when you learn that your parents have died. You know it's likely that you will, one day, have to receive this news: once, if they die together; more probably twice. You wonder which would be worse. (And you don't want to contemplate what it would mean if you never do.) You're walking home from the market on a sunny day and suddenly, for no reason, you picture yourself going in the front door a few minutes hence. You see the blinking light on your machine and push PLAY and hear the mutated voice of one of your siblings or your mum or dad, and though they probably won't give the bad news itself on tape, you know from the tone of the voice the gist of what you'll hear when you ring back. Then when you actually do push open your door, struggling with the bags, carrot greens tickling your ear, and the light is indeed blinking, your heart is a fist—my God, it's true, there *are* premonitions!—but when you push PLAY, of course it's Ralph inviting you upstairs to supper or Tony just wanting to hear your voice (though he'd never put it that way, never give you an affectionate inch) or the super wanting to repipe your loo or, nowadays, some credit card sweepstakes hang-up.

I did not have to hear about my mother's death long-distance. I was there at her side, along with my father and both of my brothers. According to her doctors, the cancer consumed her rapidly—within five months of her diagnosis—but as far as I could see, she died a prolonged, torturous death. (I have glimpsed a few, lest you doubt my powers of comparison.) Since she smoked as if tobacco were a vocation, the cancer was hardly a surprise, but she was the youngest sixty-nine-year-old I have ever known, and I couldn't imagine her anything but very much alive, electrically so, for two or three decades to come.

I flew home when she got the news, seven summers ago, and again that December, when she died. She decided to die at home—not easy, with this kind of death. She took oxygen until the day she decided, Enough. By then she spoke only in terrible gasps, and she'd given up even those attempts, probably because they planted such terrified expressions on the faces around her. So she wrote it down, that one decisive, indignant word, in large unquavering capital letters: ENOUGH.

It was my shift, and I was reading to her from a volume of Emily Dickinson I'd brought overseas from my shop, along with another two dozen books. Mum was never much of a reader—only because, I suspect, she hated all the *sitting* it requires—but my father had told me on the telephone that she liked being read to now that she was stuck in bed. So when she rapped on my knee and thrust that piece of paper across the open book, I laughed and said, "I should've guessed Emily's not your cup of tea." Mum laughed too—a brief hideous cough—and shook her head. She pointed to her chest. Emily Dickinson, everything she was and wrote, seemed so infantile for that instant, so pointlessly frilly against my mother's granite wish. I began to cry. Mum's eyes, of course, remained quite dry. She pushed herself upright from the pillows to give me her best approximation of a smile. Her breath sounded like a handsaw fighting through a dense green tree. I left the room to find my father. Within an hour, we were assembled. Except for David (who had the confounding nerve to respond, however briefly, to calls on his pager), none of us left that room for the seven hours it took her to leave us behind.

My father sat closest to her, on the bed, speaking now and then straight into her ear. His voice was quiet and caressing, inaudible as words to the rest of us, largely because of Mum's ghastly breathing, which grew louder and more urgent, interrupted by patches of gasping silence. She did not want enough morphine to put her under, even though the doctor had given my father instructions on how to "relieve her discomfort."

Of those endless hours, I remember very little other than the sound of her breathing. I remember feeling sad that her favorite dogs could not be in the room because her state would only have agitated them. They were in the kennel out back, visible from the windows but not from my mother's bed. And I remember feeling angry at David because his trousers were spattered with blood; he'd been in the midst of a difficult delivery, a breech calf, when he got Dad's call. (I thought, though I suppose it was petty, that if he could leave the room to return his calls, he could fucking change his trousers.)

It was David who rang about Dad. I was in the shop well before opening time, browsing shelf by shelf through New Fiction, to see which not-so-new fiction I must relegate to the less prominent Novels & Stories shelves. Because of that dreary human predilection for the shiny and new, I always feel when I make this shift as if I'm sending so many bright, hopeful creatures out to pasture before their youth is spent. (Though I would never condemn them, as other shops do, to a section entitled Literature, a word which to my admittedly over-schooled mind is ossified and clubby. I picture a mausoleum, filled with sagging armchairs and lamps that cast inadequate, jaundiced light.)

"Fen, it's David, are you up? I've got bad news."

"David, it's half nine. I've been up for hours." I can answer my personal phone in the shop because it's two floors below my flat and I have an extension; David would not know I was at work. He rises at dawn every day but clearly assumes I lead the stereotypically debauched life of a New York City faggot.

Why I did not think of our father, I can't say. Maybe because David didn't sound sad enough for someone with news of a death. I thought for some reason of Tealing, our family house, and imagined that it had burnt to the ground. In my mind (though our house is nowhere near that grand), I saw the end of *Rebecca,* Manderley in ruins. I waited.

"I'm afraid it's Dad. He's been found dead by the woman who cleans his house."

In my brother's expectant silence, I stared out the window and watched a young woman cross the street straight in my direction. "Dead?" I said dumbly. "He was dead?"

"Yes, it's awful, I don't know much more than that so far," David rushed on. "Had a ridiculously muddled conversation with whoever masquerades as a coroner in those parts. I'm paying him through the nose to take care of the remains, get them shipped out by the end of the week."

Remains: such a Victorian cloak of a word.

"Fenno, are you still on the line? Fenno?"

"Yes, David." Now the young woman was trying the door. When she caught my eye, I clamped the phone between shoulder and cheek and used both hands to indicate that I would open at ten. (Would I open? I supposed that I would. Running a bookshop—unlike manning a seat on the stock exchange or replacing burnt-out bulbs along the cables of a suspension bridge—is something one can manage even in fairly acute states of mourning. No one is at risk of anything more than the embarrassment of witnessing grief.)

"We'll want to do a proper funeral. You know, hundreds of people are likely to attend. Dad's still an éminence grise to the church-elder types."

This was true. Our father was influential, affluent, and genuinely loved around and beyond the Scottish country town where we grew up. For most of his life, following his father, he was the publisher of the Dumfries-Galloway newspaper. I told David I'd book the earliest flight I could manage.

"Bear in mind that you can get condolence fares; I'm not sure that's what they're called, but the rates are reduced and they'll find you seats on full-up flights if you tell them there's been a family death."

How like David to get right to the practical stuff. I wanted to ask him if he had actually realized what the impetus was behind his pragmatic overdrive. That our father was *gone*. I can't say whether David and Dad were confidants, but David saw more of him than Dennis or I—at least in the winter months, the months my father chose to stay at Tealing these past years, as if what's the point of a northern home if you don't immerse yourself in its northness? Six months before, David and Lillian had moved into Tealing, a temporary arrangement. His practice had become so successful that he'd decided to convert their cottage-by-the-clinic into an equine surgery; they'd look for a house of their own once construction was finished. Now, I supposed, they would simply stay on.

I settled on "David, are you all right?"

"In shock, but yes, 'all right' I suppose. You think I sound cold, don't you?"

"Not cold . . ."

"Someone has to get everything organized. If you were here with me now, that would be a different thing. Dennis, of course . . ." Half-heartedly, he laughed.

"You mean Véronique." On this, we were in complete agreement. There wasn't much use asking Dennis to help out in a crisis, not because he wouldn't—instinctively, he'd give you five days for every one he had to spare—but because there'd be hell to pay with his watchdog of a wife. (Dennis would ring me later that night, from France, and cry through most of the short conversation she allowed us.)

"He'll take care of food, and that's not trivial. I'm thinking we should do a luncheon."

"David?" I found myself reaching again and again for my mug of tea, though it had been empty almost since he rang. "David, can we please discuss all this when I arrive?"

By ten o'clock, I had booked a seat on British Air, called Ralph and cajoled him into looking after my animals and watching the shop for a week (he's my business partner but loves the shop as a place to make appearances, not to linger). When I unlocked the door, I saw the girl who'd peered in the window. To pass the time, she had spread a newspaper on the postbox across the street. As I stepped outside and waved to her, a blast of summer air engulfed me. June in New York, its rudely sudden heat, is something I still can't get used to. (But then, air-conditioning is one of the American luxuries I love best, the only one with which I'm profligate.)

I held the door for her to enter. Without waiting for me to offer assistance, she said, "My best friend's over at Saint A's having a double mastectomy. She loves mysteries, but only with women detectives, and nothing where anything bad happens to animals or children. Oh, and maybe, considering, no knives . . . ?"

Such presumptive demands and perversely touching out-of-the-blue disclosures, both of which I encounter often in a working day, are two things that have helped me weather the insanities and losses I've suffered since moving across the Atlantic. Like air-conditioning, they seem indigenous to these parts.

"I have just the thing," I said, which is what I say, as a stalling tactic, when I haven't the faintest idea if I have such a thing at all. I led her downstairs to Detective Stories & Thrillers—not my favorite section, though I respect its devotees—and together we filled a small shopping bag with books that would do what precious little they could to distract her friend from waking up without her breasts. Off and on that day, when I wasn't thinking of Dad, I was thinking of that anonymous woman and hoping she wasn't as young as her friend—though would age make it any more acceptable or any less painful, having to go through that ordeal without the promise of true, regenerative healing?

BEFORE I CAN MAKE the front door, Dennis has me clenched in a garlicky full-body vise-grip. Dennis and David are both noticeably taller than I am, but Dennis stands over me by nearly a head, and the feel of his embrace is inescapably parental, in the very best sense. I am never the first to pull away. "Fenny, Fenny, I can't believe it, can you? I thought he'd live to ninety, I thought he'd watch me walk wee Laurie down the aisle."

Sometimes I think Dennis ought to have been an actor or a lounge singer, but then I set myself straight, since he wouldn't recognize artifice if it were a cricket bat smashing his jaw. All the sweetness, all the loving-kindness in the two sides of our family—present in our parents, certainly, but in neither one to that degree—must have flowed like a sap through our family tree, condensing into the affectionate effervescence of my youngest brother. Dennis is that rare cliché come true: He is a gem, a diamond chiseled well beyond the rough.

If I were to list my own finer attributes, sweetness would be markedly absent. Highest on my list would be patience. (Highest on David's would be ambition. And each of us has been served quite well by his cardinal strength.)

Dennis wears one of those double-breasted nehru jackets that are the uniform of his trade, and when at last he stands back from me, I can see that it's splashed with oils and sauces and wine. Reflexively, I look down.

My brother begins brushing at my shirt. "I'm so sorry—I'm trying a balsamic marinade for butterflied lamb—I thought, because you know how Dad loved lamb—and I thought I'd grill it out back—"

"We can't do leg of lamb for fifty, you're out of your mind. I thought we decided on chicken something-or-other," says David.

"Davey, it's for us, for tonight." Dennis hears none of the sniping in our brother's voice. He's tolerated, and usually honored, David's edicts and vetoes his entire life. (Sometimes it seems obvious that's why he chose Véronique—not because David liked her, not at all, but because she has the same imperial confidence. I've wondered what might have happened if David had met her before their wedding day, whether he'd have been tactless enough to say what a bitch he thought she was. If he had, that wedding would never have taken place.) Just fifteen minutes younger than David, Dennis adores him, probably more than anyone else now that our mother's gone. I've always been a little jealous of their twinship, even though they look and act so differently.

"Well good, fine. Just please don't overtax yourself," says David. "I'll get Dad out of the boot, and then Lillian has a doctor's appointment; we'll be back after that." I hadn't realized Dad's ashes returned in the boot and am about to comment on the disrespect when Dennis cheerfully interrupts me.

"By seven if you like it rare!" Never motionless except at a meal, he takes my bags from me with one hand and pulls me into the house, shouldering open doors. *"Allô! Mes petits poires!"* he calls out. *"Il est là! Onco est arrivé!*

"You've got your old room, I made sure of that," he says as he starts up the stairs. "I told Vee I wouldn't stand seeing you on some lumpy camp bed in the library, you've come so far. The girls are all in with us, and Davey's moved into Mum and Dad's. Lord of the manor already."

"Attends! Nous sommes occupées!" Véronique calls down.

I hold Dennis back. "Just drop that stuff and get me into the kitchen. I'm famished," I tell him, though hunger and even my aversion to his wife are not my primary motives. The kitchen is where I'll find Dennis at his happiest and most relaxed, where he in turn will make me as happy and relaxed as I can be under the circumstances.

As always now when he is here, the front hall is filled with extravagant odors. Onions sautéing in butter is a constant, because his training is classic French, but invariably something less predictable will hover just above that bedrock scent: cilantro or coconut or cumin. Today I smell something I can only describe as Provençal, perhaps rosemary or fennel. Because the house never smelled like this when we were small—because our mother, though she made a dependable joint, spent as little time indoors as possible—this has transformed my homecomings for the past several years. Though the furnishings are just as they were when I was ten, the aura is altogether changed by Dennis's cooking—the pervasive mustiness of Dad's books overruled at last—so that I feel as if I'm visiting home in a dream, where everything yet nothing is the way it should be, where the best of what you have and what you wish for are briefly, tantalizingly united.

Tealing is a house beamed north from a Thomas Hardy moor: white, many-gabled, and crisscrossed, like a late Mondrian, with dark rough beams. It is charming, not grand. Its steep roof was designed to be thatched—an imported folly of the architect, kept up at great expense for decades but replaced with blue slate before we moved in. Since our mother never fussed with decor and gave not a hoot for modernization (an unusual trait in a postwar bride, and one which I suspect helped win her my father), the kitchen is still a cavernous, utilitarian room. Its chief features are a long stained oak table smack in the center and—a treasure to Dennis, who repeatedly threatens to steal it—a tarantula of a stove that can accommodate ten large pots. Next door stoops a stodgy little cooker our mother used for the plain suppers she made; only Dennis, it seems, knows how to manage the wood-fed stove. He's even turned a soufflé out of its oven.

He goes straight to the icebox when we enter and, with the habitual speed of a chef, pulls out a plate of pâté and crackers, a whole roast chicken, still trussed, and a glistening cluster of large black grapes. One foot wedged in the door, he lays them on the table, then reaches back deftly again and pulls out a beer. "Chilled expressly for my Amoorican brother."

I smile, touched by his gesture. "Cultural turncoat that I am."

He walks around the table, facing me over a cutting board and a dozen heads of garlic. "I remember your friend Mal and his little speech on the stupidity of warm beer. 'Tepid spirits for a tepid people.' I'm not sure whether he made an actual convert of you or simply shamed you into it."

We laugh at the memory of Mal's Anglophobe diatribe, delivered at this table. I watch Dennis's hands as he uses a broad knife to pummel apart the cloves, then flatten and flay them, then mince them into pungent snowy mounds. I find myself fascinated by the way he moves, so aggressively yet so gently.

"You must miss him, even that sharp wit."

"Sharp? Oh, serrated," I say. "And yes, I still miss them both—him and his high-minded jibes at the world."

"You still have that bird?"

"Felicity will outlive us all." I'm moved again by the way my brother remembers these details, without any apparent effort, about my distant life. It's as if he studied up, yet I know these things are simply right there, within easy mental grasp; it gives me the comforting impression that he thinks of me often. "She keeps Rodgie alive by sheer virtue of her constant badgering. He leaves my couch now only for short walks in the neighborhood. He likes to go to a nearby playground, sit down on the pavement, and watch the children through the fence. I think he thinks they're sheep, the way they careen about and bleat. Rodgie's not used to human beings as such relentlessly happy creatures. I'm not sure he even knows it's happiness he's seeing."

"I wish sometimes . . ." Dennis pauses to sweep the minced garlic off the board into an old chipped bowl of our mother's. " . . . that I'd taken one of the dogs back then." Rodgie is one of the last two sheepdogs we own from the line our mother bred and showed. That was her shining skill in life, her special knack. When she died, there were half a dozen dogs left at Tealing; I took Rodgie, the youngest, and David took a pair, one of whom survives to ride about like a dignitary in the back of his pickup.

"You could hardly have kept a collie in Paris while making pastry from four in the morning till dark."

"Really, though, it wasn't that. It was Vee . . . I wouldn't have said so, but I knew she'd never stand for a dog in our flat—I mean *my* flat, of course, that I was *hoping* would be ours."

"You knew her already back then?" And then I recall that they had married less than a year after Mum's death—and, in short order, produced a fusillade of children: three within four years.

"Oh, I'd just that month been smitten. Talk about ghastly timing. Mum's dying hardly seemed the occasion to tell everyone I'd found the woman of my dreams. Though when I was alone with her—Mum—I did tell her. I think it made her happy." Peeling gingerroot now, never idle for an instant even in reflection, Dennis looks up quickly to see my reaction.

"She never was jealous of our crushes, was she," I say. Not till she'd been dead a few years did it dawn on me that she'd probably noticed mine, all on schoolmates, desperately though I tried to hide them (chiefly from myself). I can't shake my bewilderment that Dennis has dreams a woman like Véronique fulfills—unless, and I suppose I could hardly fault him for it, he is overly susceptible to beauty (for beautiful, in that tautly elegant very French way, she is). Why I need Dennis to be infallible, to have no Achilles heel, I don't know—but I do. I've always imagined that his wife must be a siren in bed. There must be a golden prize nestled in all that dramatic selfishness.

"So tell me the menu, *maître frère.*" I lean across the table to put a grape in Dennis's mouth before I realize that this is a gesture of inappropriate affection, beyond brotherly, a gesture from my New York life; but he opens up happily and takes it between his teeth.

"Terrific, aren't they? 'Grapes, to be worthy, must swoon the palate,' one of my masters used to say. Alphonse Lavalle, these beauties, first of the season, straight from a vineyard behind our house. I send the children over to do my poaching. If they get caught, they'll be a lot more easily forgiven than I'd be. I'll deal with the morality later."

"Never mind the morality of agricultural goods smuggled across the Channel."

"Oh, that," Dennis says dismissively. "I'm an old hand at that."

Yes, I think, from the days when it was drugs, not food. Of three boys reared in the sixties, Dennis was the only one to push that envelope.

I get up to put away the leftover food. In the scullery, the room off the kitchen where our mother kept the whelping box for her collies, is a stack of crates that stands to my chest; between the slats, I see the sleek pearly shafts and tufted roots of leeks. "Let me guess: vichyssoise."

"God, am I that routine?"

"I've never had your vichyssoise. I'm sure it's hardly routine."

"I do it with lots of garlic and nutmeg. Buttermilk in with the cream. Then a tajine of chicken, figs, and ginger—spiced down for the elders. I poke the figs with a fork and soak them in a strong Bordeaux." He beckons, and I join him again at the table, where he slides a platter off a large bowl; inside is a Dionysian mass of fruit, pickling in a lake of velvety purple. "Then a salad, plain greens, then peaches poached in cassis with lavender. Dried from Vee's incredible garden! That course I've done—Davey hauled an extra fridge over from the clinic and parked it in the garage. He's nothing if not resourceful."

Lil's remark about my being a guest begins to ring true. In the three days it took me to get here, David and Dennis have been planning not so much a funeral as an *event,* while Lil, who takes care of her husband's human business, must have spent hours on the clinic's telephone, delivering the bad news to everyone in Dad's life beyond our immediate family.

The peaches, Dennis is telling me, are to debut on his menu when he returns to France. "Laurie did most of the peeling. Poor girl thinks she's an apprentice, but I could probably get locked away for child labor."

"Dennis, I know too many people who'd pay a small fortune to sign you on as their father—no, mother." The peaches, I realize, are what I smelled when I walked in the house. The lavender.

He laughs dismissively. "They haven't witnessed my blundering style of reading bedtime stories. Vee says I read like a caveman with a stammer." We are standing side by side, and when he looks up, he's clearly surprised to find me so close. "Oh Fen, we're not mourning Dad much, are we."

"We'll be doing plenty of that," I say, putting an arm around his shoulders. "Let's catch up first."

He closes his eyes for a moment. "Right. But no, first let's do the lamb." He instructs me to take the meat from the icebox, and as I turn around from doing so, lifting this leaden platter while realizing my back is no longer young, I very nearly drop it. Across the table, Dennis brandishes an enormous syringe filled with a green potion he's just sucked up from a jar. "Courtesy of Davey," he says as I slide the platter onto the table.

With a look of radiant satisfaction, he plunges the hypodermic into the meat and ejects its contents.

"What the hell is that?"

"Essence of spearmint and roasted garlic, reduced in balsamic vinegar," he answers, businesslike. I turn away as he fills the syringe again, feeling the sugar of the grapes rise in my throat. I should ask about his daughters, I think. But suddenly, and I'm queasily thankful, here they all are—Laurie, Théa, Christine: three, just as we boys were once three —hurling back the kitchen door and surrounding me (my knees, that is) with eager bilingual banter. I'm reminded of how Mum's collies used to greet me on the lawn when I'd come home from a term away at school. They'd never jump up; they were too well trained. They'd yip and circle me, not the predatory way they circled the sheep but with an inquisitive enthusiasm, waiting for me to roll down in the grass and invite them to lunge, wrestle, and lick me. My parents might have had money, loved each other, loved me and my brothers, but it was the loyalty of those smart beautiful dogs, when I was young, that made my home feel like the safest place in the world.

THE THREE OF US have settled well in our respective fields, in part because of money. Our grandfather had a small publishing empire, but his frugality and capitalist foresight were the key to his wealth (another cliché made flesh, considering he was a Scot). When he died, he left each of his grandchildren a chunk of that ore, to be mined when each of us reached age thirty-one, the same age our grandfather was when he bought out his partner at the *Yeoman* and married the man's daughter (oh what a logical world *that* was). David, three years out of veterinary college and working for some burnt-out practitioner in a dreary old surgery reeking of cat piss, knew immediately that the money could spare him that same fate. Dennis had been drifting from one throwaway job to another since not quite finishing university and, less wisely at first glance, blew a good deal of his share just gallivanting around the Continent. But his extravagance landed him in Paris, pastry school, and, for good or ill, the arms of a woman whose vigilance over his future kept the rest of the inheritance socked away in bonds.

I was the first to achieve this windfall, and at first I treated it as you might a lovely light that's just too bright to look at directly, half-squinting instead through a lattice of fingers. I'd glance quickly at the regular statements I received of the balance (nicely compounding away in the hands of Edinburgh's finest investors), then file them in my least accessible drawer. What was my fear? That this hundred thousand pounds or so—admittedly, a laughable sum to even the mezzo-rich of the city where I now lived—would dislodge me from the small-world groove I enjoyed not brilliantly but well enough. Further threatening to dislodge me was my parents' hope that this inheritance would draw me back to my native soil.

I had passed my orals at Columbia and was well into my dissertation. I worked more slowly than I might have, however, lingering on in New York for the wild life I constantly imagined myself about to embark on. But in the realm of imagination was where this wild life stayed, for the baths were closing, the clubs growing maudlin, an angry celibacy rearing its gargoyle head. Still, there were plenty of niches for frenzied denial; the bottom line was, politics and epidemiology aside, I never could seem to shake an innate sexual modesty that sabotaged my alter-egotistical longings and may, in the end, have saved my life.

The thought of going back overseas, even to London or some Oxbridgian polonaise of an existence, depressed me. The proximity of my family would have been fine, even desirable (especially had I known my mother would be dead in five years), but my very Britishness—

aside from my educated burr, which gave me an alluring edge at the Boy Bar and the Saint—was the part of myself I wanted to uproot and burn like a field of dead thistle. While I'd been busy, as a student, lauding the genius of Dickinson over Keats, of Wharton over Woolf, what I celebrated with far greater awe were the chrome-smooth chests of the Puerto Rican boys in Times Square, the Fourth of July smiles on the sweet blue-eyed queens who visited Mom and Pop twice a year back home, in places with breathy names like Omaha, Tallahassee, Tuskegee Falls. These irrationally contradictory objects of my craving—men who wore chains or, on the other hand, did wholesome, contrivedly daring things like ice-camp and windsurf—were not to be found in my homeland.

So as I salivated reverently over all these visceral pleasures, waiting like some semivirginal debutante for exactly the right moment to *plunge,* I came of age—fiscally speaking. I had hinted to my parents that I'd be staying on in the States after getting my degree because I felt I could snare a more glamorous teaching post than I might have back home. But the truth was that even if my dissertation was published to the acclaim my mentors assured me it would receive, even if I parlayed my upper-crusty Ivanhoe aura, the best first job I'd be able to hope for would be in a place like Pittsburgh or Oxford (Mississippi—the lynch-mob overtones made me shudder) or Portland (Maine or Oregon, take your pick; equally dull prospects).

My libido had me by the cranial balls; I was in thrall to this city and would rather, at that moment, have washed dishes in a Cuban-Chinese bodega—elbow to sweaty elbow with supple tattoos—than declaim my only slightly less passionate love for Nathaniel Hawthorne in a classroom overlooking the willow-kissed waters of the Concord River itself.

I was rescued from washing dishes by the congruent generosities of my grandfather and a professor who understood my reluctance to leave the center of my chosen cosmos. Ralph Quayle was an authority on Melville but lived a most un-Melvillian life. Along with two springer spaniels named Mavis and Druid, amidst flounced hummingbird chintzes, he occupied the attic floor of a narrow brick house on Bank Street. I knew this early on, because he liked to invite seminar students for Sunday teas. I think the custom made him feel like a don at

Cambridge, the same yearning reflected, I'm sure, in the special attention he gave me.

Typically, twelve students would show up for an hour or so of academic debate, by the end of which we'd have abandoned Bartleby the Scrivener to talk instead about the bewildering reign of Ronald Reagan, the state of AIDS research, the terrorist threat (all of it discussed with cool-headed, high-minded dispassion). Soon, a predictable attrition would set in. First, the three female students would depart; by twilight, the four straight men would make their excuses—leaving four or five of us to head out for cheap burritos or sesame noodles. Ralph would slum along with us. After dinner, still more of us would split off until, often, only Ralph and I remained. We'd head across Seventh Avenue to Uncle Charlie's, a bar that welcomed gay society into a setting so civil as to seem, at times, like a tea dance. Unlike the clubs, it was a place where you could meet people without having to gyrate shirtless in a strobe light and shout to be heard. You could, refreshingly, *talk*.

This was the only place where Ralph spoke of his personal life; where, toward the end of the school year, he told me he owned the building in which he lived. He didn't like many people to know this, because knowledge of wealth—especially in an older man without heirs—complicated relationships. Since he wasn't handsome, he said, and since he didn't have a country place, he could feel confident that all the people who acted as if they liked him really did. But if people knew he had money, how could he tell opportunists from friends?

He chose to tell me this after I told him, in the midst of some rambling solipsistic monologue, about my inheritance and the mixture of comfort and paralysis I felt whenever I thought of it. Like a forest sage from some urban fairy tale (emphasis on *fairy*), he gave me three admonitions: Don't spend the money on frivolous travel (at least for another ten years); don't spend it to captivate a lover (not even if the lover has more money); and, above all, don't tell anyone about it (as I was now doing).

Ralph was in his midfifties and planned to retire ten years later in style. His building was the least stately on its block—without its cheek-to-cheek neighbors, I imagined, it would lean like the Tower of Pisa—but it made him a killing on rent, since he let the two floors below him as separate flats and, below them, the ground floor and basement as a commercial establishment. His tenant there was a talented young baker whose challahs and tortes sent their tempting, affectionate odors up the stairwell beginning at six every morning. Any remotely classy business in that location, Ralph said, was bound to do well because it was passed at least twice a day by his many extremely affluent, high-living neighbors (by which he meant homosexual professionals with money to spend on puff pastry, orchids, and eau-de-vie in lieu of nursery school, ballet, and braces).

Bleary-eyed by this point in his lecture, I was finding my mentor tedious; why would I care about this trivia? He'd been going on and on about the baker, Armand—how promptly he paid the rent, how thoughtfully quiet he was in the predawn hours, how nicely he'd fixed up the basement for his ovens, how equally splendid his *prune tatin* and his plain-as-a-penny shortcake. . . . At first I thought Ralph was about to confess an unrequited yen for Armand—worse, I dreaded, ask my advice. For the baker was well beyond Ralph's reach. He was a tall, Italianate dark-haired young man whom I had glimpsed through the window several times on my way upstairs; of course, the scones and little sandwiches for our Sunday teas came from below, and once I'd stopped in to order a cake for a party of my own. Across the counter, I'd seen how solidly slim those hips seemed under that apron, how stunningly green those eyes. Armand was beyond my reach as well.

"He's already been in Saint Anthony's twice for transfusions," Ralph was saying when my attention lurched back, "and the drugs are demolishing his liver. There are times I wish I didn't know so much, it's so impossible knowing what to say, but I suspect he'll be pulling out soon, that he'll be too weak to do business and I'll have to find another tenant." Ralph looked genuinely heartsick—and I felt sick in my own, more generalized way. This was 1984, when everyone knew someone who was sick but you could still believe the wave would subside, the tide ebb, before your shoes were wet, before anyone who really mattered to you (like you) became ill and, worse, asphyxiated by fear. Back then, I'd known only two people who died of this plague, both just acquaintances, grad students with whom I'd shared nothing more intimate than a library carrel.

I mumbled to Ralph, "That's awful, how tragic," or something equally inane. How could I change the subject without seeming callous (which I was) or disrespectful? Just wait for a suitable pause, I decided, and tuned out again until I heard my name: "So you, Fenno, maybe that's something you'd like to take a gamble on. I'd go in with you on the initial inventory—we'd look for a seller going out of business—and you could probably have the apartment under mine within a few years, they're a couple bound to progenate any minute and they'll have to have more space . . . that is, if you wanted to live there as well, and I'd give you a decent rent. Imagine rolling out of bed and there you are at work! . . . Though I will tell you, nice as it is, we all suffer one thing together: the critic across the street and the personal dramas he thinks we should share—drunken flute sonatas and a parrot that likes to sing scales when it rains. Charming the first two or three times you hear it, but then . . ."

Critic? Parrot? The health and reproductive vitality of Ralph's tenants? I was hopelessly lost. "What inventory?" I said, groping.

Ralph burst out laughing. "Well, sweetheart, I've found out one thing tonight: being suddenly rich doesn't make you any more riveting."

". . . COMPASSIONATE, EXACTING . . . so incredibly decent—decency raised to an artform! . . . so smart and so, so *upright* in everything he did . . ." Through his raised wineglass, the candlelight casts droplets of wavering pink light onto Dennis's face as he toasts our father's virtues. His eyes blur as he struggles for only the most sincere of sentiments. "He loved us so . . . well, without demands—or at least, if he had any, he hid them awfully well. If each of his granddaughters could have just a third of his good nature, oh, well, we'd have a household of little angels." Dennis offers a sidelong smile to his wife; his free hand rests on her back.

Véronique returns his smile, but I read a touch of boredom there—though, to be fair, this could be the invention of my immovable spite. I'd known her only a few days before she heard or deduced I was gay, and though she did not treat me unkindly, I will never forget what she said to me that New Year's, happening upon me in the dining room as I looked for a platter. She was copiously pregnant with Laurie, their first, and as she stopped she spread one hand languidly across her ana-

tomical trophy (Mal called it that). She leaned toward me and said quietly, "I am as mo-dairn as zee next citizen, Fenno, but you weel never,
please, day-monstrate your preferred intimacies before my children.
Can we agree on thees?" Her dainty eyebrows were raised, like little
swallows in flight, her pursed Parisian mouth faintly smiling, as if
she'd just asked for extra milk in her tea. I raised my eyebrows theatrically in return and said, "I can't imagine our agreeing on much, but I'll
gladly comply with your papal issues. *Ça va?*"

"*Ça va,*" she said, not the least bit unnerved, damn her, and even
broadened her smile. When I told Mal about this encounter, upstairs
later that evening, he dubbed my sister-in-law the Cuntesse. Of three
visits he made with me to Tealing, he met her only that one, last time;
if he had seen her much more often, there might have been fireworks.

David actually stands. "To Dad, I owe my very sense of self, my sense
of having a weight in the world, the capacity for true impact on my fellow creatures . . . and the sense of familial continuity, the legacy not
just of this wonderful house and countryside but all the wits and smarts
we've been passed down from branch to branch of the McLeod family
tree . . ." He acknowledges each of us with a thrust of his glass; we are
an intimate five, since the three little girls are in bed. I feel as if what
he's saying belongs in a larger setting, a larger clan, as if the formality
of his words is just a few sizes too grand for our gathering. Perhaps his
toast was planned, and he'd have aimed this "legacy" bit at our nieces—
generous, I admit. Some people who long for children of their own hold
back with other people's children, too fearful that they might actually
grow to love them—and to painfully envy their parents. Others dive
right in to partake of the pleasure they still hope will one day be theirs;
and if not, they'll take whatever morsels they're thrown of someone
else's share. David, I am happy (and sheepishly surprised) to say, falls in
the latter camp. As brusque as he can be with the rest of us, he knows
how to play with the girls, to honestly amuse them: he's taken them for
jostling cross-country rides in the bed of his pickup, helped them sit
astride their first pony, milk their first cow, listen to a kitten's heartbeat
through the stethoscope he carries everywhere as if it safeguarded his
own vital signs.

I find myself wishing the girls were here at the table, and they would
have been if David and Lil had not returned so late—at nearly nine, full

of awkward apologies but no explanation, not even a veterinary crisis to blame. At eight-thirty, there was a brief disagreement between Dennis and Véronique; she insisted that the usual bedtime be enforced. As always, she prevailed without much of a row, feeding Laurie, Théa, and Christine in the kitchen while Dennis added candles to the table he'd already laid outside.

David ends with a remark about commending our father's soul not to eternity but to our lives' work, to the people whose happiness we care most about securing. I'm beginning to wonder what he's saved up for his church eulogy when I see that he and Dennis are looking at me, waiting to raise their glasses again. Feeling like a grizzled, androgynous Cordelia, I bow my head to buy time. My mind is blank as a flagstone till I hear myself say, "Here's to Mum. Here's to how she made Dad's life so . . . full of pleasures. Dad would want us to remember Mum too. May they rest peacefully together."

Glasses chink again, though the murmurs of agreement seem muted this time. Véronique is already reaching for the cheese plate. "My favorite!" she exclaims as she slices into an Explorateur, kissing Dennis on the cheek.

David leans toward me. "I do think Dad was the one who made his own 'pleasures,' you know. I just feel I ought to say that, for the record."

"Meaning . . . ?"

"Just that Mum was terrific, but she did things as she pleased, went her own way most of the time."

"Meaning she was too self-involved?"

"No more than the rest of us. But she wasn't one of those women who theoretically 'make' their men or even stand behind them."

I look quickly at Lil; she appears more intent on her salad than our conversation. Véronique, however, is paying close attention and jumps in with "Oh écoute, you pair of hens. I never met her, your mother, but if she is who Denis describes"—she pronounces my brother's name the French way, De*nee* (Lil's *Leelee-ahn,* David *Dahveed*)— "she was the right kind of woman, a woman who makes herself before anyone else, then lets the man she loves—if he is deserving it—make *heemself* to fit the curves of what it is she has sculpted."

Dennis grins. "Me, exactly!"

"You, exactly," says David, "are a pushover. Or, in keeping with your wife's metaphor, putty."

"No," says Lil. "You, exactly, are a genie. You've outdone yourself to-night, Dennis. Your dinner was magnificent, and I'm sorry we nearly spoiled it. I'm sorry the girls couldn't join us. We're so seldom together like this, the whole family." Though they've been married longer than Dennis and Véronique, David and Lil have no children, and when I hear her say *we,* not *you,* I'm reminded that she does not even have sib-lings of her own, no cousins or other kin that I know of. I feel doubly sorry for her; she deserves to be at the center of a big, noisy brood, and I know that's what she'd like, what she must this minute be wishing for; her sadly cloying manners are a mask.

It's ten-thirty now: almost but not quite dark, the generosity of the late June sun in Scotland something I always forget till I feel it directly again on my smog-soaked hide. The sun seems to pause, languorously, not hustle down as it does most everywhere I've been in the States and farther south. At this hour in this season, it seems to imply that we northerners deserve its presence more, that our company is the most en-joyable on earth. Here, the sky weaves its pinks and violets and arctic greens for more than an hour. In the lingering dusk, the candlelight flatters my brothers, who both look to me precisely as they did when we were last together. But in this medieval light, the women do not fare so well. The taut hollows beneath their cheekbones and eyebrows deepen. On Véronique's fair skin, the light brings out the nascent creases fram-ing her lips, the pucker lines that form only in French-speaking women at such an early age, that will harden into something resembling a spi-derweb. And Lil, poor Lil, looks worn out; it's obvious that at some point tonight she was crying.

Now that I recall David's mention of a doctor's appointment, I won-der if it was one of her visits to the fertility specialist they've been seeing, something David mentioned briefly, very businesslike, when I foolishly teased him on the phone last Christmas ("So when will the urge for fatherhood overtake *you?*"). Dennis—who's heard the nitty gritty from Véronique, who heard it from Lil—told me this afternoon that it's become the grim focus of their life, that Lil endures all sorts of painful delvings and injections, all timed to the crucial millisecond according to her monthly "clock."

She's put on weight, I notice now—maybe a side effect of anxiety and sorrow, but then I remember how a friend of Mal's went through this ordeal and confided every grisly detail, which he, in turn, insisted on repeating to me. "She gets the weepy blues, the raging reds, can't eat anything but lettuce and sprouts or she balloons to a *twelve*. Worst of all, her husband has to give her these horrid shots directly in the butt with a horse syringe—some hormonal brew distilled from the urine of nuns at one particular convent in northern Italy who eat a lot of rape-seed or other peasanty staple that makes their piss high in progesterone or some such fecund elixir."

Seeing my skepticism, he said, "I'll have you know I've read about them in Jane Brody. And what's so odd anyway? Monks produce jams and liqueurs for a living; why shouldn't nuns proffer up their urine, for God's sake? Or, should I say, for the sake of urban professional women who waited too long to get pregnant the usual way."

Perhaps Mal's soliloquy comes back to me because of the bit about the horse syringe—unsavory images of Dennis injecting the meat and of the expertise David would so conveniently have were it necessary in another context. . . . But stop, I tell myself, admitting as I must the odd things queens dream up about heterosexuals and their "usual ways." Jane Brody aside, Mal always did have a touch of that typically Freud-ian phobia of women's bodies and women's belongings. Once, when I tossed him my wallet so he could pull out a twenty to buy himself lunch, he laughed and said, "Takes me back to all the times I thought nothing of reaching into Mom's pocketbook to filch the loose change. I mean, a loose Ben Franklin wouldn't tempt me now. A woman's purse . . . you just never know what you'll find in there." The last bit whis-pered, with a vaudeville shudder.

It's midnight when Dennis presents a tray of frozen lime custards. In their pale blue ramekins, they look like tiny swimming pools. The color of Los Angeles, I might have mused in different company. I say instead, "I suppose I'm a little out of the loop, but I'm trusting every-thing's set for day after tomorrow—all the liturgy and whatnot." I don't wish to draw attention to how little practical help I've given (though yes, I did fill out a lot of ridiculous forms at the airport that morning), but I'd rather do it in mixed company than when I'm alone with David.

"I've reserved Saint Andrews for eleven," says David, and I'm thank-ful he ignored my pompous little *whatnot*. "There'll be two hymns, a homily, the usual prayers, and I figured the three of us could each say something brief. Brief. Dad wouldn't want this business all drawn out and sloshy."

"And the plot, you've taken care of that?" Saint Andrews is what you'd have to call the Church of Our Forebears; in the well-shaded churchyard out back are buried my father's father's father's father and those aforementioned subsequent fathers, all encircled by wives, sisters, sons, daughters. It's where our mother's buried and where, with apologies to all occupants who may have swiveled seismically down there at my instigation, I expect to end up.

"Fen, this isn't a funeral in the usual sense."

"So what was all that about having a 'proper funeral'?"

"What I mean is that we're not doing the churchyard thing. Do you know how many people are showing up?"

"You keep harping on that, as if we're holding some affair of state. So fine, we just do the immediate family 'thing' while they all go freshen up their faces and meet us back here. Isn't that how it went with Mum?" I think of the broad stripe of green awaiting Dad between our mother and his father. Quite the estate for a box of ashes.

"Dad *did* ask to be cremated . . ."

"Well no. No, he didn't. But you imagine getting a whole body, in the subtropics in June no less, shipped from a technologically prehistoric island where the only English most people know is 'Go ahead, make my day.' You didn't exactly volunteer to go over there, and I couldn't leave, so I—"

"I'm not cross, David. I'm just curious about what he wanted. It's a safe assumption, isn't it, that he wanted to be in the family plot? What's Mum doing there otherwise?"

Using his spoon like a scalpel, David works carefully at peeling the last entrails of custard from his dish as he mutters, "I'm not sure that would've been Mum's first choice, either."

"There's plenty more!" says Dennis. "I made ten!"

David smiles briefly at him, then looks at me. "You're going to think I'm irrational at best, but I've been thinking of taking his ashes back to Greece—after all, we will, or I will, have to deal with his belongings in that house—and spreading them there, out to sea, maybe in view of the house itself, where he—"

"Oh, we could make it a family trip; we close the restaurant for two weeks in August . . ." Véronique, putting in her personal tuppence.

"Where's all this allegiance to the 'McLeod family tree'?" I say to David, running her over.

He stares at me, and in the candlelight it's hard to make out whether he's cross, distracted, or confused. "Look, Fenno, if you're going to insist . . ."

"You say that as if I made a habit of insisting on things."

Dennis begins to look concerned. "Well I always assumed the family plot was where we'd all wind up, like a permanent reunion."

Véronique says, "Not *our* family, *chéri*. Our family will rest at Neuilly."

This calls us all to an awkward halt. Lil, who's stacking plates, says, "To be crude about it, Davey, ashes don't spoil. You can think about it after the service, can't you?"

Dennis stands. "Well, everybody, a soup's waiting somewhere for me to make it." He heads for the kitchen and, with the ease of a relay runner, scoops the stack of plates away from Lil.

At the same time, Véronique snakes a sisterly arm around her waist. "*Viens.* We will go up and look on the little ones." Ah, dull-witted fertility, I think. In all likelihood, Véronique is expecting again. French women can hide a pregnancy halfway through; just a minor one of their deceptive arts.

And I want Lil to stay, want to spirit her away for myself. We barely talked on the drive from Prestwick because David wanted to give me the details (none surprising) about our father's will.

Lil is more to me than a charming relation. She represents an emotionally precipitous moment in my life, a point of no return. Before she met David, I knew Lil from a distance at Cambridge. I was in my last year when she was in her first; she was pointed out to me, at a crew match, as not just a countrymate but a countymate of mine. She, too, was from Dumfries. That in itself earned her no distinction with me (I wanted *out* of that county, that country, the entire befuddled empire— though it would take me a few years yet to plot my escape). What did impress me, months later, was Lil as a performer. This was back in the allegedly world-changing early seventies; her small claim to avant-garde fame was starting a modern dance troupe. I've never cared much for dance, but when word got around that a few blokes had joined, the audience for Lil's troupe swelled. With different though equally philistine motives (from ravishment to ridicule), we male spectators were eager to leer at our peers in leotards—as if the sight of ourselves in bellbottoms wasn't loony enough.

But what Lil had accomplished disarmed us, and no one so much as snickered. Lil herself was astonishingly graceful—and, in retrospect, brave. I'm sure the whole production was sophomoric at best, but the mere look of the unorthodox movements she staged was something even the most skeptical among us had to sit back and admire. Musically, for one thing, it wasn't what we expected: instead of Stravinsky or Copland, we heard Hendrix and Holiday—familiar, all of it, but new in this context, and new, also, as only American things could feel new in those days.

"Don't Think Twice, It's All Right" was the last song in the programme. Lil danced solo, in skintight indigo blue, and I remember sitting forward in my wooden folding chair, almost the instant she came onstage, with the ecstatic shame of public arousal. At the time, I was sharing my narrow bed with a fellow literatus (my first prolonged if still closeted liaison), and the sensation that Lil's appearance caused me was electrically hopeful. Was normalcy within my reach, despite my having renounced it? Could I circumvent the subterfuge and mortification I'd just seized as my martyrly lot? Four minutes of this apostatic relief, another four of enthusiastic ovations and bravos (the loudest a frenzied *brava* for Lil; I wasn't alone), and then I was out in the prim scolding of February air. As I walked alone to my rooms, as the crowd thinned away quickly, I felt a kind of falling. Leaving the warmth of the makeshift theater, I had been imagining how to tell Rupert—who would be waiting—that my passion had been an aberration, a computing error made by a wayward gland. There would be awkwardness, anger, apology; I would be ostracized by a certain clique which held court at a favored refectory table. How joyfully I would brave this social flaying!

But looking up at the lights in the Gothic towers around me, I thought again of Lil and saw her effect on me turned inside out. I saw her, ironically, as an icon of everything I had begun to accept, not of what I wished to turn backward and choose instead. I saw her Peter Pan torso, her newly militant hair (flame red and shorn to a boot camp bristle), and I saw, sadly, the fine chameleon act her dance had been: the way her body had seemed to absorb and then refract, like a genuine glow, the acrid five o'clock shadow of Bob Dylan's voice. She proved to me exactly, now, what she had disproved not twenty minutes before.

From a distance, every few weeks, she still captivated me as a creature of spirit. When the weather grew warm, I enjoyed catching sight of her on her bicycle, dressed in some filmy neo-Isadora dress thrown over a leotard, bangles jingling at her wrists. She became a Girl to Meet—for boys who wanted to meet girls. For me, she was a remote, nostalgic breeze, a favorite artifact in a favorite, familiar museum.

That summer I moved to London to read manuscripts for a scholarly press (cruelly giving my father hope that this would lead me on a dignified independent path to the *Yeoman*). Proudly, childishly out of touch with my family for months, I returned home at Christmas to a shock of simultaneous delight, petty rage, jealousy, and awe when David walked in the front door of Tealing with Lil, who wore a red brocade dress like something out of *The Faerie Queene* and beaded earrings so long they brushed her clavicles. They had met in town over the summer; our grandfathers, they reported to me quite giddily, had played tennis together at university way back when. "An unbeatable doubles team!" Lil exclaimed, at which my mother threw me an offstage roll of the eyes, but one which told me she'd long since given this girl her seal of approval. Years later, in an irrational corner of my mind, David and I are still (as if we ever were) jousting for Lil's affection—just a symbol, some shrink would say, of our mother's approval.

Now, the sudden departure of everyone else from the dinner table leaves me alone with David. We size each other up; David, to give him credit, is the first to give in and laugh. "We do know how to break up a party."

"Speak for yourself, Dr. McLeod."

"Which reminds me." He stands and pours us each a glass of wine; the bottle is all that remains on the table between us. I think he's about to propose a private toast, but he says, "Have to call in; I've taken on an intern to cover after-hours emergency calls, at least for small-animal stuff. Lillian talked me into it; she's been reading some insidious American book on stress. She thinks I need what she calls 'down time.' All I can think of is 'putting down' and 'going down'—terms of death in my profession." He laughs self-consciously. "I suppose you'd agree with her, though."

"I'd agree with anything that buys the two of you more happiness." I realize that in my own discomfort, which mirrors his, I must be wearing a smirk. Which earns me David's retort.

"Q.E.D., Fenno. Only Americans see it as a commodity."

I let him have the last, glib word; obvious to you and me, perhaps, but he hasn't the slimmest notion how different life would be if happiness could be bought and sold. Or simply bartered.

FIVE

CLEVER HOW THE COSMOS CAN, in a single portent, be ingratiating yet sadistic. The day my dissertation was approved, Ralph
and I found Armand, a few hours dead, in the little flagstone garden
behind the bakery. He was slumped at one of the bistro tables he'd put
out for customers once the weather turned warm. And warm it had
been, unseasonably so, but even in soaking up the sun, Armand had
worn a thick wool jumper, the sort of sumptuously patterned garment
native to the slopes of Davos. It was Monday afternoon—he was closed
on Mondays—and but for the bright scarlet of that jumper, he might
have lain there overnight. I had dropped by Ralph's flat with a bottle of
champagne, and as he reached for flutes on a shelf above the rear windows, he happened to gaze down through the branches. His first reaction was a small cry of delight; he mistook the flash of red wool for a
box of the geraniums Armand loved to plant out back every spring.

Armand had tried, too late, to sell his business; now, a sister showed
up from Connecticut to sell off its artifacts: the antique display case,
the milk-glass cakestands, the ovens, the garden furnishings, even the
arsenal of elegantly industrial whisks, mixing spoons, and ceramic
basins in which puffs of ethereal dough had once risen, awaiting meta-
morphosis into brioche. I would miss Armand's almond brioche; Ralph
would miss his habanero cornbread.

It was Fleet Week of 1986, and we had just bombed Libya; that I
thought "we" on hearing this bit of news, and not with pride, startled
me enormously. I was, apparently, home. I was thirty-three and working halfheartedly as the research assistant to a biographer of the artist
Joseph Cornell. The job was beneath me, but it paid my lease on the
studio flat I'd had since coming here. For two years, stubbornly and
sparingly, I had taken from my windfall dividends only the necessary
funds for groceries, other everyday sundries, and airfare for a yearly fortnight in Scotland.

Just after dark on a night too lovely to spend indoors, Ralph and I sat together on the front steps of his building to talk about the bookstore. He'd done some research and worked out expenses, he said, showing me his calculations. Then he sighed and clutched the pad of paper to his chest. "It's only fair to confess that I could get you an interview—and I mean a *significant* interview—down at Hollins. I just got wind that their Edith Wharton expert up and had an infarction." Another sigh, in case I'd missed the first. "But it's practically the Bible Belt, and the nubility is not of our persuasion."

He looked at me as balefully as one of his spaniels might, and just like that, suppressing a vision of my father's horrified face, I threw over the possibility of a respected academic career for a future in trade (the second horrified face which swam into view was that of my father's father, with whose money I'd finance my fall from grace). That taken care of, Ralph began reciting figures. I listened carefully enough while watching passersby with a strangely sharp attention, as if this were a fateful moment in need of memorization.

Four teenage girls in platform shoes came by, talking loudly about the oafishness of their boyfriends. Dogs, one after another, strained leashes ahead of their owners, pressing hopefully west toward the rich smells of the river. The tallest trees made a watery swishing, like an overhead creek; emerging repeatedly from their shadows, white shirts and dresses glowed in the streetlight. Once in a while, there were little bands of delectably young, well-scrubbed sailors; their uniforms would change from lavender to citron and back as they swaggered through the eddies of shade, laughing to broadcast their freedom.

Older couples, dressed for Palm Beach, emerged from Ye Biddecombe Inn, a restaurant with deliciously old-fashioned decor and not so deliciously old-fashioned food. (Mal, who made it a habit to retitle all establishments he deemed self-important, called it Ye Better Come *Out*. Within a few blocks, Venezia Mia! became the Gondolier's Pantyhose. La Chambre Rose—they do make a good coq au vin, I used to protest— is still in my book as Le Codpiece de Santa.)

From a distance, I watched an old man make his way carefully in our direction, leaning on a patient young companion at his side. When they drew near, I saw that the "old man" was in fact young, probably younger than I. His clothes were quite fashionable but hung as if damp from his shoulders and hips. He wore terrycloth slippers—also fashionable, but meant to be worn at a spa, with a bathing costume, not on crooked pavingstones. Meticulously, he watched his footing.

I had just beaten back the fear that I might face this very decline, yet paradoxically, I'd had to make myself an old man of another sort to achieve such secret, shameful triumph. Within the past year, three men I could certainly call friends (and I did not have legions of friends) had died of AIDS—of its complications, as obituaries now properly read. I had spent small stretches of time with all three while they were very ill but had not been present when they died (all in hospital). Still, I heard stories—both wanting and not wanting to hear them—and was assured that my friends had felt no peace, no acceptance, not even resignation. Frederick, toward the end, yanked the mediport out of his chest. George, whose meek nature was consistent with his expertise in Sara Teasdale, fought the onset of his coma with uncharacteristically tigerlike strength. Luke was forty-eight when he went: ancient to me at the time, but what kind of consolation was that? In fact, these men had yet to see a single gray hair in the mirror.

Before the first of those deaths, I had stopped going to clubs altogether. I told myself I was relieved not to have to battle the modesty I'd once found so frumpish; I could now cultivate this irritating foible with pride. But of course I wasn't relieved at all; I was queasy with dread. I would still go to Uncle Charlie's, with and without Ralph, because everything there felt mannerly and controllable. I needed, still, to know that I could draw an invitation, and often I was sorely, achingly tempted. I was like those weekend anglers who find pleasure in the fishing but throw every fish they hook right back in the water. Yes, I was the king of catch-and-release courting.

Upright, I would tell myself as I savored the visual innuendos of a trimly mustached business student, as I pictured us falling together into my bed. *Stay upright and you will stay alive.* Mornings after these encounters, I'd take long walks: "Constitutionals," my Presbyterian forebears called them; frustrationals, I renamed them. *Upright, upright, upright,* I'd silently chant, a little mantra to the beat of my stride, until one day I recalled that this was the word used most often to praise my father. Upright, upstanding, upbeat. (In retrospect, I can't help imagining Mal's retort: "Christ, I'd rather *upchuck.*" But this was before I'd met Mal.)

When I moved to Bank Street, into the flat below Ralph's, I began to walk nearly every morning. My preferred route was down along the piers into TriBeCa, across Desbrosses and back up Greenwich Street. When the river route was too bitterly windy or tropically scalding, I'd head south on Washington instead, toward the distant skyscrapers of Wall Street (uprightness deified). This took me past the Federal Express terminal, where uniformed drivers lined up awaiting their freight. In warm weather they wore shorts, and as I passed alongside the vans I could see their exposed legs through the open cabs. Those calves alone, without exception so exquisitely muscled and tendoned, just the sight of them, would send a forlorn heat up the backs of my own less admirable legs.

On good days, when that unselfconscious display became a virtual chorus line of choice male gams, I would think of a darkly impish man named Hubert whom I'd met at Uncle Charlie's. After a couple of friendly drinks, I asked him about a manila envelope which he held by his side, never setting it down. He laughed a little manically and told me—though he did not show me—that it contained a large black-and-white glossy displaying him in his full (and I gathered impressive) naked glory. If Hubert encountered anyone, anywhere, who struck his fancy—waiter, housepainter, loiterer, clerk—he would introduce himself by presenting the envelope with a courteous smile and an invitation. I was astonished to hear that the worst trouble he'd incited was a kick in the groin from the superintendent of his apartment building after Hubert offered his pictorial tumescence to a fetching young man eating an ice cream cone in the building foyer; the young man was the super's sixteen-year-old son. Only Hubert's articulate, convincing remorse and his record of prompt rental payments spared him eviction. Thereafter, he had to repair his own leaks.

At the FedEx terminal, I would laugh at the thought of making such a presentation to one of the drivers lined up reading their *Playboys* ("Ah, just for show. Queens, every one!" Hubert would have insisted). Not in the blue moon of a more carefree era would Fenno McLeod have been so tempted, let alone so bold. Ironically, I was to meet my own sexual downfall a few blocks northeast on this very route. But in the first days of these walks, I was sure I had insulated myself from the fooleries of desire, sure by the same sad token that I had met another fate I once, much earlier, feared: that of boy as old maid. And whatever sense of defeat I did not march to exhaustion on the streets I could now pace to a fare-thee-well in my expanded accommodations.

The flat vacated by the happily fertile young couple (Ralph's guess had been correct) was what New Yorkers call a railroad, but in its most presentable guise. In the back, one floor below Ralph, it overlooked the garden where Armand had died. Where he had placed café tables and flower boxes, I now envisioned two armchairs and a sale bin, all on casters. No plantings were necessary to beautify this niche, for it was sheltered by a large, virile magnolia tree. As I moved in, the last of its lavender trumpets brushed flirtatiously against the windows of my new bedroom.

I do not believe in ghosts, but I am not without a conscience. What did haunt me was the vulturish guilt I felt at having swooped in so soon after Armand's death (how shallow my acquaintance with guilt was back then). I ran into his sister all too often during the awkward transition downstairs, and when she asked if I wanted to buy the velvet settee he'd kept up front as an elegant touch, I accepted on the spot and gave her the price she asked—though I had no intention of allowing this potentially necromantic object into my home. I paid for a lorry and had the driver deliver it promptly to a furniture auction benefiting the Gay Men's Health Crisis, an organization whose T-shirts and posters and petitioning foot soldiers confronted me everywhere in the neighborhood, keeping me upright as ever.

My first night in the flat, I lay awake a long time making plans. Ralph had suggested we find an "angle" for the shop. The Barnes & Noble megabibliopoli, with their cappuccino mezzanines and hangar-like vacuity, had yet to overtake New York, but quaint bookshops, places where a whiff of mildew incites only pleasant nostalgia, were as common in the neighborhood as mock French cafés. Earlier, unpacking my clothing, I had watched a bluejay squabble with a squirrel in the branches of the magnolia, and it brought back the fascination with birds I'd had for a time in my teenage years. Rather stodgily (the old maid ascendant), I'd kept painstaking records of all the species I spotted roundabout Tealing, and one Christmas my parents gave me a folio of Audubon prints Mum had bought at one of those jumble sales for which local aristocrats shook out their attics. I kept the prints under my bed and would look through them periodically with the material satisfaction another boy might find in a collection of coins or rocks; now and then I'd find other bird pictures on sale at frame shops (usually torn from old ornithology texts). Once at university, however, I forgot about anything so banal as birds. It was my mother, cleaning out the attic of Tealing (probably for one of those jumble sales), who'd shipped me the folio just a year before.

Knowing from her letter what the package contained, I hadn't even opened it. At this moment, it stood tightly quartered in a box of framed pictures in my living room. So, I thought now as I began to learn the filigree of leaves and flowers that swayed across my ceiling, what about a bookshop hung everywhere with birds, perhaps with a special section of books about birds? I'd heard someone say at a party that there were quite a lot of diehard birdwatchers in this city of cities, people who rose at four in the morning to spend their dawn hours in Central Park or along the two rivers, scanning the sky with binoculars. There were, apparently, ospreys and egrets, cormorants and cranes, hummingbirds and exquisitely colored finches, all to be seen leading urban lives by those who knew how to look.

It was in fact just shy of four in the morning when I had the overpowering urge to unpack that folio of birds and see how they had weathered the years of neglect. To make myself fully alert, I groped about in the kitchen, by the tailings of streetlight traversing the parlor, to make myself a cup of tea. As I waited for the water to boil, I wandered to the front wall of windows. Directly across the street, lights burned in what I could see must be a handsomely furnished flat; at its windows, gray velvet curtains were pulled back with heavy gold tassels, and on the facing wall hung a beautifully figured carpet—Chinese deco. What drew my eye, however, was not so much the light as the surprising amount of commotion I could discern: From the play of light and shadow, it looked and sounded as if someone was dashing about in the recesses of the flat, to the dual accompaniment of music and shouting.

I opened one of my own windows and sat on a crate of books to have a better view. The music was opera, though I couldn't make out the language. The shouting, however, was decidedly Italian, the gist translatable by anyone. *"Basta, basta,* motherfucking *BASTA!"* I heard. A man's voice.

There was, then, a silence (except for some diva singing blithely on) of a minute or more. I was about to get up and look for my birds when I heard from across the street the unmistakable smash of china, probably on a tile floor, followed by a single decisive *"Basta!"* Another smash. *"Basta!"* Smash. *"Basta!"* This continued quite rhythmically—smash, expletive, smash, expletive, smash—till I (and surely most of the neighborhood) had heard a dinner service for a small batallion hurled to smithereens and something, there was no telling what, declared to be monstrously, outrageously *Enough.*

I was leaning out my window by now, certain that a domestic dispute was about to turn physically violent (had it not done so already), wondering if I should ring the police. I listened for protest, argument, cries of pain. I could see nothing but the handsome curtains and carpeted wall, before it the surface of a table and a lamp (Arts and Crafts, from the shape of its shade).

Nothing. There was a long electric silence, and then I saw a hand in a green sleeve slip under the lampshade and turn out the light. A moment later, the flat was dark.

In the next few minutes, I realized that no other lights had gone on in response to the outburst I'd heard. Like the sleepwalker which I began to suspect I must be, I opened the box I had come to find, pulled out my mother's package and began to work at removing the tape. Too stubborn or exhausted to find a knife or scissors in the kitchen chaos, I cut my fingers twice but finally bared the old folio. When I opened it, the first print I saw was Audubon's Greater Flamingo. How breathtakingly sexual, I realized, not having looked at it since I was sixteen or so. I leafed past it to see his Trumpeter Swan, swimming black-footed through water like pleated chartreuse silk, turning its neck to marvel at a moth skimming its wake. Then a Whooping Crane, preying on small lizards. A brace of cross-eyed Great Horned Owls. Barn Swallows, breasts feathered tangerine, in their high-rise nest. Carolina Parakeets (long extinct), Common Grackle, Magpie Jays, and an American White Pelican which looked to me, under the intoxication of sleeplessness, like a comedian I'd seen on Ralph's telly named Jay Leno. Peculiar the artifacts our memories unearth at such hours.

By the time I finished admiring the prints—all unharmed by exile— the sun had risen. I went to the kitchen and reheated the kettle (I'd left it to shut off and cool, never making that first cup of tea). I warmed and filled my pot and carried it back to the front room. I reseated myself on that crate of books and stared across the street but of course could see nothing more than those curtains, that lamp, that hanging rug. Eventually, I showered, took a nap, and went about the day's tasks: measuring the downstairs space for bookshelves and finding the least costly way to have them built.

The predawn tantrum I had witnessed assumed the aftertaste of a potent dream. But two mornings later, returning from my daily frustrational, about to cross the street to my building, I happened to glance into an enormous cardboard carton sitting on the pavement beside a row of dustbins. The carton was filled with broken plates. I caught my breath. Though the fragments were many and small, they were the remains of the same pattern—a Victorian flummery of Chinese pheasants and tropical blooms—that my mother the new bride had selected as her formal china. Through my childhood, they had been on display in a breakfront at Tealing, hardly ever used. By my teenage years, I could already see how bafflingly unlike my mother those dishes were; by the time I left home, I came to realize she must have chosen them out of sheer (and uncharacteristic) insecurity, as a young woman marrying decidedly up, choosing what she presumed would be chosen by the kind of young woman my father had been expected to marry. My grandparents were not so antediluvian that my father's choice became a scandal, but Mum was essentially a maid and barkeep. Even today, that sort of match would cause a catty whisper or two.

Last Christmas, when I remained in New York, Dennis sent pictures of his family. Looking at the happy group posed in his dining room in France, I felt a jolt of envy when I saw, displayed in a rustic hutch behind my pretty nieces, that very set of plates. Of course, they suit Véronique perfectly.

IT'S TRUE: I can't resist spying on people—though I won't go out of my way to do so. So once the two couples have gone indoors, I sit back at the table with a glass of good wine and gaze at the house as if it were a mechanized dollhouse in a Christmas display at a swish department store. Through the kitchen windows, Dennis seems to dance at his chores, and I wonder if that might be how a chef gets through a long night on his feet. (A mazurka to sauté the garlic, a jig to grill the meat; then foxtrot the soup to a simmer and waltz the chocolate glaze right onto those tortes.) I watch him dump leeks by armfuls onto the table and palm a stone to sharpen a knife the length of a small umbrella.

Upstairs, the light in the library spills out the window. This is now as much David's room as it is—was—our father's; he moved his files in months ago, though news cuttings from Dad's days at the *Yeoman* still cover the walls. I watch David lift the receiver from the telephone. In a moment he frowns, then laughs, then walks along the window surveying the night as he speaks to his underling. Though, it occurs to me, suppose he's ringing a mistress?

With this thought, I look left, to the room at the end of the house where Dennis and his family are staying. There, the light is low. Side by side, my two sisters-in-law stand in silhouette. They look down together—at one of the children, no doubt. What wouldn't I bet Véronique is busy extolling the perfection of her child's fair skin, silky hair, eloquently curling toes.

I might have insisted the children have my old room, but the room where they are staying, the one Dennis once shared with David, is by far the largest on the second floor. Even with a cot and two mattresses spread on the carpet, there's plenty of space to move about. When we were children, the room felt even larger because, for some unknown reason, there's a ladder which ascends through a trapdoor to a tiny self-contained room with a huge fan-shaped window. I envied my brothers this funny little attic, which Mum named the foxhole; she'd call from below, "Any soldiers brave enough to dodge the bombs for a spot of tea?" or "Retreat for supper, troops!" But she seemed to respect its privacy, so it became like a treehouse, a repository for all manner of boy debris: fossilized cowpies, rodent skulls, comic books, homemade weapons, rusted horseshoes, and probably, long after my last ascent, racy magazines.

From this aerie, you can view the acreage out back for miles. When we were young, Angus cows and Shropshire sheep grazed this land, most of it open fields. (Now, two vast modern houses look back at ours, though from a stately distance.) Two or three mornings a week, in autumn and spring, the livestock would be confined to the barns and a foxhunting club would send its entourage thundering through. For a few years, until I lost interest in sport altogether, the three of us would rush up the ladder to watch whenever we heard the huntsman's approaching horn.

There is also a peripheral view of the kennel my mother had built for her collies in a field across a stream. The brick structure still stands, but after Mum died, Dad removed the fencing from the space she set off as a dog run, and it quickly grew over in long wild grasses.

"Turning to stone out there?" Dennis is leaning out the kitchen door and waving a wooden spoon to get my attention.

"I'm spying on the household."

"I don't mean to complain about the work, but I am lonely in here. You don't have to lift a finger, but you do have to keep me company."

In the kitchen, he hands me an apron of Mum's and says, "I lied— but there's only one job I'll force on you." He's filled the scullery sink with water and hands me a giant collander filled with chopped green leeks. "Rinse. There'll be four or five of these, and you can roll them up in Mum's old tea towels—second drawer down, next to the cooker."

Grateful to have a purpose, I roll up my sleeves and pull out the towels. Dennis has plugged in a tape player and hums along to some hideously sappy Elton John collection. Only after I've rinsed and wrapped about two bushels of leeks do I suggest a change.

"But doesn't it take you back?" says my compliant brother as he ejects Elton midstanza and shuffles through a pile of tapes.

"Not in any way I find pleasant." I'm smiling when I say this, but Dennis stops to give me a look of apologetic alarm. I know what he's thinking. In his rush to empathy, he's worried that all my darkest memories are connected with Mal (whose place in my life he doesn't fully understand, but why should he—or anyone—when I volunteer so little and do not encourage questions?). In fact, this particular Elton John is so old that it takes me back to misguided gropings with a particular girl, a determined consummation ranking very high among things I'd like to erase from my hard drive.

Dennis invites me to choose but then seizes a tape himself. "No, this! This is just the right thing for the occasion. Laurie picked it out when we visited Dad—drives her mother around the bend, so we listen to it in the car when I take her with me to the *marché*." All at once our mother's dour Scottish kitchen reverberates with bouzouki music and a plaintive tinny voice singing in Greek. Grating nutmeg with his hands but gyrating with his body, Dennis sings along in gleeful gibberish: "Yamos, yasmeero smeero yaka!"

I bend over the sink and laugh harder than I have in a long time, and just as it hits, this incredible release, so does the comforting, Christmasy smell of fresh nutmeg and the realization that I had no idea Dennis (or anyone) visited our father in Greece.

"When did you visit Dad over there?" I ask when we've both calmed down (Dennis casting a guilty eye upward and lowering the volume).

"Last August. Vee had a huge formal wedding job, a gala château affair requiring half a rainforest of orchids, and I thought I'd get ourselves, the girls and me, out of her hair for a week."

"I thought he was into the monkish retreat, that he went there to ruminate."

Dennis laughs. "Well he liked that part, absolutely. But it's not as if he set up rules about the place or wore some kind of hairshirt. What— did you want to go but you just never asked?"

No, I have to admit. I never asked to go to Naxos and probably never would have. I assumed the place to be our father's sanctum sanctorum, inviolable by family. Now I see this was pure extrapolation, based on a few surprisingly expressive letters he wrote me his first summer there (letters of any sort from Dad were rare), in which he went on about how much he liked the solitude. Liking it, of course, does not mean that you require it.

"You know, he made friends there," says Dennis. "He had a super dinner party, in fact, and I taught him to make a few simple things like tzatziki and a loin of pork baked with yogurt, cinnamon, and potatoes; ordinarily, he hired a neighboring widow to cook for his little affairs."

"His 'little affairs'?"

Dennis laughs at me again. "Fenno, what's life without dinner parties?"

"So who came to this dinner party?" My tone is that of a spurned ex-wife (having no reason to expect an invitation but hurt and indignant nonetheless).

"Who came? This professorial type and his wife who have a bungalow down the road—the fellow taught playwriting, I think. Local Greek gentry or some such distinction. And then two other couples, all British expats—ha, like yourself!—who live there year-round. One of the couples had a wee lass around Laurie's age who came along, and the other couple were two men about Dad's age. Or rather, I suppose, they shared a house . . ."

"Oh you mean they might have been mere *flatmates*." Having finished my assigned task, I've hunted down another bottle of wine and yank the cork out for emphasis. The wineglasses from dinner have been washed and upended to dry, so I take a tumbler out of the cupboard.

"They seemed, I don't know . . . they were both landscape architects and we got to talking about flowers, I liked them very much . . ."

I touch him on the shoulder. "I don't mean to give you a rough time."

Dennis collects himself. "In fact, Dad had just got permission to have them design a small garden of succulents around his patio. I was sorry Vee couldn't meet them, exchange a little shoptalk."

I smile. I like the notion of my father's engaging a pair of florally minded queens to shape his surroundings. I don't mean that nastily, either. I know I made my father uncomfortable (though, again, did I tell him anything of my life, directly, to confirm his hunches and make them easier to live with?), but I do not think I enraged or disgusted him.

"The wee girls went to sleep in Dad's bed," Dennis is saying now, "the two women walked each other home, and the party ended very late with Dad, me, the playwriting prof, and the two gardening blokes standing out under the olive trees trying to name the constellations. We were all terrible at it, so we just . . . invented. Dad found the House of Parliament up there somehow, I seem to recall pointing out a large duck, someone I think actually did peg Orion or the Plough . . . well, there was plenty of ouzo to go around! Next day, I had a monstrous crick in my neck."

I wait for something more, but Dennis turns his happy attention to tapping the last of the nutmeg off his grater into a tiny bowl. I have two simultaneously mournful wishes: that I had been at my father's dinner party and that my brother could describe the scene, the experience, with a precision more worthy of his emotions. There were moments, as a boy, when I wondered guiltily if my father wished the same of Mum. (Dad's eloquence, though he was not a big talker, outstripped hers by far.) Dennis's passions begin to resemble our mother's: many and large, but not subtle.

I watch him work a bit longer before saying, "So you, then, ought to know what Dad would think of David's idea about the ashes."

Predictably (to my satisfaction), he is caught off guard. "Well Davey's right he loved Greece, I mean that particular place. He did love it."

"Enough to forsake family tradition."

"Tradition? Well, ha Fenny, you're hardly one to talk about toeing up to tradition, wouldn't you say?"

"I don't know why not," I say slowly. "You know, I'm regarded as quite stuffy by many people I meet in America, and I can't say I mind. I come back here and I'm suddenly, inexplicably, an iconoclast by virtue of my long absences and my alleged sexual preference."

A look of confusion crosses Dennis's face. He's struggling, I realize, to recall the meaning of *iconoclast*. "Alleged?" he says quietly and then looks frightened, as if he didn't mean to say it aloud.

"Dennis, you haven't had enough to drink," I say. I get up to pour him a glass of wine as well, aware that I am, to borrow one of Mal's colorful expressions, sloshed as a foundering yawl.

"No thank you," he says, sounding demure and cold.

I sit down again. "But the ashes. Seriously, Dennis."

"I think we should do whatever causes the least contention. Bury them in the churchyard by Mum or take them back to Greece, I won't lose sleep either way."

"So you'd leave Mum with Dad's family and no one to defend her integrity."

Dennis smiles at me with a touch of pity. "Where does Mum's integrity come in?"

I laugh. "Can't say."

"None of us can, can we?" Dennis doesn't look up as he says this, and I begin to think there's more to it than the concentration he's using to pour us each a cup of verbena (the dried leaves taken from a satchel of herbs he's carried over from France; I peer in and see bundles of thyme, oregano, chives).

He hands me my cup, more than a little pointedly. "Go to bed. Tomorrow you'll thank me."

"I haven't been much help here, have I?"

"Nonsense," he says, jovial again. He points to the linen-wrapped leeks on the scullery washboard.

I leave the kitchen meekly, carrying my tea as bidden, one hand holding the saucer, the other bracing the cup. In the front hall, I see Dad's ashes on the table where David left them, as if to greet guests when they enter the house. The ashes are in a plain wooden box—a box which, when I pick it up, turns out to be plastic with a false wood grain, warping apart at the seams. In size and color, it reminds me of the real wooden box in which my mother kept her few pieces of jewelry. A fragment of a Strauss waltz would play every time she opened it.

On a whim, I leave my tea behind and carry the box containing my father upstairs to my room. Without turning on the light, I set the box on the windowseat that overlooks the stream—the burn, it's called hereabouts—which once defined a border of Tealing's modest property. Not long after we moved in, Dad bought the large field on the other side, so Mum could build her kennel there and graze half a dozen sheep.

On a clear midnight with a good moon, the line of birches on the far side will glow. I've always thought it's the best view from anywhere in the house; on so many nights it enticed or consoled me to sleep.

As I—or we, I can't help thinking—sit there in the dark, voices materialize through a wall. I listen as acutely as I can; I walk soundlessly toward the wall and lean toward the conversation. It's Lil and Véronique in my parents' old room, now David and Lil's.

"We had a very long talk, very long, and he has said no. He is sorry that he is saying no, but I think he will not be moved." Véronique, in her lilting purr. "I told him I had thought of it and it would be agreeable for me—I have three children, I will not be having more."

"Dennis doesn't long for a son?"

"Oh Denis, he, *comment dirais-je?*"—a small and I suspect inappropriate laugh—"*il nage bien en fémininité—tu comprends?*"

Lil, bless her manners, laughs along. "I've often thought something similar about Davey, he has his element too. I'm not sure I could say he 'swims well in animality'—sounds ghastly in English—but that's rather what it's like. He seems to so many people so . . . gruff. But to see him with a lamb or an old swaybacked mare, the tender concentration in his hands and his eyes, I've had this fantasy almost since I met him that I'd love to see that particular tenderness replicated in a son—or a daughter. I suppose now . . ." Even through the well-built wall, I hear her voice quaver.

"You will, you will," Véronique is saying. "You will still see this, Liliane, I believe you will. You must believe it, too, chérie."

"Oh Vee, all the things they've done, I feel like I'm in some science fiction novel, abducted by bug-eyed aliens in white laboratory coats; the things they've been doing to us, to me, and after all I went through, what was the point? They did something centrifugal this time, and I just couldn't listen to the results. It's awful to admit, but up till now, even when it was me they were dissecting, I've just always thought, well *David* understands these things—he's as good as a human doctor when it comes to all this medical knowledge—so I stopped paying attention ages ago and figured, David's brilliant, David will solve it. But this is the absolute limit, and of course I'm just as responsible. . . ."

"*Ecoute*. This is *your* joy of which you must take care." Lil has been sobbing awhile now, and Véronique goes on talking in a singsong voice, probably just to keep the grief from ballooning. She speaks so quietly now that I can't make out a word, and I stop short of pressing my ear against the wall, an arm's length from where they sit. What I'm doing is obscene, but as Mal would say, this is scalding stuff. Sad stuff too, though I can't help feeling relieved that Véronique will apparently not be donating an egg to blend her genes with David's (the inverse of my spouse-swapping fantasy!). I note with surprise and gratification that Dennis had the power to refuse—that she even asked his permission.

There are footsteps in the hall now, a knock on the neighboring door. "Lillian? Lil?" It's David. Down in the kitchen, I had myopically assumed that everyone else was sleeping; now I'm wondering, paranoid but never mind, whether they were in fact avoiding Dennis and me (or simply avoiding me).

Lillian answers her husband. The door opens and closes. Véronique says good night; the door opens and closes again. Silence, shuffling; Lil resumes crying. I hear the bedsprings surrender to David's weight. Then I hear another sound that might be—and I don't want to know if it is—my brother crying, too.

I go to the windowseat and crank open the casement windows, not just because the room and I both need a dose of June air. The lead joints of the windowpanes always object; having finally reached the limits of my prurience, I'm hoping the noise will alert David and Lil to my waking presence.

The birches cast mossy shadows across the field, and the waters of the burn warble quietly along. Carefully, I open the box. My father's ashes are contained, flimsily, in a plastic bag closed by a wire tie. Through a tiny lesion in the bag, some of the ashes have leaked out. When I close the box—quickly, a little horrified by my childish curiosity—a puff of gray dust escapes. I avert my head, to avoid inhaling the ash. I set the box on the windowseat and retreat to my narrow bed, undress without hanging or folding my clothes, don a pair of pajamas, and slip between the old-fashioned stiff linen sheets.

I am against spreading my father's ashes in Greece—spreading them anywhere—in part for a simple, selfish reason irrelevant to my anomalous respect for family traditions.

Before I ever did it, I thought the notion of spreading ashes on water highly romantic, the best and most mannerly way to get past the horror of funerals. Having partaken in this ritual twice now, I dread and despise it. Inevitably, the faintest breeze against the water sends the finest ashes back into your eyes and mouth; you have to brush the residue of your loved one's bones, organs, viscera, and skin from the folds of your clothes, excavate it later on from the seams in your shoes. You have to wash him from your hair and down the drain of your tub, as if he were soot from a campfire, dust from an attic, diesel exhaust from an ill-muffled bus.

Ever since, I've begged off such outings by claiming that I get rabidly seasick and thus would spoil the solemnity of the occasion. (In truth, I love to sail, so long as someone else knows how to navigate.)

THE SHOP WAS CHRISTENED PLUME. I wasn't happy about this coy pun Ralph cooked up to evoke both scholarship and ornithology, but it was preferable to Books of a Feather, Feathered Folio, and Bibliobirds, three other suggestions which should not have surprised me, coming as they did from a man whose bed wore a bonnet of chintz. (I wanted, simply, Books & Birds, to which Ralph snorted, "Sweetheart, you are a font of insight, but you infallibly err on the side of dull." Which I would not dispute.)

We opened quietly in July, postponing the christening party until September and what the French so succinctly call *la rentrée* to ensure the attendance of half the humanities faculty from Columbia and, by extension, their spousal and rivalrous complement from nearby NYU. Even a few Princetonians made the commute. By then, we had also attracted our neighbors' attention and made them sufficiently comfortable to wander in for a free glass of wine. As a featured guest, we had the aging but still robust Roger Tory Peterson; by the time our soiree was in full swing (full flight?), a queue had curled toward the corner of the block, each occupant holding one of Mr. Peterson's guidebooks.

A major expenditure turned out to be the proper framing of my bird prints, but the investment was wise. Though even a sliver of unshelved wallspace in a bookshop might seem like folly in these parts, the view from the street was seductive. Here and there between the shelves, like portals onto a lost world, hung Audubon's grand, effetely poised birds. In the glass that brightened their plumage was reflected the greenery on the street and in the garden, lending our low-ceilinged quarters a touch of the arboreal that made it feel, at times, akin to a treehouse.

By the door to the garden stood a display case holding, on green velvet, fine binoculars and portable telescopes with featherweight tripods, along with compasses, camping knives, and even upscale picnicking gadgets. (To Ralph, I gave a firm veto on T-shirts bearing the logo he longed to commission.) I kept in stock the complete ornithological guidebooks from several respected publishers, along with whatever used books of interest I could find in backwoods shops on the rare occasion I left the city. The week we ran our first ad in a birdwatching journal, our foot traffic doubled, and for the first time we talked of hiring an assistant, at least for weekends and evenings.

By the end of that summer, we'd already earned a number of regulars, some of whom bought and some of whom didn't. I realized the value of this place as a drifter's or procrastinator's paradise, destination for a dreamy lunch hour, meeting place for illicit lovers, oasis for unhappy spouses who wanted to postpone the evening's squabbles. We had a handful of lonelyhearts, none too daft or unpleasant, who wanted not the shop's atmosphere but my free-for-the-asking company. I didn't mind this as much as I'd have guessed, and Ralph, who dropped by every day for about an hour, was more than willing to contribute his practiced charm. Mavis and Druid would doze about his ankles, lending us their hunting lodge cachet.

Come September, this troupe of regulars expanded to include a few more stylish, polished types, people who'd had the luxury of fleeing the city for a month or more. One was a man, about my age, who paid his first visit as if he were the bookshop equivalent of a health inspector. After a smug hello, he turned slowly about, lighthouse fashion, and regarded the shop as if alert for violations. Next he began appraising my Audubons—and I do mean appraising; I could see him searching, eyes about an inch from the glass, for watermarks or registration flaws or whatever it is that art experts search for. At first I thought he was a dealer, and I hoped he would mistakenly declare the prints of great value so I could happily tell him they were not.

Once he had finished scrutinizing the prints, however, he gave equal attention to the vitrine of birding accessories and then wandered out to the garden. I could only imagine his busybodying examination of everything, from the fading blossoms of the Armand Memorial Geraniums I'd planted that summer to the cracks in our flagstones and rotting stockade fence.

At last he turned to the books, stopping throughout the shop to scan shelves (I mapped his sojourn by the creaking floorboards), though I never saw him take down and handle a book. He went to the basement as well, emerging after just a few minutes. Well, I thought with begrudging approval, no Raymond Chandler or bloody *Dune* for that one.

After looking out the front window with a dreamy expression, he finally focused on me. "I didn't know Ralph had a thing for birds."

Refusing to be startled, I answered, "He doesn't."

"Then, I take it, you do?"

"I'm not a birdwatcher, if that's what you mean."

He nodded, as if I had given the correct answer, and pointed to the Carolina Parakeets hanging behind my desk. "Parrots. Do you know parrots?"

I couldn't imagine where this conversation was headed, so I said, "You know Ralph?"

"Oh everyone in the nabe knows Ralph, he's so civic-minded. Makes sure our trees are never thirsty, the sewers never clogged. Even without those droopy old dogs . . . Spaniels look rather boneless, don't you think? As if they've been fileted?"

I wished we'd stayed on parrots.

"People must inquire about your accent," he said. "I'll bet they drive you nuts by assuming you're Irish."

"That does happen," I said. "Irishness seems fashionable here."

"But not in Scotland."

"No." The telephone rang. It was Ralph, asking me to supper, and I longed to describe the man now meandering his way among the books again. I agreed to pick up duck breasts at Ralph's favorite butcher.

When I rang off, the man returned to me like a magnet. "I'll be frank: Your music section is deplorable. Deplorable and understocked. It's not even as long as I am short!" He smiled at his self-effacement. I wouldn't have called him short, but there was a slightness to the man which might have led people to underestimate his stature—that is, until they heard him express a few opinions.

"Ralph and I don't know a great deal about music." I was about to add that we were planning on getting some outside counsel on this and other subjects when I realized that if I did, this fellow might volunteer himself.

"Evidently," he said, concluding yet another subject. He sat in the armchair next to my desk and returned to the subject of myself: where exactly I was from, how long I'd been here, how I knew Ralph. He knew that I lived upstairs, and as he never asked my name, I had to assume he knew that as well. My terse answers did not seem to deter him—but then he looked at his watch and said, without a trace of irony, "I see it's teatime and I see you're not offering any, so it's a fair guess I've overstayed my welcome." He stood and looked around. "I do love your birds."

"Thank you." I fought the well-bred urge to stand as well and shake his hand. Sensing my churlish resistance, I'm sure, he took out his wallet, removed a business card, and placed it in front of me. "Leaving my card is a habit, I'm afraid. Indulge me, please, by accepting it."

The card read, in a surprisingly plain typeface, Malachy Burns. I admired the discreet, antiquated nicety of this object, the absurdity of the gesture notwithstanding. And then my visitor added, pointing to the card, "I've thought of inserting a little fill-in-the-blank below my name so you could embellish it to your liking: With Passion. His Bridges. In Hell. Of course, you'd have to know me better than you do."

At the door, he looked back and said, "I regret to inform you that a large rodent or a lapdog has recently defecated, not unjustifiably, in front of the novels of J.R.R. Tolkien." This parting shot left me speechless, as I'm sure it was intended to do, but it also proved to be true (and I knew at once that the perpetrator was the latter creature he'd named, since one of my lonelyhearts had dropped by with her shih tzu). Before I went downstairs to check, I stood by the front window and watched my visitor depart. He crossed the street and let himself into the brownstone directly facing this one. I couldn't see his ultimate destination, but I would have bet the remainder of my inheritance that it was the apartment in which someone (I now had an excellent notion who) had so dramatically—so operatically—shattered that set of my mother's good china.

SIX

I AWAKE TO THE PENETRATING STARES of my four- and five-year-old nieces, Théa and Laurie, and the shock of cold metal on my neck.

"*Sa poitrine!*" Laurie whispers bossily at her little sister and then, seeing my eyes have opened, switches to English. "Onco, we're listening to your heart." She is busily removing what must be David's stethoscope from around Théa's neck.

"Darling," I say, "my heart's not in my throat. Not now anyway."

"I *know*. I was telling her that."

I start to rise, reaching out to touch their blond heads. Their hair is the absolute texture of innocence, smooth as Venetian glass, yet also erotically stirring, like the warm skin of a lover's inner arm.

"No, no. Lie down," commands Laurie. She pushes me back.

"All right, I'm your patient."

"Théa, *son poignet*." Complying, Théa grabs my nearest wrist in both hands. I note with pleasure that she is wearing the black silk dragon pajamas I bought for her in Chinatown (for Laurie I bought one of those stiff lacquered parasols painted with chrysanthemums, for Christine a doll with long black hair and a rice paddy hat; it was Mal who taught me to shop with a theme).

"*Pas comme ça.*" Laurie rearranges her sister's hand on mine. "Davi showed us how to get a pulse," she explains.

"Ah." I give in to her prodding. I'm glad I wore pajamas to bed, but then Laurie orders me to unbutton the top so she can get the stethoscope to its target. As she finally locates my heart and listens, wide-eyed, she wears an astonishingly unlined scowl. I glance sideways at Théa, who's let go of my wrist, and wink. I have the urge to seize both girls and pull them into my warm narrow bed, but I know Laurie wouldn't take kindly to my interfering with her exam. Back in New York, I've met enough children to recognize the age of martial law. I wrap my arm around Théa's bony shoulders and hold her against my side.

"It's very fast, I think," says Laurie. "Very very fast. I think it's too fast."

"Well if it isn't Lord Layabout and his concubines." David stands in the doorway. He's smiling, but I'm embarrassed he's found me in this position, however innocent.

"Davi, his heart's way too fast, I think."

"Well, lass, we may have to arrange a transplant." David looms over us now, a hand on Laurie's shoulder, and I pull myself to a sitting position. He taps his Jacques Cousteau watch. "*Eleven,* Fen. I've already been to the clinic, pilled a few cats, stopped on my way back to castrate a bullock and then to pick up the tables and chairs. Think you could dress your leisurely self and help me unload them into the garage?"

"Listen, Davi, *listen,*" says Laurie, thrusting the stethoscope at him with un-derailable purpose.

David takes the stethoscope and sits on the edge of my bed. Concealing my reluctance, I comply. Théa, hearing her mother's voice downstairs, lost interest and fled, so David and Laurie now huddle in silent consternation over my body. David pushes back the left half of my pajama shirt and positions the stethoscope firmly. He holds the disk between two fingers so that his entire hand loosely cups my breast. I can feel my nipple harden, out of nervousness, under his palm. Since I rarely go to doctors (sinfully taking my health for granted, and no, I have never been tested), I'm feeling doubly peculiar, worried that as my brother listens so studiously to my heart he will accidentally diagnose some fatal arrhythmia or murmur.

"Well, Dr. Dah-vi?" I say, trying to sound playful by echoing the pet name for my avuncular rival.

"Well, you're not a pig. And decidedly not a Shetland pony. Every species, you know, has a unique heartbeat, so in fact I don't know much more about what I'm listening to than you would."

"Is he sick?" asks Laurie hopefully. I decide not to take this personally.

"He's just a bit lazy. That's his only ailment today."

"Oh." She checks her disappointment, seemingly aware how rude it is, and says to me, "Onco, I'm glad you're well." My nieces do have marvellous manners, which, like so many other things about them, make me feel surprisingly proud—genetic reflex, I suppose.

As I get out of bed, David is staring at the box on the windowseat. "What's Dad doing up here? Afraid he'd flee the reunion? Afraid I'd spirit him off and have my obstinate way?" Laughing, he leaves without waiting for an answer.

When I make my way downstairs, I hear no voices. The dining room table is covered with an array of Mum's best china pitchers, soup tureens, and teapots. Véronique walks into the room and says, "Your mother, she never arranged flowers? I do not find a single true vase in this house."

"I must say, I don't remember," I tell her honestly.

Véronique regards me with an uncharacteristically neutral stare, as if she's forgotten whether she knows me. "Have you eaten? Denis has saved you coffee, I believe."

"I'm a tea loyalist, but thanks." She is still staring at me, and I can't read a thing in her gaze. I'd have expected her to remark on my laziness or my lack of helpfulness. "You might check the scullery," I say. "For vases."

"Oh, *merci*." She smiles quickly and goes into the kitchen ahead of me.

Dennis is busy at the table—exactly where I left him the night before. "Water's hotting up; I heard your voice," he says. Christine is sitting on the scullery floor nestling a dingy stuffed cat into a bed she's made of linen napkins (I resolve not to be hurt that my rice paddy doll is nowhere in sight). Her mother climbs onto a stool, searching high shelves. "Brilliant, Fenno." She turns and holds out two cobwebbed vases. "May I hand them down?"

Once again relieved to be useful, even to Véronique, I offer to wash them. She pulls Christine onto a hip and heads outside. Too late, I try to stop Dennis from making my tea.

"You know, I do all these things ten times faster than anyone else, so why not?" After he hands me my cup, he looks at the seven vases next to the sink. "I don't recognize a single one of those, do you?"

"I suppose Mum never did arrange flowers."

"She wasn't keen on domestic things, was she?"

"And yet she produced you." To my digestive dismay, Dennis is now skinning and boning a small mountain of chickens.

As I turn over a vase to rinse it under the tap, two objects fall into the sink: a house key, the large old-fashioned kind, and two military medals.

Behind me, Dennis sighs. "Isn't it strange to think that just a week ago—less—Dad was living his life on that island, making his meals, reading his books, enjoying the sun?"

"Well, as Mal loved to say, we're all alive the day before we die." I rub one of the medals between a thumb and forefinger, trying to remove the oxidation that's darkened its face. The striped ribbon is crumpled and dirty.

"Yes, but *how* alive is another question. I imagine Dad was extremely alive, as alive as could be, to the end. Do you think that's good or bad?"

"Do you mean, would I rather go slowly, and have the leisure to contemplate my demise while in excruciating pain, or get whacked by a lorry while I'm fretting over my tax return?"

"I just keep not believing he's dead, because, well, it wasn't time yet, was it? Wouldn't you say it was premature?"

Under any circumstances, I'd find it hard to answer this rather obtuse question without sarcasm, but now I have an excuse not to answer at all. I turn around and hold out the medal. "Recognize this?"

He leans close to examine it but does not take it. His hands are wet with poultry juices. "Must be Dad's, from the war."

"In an old vase on a shelf in the scullery?" I show him the key as well, though keys in odd places, hiding places, are not so unusual. But this key is not a key to our house.

"Well, you know, maybe we were having one of our treasure hunts, Davey and me, or playing a trick on Mum," he says. "There was a period when we used to 'borrow' things from her handbag or her chest of drawers and hide them. See how long it would take her to notice them missing."

I am about to pocket my finds as David walks in from out back. "Going a little daft already, Fen?" He's struggling not to lose his temper. Only then do I remember the tables and chairs.

"Oh! Show the medals to Davey," says Dennis. "That was a fancy of his way back when."

David's scowl lifts as I hold out the medals. He takes them and lays them in the palm of a hand. "I say, this is a Distinguished Service Order."

"Dad's?" I say.

"Oh Dad wasn't that brave." He laughs fondly. "Brave he was, I'm sure, but a D.S.O.—we'd know about that. Mum would've made him wear it to go to the loo." He holds up the other medal, rubs its soiled bit of ribbon. "Nor, might I add, was he in Africa. Where did you find these?"

"In a vase, of all places," I say. "Africa?"

As David hands the medals back to me, he says, "The Africa Star, that one, for service in North Africa during the last war," but it's clear he's lost interest. "Must've been left by the occupants before us. Curious." Then he holds the back door open. "The day, like life, is passing us by!" he announces to me with an accusatory smile.

THAT OCTOBER, an icy rain fell with vindictive force for nearly two weeks. Each morning I would head straight for the basement to check for flooding (we were watertight, as it turned out, thanks to work that Armand had done when he put in his ovens). Outside, leaves that had barely turned yellow were ripped from the trees and papered tight against windows. Inside, it was so humid that the glue binding the cheaper books softened and filled the store with a medicinal, rubbery smell.

During this fortnight of damp gloom, I was often alone in the shop and found it hard not to brood about my socially straitjacketed life. Perhaps I was lazy, but most evenings after closing up (then neatening and reshelving books), I would go upstairs—half the time to a solitary simple meal in my flat, half the time for a chatty rich meal at Ralph's, sometimes with a colleague of his (in which case most of the conversation amounted to academic dishing and griping; I had no regrets about passing up *that* life). I kept up my early-morning walks, even in the rain, and on Mondays, when we were closed, I would go to a film or out to lunch with one of the few friends I'd kept from grad school (whom I would forbid to gripe *or* dish). And because the business was new, I declined the few invitations I received for weekends away.

The readings Ralph wanted us to stage would not start until after Thanksgiving, and I seemed to be living in suspension till then, as if that one change in my routine would vastly enrich my existence.

One late afternoon I decided to close early; I hadn't seen a soul in over an hour. To air out the place before locking up, I opened the door to the garden. I leaned in the shelter of its frame to catch the scents of wet moss and magnolia leaves. The rain fell hard, sluicing from our gutters onto the flagstones with a punishing din. Sparrows huddled, fluffing their feathers for warmth, on the perches around the feeder I had hung from the tree. As I took in this scene (morosely likening myself to one of those sodden immobile birds), someone spoke, just inches from my ear. "I was beginning to think the place abandoned." In response to the alarm on my face, my visitor continued, "I might have pilfered a thousand dollars in art books without your being any the wiser; perhaps you should install one of those tinkling bells." My visitor was (and it did nothing to improve my mood) Malachy Burns.

I smiled tersely. "Any other advice?"

"Not today," he said cheerfully. His shoulder nearly touching mine, he turned his attention to the garden, as if we were companions in contemplation. "That's a splendid feeder. Very Kyoto-esque. I know exactly where you got it and it can't have been a bargain."

I said nothing in reply to this backhanded compliment. The birdfeeder was a Victorian pagoda whose perches seated twenty under deep scalloped eaves. It had come from a pricey antiques shop a few blocks away. I had justified the splurge as a thematic accessory, writing it off as a business expense.

Malachy Burns stepped back inside. "Listen. I've brought someone I'd like you to meet. She's waiting up front."

Full of sour, weary speculation, I followed him through the aisles of books. His cranky senile mother? A neighbor with a complaint? Another lonelyheart he wanted to fob off on me?

Against the silver light from the front window, I could see only that there was a sizable object on the armchair next to my desk. Malachy Burns had draped his mackintosh on the chair and was now bent over the object, murmuring as if to a baby. As I came nearer, I saw that the object was a cage. When my visitor turned around, a bright red bird the size of a small dog was perched on his shirtsleeve.

"This is Felicity," he said. "Felicity, this is Fenno. I think you'll like him. He's very classy."

The bird regarded me intently. She tilted her head in that quizzically avian way, and I heard a faint clicking in her throat, a cantankerous tut-tut-tutting. She was, on closer inspection, not entirely red but had a deep blue-violet belly and gray feet that looked as if they were covered with crocodile skin. Her beak and eyes were the soft black of stones pummeled smooth by the sea.

I will admit that I was half-besotted, there and then. I had never owned a bird, though I admired the beauty of birds in the wild, and I had never laid eyes on a creature like this one.

Malachy Burns was raptly watching us both, man and bird. He said, "She's an eclectus. I named her for the virtue I'm least likely to acquire—that is, after deciding that Fidelity smacks of finance and that I simply couldn't love a companion named Prudence."

Having no idea what was expected of me (was this a prank?), I was mute. Now Malachy Burns extended the arm with the bird. Felicity half-unfurled her wings, then closed them again. "Let her sit on your shoulder. Go on, Felicity."

Certain this must be a prank, I backed away.

Malachy Burns laughed. "She won't bite your ear off. More than I can say about some of the people in my life."

So I let Felicity—and she was quite willing—vault from his sleeve onto my shoulder. Immediately, she began to explore my hair and my right ear, gently, with her beak. She did not cackle or chatter, which made her touch feel more amorous than playful. I turned my head toward her, trying to see her, and noticed that her feathers gave off a pungent smell, a pleasant musky mixture of nutmeg and lilies.

"She's gorgeous, isn't she. And she loves people, a true socialite. I used to give big fabulous parties, literal crushes of people, and she'd sojourn from shoulder to shoulder the whole evening long."

I had finally remembered to ask Ralph one night, having emptied the pockets of a jacket and pulled out the card. "Oh dear God," Ralph had groaned. "So the bitch deigned to darken our doorstep. Emphasis on *darken*." Malachy Burns, Ralph told me, was chief music critic for the *New York Times* (a title Ralph was astonished not to find on the card, since the man was as conceited as, Ralph had to admit, he was perceptive). He specialized in opera, which explained why half the neighborhood had to listen to Callas and Domingo at top volume till two in the morning or starting at six. He compensated for these disturbances of the peace by inviting all his neighbors to the grand parties he gave ("and darling, you have never seen so many A list queens under one roof since the days of Fifty-Four"). Though come to think of it, Ralph said, the parties had not resumed after the summer, as they usually did. Predictable rumor held that Malachy Burns was ill.

This was the first I had seen of the man since his earlier visit, and I did not regard him much differently. (To look at his clothes and his sharp, clever haircut, I had guessed he held some important post, and to learn that anyone was ill these days elicited, sadly, more resignation than shock.)

"Felicity, sing a little for your new friend," he said. His voice was soft, ample with affection, whenever he spoke to the bird.

Felicity straightened herself up on my shoulder and let out a clear ululation of notes that mimicked perfectly a singer's warm-up. I had heard this before, this particular range of scales, especially during these rainy days. Whenever I heard it, I could tell only that it came from somewhere else along the street, and I had assumed someone was taking voice lessons (though I had not thought her a talented singer, I had never doubted that she was human).

"That's remarkable. Does she talk?"

"A few words here and there, but never very intelligible. Eclectuses aren't fancy talkers like Amazons or grays."

"So you know your parrots."

Malachy laughed. "Only perforce. Felicity was a gift, a few years ago, from an Italian tenor whose wife breeds these birds. I think they all sing scales because they hear it all day, every day, from the minute they hatch."

Felicity had returned to grooming my ear, running the tip of her beak around the inside perimeter. It tickled terribly, but it was the most tangible affection I'd felt in months.

"If you have a bird, anyone you meet will tell you everything they know about whatever other kind of bird they or their acquaintances have. Achingly boring." Malachy reached out and took my arm. "Hold your hand up like this and she'll hop on." She did, and her weight was impressive. She looked me in the eye and made her tutting noise.

"She's scolding me."

"Oh no, that's love—or courtship at least." Malachy laughed again.

The bird set him at ease around others, I could tell, and made him far more likable.

Suddenly, Felicity turned and leaped onto his shoulder. She began to groom busily under a wing. As she splayed the feathers, they made an elegant dry rustling, the sound of a stiff satin gown in motion across a dance floor. Malachy moved the cage to my desk (heedless of my papers) and sat on the chair. "I have what will sound like a preposterous favor to ask." When I did not move, he said, "Please sit down. You're making me feel crazier than I already do."

I sat. "Yes?"

"I'd like you to take Felicity on as a boarder—and maybe, if the two of you get along, you'd take her home with you at night. I'd pay for her upkeep—it's not expensive—and if you have to leave town, there's a boy across the street in the apartment below mine who likes to take care of her. I'd pay for that too." Both Malachy Burns and his bird regarded me across my desk. When I did not answer, he said, "I hate to belittle her so, but she could be a sort of . . . mascot here, don't you think? Even, perhaps, an attraction."

"So you're tired of her. Someone gave you this novel gift, and now that the novelty's dimmed, she's a burden." I doubted this even as I said it, but wasn't that the obvious explanation for such an offer?

He sighed. "I can understand your guessing that, but nothing could be further from the truth."

"You're expecting me to take this bird from you, just like that—this bird who will probably live a hundred years—as if you were handing over a parcel of secondhand books to sell on consignment?"

Mal's eyes were his most striking feature. A very pale blue, the color of shaded snow, they could appear almost pure white, like a blind man's eyes, when caught in the sun. Now they brightened with tears, and a ghastly silence spread between us. He said at last, "I am regrettably, to use the medical softsell, 'immuno-compromised,' and as if to add insult to injury, my all-knowing doctors informed me awhile back that I simply cannot have a bird, not so much as a chickadee, in my home. I refused to believe them until I read about it last month in my colleague Jane Brody's column. Seems there's some deadly ornithological pneumonia that may strike me down if I inhale poor Felicity's vaporized guano."

It was now raining so viciously that Mal had raised his voice. The word *guano,* spoken in righteous sarcasm, rang out like an ultimatum.

"Now is where you apologize and are mortified into submission," he said before I did exactly that. "Which I won't have. I don't know why I expected not to be blunt about this." He leaned forward. A mistress of timing, as I would learn over the years, Felicity began to sing her scales again.

"I do like her," I said, "but . . ."

"Oh please do not tell me you have to ask permission from that old biddy Ralph."

I'm afraid this made me laugh. "I suppose I don't."

Malachy Burns stood. "Well this is a relief, and I'm leaving before you change your mind."

"I'm not prepared . . ."

"You're not getting her now," he said as he arranged a brocade cover over the cage. "I'm planning to have a few last bittersweet days of her morning company, fuck their epidemiological doom, and I'd like you to come for dinner tomorrow if you're free. It's clear you don't like me much—no one does at first—but I am an excellent cook." He pulled on his mackintosh. "Once Felicity moves over here, I'll be spying on you constantly. But I also promise to send lots of spendthrifty bookworms your way. Maybe a little ass in the bargain. I may not have my health, but I still have my cultural clout."

I walked him to the door, to lock it behind him. Before leaving, he held up the cage and pulled aside the cover so that I could have a last look at Felicity. "In answer to your speculation, it's unlikely she'll live a hundred years. But decades, yes. She's just four. In my will, I've left her to my mother, but I'll have to amend that, won't I?"

AFTER WE'VE STACKED THE TABLES and chairs in the garage (and after David's counted them at least twice and fussed over the bad manners of people who haven't yet responded to their telephoned invitations for lunch), we head behind the house to decide where we'll arrange them tomorrow. Meteorologists have forecast the kind of June day that Wimbledon competitors pray for; indeed, Dad's mourners will have to miss the women's finals.

David does a lot of pacing and thinking out loud, and I agree with everything he suggests. My three nieces are playing under a cluster of lilacs which separates Tealing from the bed-and-breakfast next door, and Véronique is inspecting the gardens that Dad revived in recent years. Peonies and irises are in full sanguine bloom, along with the requisite roses and a few smaller plantings I couldn't identify at gunpoint. Véronique is actually taking notes; you'd think she was planning a military campaign. Claiming she can't use the ferns because they have some sort of blight, she's sent Lil into town to buy the greenery required to show off the flowers. This irks me not just because I think it frivolous but because I've yet to spend any time alone with Lil.

Satisfied with his plans, David wanders toward the burn. I follow him across the footbridge our father built to the meadow on the other side. With the sheep and the collies long gone, it's grown over, but beautifully, in wildflowers and timothy. Stray birch saplings encroach from the edges.

"Dennis wanted me to mow a big swath so we could have the lunch here. Nothing's an impediment to his romantic vision."

"And you'd have done the mowing."

David nods. "Although, you know, I do want to put a vegetable garden out here for Lillian, now that we'll . . ."

"Now that you'll be taking over." I say this lightly.

"Taking over, yes, I suppose we are," David agrees. "And the first thing I plan to do, next week, is take down that old ruin." He points to the abandoned kennel.

"I wish you wouldn't. That place is the last vestige of Mum."

"But useless, and an eyesore. I think it's full of bats."

"O ye of little sentiment." I try to sound like I'm joking, but David picks up on my spite.

"You'd like, what, a temple here? A sheepdogging shrine?"

I decide on silence as my best option. Practically, he's in the right.

"You know, Fen, our parents didn't have this dishy harmonious union you imagine."

"'Dishy'? Who was talking about anyone's marriage?" Should I be flattered that he even bothers to imagine what I imagine?

"There wasn't a single picture of Mum in the house on Naxos," he continues. And here it comes, I think. David, too, visited Dad in Greece and partook of his "little affairs." Of course he did.

"Sometimes," David says, "except for the fact that Dennis so clearly inherited Grandfather's enormous ears and nose, I used to wonder if the two of us were really Dad's."

Assuming he's referring to some Freudian teenage delusion, that age-old desire to disown our fathers when they refuse, maddeningly, to disown us, I say, "And me? Did you stop to wonder if I was really Dad's?" (I look, as our parents' friends never tired of remarking, exactly like our mother: fair, blue-eyed, wide-faced. My brothers both have Dad's darker hair and windblown complexion.)

David's laugh is contemptuous. "Well now, Fen, you'd be the love child, wouldn't you? The oldest offspring is rarely illegitimate. That is, in postfeudal times."

Like most brothers, as children the three of us would wrestle at the slightest provocation (and unlike most mothers, ours rarely forced us apart, letting us hash out conflict, real or symbolic, on physical terms). Just before I went away to school, David became strong and wily enough to beat me. Yet I would refuse to cry uncle and often came out the worse for wear, limping or nursing a sprained wrist. Now, never mind that I'm old enough to know better, I let the same instincts goad me on.

"Oh, and I suppose this reproductive expertise comes from being paid to oversee innumerable fuckings in farmyards. Though what a relief to hear you think me *legitimate*."

"Did that lover of yours bring out this nasty streak? You never used to be so brittle."

"In point of fact, he wasn't my lover."

"Whatever."

"Yes. Whatever."

David sighs. "Fenno, I'm going to regret this, but bloody hell, you're like a textbook poofter, blindly worshiping your mum and looking down your aesthetically superior nose at the rest of us heterosexual rubes."

"David. You a rube? Down at the Globe, I'm sure a few of your best mates are flamers." Behind him, I spot the three little girls headed toward us across the bridge. I wave to them, and David glances around.

He turns back to me and lowers his voice. "From up there"—he points to the highest window of the house, the foxhole above his bedroom—"I saw more of the world than I was meant to."

Unwittingly, I make a snorting noise. David ignores it.

"I saw things that wouldn't have pleased Dad."

"Just what, precisely, do you mean by 'things'?" My voice sounds frightfully mincing, as if to confirm David's vision of me as a poofter.

Laurie grabs our sleeves, both of us at once. "Papa says come, *à table*. He's making omelettes! You have to eat them while they're still puffed up!"

Without looking at me again, David lifts Théa, seats her on his shoulders, and starts for the house. I pick up Christine, who at two and a half keeps up valiantly with her sisters. Laurie scowls at me, as if I've snubbed her, and I say, "I'll be your pony later, after lunch. I promise."

Her scowl deepens. "I'm getting a little old for that." She bolts toward David, who's turned back to extend her his hand.

Abruptly, Christine starts crying. *"Où est mon chat?"*

"Oh, sweetheart, we'll find him, we'll find him," I say. As I carry her across the bridge, I hold her close to my body out of self-pity and loneliness as much as love. Grateful that she's bought me even minutes away from my brothers, both of them, I let Christine direct me round the lawn to search for her sorry little cat. We find him under the lilacs, where the older girls have laid a play picnic for their dolls, using one of my mother's best linen napkins as a blanket and a clutch of tiny silver ashtrays as plates. Grapes and quartered biscuits have been carefully apportioned all around. In the center of the napkin, a crystal saltcellar holds violets.

As we kneel on the ground, I take out my handkerchief and wipe Christine's wet face. When I put it back in my pocket, one of the mystery medals pricks my thumb, as if to taunt me about how little I know. I look toward the house and steel myself. It's as if I am standing on an ice floe that's drifted too far south; the illusions that keep me high and dry are busily melting toward nil. And I am not the world's most confident swimmer.

MY FIRST REWARD for taking in Felicity was her very company, which I loved at times to the point of doubting my sanity. I loved her weighty presence on my shoulder when I reshelved books. I loved the way she craned her neck (a busybody, just like me) to watch people passing the shop window, the way she might suddenly up and fly, her wide wings narrowly but infallibly clearing the tight spaces of the shop. I loved her occasional bouts of gratuitous laughter, and sometimes while I was on the phone—in her eyes, I must have been talking to her—she would shuffle about on my opposite shoulder and murmur in my ear a muffled phrase that sounded like "Didn't I say so, sweet?" I should probably not confess that at moments I felt as if I'd found a soul mate.

The second dividend was that I now had three kinds of evenings (four, if you counted our now weekly readings by the novelists and poets du jour). Two or three times a month, Mal would come to dinner at my flat so that he could spend more time with Felicity than the visits he paid to her in the shop (most days he wasn't traveling). Pronouncing the first meal I cooked him "anglotypically atrocious," thereafter Mal brought the food and cooked it. And though my ignorance of opera nearly led to Felicity's repossession, an occasional pair of tickets to a chamber concert, a recital, or the ballet would show up on my desk. Ralph, often a beneficiary, decided that perhaps Mal wasn't a bitch after all. (Mavis and Druid, on the other hand, were anything but pleased by Felicity. Whenever they entered the shop, she would squawk loudly— out of pleasure, I insisted, but they could not agree.)

Our evenings together were awkward at first. For one thing, I had seen Mal's flat, if only once. It wasn't a great deal larger than mine, but its architectural details were more refined, and the beauty and meticulous placement of everything in it were meant to astonish. Each of the three rooms beyond the kitchen was painted a different shade of leafy green. In the small dining room (a room I did not have), the chairs were upholstered in velvet.

I did not like the covetous urges it stirred, but this was a lovely place to be, a sanctuary of the material sublime. I found myself, like some eager bumpkin, unable to resist asking about each object, from the green-shaded Stickley lamp and the Italian watercolors of costume designs for *The Magic Flute* to the blue deco rug I had spotted months ago from across the street (depicting not dragons or pagodas but handsomely woven domestic animals, my favorite a trotting horse with a flower in its teeth). In one corner of the living room stood a primeval-looking chair, an exception to the consolingly plush upholstery everywhere else you might sit. The scarred wood looked as if it had never been finished, and the curved arms ended in a pair of vertical spindles, worn smooth and pale by some kind of friction. As I felt their oddly silken surface, Mal said, "The clenched hands of women in labor." He smiled at my confusion. "It's a birthing chair. I found it in a junk-shop in Quezaltenango." He pulled off the flat seat; below was a large aperture.

Each object promised a tale: an unwise but incendiary affair, a fabulous find in some uncharted bucolic hamlet, a plane detoured by foul weather to a spot even more delightful than the intended destination. I disliked the role of neophyte but had only myself to blame. No, I had not been to the South Pacific; no, not even to Covent Garden. I had never tasted star fruit, never heard of orange roughy (yes, Mal was an excellent cook and effortlessly so).

My flat, though clean, was furnished with carelessly mingled things I'd purchased mostly in charity shops (in Brooklyn, not Quezaltenango). Politely, Mal began his first visit perusing my bookshelves, Felicity touring along on his shoulder. I learned, with minimal gratification, that he was not well read and not at all sorry about it. He turned to the pictures of my brothers and parents which I had placed on the mantel above my nonfunctioning fireplace. Lil was there, too, just having married David; Dennis was yet to meet Véronique.

Through an asphyxiating silence, Mal pored over my relatives; his manner reminded me of the first time he'd come to the shop and scrutinized the bird prints. At last he looked at me and said, "You're a sentimentalist. I admire that. In others."

"I wouldn't go so far as to put an -ist on it. I don't adhere to any sort of manifesto. They're just my kin. I happen to like them. I like being reminded of their existence."

Ignoring my testiness, he said, "I'm sentimental about nothing; I just didn't get that gene. Except perhaps for one thing: Maria Callas, her voice and her life—two things? Responsible or not, that Jackie O will not be forgiven by me, nor can I understand the fawning fuss made over her every sigh. Such a whisper of a woman under that pilfered Chanel veneer. Such a niente, a zip, a zero. American women set such petty standards in their heroines. So this woman stood by a man who couldn't keep it zipped! So she has nifty taste and upped the thread count of sheets in the Lincoln Bedroom! So she allegedly saved Grand Central! So she knows how to keep mum!"

He lifted my parents off the mantel. "Well, Grand Central is grand, I'll give her that," he murmured. "But *someone* would have thrown the Colony Club in front of that demolition ball." He set the picture down without a word. Someone braver than I might have defended the exquisite charisma of Mrs. O or asked Mal about his family. It took a few evenings for me to learn how to ride these conversations, how not to be left in the starting gate, my horse bolted out from under me.

Mal never mentioned his health, yet the reason for our artificial friendship was rarely far from my mind. One evening the following spring, I noticed a mark on his forearm, a purple amoeba, when he rolled up his sleeves to begin a risotto. As we ate, he noticed the direction of my gaze. A cunning smile flared across his face (and a prominent blush across mine). "A door, dear Fenno. I literally, honest and truly, bumped into a doorjamb while getting up to piss in the middle of the night at a new hotel in Rome. My favorite was booked." It did look like a bruise. I apologized.

Mal leaned back in his chair. "Kaposi. Now who do you suppose that fellow was? Isn't it an odd, exotic name, almost jolly, for this deadly creeping thing of which I must live in terror? I picture some seedy ingratiating Arab type wearing a motheaten fez, some shady extra in *Casablanca*."

"Actually"—I tried to sound equally cool—"he was a turn-of-the-century Hungarian dermatologist. His first name was Moritz." It so happened that in a morbid moment, when Luke was ill, I'd looked up Kaposi's sarcoma.

"I stand enlightened." Mal laughed and tossed his napkin on the table. "Anyone for a touch of sorbet? Felicity won't say no."

Often, if talk of current events, celebrities, or art took us to the edge of this topic, Mal would bring up Felicity, as if to remind me that her companionship was the sole intimacy we shared. Yet even here he could cut me short. One evening, watching the two of them greet each other, I said, "She's very much your child."

Mal said coldly, "She is not a child. She's a bird." After an awkward space, he added quietly, "Parenthood is a kind of love unto itself. I don't subscribe to the idea of animals as children. But yes, of course I adore her."

I knew nothing about Mal's medical care except, of course, that his doctors (I noted the plural with conflicting alarm and relief) had forbidden him one of his greatest everyday joys. That joy—waking early to Felicity's warblings, letting her dash across the table to steal a piece of fruit from one's plate—was now mine, and when I enjoyed it most, I felt like a thief. The day Mal gave her to me, he stroked her luscious feathers and said, "One of the things I'll miss most—and it's vain, I know—is waking to a breakfast companion who's dressed every single morning like Jessye Norman at Carnegie Hall."

Sometimes he looked perilously thin, his pale brown hair parched and dull in a way no costly styling could conceal. Other times he looked wiry and strong, his freckled skin luminous and supple. He told me once that he'd always avoided the sun, so pallor was a constant. And when he came to dinner, he might drink quite a bit of wine or he might abstain. He might look weary and leave at nine; he might stay past midnight, until I kicked him out. Sometimes I was certain he aimed to be unpredictable.

One night after he left early, I found a plastic pillbox on my bathroom sink. It held several different kinds of pills in separate compartments. Mal had left not ten minutes before, so I simply took the box across the street and rang his bell. As I climbed the stairs, I could see him waiting in the open doorway to his flat. "Fenno?" he called down uncertainly, though I had identified myself on the intercom.

At the door, I held out the box. "Oh yes," he said quickly, and put the box in his pocket. He hesitated, perhaps about to ask me in, but then he said he was finishing up a review, and it wasn't kind, and the object of his scorn deserved his full attention. "If I write a rave," he said, "I can do it stone drunk on a dance floor. But cruelty requires astute respect. In my field at least."

We said goodnight for a second time, and the next day I searched the paper till I found Mal's review. It was mournful in its chastisement of James Levine for grossly overplaying the singers in the Met's latest *Traviata*. When Mal came by the shop, I commented on his diplomacy.

"That was draft five or six," he said. "Draft one expressed my true and perpetual opinion of that man and his mediocrity: Yoohoo, Jimmy dear, did someone neglect to inform you you're basically background? Why do you suppose you're not in the garters of Seiji Ozawa?"

This was when I noticed that, conceited or not, Mal was immune to praise. Like the photographer who can't stand having his picture taken,

Mal had chosen the one profession which spared him his deepest aversion. By now, I had been seeing the man nearly every day for a year, yet simple truths like this could still elude me because I did not, really, know him at all.

Did I want to? On the evenings I was home in my living room, a glance across the street at his darkened windows would tell me he was out. Being out was a large part of his job. If, much later, I happened to see that his lights were on, I imagined him working then as well. Had we still lived in the age of the typewriter, I might have, if I leaned out my window, heard one clacking cattily away. But on two or three other nights that first year, I saw faces behind Mal's windows: men and women dressed up and laughing. If he had parties at all these days, Mal had said in my kitchen one night, they were small dinner parties for the few people he honestly liked. I was surprised how much his remark stung; what made me think I was more to him than a glorified zookeeper or, effectively, a tolerated son-in-law? To literally witness these parties to which I had not been invited—yet at which I could practically hear the conversation—stung even more, leaving me spiteful and sad. Though feeling left out, you will have noticed, is second nature to me.

SEVEN

L AST NIGHT I REMEMBERED to set my alarm, so I'm downstairs by six o'clock. For the first time since my arrival, the kitchen is vacant, the table cleared of cooking preparations. I sit down and enjoy my tea and my childhood house in sweet, solitary silence. I feel deliciously smug. At a flash of motion from the garden, however, I realize that I am not the first one up.

Véronique spots me as I spy on her from the window. Without calling my name, she beckons energetically. Left no choice, I head across the grass; within a few mincing steps, I am soaked to the shins with dew. Véronique—a grown-up Continental Girl Guide—is wearing wellies.

She stands among the white peonies exercising a pair of shears; dozens of cut flowers lie in the grass. Her eyes are obscured by stylish wraparound sunglasses, and her yellow hair, usually twisted back, hangs loose across a white cabled jumper which I recognize as Dad's. It's kept, free for the loan, on a rack in the scullery, but I feel possessive.

When I'm standing close to her, she says, softly, "Newspapers, Fenno? Would you be so kind enough as to bring me some newspapers?"

"Well," I say, pointing at my trousers and pretending to pretend indignation, "you might have let me know before I crossed the great swamp."

"You will be no more the wet for going two times. I do not wish to wake Denis and the children." She points up at the house. "I will then accomplish *zéro,*" she says tartly, but she thanks me.

I do as I'm told, pulling piles of old papers out from under the scullery sink—copies of the *Yeoman,* two and three months old, which Dad would have read before leaving for Greece. The *Yeoman* is the newspaper my grandfather founded. Dad took it up next, as expected, but sold it after Mum died, after our convening as grown, bereft men made him see at last that none of his sons—least of all this one—planned to take on his work.

Véronique asks me to lay out several sheaves. The instant the paper touches the grass, it darkens thirstily from the edges. I think of how many substances this very newspaper has absorbed over the years: mud from our boots and shoes, blood from newborn puppies whelped by our mother, the stains of leavings from meals which I would carry out back in the evenings to empty over the wall for wildlife to scavenge.

Véronique startles me by saying, "You have lived in New York how long is it now?" She is bent over, rolling the peonies into the paper.

Seventeen years, I tell her.

She asks, again without looking up, if I'm happy there.

"Oh yes," I say dismissively. I wonder if she's going to start asking pointed questions about my life, but I have to confess she's been little other than polite to me during this visit. Have the hormones of childbirth made her fair-minded? Am I vaguely disappointed, itching for a fight?

"So then you will stay there, you believe. Forever?"

"That's a grandiose word in my lexicon."

Ignoring the jest, Véronique instructs me to hold out my arms and begins stacking cones of flowers against my chest. They're for the church arrangements; will I carry them please to Davide's pickup?

Together, we lay them in the bed of the pickup, securing them in one corner between a spare wheel and a toolbox.

As we start back, she says, "So you think no longer of returning back here, of settling here yourself?"

"I don't think I've ever thought that. Why—is there some fear I'll try to horn in on the status quo?"

"At the contrary. I think everyone would like to see more of you."

"Everyone?"

As we enter the kitchen, she says, "Fenno, you are not compellent enough to be a villain. This is perhaps an insult to you?"

Before I can answer, she points to the newspapers on the floor and says, "Now I must bring irises. Could you please?" She marches out the door.

It is, as predicted, a day of alert, exquisite beauty. Oblivious now to my drenched ankles, I stop in the center of the lawn to listen to the escalating birdsong: I can distinguish yellowhammers, chiffchaffs, a collared dove, a mistle thrush—old familiars, friends of my youth. The shadow of the house, which covered the entire lawn just a few minutes ago, has retreated dramatically, making the house look taller, as if it is literally rising to the occasion. Above its steep roof, the sun is rapidly drying the grass on which Dad's memorial luncheon will take place a few hours hence.

On solar cue, a small lorry pulls up and three young men climb out. They head for the garage and begin ferrying tables and chairs to the lawn, setting them down around me. They acknowledge me with only the briefest nods (ignorant, I suppose, that their gratuities may depend in part on me).

The next three hours are filled with a careful rush to overcome chaos. Dennis puts two large pots on the stove for rice, places the casseroles of meat on the kitchen table, shows two hired girls how to serve the soup. Véronique fills the house with our father's own flowers, then dresses her daughters in starched and crinolined dresses, three different shades of respectful blue (Véronique wears simple but shapely black). Lil is absent yet again, retrieving an Edinburgh contingent at the Lockerbie rail station; she will meet us at Saint Andrews. David makes the boys who arrived in the lorry rearrange all the tables and chairs. Hewing to his specifications as well, I lay a drinks bar on the terrace behind the kitchen. I find a silver ice bucket that is so deeply tarnished it looks positively archaeological. My grandfather's initials appear after a third go-round of polish, and somehow this omen delights me. (Following Lil's advice, we will not be collecting in the churchyard after the service; we plan to fight about our father's resting place later tonight.)

Véronique drives Dennis and the children in Dad's car. Behind them, I ride with David in his truck. We say very little, and I watch not the green hills and woods as they lose ground to the reach of the city but my nieces' bobbing heads. Every time they kneel on the backseat to wave and make faces at us, their mother's slender arm reaches back and warns them into place. When they pull ahead, I can see Dennis looking at Véronique, talking gaily, hands expressive, probably strategizing a new ragout or fricassee.

The vicar stands outside, already robed, eyes closed and face tilted up to catch a few heavenly rays from his Alleged Maker. He lets us into the church and props open its broad medieval doors. Inside, the cool, grave stillness overwhelms me. The church has such a parental smell: admonitory yet consoling. Church was one of the few places to which my mother wore perfume; magically, I smell that particular sweetness too. To distract myself from these hazardous sensations, I take Laurie's hand and lead her to the baptismal font. It's made of a white marble, glacial and ghostly, whose faint markings look like subcutaneous veins. This is where Laurie's father, David, myself, and the grandfather whose loss she hasn't yet grasped were christened. She (but not her sisters) was also christened here. When she stands on tiptoe, her nose just clears the rim of the basin. "When babies don't need it, do they let birds come in for a swim? The size is exactly, perfectly perfect."

"Perfectly perfect," I agree with melancholy satisfaction. I dip a finger in the water and touch Laurie's nose. "No dripping on my dress!" she exclaims with a grimace. As she runs back out toward the sun, I hear David quarreling gently with the vicar over hymns.

A YEAR AND A HALF after we opened the shop, it was showing a decent profit. Ralph's money (and ego) allowed us to serve good wine after our readings, and half a dozen mentions in wildlife magazines led visiting naturalists through our door (to which I had affixed a bell, compliments of Malachy Burns). We added to our merchandise one-of-a-kind birdhouses made from the tragic remnants of newly felled national forest in northern Idaho (ten percent of the proceeds went to the Nature Conservancy, another scheme of Ralph's).

As the air warmed that spring, steeped in the fragrance of crowning hyacinths and budding trees, my morning walks shed their puritanical purpose. I fancied that they had begun to signify the well-trodden path of my life, which I had grown to like. Uncringingly at last, I enjoyed my apparent health and drew from my hierarchy of alliances a superior sense of order (even Mal's niche seemed clear). Thanks to Felicity's ruckus at dawn, I rose earlier than most of my neighbors and took my route slowly, with relish, feeling generally thankful rather than sullen. I looked forward to browsing the untouchable wares in the FedEx lorries (reliably trading their trousers for shorts). I stopped to contemplate buildings and plantings I'd never noticed before.

A true curiosity was the tiny white weatherboard house at the corner of Greenwich and Charles. Set back against a mammoth, nondescript apartment building, it had its own little lawn, partitioned from the street by a tall wooden fence; to see the house properly, you had to squint between the slats.

In any other setting, you'd pass this house right by as a runty ramshackle thing, its roofline flat, its windows and doors pathetically crooked, its rooms surely not much larger than cupboards. It reminded me of windbeaten cottages in the poorest seaside towns along the Firth of Forth. But here, in this muscular setting, it was breathtakingly quaint, and its lawn, though minuscule by suburban standards, was magnificent for such a crowded, coveted corner of the world. So while the place looked as if it had sprouted like a carbuncle from the dull cement skin of the building next door, you could well imagine it as the third or fourth pied-à-terre of a film star.

There was a child's swing set and, parked in the driveway, a blue station wagon. I had never seen any sign of activity until one morning that May—when, for the first time I could remember, the station wagon was gone. A woman with a long dark ponytail was crouched on the grass; for several seconds, her back to me, she remained in this attitude. She appeared to have lost or to be planting something.

When she stood, I saw first that she was holding a camera and, second, that she was a man. He looked straight at me and said, "You with the invisible dog. If you've got half an hour, I could use an assistant."

I froze; my white shirt had given me away through the fence.

The man laughed. "I don't lure in suckers to bury them in the basement, if that's what you're thinking." He walked to the driveway, opened the gate, and leaned out to look at me more directly. "Well, come on in there. I've got coffee and such."

I started in on some fable about an architectural critic friend who'd told me about this house and I was just having a look and perhaps I'd looked a bit long and—

"Looking's no crime," said the man as we came face-to-face. My embarrassment amused him.

He did not take me into the house but offered to bring me a cup of coffee. He came out a moment later, carrying a lawn chair as well. He took it to the place where he had been crouching, unfolded it, and told me to sit. "This is tedious," he said, "so go ahead and sunbathe till I'm ready."

A large silver spoon was lying in the grass. My host now began to play with its position, repeatedly standing back to look at it through the camera. Then he knelt down, leaned close to the spoon so that his face was just inches away, held the camera at arm's length and clicked the shutter.

Other than sipping my coffee (which I did not enjoy but had felt compelled to accept), I sat quite still. I felt awkward but safe, not because of the man's disavowal of criminal intention but because I knew that innumerable flat dwellers could look down upon us from three sides as they showered, made their breakfasts, and dressed for work.

"Now here's where you come in," he said abruptly, holding out the camera. I put down my coffee and took it. He squinted at the sun and held a light meter near the spoon. As he leaned down, his T-shirt rose above his jeans. Beneath the shirt, his skin was pale and smooth. A sparse patch of brown hair grew in the small of his back.

He walked behind me, twisted the lens and adjusted a few small knobs on the camera from over my head. His hands were all knuckles, graceful but well worked.

I felt as if I were underwater, forbidden by the elements from speaking. I leaned forward, clutching the camera, waiting for orders as my nameless director walked beyond the spoon, folded his arms, and stood facing away.

"Center the spoon," he said from this stance. He had an accent strong enough that even I could recognize it as midwestern; I'd had a classmate back at Cambridge who uttered those prairie-wide vowels. He was from Chicago.

This man was probably in his thirties, but he had a full youthful face, like pink-skinned Italian boys in Caravaggio's paintings. His eyes were cinnamon-colored, and his hair, pulled back, revealed an off-center widow's peak that gave his expression a cynical touch, as if one eyebrow were permanently cocked. He wasn't particularly tall or muscular, but his body had a loose wiliness that gave him a presence as good as brute strength.

When I clicked the shutter as ordered, it became clear what he was doing: photographing his reflection in the spoon (or having me do so). His image was little more than a black sliver in the spoon's broad convex face. The sky with its roiling white clouds prevailed. After I clicked the shutter, he turned, raised his arms, and told me to shoot again. He changed his position or changed the spoon itself twenty or thirty times, at each pose saying, "Shoot," as if I were a marksman at an execution. At the end of the roll, he reloaded the camera and handed it back for another round.

After the second roll, he took the camera and said, "You make a decent assistant, no chitchat. Be along here tomorrow?"

I said that I would, though I feared my voice was trembling.

"Great," he said, smiling. "My assistant have a name?"

I told him. He shook my hand and said, "Tony Best. I'd invite you to hang out, but I have a rendezvous." He lampooned the French word with a hick's pronunciation, and I did not know if this meant he had no rendezvous at all or had somehow noticed my appraisal of his accent and wanted me to know he could not be patronized. I thought about that off and on all day.

That night, I was boiling potatoes and reading Roethke at my kitchen table when the phone rang. "Do you own a tuxedo?" Mal asked urgently. "All I need are the shirt and cummerbund."

I told him I owned a tuxedo that had belonged to my grandfather, but I hadn't worn it myself in years.

The apartment door was open, and when I walked in, I heard retching. Mal was bent over the kitchen sink. His arms, braced on the countertop, shook. I stood there, uselessly passive, clutching my jumbled garments.

"Christ, what time is it?" Mal gasped when he stood up. "Christ," he said again when I told him it was ten past seven.

Mal was naked from the waist up, his shirt thrown aside near my feet. It smelled of vomit. After wiping his face with a tea towel, he threw it on top of the shirt. He told me, in a businesslike but strangely earnest tone, that he needed my help.

He asked me to hold up the shirt I'd brought. I'd expected petulance or sarcasm, because it was so rumpled, but he merely took it and said, "In the bathroom. There's an iron on the highest shelf over the sink and some of that lurid pepto-bilge in the cabinet. I have an eight o'clock curtain. Kiri Te Kanawa is singing."

I found the Pepto-Bismol at once, glad not to have to rummage through the crush of apothecary labels I encountered (that kind of prurience does not afflict me). But to reach the iron, I had to stand on the toilet, and as I leaned awkwardly over the sink, I knocked a jar of cotton balls and a small wooden box off the top of the medicine chest. I decided to take Mal the iron and the medicine first, then come back and clean up.

Mal had set up an ironing board. He downed a swig of Pepto-Bismol as if it were whisky, said "Christ, I don't even know if I can take this stuff," and set about ironing the shirt. "Thank God Gramps didn't go in for ruffles."

The jar had not broken (falling on a fine if threadbare purple kilim), and I jammed in the scattered cotton. The wooden box, lid thrown aside, had landed face down behind the toilet. When I picked it up, a sheaf of Polaroids spilled out like a pack of cards.

Surprisingly, they were not pornographic. Even more surprisingly, most of them included someone I recognized. Looking happy and healthy, here everywhere was Armand, the doomed alluring young baker. At the seaside. In a tux—ruffles, canary yellow. On Mal's green velvet chaise longue—lips pressed to Mal's cheek, Armand holding the outstretched camera. Grinning flirtatiously from between two stately cakes on pedestals—in the shop which was now mine. I thought of the day I'd met Mal, the way he'd scrutinized every inch of that altered domain. He wasn't seeing; he was remembering.

"Andiamo!" called Mal, so I fumbled the Polaroids into their box and back to their appointed Siberia.

The shirt looked crisp now and fit Mal perfectly. Hastily, he pulled on his jacket. I realized that we were the same height, the same size all around; even the same coloring, but for our eyes. He looked more like a brother to me than either David or Dennis. As I followed him out, it occurred to me that I had expressed little concern. I said, "Was it something you ate? Will you be all right?"

"My newest wonder drug. They like to sneak up on you, exact a little penance now and then. Remind you how grateful you'd better be not to be dead." He hurried downstairs ahead of me.

Mal jogged toward Hudson Street to find a cab. At the end of the block, he turned around and called back, "Thank you! You saved my sartorial life!" Felicity heard his voice from her perch in my living room; I could hear her muffled squawks of excitement as I crossed the street—but she liked my company, too, and did not seem disappointed when I came in alone.

————

DAVID WAS RIGHT: the church overflows with bodies, seated and standing. The hymns, from the mouths of all these singers, resonate so fiercely against the stone walls that I wonder if they could crack. And I am right, in that we fulfill some kind of classic family template. I, Literary Chip Off The Old Block, remember my father (briefly, briefly, as David's austere gaze from the front pew reminds me) as a man of intellectual hunger and professional integrity. (I might have given a different eulogy as the Black Sheep Returned From Abroad, but it would be no less flattering.) Dennis, Happy-Go-Lucky Perpetual Youth, tells fond, funny stories about our home life, most of them involving genial mishaps rather than pranks (our father having been born with a somewhat recessed funnybone). David, Heir Apparent, performs an homage to our father as granite cornerstone of family and community (no talk of family trees this time—wary, perhaps, of commingling clichés).

Afterward, the vicar flicks a switch that sets the bell tolling, and we stand on the small front lawn of the church, accepting the respects of everyone from old schoolmasters I'd thought long dead to dozens of strangers who worked at the *Yeoman*—driving lorries, operating presses, copyediting late-breaking stories at dawn. I am reminded of the small kingdom my father ruled (fairly, by all accounts), a kingdom I can remember visiting a shabby two or three times once I'd grown up and consciously turned that life down.

In the reshuffling of transportation, I am once again in the pickup but this time with Lil. David sent Dennis home, to meet the first guests and get the hirelings under control, then went back into the church to pay the vicar.

"God I've missed you, where've you been?" I gush, leaning across the seat to kiss Lil when she climbs in beside me.

Lil blushes. "Dramatic as ever, Fenno." She frowns at the small thicket of keys David gave her. "What are they all *to,* I always wonder."

I pull out two that look like they'd start a car. "Cages, I imagine."

She laughs lightly but doesn't look me in the eye. I feel as desperate for her attention as a teenage boy courting an experienced woman. She looks more rested than she did the night of our family dinner, but the lines in her profile seem too numerous. She is still compact, but not with the fawnlike figure she had in her twenties. After marrying David, she let her brilliant red hair grow out into its natural waves, which she ties in back with a ribbon. The earrings she wears are far less gypsyish than those of university days, and only the slightest dimples on her earlobes betray the extra piercings which she was among the first to flaunt.

David and Lil married the summer they both finished university; David went straight to veterinary college, while Lil found a job in a girls' school teaching history (her "modest but heady ambition," she'd told me that long-ago Christmas Eve, wearing her Faerie Queene dress: "My plan's to oil those imperial cogs with a drop or two of anarchy!"). But when, several years later, David used his inheritance to start his own surgery, she resigned her teaching post and joined him, taking care of everything from decorating examination rooms to charming David's banker. It mystified me how she could make such a sacrifice, do such menial things, but I have never seen any sign that she does not love this work as much as she loved her teaching.

"Do you know, it's been more than twenty years since I saw you on that stage making love to Bob Dylan."

"You always bring that up, as if I were Queen of the Hippies."

"You were!"

"I was going with the flow."

"Better than standing numbly onshore—that's where I was."

"We were all so impressed with ourselves. We thought we were overcoming obstacles. We hadn't a bloody clue about obstacles." Lil looks worried as she pulls into a knot of traffic entering a roundabout. The gears grind as she downshifts for a lorry that's cutting us off.

"I hate this thing; it's a tank," she says, putting an end to my reminiscence. I offer to drive, but she refuses, crowding the wheel like a novice. When we pass the last traffic light, she relaxes a little.

"I think David's disgusted with me," I say. I wonder if there's any way I could tell her what David said about our mother, ask her exactly what he meant. I thought about it through much of the church service, where she was mentioned not once by family, not even (appallingly) by me.

"No, he's just preoccupied—and very sad. He really is. He gets all officious, but it's camouflage. You forget how much time we've spent with your dad since moving to the house. He was still so . . . hardy when he left last month. I think it's more of a shock to Davey than it is to you or Dennis."

Though her tone is sympathetic, I feel chastened. "I suppose I sound like the child who still fancies himself the bang at the center of the cosmos."

"You know you don't. You're just not . . . here very much. I think you underestimate David."

"Well I think he underestimates you."

She looks at me, fleetingly. "I don't know why you'd say that."

"All this 'preoccupation'—Dad's death aside—is any of it with you? Anyone can see you're distressed."

"Business is almost too much for us to handle right now, since we built the extension with all that high-tech equipment. Which isn't a bad thing. So I did convince him to get more help, but he's terrible at delegating, terrible."

"Oh fuck the business, Lil."

The look she spares me is hurt, then angry. "Well fuck you, Fenno. The business is our life." Her voice trembles.

"Should it be? Do you want it to be? I doubt it." This is terrible timing (a curse of mine), as Tealing gleams ahead of us in all its rustic conceit. One of the hired boys is directing cars to park up close against the hedgerow.

Lil says nothing further until she's parked. She apologizes for losing her temper, but she's looking at her lap, fiddling with David's keys. "We'll talk, really really talk, before you leave. Right now I'm hopelessly . . ." Her voice trembles again. I slide toward her across the seat, but she turns away to open her door. "We have to be hosts, that's our job right now."

I'm forced to agree with her there; from the line of cars sidling up on the verge of our country lane, it looks as if even the delinquent nonrespondents are here. "Let's hope no one wants seconds on vichyssoise," I say as we cut through the hedgerow like crashers. Immediately, we are recognized, separated, set upon with elaborate sympathies.

My two aunts and their grown children have arrived en masse, an explicitly united front. Pointedly or accidentally (who cares which), they missed the church service but are among the first at Tealing. Dad's sisters never quite forgave him for selling their ancestral home so that he and Mum and the three of us could move out here to the country. Dad once told me that both of their husbands (now dead) had the means to buy him out, but they were established professionals, and from the castled enlightenment of Edinburgh, Dumfries was little more than a glo-rified village.

After going through the grief-stricken motions with my aunts, I manage to make it undeterred to the drinks bar, get myself a whisky, and flee into the house, quiet and dim except for the heated bustlings in the kitchen.

As if to get my bearings on the occasion, I go to the front hall, where we have placed our father's ashes on the table below the mirror at which he would customarily adjust his hat before leaving for work. Next to the box stands a tiny crystal pitcher brimming with violets. I sip my whisky for a few long moments, closing my eyes to enjoy its astringently sugary scent. I lift the glass, make a Roman toast—"Hail, Father"—then wan-der into the dining room. Save for another of Véronique's bouquets (this one gaudy with roses), it feels forlorn, a place which ought to be in-cluded in these antifestivities but has been shunned. As I'm trying to re-press such maudlin sentiments (and trying to remember the last food I ate, necessary to absorb these spirits, literal and otherwise), I hear the unmistakable *thwock,* pause, *thwock,* pause, *thwock,* pause, ROAR of ten-nis on the telly. In the living room, I catch one of my cousins (Will, a salesman of sporting equipment) cheering on Steffi Graf.

"Oh, hullo, hullo, it's been a dog's age!" he gushes. His sister Gillian giggles sheepishly from my father's leather armchair.

"I dread these things, too," I say as I shake Will's hand (having gra-ciously decided against "Got a few quid on her, have you?").

"We are so sorry," says Gillian. "How sudden!" Behind her looms a close-up of Steffi—wearing, as usual, an expression of disingenuously Sisyphean angst. I'd trade places with her in a minute.

"How's the sports biz?" I actually hear myself say. (It's shamefully American to talk about jobs, but I cannot for the life of me remember the names of my cousin's children, and I overheard after the service that he is in the midst of a craven divorce.)

"Never better. I'm concentrating on golf; there's a revolution in footwear."

"A revolution. Ah!" Lamentably, not a drop of my whisky remains.

"He's covering France and Spain—booming new markets," cheer-leads Gillian.

"Nice ground to cover," I say.

"Indeed. I'm a fortunate man."

"Very," I say, at which point we collide with silence. "You know," I finally manage, "I mustn't abandon my brothers out there."

"Oh we must catch up with them too!" says Gillian, relieved. Will has the nerve to turn back to Steffi.

I do intend to go outside, but my obstinate feet take me through the kitchen and up the back stairs. En route, I nab a handful of biscuits from a platter of cheeses. This is utterly childish, I say to my hopeless self as I ascend.

Sunlight falls through the open door of the library. With the excuse that this is a vantage point from which to keep an eye on events below, I take my squirreled biscuits in and close the door behind me. From the window, I see our guests strolling every which way in threes and fours: out to the once-farmed fields behind us, over the footbridge across the burn. You'd think they were attending a property auction. Bowls of vichyssoise are being carried out on trays, and some of the elderly guests have seated themselves at the tables, but there is no other sign that the meal is imminent.

As the soups are placed, I see that Dennis, too, has his moment of rightness: The meal he prepared already appears, as his daughter would say, perfectly perfect. In the center of each table is a small cluster of white peonies. On white plates on white linens, each bowl of soup, also white, is garnished with a pink chive blossom (ah yes: dried from Vee's incredible garden). Very archetypal, very Snow White, Mal would have said approvingly. In some cultures, he would remind me if he were here, white is the color of mourning. "Blood shows up better on white," he might have remarked.

Having wolfishly consumed the biscuits, I look down and see crumbs on the carpet. Looking for a means to sweep them up, I scan the desk. Squared pertly on the blotter is a pile of catalogs, from which I borrow a laminated price list (ultrasound equipment, I'm impressed to see—so my brother's one-upping James Herriot). After transferring my crumbs to the wastebin and replacing the price list, I find myself sitting at the desk. Not one to drink at midday, I am a wee bit drunk, and when I am drunk I am cowardly.

When this desk was Dad's, there were story files and cuttings strewn about the perimeter, leaving only a small green clearing on the blotter for work. Here Dad wrote his correspondence, and the surface of the blotter was speckled with ink from his fountain pen. Now the blotter is unstained (the paper brown, not green) and cleared of everything but the catalogs and the slimmest of notebook computers (closed). Lined up beyond are a pewter cup of colored pencils and Biros, a calculator, a stapler, and a notepad printed with the unpronounceable name of some veterinary anesthetic.

In the drawers to the right (yes, I open them) are color-coded folders with labels like LAMINITIS CASES and PARASITES, CURRENT LIT. and DYSPLASIA—ACUPUNCTURE/ALTERNATIVE. I laugh at one labeled EXPANSION IDEAS. (You Boy Scout, I think, and then remember my similar impression of Véronique the Girl Guide in those wellies. Yes, my spouse-swapping notion's not half bad: these two seem made for each other.)

But the drawers to the left still contain a jumble of my father's things: in the top drawer, his pen, a pair of reading spectacles, a tin of anise drops, a battered empty wallet, a pocket notebook with the telltale curvature of a hind pocket (used pages all ripped out).

My mother's last passport.

Barely distorted by the raised characters of the Crown's official stamp, there she is, so happy she's almost laughing. There are only a couple of countries recorded: France, the Netherlands, France again. The passport expired three years after she died.

I pocket the passport and close the top drawer. I am just opening the next one, just seeing my name in my father's handwriting on a bulky envelope, when the pitch of noise from the lawn changes. The conversation rises an octave in excitement and I hear the clink of cutlery on glass. Going to the window, I see that nearly everyone is seated and that David is standing expectantly, waiting to welcome his guests. I doubt he's noticed my absence.

I slam shut the desk drawer and bolt down the back stairs. In the kitchen, the servers are seated for a break around the kitchen table, reading magazines and chewing gum. I must look like a madman, dashing through the room and out the door, but they barely notice.

David has just finished his (brief, brief!) welcome, and people are lifting their spoons and tasting the soup. I slip into the nearest empty chair—empty, I see too late, because it's in a spot most people would likely avoid: between a woman one might size up as a lonely aging bore and an alarmingly elderly man who must devote what little energy he has to getting the vichyssoise, unspilled, to his mouth. He does not register my arrival.

I'm barely seated, however, before the woman says, "Fenno. You are Fenno," with a smile too flattering not to like. Though initially I thought her old enough to be my grandmother, she is probably my father's age. Her hair is white, cut in a sharp pageboy that looks more utilitarian than flapperish or chic. She wears a gray linen dress—its sleevelessness daring, since she is not slim—and no jewelry other than a dainty wristwatch, which serves only to make her arms look thicker than they already are. Nor is she wearing the customary hat. (Not, hence, a member of our church. She is English, in fact.)

"Guilty as charged," I say.

"Photos. I have seen photos. Handsome runs in this family, no doubt about it." She lifts her soupspoon and pauses. She looks as if she's about to conduct a symphony. "I will miss Paul." She sweeps the spoon in an arc. "But that is what we are all here to say, by our simple presence, is it not?"

She is Marjorie Guernsey-Jones, all the way up from Devon. She saves me the predictable inquiries by declaring that she met my father six years ago—to the week, if she is not mistaken—on a tour of Greece and that she is proud to have helped convince him to lease the house on Naxos the following year. Two years ago, she visited him there (Well who *didn't,* I groan inwardly), and it's a journey she will always remember for the invigorating hikes they took. "We might as well have mapped that island, I tell you. Not a mythic stone unturned. Paul is the ideal touring companion because he never argues and never complains. And— not insignificant, mind you!—he can read the most wretched map like a migrating goose reads a coastline."

From my right, I hear the gentle snoring of the very old man. A bee hovers near the flower in his abandoned soup, then spirals harmlessly away. Thus forced (or freed) to give this woman my undivided attention, I find after a few minutes that I do not mind at all. I like the way she calls Dad by his first name (not "your father," incessantly, as if his name died with him), and I like the way she never corrects her own use of the present tense in describing him. If I could fully admit how sad I am that he is gone, I could fully admit that these habits of hers are a comfort to me.

"Paul told me you are a devotee of American letters."

"Yes. Well, I was, in a more serious way, some years ago."

"I do love Willa Cather."

I smile. I've never much cared for Cather.

"Taught *Death Comes for the Archbishop* to my girls a few years running. Might have taken place on the moon, it was that fantastical to them." She laughs. She pours us both a second glass of wine. "Paul told me how much he'd have liked you to take his place at the paper."

"I disappointed him there."

"Oh no, no. He just had a brief period of needing to air his minor laments—and he knew, let me tell you, that they were minor. I told him he was a fortunate ingrate. I didn't have a single child to do so benign, so absolutely correct a thing as to go his own self-sufficient way. But then, I was just getting back at him that night."

"Getting back?" I begin to feel, from the intensity of her gaze, as if this woman sought me out—though hadn't I stumbled onto her?

"Well, that I don't have children—people can look at me and guess that, young man, don't you think? Aren't the words *dear old aunt* as good as tattooed on my brow?"

Probably blushing from guilt, I protest.

"No. Don't deny it. Well I said as much to Paul—about the tattooed business. And he laughed and said that the first time he saw me, the words he saw there were *old maid.*" When I tell her that I cannot believe my father would be so rude, she lays a plump hand on my arm and says, "Paul is a bit of a hazard on ouzo and we both had far too much. It's the antiwhisky, you know—wicked as the Antichrist. It's the Greeks' revenge on everybody else's colonial grandiosity, trampling what little foliage they have, carting off their history pillar by pillar. One day I hope they sack the British Museum."

"What about Alexander?" I ask—and receive a headmistressy look.

"Dear one, your history is woefully blurred. Alexander was the king of Macedonia. He *conquered* Greece."

This woman tells me nothing about my father that I did not know—nothing I can put a finger on—but when I begin to realize what an easy kinship they had, I am fascinated yet disapproving. Disapproving, it dawns on me with a third glass of wine, because I'm wondering just how close she was to Dad. My mother was pretty and seductive almost to the end, and even if my father's affections for this woman blossomed after Mum's death, they feel like an aesthetic affront, a desperation. I'm appalled to be thinking such thoughts—and I don't even know if this woman was more than a friend. Probably not, as she tells me that she knew Dad mainly through letters.

I'm so caught up in our conversation that I gasp when I feel the old man's head fall onto my shoulder. Marjorie Guernsey-Jones leans nimbly across me and grasps the man's arm to keep him from slumping to the ground. "Welcome back, comrade," she says in answer to his haplessly darting gaze. She goes behind me and helps him regain his balance. Indicating with a nod that I should move to her seat, she takes mine, pours the man a glass of water, and gaily introduces herself as if he's just dropped in from a nearby table, not from an untimely snooze. This puts me next to a man I recognize, after a mental struggle, as a past picture editor of the *Yeoman* and, beyond him, his wife. We reacquaint ourselves awkwardly, and for the rest of the meal we discuss the ways in which news reporting has changed (for the worse, to be sure) since my father's day.

After the sweet earthy tajine and tart green salad, the peaches in their purple liqueur are served, along with plates of thin chocolate wafers. The peaches look (perhaps through a scrim of too much Margaux) like tastings of a sunset. While we eat this morsel of divinity, a few guests stand and give tributes to Dad, none too drunken, and then, as people finish their tea and mill about to take their leave, a piper in full ceremonial dress steps out of the house (a complete surprise to Mr. Yet Again Out of the Loop). All these transitions are ordinary features at such occasions, yet the seeming spontaneity of each is a marvel—orchestrated by David, I know without asking. The piper is one of my father's closest friends, the *Yeoman*'s managing editor for decades. Squinting into the afternoon light, he plays "Flower of Scotland" and "Skye Boat Song," undaunted by tears that seep from his eyes (and, predictably but honestly, from everyone else's too, all but those of the teenage help as they stack and ferry plates; death, to them, would be reassuringly quaint).

In the crush of good-byes, as doors slam and people traipse in and out of the house to use the loo or fetch their jackets and shawls, I cruise along in a mild alcoholic muddle, shaking hands, embracing women I've barely met, helping old men fold their stiff bodies into their cars. Most of them are gone when I feel a firm grip on my elbow. I turn to see

Marjorie Guernsey-Jones, whose earlier disappearance left me feeling wounded.

"Dear one, I'm off to pester friends in the Lake District before I head home, but I'd wanted to leave you with something." She's holding a packet of letters secured with postal twine. I see her name scripted in my father's hand.

When I reach for the letters, she withdraws her hand and smiles, shaking her head. "But I am a weak woman, and I changed my mind," she says. "So what I would like is your address, if you will, so that I may relinquish them farther along the road or, at the least, have them forwarded after my own demise."

"May I have your address as well?" I hear myself ask in an uncontrollably robust voice.

Marjorie Guernsey-Jones breaks into a spacious grin. "Dear one, you certainly may." She opens her pragmatically large handbag, tucks in the packet of letters, and pulls out a notepad to which a pencil is tied.

After exchanging addresses, we look at each other expectantly, not quite able to say good-bye. "May I ask you something else, something blunt?" my ventriloquist's dummy utters. When she nods, I ask, "Are those love letters?"

She looks stunned, and at first I'm sure I've offended her. "Yes," she says. Her eyes glitter. "Love-of-life letters. That's what they are."

After I help her into her car, Marjorie Guernsey-Jones rolls down her window and says, "You'd have been my favorite, too."

AFTER THE TUXEDO, things changed with Mal; I had crossed some invisible membrane. The next week, he invited me to the debut recital of a cello prodigy. He said, "The cello is too sad an instrument to listen to alone."

He might as well have gone alone, however, for all the attention he paid me at the concert. Mal was recognized by a dozen people in the lobby beforehand, spoke briefly with each one, and never introduced me. During the performance, he took occasional but fervent notes in a small leather book and otherwise kept his fierce gaze aimed at the young man onstage. Toward the end, he closed his eyes—transported by pain or pleasure, I couldn't tell which. Halfway downtown in a taxi, he finally addressed me. We were stuck in a traffic jam, bathed in the pre-Disney neon of old Times Square.

"I went through that rigamarole myself, you know—or the earlier stages that might have been a prelude to that life."

I suppose I looked moronically blank, because Mal laughed and said, "Confusion is like yawning, my dear. In all walks of society, you're best off covering it up." Then he told me about his childhood career as a prodigy flutist. "Not, thank heaven, a *flaut*ist. For which I have my parents to thank." His parents, Mal told me, had been fans rather than impresarios. Mal had been the one to research the music camps and competitions, find a good teacher to act as a mentor in the literal and cultural backwoods of Vermont. Mal's father was a lawyer and made enough money to pay all the necessary fees, to allow his son to forgo the summer jobs his classmates and his own siblings took as waiters and lifeguards and campground attendants. But that was a lifetime ago. He hadn't made the bigtop.

"All I did for years, all I remember doing, was practice. Practice: such a limp word for the context. You do not, if you are serious, *practice* your instrument. You flay, eviscerate, excoriate the thing until it surrenders its thingness, until its carapace cracks open and it bleeds. Even a voice. You belabor it until any sound but the sound of that instrument is, to your ears, gelatinous babble." As he lectured me, he gazed imperiously at a billboard showing a tight-bodied boy in underpants that were tighter still. Mal's face glowed blue, then red, then orange as trade names winked above the avenue before us.

"And so?" I said, though Mal clearly meant the story to end there. "So what happened?" Irritated at the way he'd ignored me for most of the evening, I felt like needling him.

"Family matters." He sighed. "Ancient history."

"What family matters?" I said. "What would stop *you* from pursuing any ambition?" At this backhanded insult, or so I assumed, Mal set his jaw and looked stubbornly out the window.

But then he told me, still gazing off into the symphony of artificial color about us, that when he was seventeen he made the finals of the first competition that would take him to New York. The week before he was to go (accompanied by his cheerleading family), his little brother was diagnosed with Hodgkins disease.

"I turned down Juilliard and went to the University of Vermont. It seemed callous, even to me, to leave home right after a virtual tornado had ripped away everything but the foundation. But you know, why I stayed hardly matters, does it? Maybe I didn't have enough hunger for that life. Maybe I was secretly relieved. The little cellist we saw tonight? Voracious as the dickens."

After another silence, I asked if he still played. He said, "Only in a state of thorough inebriation, a state I am now forbidden to visit."

As we were getting out of the cab, I remembered to ask about his brother. "Oh cured, cured," he said idly, as if this part of his story was a trivial postscript. "And grew up to be a royal pain in the ass leading a rather lackluster life. But who am I to judge."

For a few minutes, we talked on the pavement outside his door. He told me (after I asked) that his father was now the senior state senator and majority leader in godforsaken Montpelier, his mother a social worker who counseled teenage mothers. "My mother would gladly be mother to the planet," he said. "Last year she started a group called Mother The Mothers! The name's printed in fuchsia, with a big fat red exclamation point, the bottom of which is a heart. I have bumper stickers with the toll-free number I'm supposed to be distributing to friends." He smiled sheepishly.

Mal had an older sister who had married, produced the requisite grandchildren, and settled less than two hours from Mom and Dad— which left Mal with no patience for the younger brother, who still refused to come out (his excuse, that one gay son was "heartbreak enough").

"I can't tell you how many faux fiancées I've made nice with over turkey and stuffing. I hope you've never inflicted that indignity on your clan."

I laughed. "No, not that one." Then we parted, so that he could write his review. At home alone, thinking about what he'd revealed, I remembered that there was not a single photograph displayed in his flat, family or otherwise. I thought about the box of Armand in the bathroom and wondered whether Mal simply felt that photographs of any kind would vulgarize the beauty of his surroundings. This was, certainly, the first time I'd heard him acknowledge blood ties at all (except for the remark he'd made about leaving Felicity to his mother the day I'd agreed to take her).

Late that spring, I began to see Mal as ill, not just frail and tired. He came for dinner as often as ever, but sometimes he would not touch the food he cooked; he might not even serve himself a plate. If he wore a short-sleeved or open-necked shirt, I could see from the bones at his wrist and beneath his throat that he was becoming gaunt.

One night in July, he did not show up. (That he was in the city at all that month was a sign of illness as much as anything else. It had been his habit, I knew, to go to Europe for the midsummer festivals and then, in August, to pack up Felicity and lease a house on Fire Island.) As Mal was always punctual, I phoned him after half an hour had passed. I got his machine—even though, standing in my living room holding the phone, I could see that his lights were on.

It took me ten minutes to get up the courage to cross the street. I rang the bell and waited. Eventually, he buzzed me up. As on the night I took him my tuxedo, I found his door ajar. He called to me, and I followed wet footprints back to the bathroom.

Mal was crouched in a steaming bath. Never having seen him naked, I was shocked to see how thin he really was. To call him gaunt was tactful. But in that moment I noticed, too, that his torso was perfectly smooth in a way that had once been beautiful, his nipples strikingly dark, large and smooth as antique coins.

He was smiling. "You see me in the tatters of my God-given splendor."

"Can I do anything?" I said, unable to hide my terror.

He asked me, evenly though he was shivering, to bring the phone from his bedroom. When I brought it, he asked me to punch in the number of one of his doctors, a number he knew by heart. I handed him the phone and left to give him privacy (this conversation I had no desire to overhear). In a few minutes he called me back and handed me the phone.

"She'll call back," he said calmly. Then he winced and leaned forward, hugging his knees. A dark plume spread through the water behind him; the florid odor of diarrhea filled the room.

"Oh Jesus," he said. "Will you please close the door behind you and answer the phone if it rings?"

I sat on the green velvet chaise in Mal's living room and pretended to look at a large, flamboyant book on the architect Gaudi. His buildings looked to me, at that moment, as buffoonish as cartoons. Listening to water draining, water running, to muffled scrubbings and rinsings, I began to shiver, too.

What should I ask? What could I offer? Wasn't this exactly the sort of nightmare I had made myself a snail to avoid living, to avoid even seeing? As if to mock me, there in full view sat Mal's collection of conch shells, displayed on a table by a window to reflect the daylight in their fleshy veneer.

Mal appeared quietly and suddenly. He wore a thick white robe and had combed his wet hair. He sat on a sofa that faced mine from the opposite side of the room. He just looked at me, as if looking would be the best way to know what I was thinking.

"She hasn't called. Your doctor."

Mal pulled his feet up, enfolding his shins in the robe. "This is the last place you'd like to be, isn't it." His voice seemed drained of its habitual irony, as if that, too, had been expelled by his body into the bath and rinsed down into the sewers beneath us.

"I'm awfully cold," he added. "Would you throw me that throw, the one you're leaning against?"

I blurted out, "Shouldn't you have one of those helpers from the GMHC? Those . . . buddies?" The word itself must have sounded as ridiculous to Mal as it did to me, because he laughed.

"Oh, you mean a human golden retriever? Someone who'll come when I call, fetch my meds, and never soil my rug with indifference or fear?"

"Well shouldn't you . . ." I paused, trapped.

"Shouldn't I . . . ?" he echoed.

"Shouldn't you have someone, someone to . . ."

"Someone to watch over me?" Mal hummed Gershwin's notes.

"Doesn't your family . . ." Everything I said trailed off, because all of it was disingenuous. None of these questions was the one I ought to be asking.

Mal leaned toward me and said, "Do you mean: proposition one, I tuck tail and head to Vermont, to die beneath my childhood blankie, or proposition two, some member of my family drops his or her entire life and comes down here to mop my brow till it's cold enough to be embalmed?" Abruptly, Mal launched into a raging litany of his personal medical statistics: T-cells, white blood cells, liver this, kidney that. "I am living my life! I am far from dead!" he concluded, and the color his rage had brought to his face supported him.

On the table between us, the phone rang. Mal seized it. "Susan, hello, yes me. You are too dependable," he sighed, almost amorously. He carried the phone back into his bedroom and closed the door. I sat, paralyzed, Gaudi crushing my thighs.

Every beloved object in that room, from the Tibetan thangka to the Guatemalan birthing chair, pointed a finger at me. Selfish, selfish, selfish. Yellow, yellow, yellow. Blind, blind, blind. Each had a different, equally justifiable accusation.

The problem was, something had reentered my life—or, in truth, had entered my life for the very first time, though I refused to see how unfamiliar it was. It was sexual longing, both fulfilled and unfulfillable, the kind of sustained tensile lust which accelerates until it will not be contained or diverted. Let loose to have its way, it can build a palace or sink an aircraft carrier.

Back in May, every morning for most of a week, I had gone through the sham of acting as photographic lackey to Tony Best, the odd midwestern man in the odd carbuncular house. He was businesslike and ironic about our arrangement. He was shooting reflected self-portraits in antique porcelain, in wrinkled windowpanes, in large iridescent bubbles blown with a child's plastic ring (I did the blowing). Not until the fourth day, when it was drizzling, did he invite me into the house.

I was surprised to see how literally Victorian the furnishings were. They seemed to have nothing to do with this coyly relaxed character. In the tiny kitchen, lace curtains hung at the crooked window and a collection of matronly teacups lined a shelf above the sink. I wedged myself into a chair at a dainty table while Tony toasted bagels in the oven and reheated a pot of coffee, which I was still pretending to like.

"So tell me *your* story," he said, as if I knew so much as a chapter of his.

Because I had spoken so little in the few mornings we'd spent together, I began by half-stammering my affiliation with the shop.

Tony, smiling with those flashy American teeth, interrupted me. "Still think I'm a psycho, don't you, waiting for just the right moment to fit you, piecemeal, into a freezer."

I laughed feebly. "Well, do you always pick up strangers this way?" I blushed, because so far he had given no indication that there was anything sexual in his intentions. I did not want him to know that I wished desperately there were.

"I meet different people in different ways, don't you?" As he wedged himself in at the table, his knees touched mine and then pulled back.

"Not in this way," I said.

"Well you just have. Haven't you?"

From the next room, an old clock with a pendulum creaked. I wanted to flee, but my fear was only of this man's teasing intensity.

"I've been walking this route most mornings for more than a year," I said, "and I've never seen you before."

Tony shrugged and smiled. "Here I am now."

"Here you are now," I echoed stupidly.

He asked abruptly, "Do you want a tour?"

He showed me only the ground floor: four miniature rooms crammed with dark, silk-upholstered furniture. Worn Persian rugs overlapped on every floor save the speckled lino of the kitchen. No two lintels hung at the same angle. He walked me through almost without a word, as if he'd been hired for the job.

In the living room, as I inspected a painted pastoral scene on the face of the old clock, I felt his body enfold me from behind. He said nothing as his long chilly hands slipped under my shirt and across my chest. "Oh God," I heard myself whisper. In reply, I felt his mouth on the back of my neck. He had unbuttoned my shirt and pulled it down to my elbows, briefly pinning my arms, pausing to keep me passive, before he pulled the shirt away from my body and turned me around.

He did not look me in the eye, not once. He slid to his knees after swiftly releasing my belt. Protest after protest filled my head but made it nowhere near my lips, which were parted and gasping. I must have sounded and looked like a sea creature yanked from the water, and I was exactly that: snatched from my monastic element as rudely as a trout fooled by a fly. "Oh God," I heard myself utter inanely again and again, like some over-the-hill virgin, but Tony was stealth made flesh. In the end, I was the only one entirely naked, slouched horizontal at the foot of the clock, its antique groans palpable all along my spine. But for the fact that my cheek lay against a Persian carpet, not piss-rinsed macadam, this was a position as far from upright as I could have dreamed of achieving.

I lay there, stunned and immobile, as Tony slipped into the kitchen.

I could hear him at the cooker, the thump and whoosh of a burner ignited. By the time I had pulled myself up and reassembled my clothes, he came back in and sat on the couch. "I'll bet you really prefer tea," he said through a one-sided smile.

"I do," I said, grateful for an easy question. I looked with panic at the clock that had witnessed my undoing. I was relieved and dismayed to see that only an hour had passed since I had entered the house. I did not need to open the shop for another two.

We had tea, both of us. Tony told me about an upcoming show he had at a gallery on Avenue A. His relaxation was infectious, and I took up where I had been interrupted in the kitchen, telling him about the shop. When I left, we made no plans. Halfway back to Bank Street, letting the timid rain soak me by inches, I recalled, and thought it strange, that not a single picture of Tony's—not one photograph of any kind—hung on the walls of his house.

I vowed not to return the next morning, and I kept this promise, cleaving to the river instead and walking the edge of the island all the way through Battery Park. But the morning after, I was back at Charles and Greenwich; by the end of the summer, I was meeting Tony three or four times a week and, rain or shine, going through the same animal rites over and over, predictable as marital intimacy (though who am I to compare?). I did not try to take our meetings to another setting, nor did he. I probably believed that they were safely contained by that arcane parlor, dark and crimson as a beating heart. Nothing which happened in there should count as real. The rest of my days and weeks progressed as usual, though I would sometimes fall asleep an hour or two earlier than I had. No one remarked on any difference in me—no one but Felicity. When I returned from my liaisons, she flew at me more eagerly than usual, even roughly, as if to repossess me. An animal behaviorist would probably say that this possessiveness was just the instinctive response of her biological clock, so much more keenly tuned in animals, to my longer-than-normal absence on these mornings. But when she beaked my ear and murmured her odd little "Didn't I say so, sweet?" the question, now a warning, seemed more than coincidental.

EIGHT

WHEN I AWAKE for the second time today, it is still light. My head throbs and my consciousness is as sodden as the pillow on which I've drunkenly drooled after (apparently) passing out on my bed. One of the flower arrangements from lunch sits on the bedside table: white peonies, the metaphorical antonym of my psyche at this moment. I do not remember coming upstairs after the guests' departure and am seized by the mortifying thought that my brothers may have lugged me up here like a sack of horse feed.

But then I see the envelope on the floor, next to a glass of water.

The help did most of the tidying up; my one task, the reverse of my morning assignment, was to dismantle the bar. As I ferried bottles back into the house, I thought of little other than the envelope in the desk upstairs, the envelope addressed to me. With the panicky obsession conferred by booze, I could not imagine postponing that investigation. The last tumbler replaced on its shelf, I dashed straight up the front stairs. I could hear my family gathering in the kitchen, to rest their feet and gossip about the afternoon.

My watch tells me it's half seven. I sit up and listen. Outside, the burn trickles carelessly along; inside, nothing.

I reach down and lift the envelope. It remains sealed. (So I did pass out.) Because my drunken impatience has now been eclipsed by sober hesitation, I lay the envelope on the bed and decide to leave my lair. After literally pissing away the day's anxieties, I stand in the hall and listen again. This time I hear music, just barely, from the kitchen. I return to the loo and rinse my face, comb my hair.

But the kitchen is deserted. On the table, my mother's serving dishes lie cleaned and draining on tea towels, face down as if in penance. Dennis's boom box sits beside the sink, tuned to a classical station. This mystifies me until I see that David's old collie, Cal, has had his bed restored to a corner of the scullery. He does not stir when I enter, and I wonder if he's going deaf. Seeing him reminds me that I have not called Ralph to check on my own animals. They will be fine (Rodgie, nostalgic for his virility, avidly courting Mavis), but I feel negligent nonetheless.

The music pauses, and I am acknowledged with a reminder that this is "Aria Afternoon" (never mind that it's evening) and that listeners like myself shouldn't be shy about calling in requests. Maria Callas, I am told, will now sing Violetta in Act Three of *Traviata*.

I say, "Not in this house she won't," and change the station. My voice does wake Cal. He looks up at me, briefly concerned, then lays his chin back on his paws. Oh, just you.

As I fine-tune a station playing soft pop (for Cal, not me), I see a note under the boom box. *Sleeping Beauty: We've gone to that pub across from the petrol pumps. Join us if you're roused from the spell.* (". . . if you're kissed by a prince," he was probably itching to write; the cretinous medical scrawl is David's.)

Relieved and disgruntled, I step out the back door. The sun is still surprisingly high; birds are still busy in nearby branches. The tables and chairs have been carted away, and the only sign of the luncheon is the hectically trampled grass, like the footprint of a Hollywood spaceship. This time tomorrow, that too will have vanished.

In the refrigerator, I find a pot of leftover vichysoisse. Reaching for the nearest receptacle, I use a teacup as a ladle and gluttonously drink it down. The aftertaste is pleasingly earthen. I rinse the teacup under the tap and fill it with water again and again, drinking until my belly feels taut. Pointedly, I leave the cup in the sink without washing it and then, as if I've been given another task, return to my room.

I shake the contents of the envelope onto my bed. There isn't much (again, I feel both relieved and disgruntled). A schoolchild's composition book, used but untitled. A birth certificate (mine). A letter typed on two sheets of that gauzy blue paper used for air letters. A pencil drawing. A lipstick.

I pick up the lipstick. I pull off the top. Though the simple mechanism resists at first, I deploy its delicate missile—a festive red, unused— until it stands fully erect. It smells old, like cheap stage makeup, and when I touch it, a small fragment flakes off the shaft onto my trousers. I twist the lipstick closed and feel my pulse quicken, as if I've defaced an heirloom.

The lipstick is French, embossed with the emblem of a perfume house whose prices my mother would never have paid. So then . . . my father had a mistress? This is the only other explanation I can find for such a souvenir. But why save it for me?

The composition book, filled with Mum's round girlish handwriting, *is* hers. Now I remember: her kennel book. Here, she kept careful track of her dogs' lineage, of stud fees paid, of performance at trials, of heat cycles for her bitches. One of the last entries is Rodgie, my dog; out of Cora, by Buck (a national champion), he was the most promising pup from her next-to-last litter. *Avid temperament, unusually eager to please. C's keen white nose, B's square hindquarters (built for speed!) Testicles late to descend, but Dr. B says sterility unlikely.* Rodgie, my thoroughly citified collie, has of course been (in petspeak) "neutered"; I can hear my mother scolding me: a line of champion herding dogs nipped in the bud!

I close the book and hold it to my chest, glad to have it.

This leaves the drawing and the letter.

The drawing shows a tree with intricate branches. When I turn it over to look for an inscription or signature, I find instead a watercolor sketch of a mother and child (the mother's face a little smudged). The artist's line is practiced and fluid: beyond the work of a student but short of masterly. I lay it on the bed next to the lipstick. Two artifacts of enigma.

The letter is dated 4 July 1989.

Dear Fenno,

I may or may not send you this letter. If I do, it will betray a certain weakness. If I do not, blame it on another. I have a goodly share.

I am back from Greece, still painfully sunburnt, molting like a snake, and in my cups. (The pain is my excuse.) This house has been empty before, but never so thoroughly as it is tonight. Your mother's absence has many meanings. I confess that it is now not entirely unwelcome.

Today, I have realized upon dating this letter, is your newly embraced Independence Day. Independent you certainly are. In that and other respects, I thought of you often while I was away. I thought of your perfectly reasonable impertinence last winter (though quite unlike you), and I thought childishly of ways to give you a taste of the responsibilities you assume I should continue to shoulder. I thought of how I ought to visit you

*over there but of how I might prefer not to see your life up close. My
particular cowardice: yet another weakness. Still, I should like to see
your shop. I am half envious, you know. And admiring. I must not
leave that out.*

*The last six months have been filled with irrational acts, beginning
with a petty theft, ending with a petty betrayal. (I am constantly told
that erratic or inexplicable behavior is "normal" in the wake of a "loss.")
At the Lockerbie air crash site, I stole a small object: a lipstick. Can I say
that it is "insignificant"? (Might it not carry the trace of a signature
explosive brew?) In the months since, I have fetishized this object, carrying
it with me in a pocket or standing it up on my dressing table, like a work
of art. Perhaps it gives me a pathetically dim taste of criminal thrill.
Perhaps it speaks to me of death, personally, as your mother's death
should have but could not.*

*Another fixation I have developed is an appetite for the same unvarying
dinner at the same unvarying pub, one I had never been to but discovered in
Lochmaben on a return trip from a funeral. (I go to so many these days.) I
drive there three or four nights a week and order the trout and peas. Plain,
but cooked well. I like knowing no one, though the barman has become too
familiar and tries to chat me up. I dread what he will expect by way of
conversation upon seeing my sunburnt self after a three-week hiatus. I
am not in a mood to be teased.*

*Greece was like the most irresistible of women: a beauty and a trial.
The tour itself was a mistake. That was a large part of the trial. I
befriended a young man your age, or so I believed, yet when I returned
here, I used my connections to terminate his employment. I dislike how
satisfying this unkind deed continues to feel.*

*I am selling the paper. I will be parceling out some of my profits to the
three of you in the coming year, for obvious tax benefits. You will hear
more from me on this matter (when I am sober).*

*Thank you for taking Rodgie. I hope he is faring as well as can be
reasonably expected with such a change of setting. The dogs that remain—
Gem, Jasper, Bat—I am sending to the farm at Conkers, for good, though
I have heard the farm may soon be split up and sold. The businessman who
bought Conkers has no agricultural bent. He liked the idea of a tenant farm
but, in practice, cannot abide the stench of manure that wafts his way each
evening to taint the rapture of sunset. (This is all extrapolation from rumors*

exchanged at the petrol pumps.) Nevertheless, the foreman assures me that the dogs will have a good place regardless of land dealings. He would take them to an excellent farm up near Kilmarnock. This way, they will be worked. They need to be worked. (You may have trouble from Rodgie on this front, but perhaps he is young enough to adapt to indolence—not yours but that of the city dog!)

Before you call me a traitor, let me say that the dogs would be neglected as I undertake a new project in my latter life. I have always wanted to know one thing well (as your mother did, and here by the way is the closest thing she kept to a journal, which I believe you might treasure more than your brothers would). As a journalist, I have studied many things, but not one of them well and with the circumspection of prolonged study. So I have decided to know one place, a new place. Next month I plan to return to Greece, to Naxos, an island I have seen but on which I have not set foot. From what I have read, I believe it will suit me. I will look for a house, something simple. You may conclude I have gone slightly daft. I could hardly prove you wrong!

Please be in touch with your brothers. As a favor to me if necessary, please compensate for the geographical distance you have chosen by, at the very least, wholeheartedly observing the right occasions. (Am I sounding too much the "Brit" you have called me out for in the past?) On the subject of occasions, have you received word from Dennis about his wedding? A French bride! I shall have to bury my prejudice from the war, and I am too old-fashioned not to be unsettled that I have yet to meet the girl, but about Dennis I have always had the feeling that some cosmic force protects him from all the foolish and illogical things he's chosen to do. So if the girl is dross, then gold she will become. But that sounds cruel. What I mean to say is

There the letter ends, as if he wrote himself over a cliff.

What prevented Dad from finishing the letter and sending it? I can see nothing earthshaking about his confessions, yet they would have touched me. Or would they, back then? I try to remember where, as they say, my head was at that summer, and I do recall that I was still cross at my father for little more than acting like himself—always composed, rarely tearful, impersonally giving—through the dark hole of time surrounding Mum's death.

I put the letter down, alongside the rest of my booty, and I push my face into the peonies beside my bed. They are still regal and fresh, but to my hungover nose, they smell faintly like mold. When I recoil, my thoughts veer elsewhere: Why hadn't David given me this package? Had he pawed through it himself and been jealous? I imagine confronting him—until I realize that I am just as much the offender here, having poached the package from his desk. More likely, he hasn't gone through the drawers containing Dad's things. It's been, remarkably, less than a week since there would be reason to do so.

I replace my bequests in their envelope. Twilight has drifted, sneaky as a tide, over my view of the meadow. I reach for the lamp chain but stop short. I am tired, and if I make myself fully awake, I will work up a miserly sulk.

In my boyhood bed, I sleep the sleep of the overindulged, waking twice but briefly: once, to Véronique's melodiously autocratic voice— "*Regardez l'heure, enfants, au lit!*"—and then to David and Lil's murmurings beyond our common wall. Their voices are soft, their words a blur, yet I have the fleeting impression that it is far too late at night for a married couple to be discussing anything but matters dismal or thorny.

TONY GREW UP IN MILWAUKEE. His mother still lives there. She is blind and always has been. His father died a few years ago.

Tony was sent to a military academy at age sixteen after burning down his parents' garage on purpose.

The summer his peers were in Woodstock and Berkeley, he drove a combine for a Mormon farmer in Missouri. He slept in the hayloft, where the strong smell of silage masked the fumes from the quantities of dope with which he smoked away most of his wages.

He started taking pictures after working, the following summer, in a commercial darkroom in Seattle and despising everything that passed through his hands.

He never finished college. He lived in France for a few years but never really learned the language. (He is too vain, it's clear, to run the requisite risk of making an ass of himself.)

These were the raw, disjointed facts I gleaned about Tony's life that long, exhausting, duplicitous summer. Why do I say duplicitous? I was never, after all, deceiving anyone . . . except, as it turned out, myself. At some level I must have known this, because I felt heavy with secrets whose secrecy had no rational justification.

It was, as I said before, not a good summer for Mal. If I happened to spend a morning with Tony and then the same evening with Mal, I would sleep ten or more hours that night, dragging myself out of bed only minutes before I was due to open the shop. I would sleep through Felicity's celebration of dawn and her greetings to the birds in the trees out front. She would scold me as I slammed my way through a break-neck version of my routine (tongue-scalding tea, untoasted bread, a one-handed mirrorless shave while filling Felicity's cups with seeds and fruit).

Two or three times a week, I would go over to Mal's. Felicity was banned from his apartment, so it was clear that our friendship had taken on another dimension: not socializing, but a tentative form of caretaking. It was as if my assuming Felicity's care had been a dry run for my taking on, more gradually, Mal's. To speak of this explicitly would have been too awkward for either of us, but one task at a time—carting out laundry, shopping, making photocopies, renting the occa-sional film—I quietly assumed the more banal aspects of his upkeep. To see Felicity, he still came by the shop, but dinner at my flat was rare now; Mal's two flights of stairs were labor enough without mine.

One day in July, I was unpacking a shipment of books after-hours when Ralph came into the shop. In the last week, I had refused two dinner invitations, and I knew he felt slighted. But that day, without so much as a greeting, he said, "So, are you fucking him?"

Wondering what spy could have reported on my mornings with Tony, I felt my face redden and kept it aimed down at a carton of guides to the birds of North America.

"Are you fucking our little critic? Is this why your glands are so patently aglow?" he said. "I ask because your welfare concerns me." This he said more gently, like the ideal father I no longer wanted him to be.

I straightened up and looked at him coldly. "What if I were in love with him?"

Ralph's face flinched in surprise. "You're in love with the man?"

I laughed. "If I were in love with anyone, you would be the first to know." A lie, but one I believed harmless. "No, I am not fucking Malachy Burns, if that's who you mean. And I've never thought of him as 'little.' "

"I didn't mean to pry."

"Yes you did." I was smiling, my secret still a secret.

"I never see you except in here," said Ralph. "You seem to spend more time with that bird than anyone else."

"I have a life outside your charming house. Barely, but I do."

He apologized, but as he paced, fussing with books, he seemed sullen. "Are you still happy with our arrangement?" he asked when he was hidden by a barricade of shelving.

"Of course." I took out a rag and glass cleaner to wash the day's fingerprints from the vitrine of birdwatching gadgets.

"I mean, you don't feel it's altered our friendship."

"No." Tools of espionage, I mused as I gazed down at all the devices of magnification we offered for sale.

Mavis and Druid brushed the backs of my legs as they pushed past me toward the garden.

"Well that's good. Business shouldn't become a wedge between comrades," said Ralph, still out of sight. I laughed quietly at his frumpy reference to the two of us as *comrades*—as if we had shared a war or an expedition through uncharted jungle. I was accustomed to Ralph's primness (a side effect of daily immersion in nineteenth-century prose), but after a morning of Tony's cryptically blunt passions, it began to seem positively doilyesque, much like Ralph's taste in decor.

A certain primness, too, had crept into my relations with Mal. The more intimate I became with his precarious physical state, the more distance he put between me and the rest of his life. And like a number of men I'd known who'd fallen ill, he had taken up a new, monastic diet—for which I often shopped. Twice weekly, I would emerge from the Integral Yoga market with string grocery bags (a gift from Mal's ecofriendly mother) ballooning with kale, collards, locally pressed tofu, daikon root, and rolls of dried seaweed.

Mal embraced his new cuisine with sardonic ardor. He'd hold out a fistful of freshly rinsed broccoli sprouts and say, "Crème brûlée, anyone?" We'd share the laugh, and I'd stick around for a meal that smelled alarmingly barnlike during the cooking. I tried not to remember how the very same diet had done nothing to revitalize Frederick or Luke—though they were farther gone than Mal (I could not suppress the thought of "goneness" as if it were a process already under way).

But when I tried to get Mal to tell me more about his family or his childhood or his years as a musical prodigy, he would change the subject. He would talk more than he ever had about performances he was reviewing, foreign events he hoped his body would cooperate in letting him cover. One night he railed on and on about a *Sleeping Beauty* he had thought "beyond tacky" in its production values. At the end of his verbal scourge, we were silent.

Mal said, "Nureyev may be dying."

I said, "Do you know him?"

"No," he snapped, "I'm not dropping names. It's just that I don't take such news with equanimity."

Mal sat on his beautiful green chaise longue, stroking the velvet like the pelt of a cat. The windows were open, and the air was infused with the humid perfume of flowering Callery pear trees. "You think about my dying, and you hate yourself for being so morbid," he said. Knowing him as I did now, I could see that from the first mention of *Sleeping Beauty,* he'd been steering our conversation toward this, and I hated him for the manipulation. When I refused to reply, he did it for me.

"This is where you protest, because it's only polite, and then after I tell you it's all right to confess your worst fantasies—you've been too kind and generous for me to refuse you that, and it would be true— you ask me if I've made any plans, if I have a will, if I want my family with me—"

"Or, if I'm cruel, I tell you that everyone dies alone, no matter how many people there are in the room."

Mal's watch beeped. As he walked to the kitchen to take a pill, he said, "My family will have all sorts of plans about what to do with me after I'm dead, but I care more about my dying than my deadness. With that, I don't want them to interfere."

"Interfere?" Sucked in after all, my resistance in shambles.

"Like any good fag, I adore and idolize my mother," Mal said when he sat down again. "But she is the most perilous kind of liberal: a devout Catholic liberal. Saints' bones are sacred, embryos are sacred, death throes that last an eon are sacred. My father must adore her, too, because her activism—though never the least bit angry!—has kept him from national office. I'm sure of it. And me"—he laughed—"me she did a job on, too, in her own way. And I won't let her do another."

His speech confused me, and I blurted out, "I didn't think you were dying quite . . ." I stopped myself.

"Quite yet." Mal laughed again, and this time it made him cough. When he had recovered, he said, "I'm doing this on the advice of my theoretically optimistic favorite doctor, who said that everyone would be wise to make these plans. She's promised me new drugs this fall— back-to-school special—and says I'll be right as rain again. For however long."

"But what plans—"

"Oh Fenno, your education has left your brain too full to be smart. I am asking you to be the—I think it's called, ironically, 'health' proxy— on my living—ironies everywhere—my living will. The job is, basi-cally, to keep me from getting stuck full of tubes." He walked to a window. "You needn't answer now. In fact, please don't. I've chosen you not because you're my oldest or most trusted friend, don't get me wrong, but because you're *around* more than anyone else I know."

"Too dull to be invited anywhere, is that what you mean? How flat-tering."

He sighed. "And I find you dependable, and I like you, and you have a cold enough eye not to go all rubbery if and when you have to pull the plug." He laughed again, and coughed again. He leaned out the win-dow until the coughing had passed. When he turned back to me, he said, "I wish the pear trees would bloom all summer long."

A month later, I found out that my mother had been diagnosed with cancer. While I went to see her, Ralph would take over the shop; the boy in Mal's building would take Felicity. Mal was scheduled to go to London about the same time, to write a profile of Jessye Norman at home. On an inexplicable whim, I asked if he wanted to fly to Scotland with me, spend a few days, head south from there.

What was I doing? Was I somehow frightened of being alone with my parents under such ominous circumstances, or had I begun to feel protective of Mal? His fragility did appear to wax and wane from one day to the next, and by now I had accepted his request and signed a document which would allow me to insist that doctors stand aside and let him die if matters became too dire. Solemnly, Mal sealed my own copy of the document in a clean envelope and handed it to me. "I suppose you should meet my mother," he said. "Because if the worst ever happens, she's the one you'll have to overrule. Legalities be damned."

Now, having sprung my impulsive invitation, I saw Mal, for the first time ever, express surprise. He gasped slightly and set his glass of water down by the sink. "I have never had the desire," he said carefully, "to visit a country that has such a brutal past."

"What country doesn't?" I said lightly. I was relieved he'd be turning me down.

"'O cold is the snow that sweeps Glencoe—'" he began to recite. A ballad I hadn't heard since I was a child.

"Yes, yes, where the Campbells slew the McDonalds. Old news."

"But really. Invite yourself over to make up and kiss, then kill the women and children in their sleep? Over the top, wouldn't you say?"

I laughed. "Well enjoy yourself in pacifist Maggie Thatcher Land."

"But I accept," said Mal. "I'm older and more broad-minded now. Thicker-skinned. I'd love to see the blood-soaked moors. I'd love to eat sheep's bladder stuffed with lard. Maybe that'll cure what ails me."

"*LE VOILÀ!*" Véronique greets me in the kitchen, clapping her hands together and clasping them at her throat, as if my late appearance has made her day. "I kept the baby wolves from your door; they wished you to bring them to that little farm and make them a tour of the animals." She hands me a cup of tea. Out the window, I see the three girls playing together under the great old lilac bush which seems to have become their headquarters. David and Lil have left for work. Dennis is nowhere in sight.

"I'd be happy to do that," I say.

"Not now. There are other plans now."

With my back to her, I roll my eyes, wondering when I will cease to be so predictably passive. I'd intended to take a train down to London for a few days, just to slouch sentimentally about, but the thought of announcing this departure makes me feel guilty, perhaps because I missed last night's gathering (something Véronique doesn't mention).

As I make myself toast, she tells me that she's promised to deal with the checks left by guests in memory of my father—to drive them to the hospital where my mother's cancer was treated (and, I note sourly, not cured). The hospital is in town; Dennis has told her I know the way.

"Why don't you just post them?" I say. "Or why doesn't Dennis drive?"

"Denis, he wants to take the girls to this famous Annie Laurie's house. That is not an endeavor for me. And the director of the hospital, he is anxious for the funds to begin."

"What, they're desperate? The hospital's broke? What kind of an object for charity is that?"

Véronique looks at me with courteous indulgence. "On the return, we will market for tonight. Denis will roast hens on the fire. It will be beautiful again for dinner out in the air—though Davide and Liliane, they have engaged themselves elsewhere. Old friends of Denis from school, he says you may know them, they will join us."

At the thought of negotiating a Scottish town grocery with a Frenchwoman married to a professional chef, I begin to see my brother's expertise as a prison of sorts, condemning us to spend most of our time shopping and eating, digesting and praising. I would rather play doctor with my nieces.

This is what happens when you get up too late, I admonish myself. Other people make your plans.

"We will leave in half an hour?" Véronique asks brightly, though it's not a question. I nod, and she heads outside to check on her daughters. I reach for the day's papers—the *Times,* the *Guardian,* the *Yeoman,* all still delivered to Paul McLeod. As I settle into my habitual slouch, my foot nudges something on the floor. I look under the table to see the doll I bought for Christine. When I pull it up, I see a dark smudge where its cloth face was stepped on. Its rice paddy hat is coming unglued. Resist identification, I tell myself sternly as I prop the poor thing in a sitting position against a bowl of red roses.

So it is that, four hours later, I find myself receiving olfactory orders from my sister-in-law. "Smell this one. No, actually place your nose within the chamber. Do not be timid. *Comme ça!*"

Only Véronique would have the nerve to place her manicured hand behind someone's neck (mine) and push (however gently) until I am nasally submerged in a large copper-colored iris.

"Do you smell it? For that, these are among my favorites, the bearded ones. But this scent has never been captive in a perfume. Never."

Silently, I have to agree that the scent of this flower is wonderful, a blend of moss and honey.

I have been led by the nose (now literally) to the fortunately tithed hospital, the grocery, the apothecary, and, unexpectedly, to an explosively colorful garden. We are surrounded by towering larkspur, foxgloves, and irises, following a narrow brick path which winds toward a small grove of cherry trees. The garden, on the outskirts of the town, belongs to an old friend of Lillian's who is off on holiday; Lil told Véronique that she must make a detour to see it. Like many gardens of the well-to-do in these parts, it stands separately from the house, across the road. We enter by an iron gate, which is probably never locked.

On our drive, Véronique kept up a stream of chatter that, by its glittering cheerfulness, nearly won me over to liking her. She spoke with loyal enthusiasm of Dennis's plans to expand his restaurant, talked happily about her daughters' nascent talents, and did not forget to ask me about (and appear genuinely interested in) the bookshop. She even asked me to recommend a few novels—"light, if you please!"—to help her perfect her English.

Still, I feel uncomfortable being alone with her and long to be back at Tealing. When she announced this last stop, I tried to refuse. *"Dis donc,"* she scolded, "there is always time for beauty, would you not say?" Yes, I conceded, I would have to say.

Under the cherry trees, Véronique stands with her hands on her hips and surveys the sea of flowers. This, I realize, is a trait of hers which grates on my nerves: the appraising poise of the tireless critic. She glances at the branches above us, heavy with petaled starbursts. She sighs. "Ah, no apple. No pear. A small pity."

"It's magnificent," I say. "What do you mean?"

"I mean"—she taps me on the arm, as a mentor would—"no fragrance. This garden is, safe those irises, made for the eye."

Here we go, I think. What harangue on inferior gardening will follow?

"This garden, you know, it reminds me of my life before the girls. Oh, a lovely life, a life of pretty colors and passions. And this little wood of *cerisiers* I could say is like my marriage to Denis. But to have children . . . to have children is to plant roses, *muguets,* lavender, lilac, gardenia, stock, peonies, tuberose, hyacinth . . . it is to achieve a whole sense, a grand sense one did not priorly know. It is to give one's garden another dimension. Perfume of life itself."

After noticing her impressive command of flowers in English (many of her Provençal clients will be Brits or Californians), I absorb with a small wry shock that her fatuous metaphor is, to me, an insult. Does she know this? Is she assuring me, or herself, that her life has greater dimension than mine? For all her new courtesies, nothing much has changed. I think of a remark she made a few days after I met her, when she was pregnant with Laurie and I asked whether Dennis would want to name a daughter after our mother. "Maureen?" she said. "Is this not, in your culture, generally the name of a servant? And it would not ring so well in French, I believe." Here she pronounced my mother's name in exaggerated French, so that its rolled *r* sounded contemptibly rough, its Celtic ending snippishly nasal.

I am reviving my anger at this bygone offense when Véronique says, "I am sad for Liliane, because she knows this without knowing it. She would prefer that richer garden to this."

I say nothing. Despite her apparent kinship with Lil, I have no desire to gossip about Lil's heartaches.

I look openly at my watch. It's half three and I thirst for my tea. Véronique sees my look. A breeze ruffles the branches and casts a handful of petals onto our shoulders. Hardly the bride and groom.

Véronique sighs a capaciously French sigh and touches my arm again. This time she does not remove her hand. She looks me fiercely in the eye. "I am coming to you as an ambassador."

"Ambassador?" I repeat blankly. *Representing what military junta?* I think, but I smile and say, "I never thought you the diplomatic type."

"I am dreading this all morning," she says, "so please will you not make it more difficult from what it already has been."

The ashes. Of course. Marveling at my brothers' cowardice, I say, "Oh for God's sake take the bleeding ashes back to Greece. I don't know why I ever professed to care about where they get heaved."

Véronique's eyes are wide and glisten slightly. She looks puzzled and frightened, as if she's lost the ability to translate my language into hers.

"Oh not ashes, no. I do not speak of ashes."

"Then what do you speak of?" I snap.

"I speak of Liliane. I speak of Liliane and of her babies."

Her babies. I now need tea with the sweaty desperation of an addict.

There is a stone bench behind us. Véronique sits. "Your brother cannot make babies. Do you know this? I think you do not."

"You think right. I do not know much of anything that goes on in these parts anymore. Certainly nothing that goes on in anyone's private parts."

With a calm that shames me, she says, "I will ignore this anger you must always jettison. I will say what it is I have been asked to say. You will do as you wish." She glares at me until I tell her I'm sorry and ask her to finish.

"These male doctors to whom Liliane has consulted spent a year to discover that it is David who will not make her pregnant." Véronique speaks slowly, as if she must be careful not to err.

I sit beside her. The stone's damp chill is a shock. "Sad."

"*Oui.*"

"Is it absolute? That he can't . . ."

"It is no longer meriting the effort, they are told."

"And you were asked to tell me this news?"

"I was chosen to ask you to consider a favor. The favor of helping Liliane to have a child." She pulls subtly away from my body.

I look out at the flowers before us. They are so tall—so fertile, it occurs to me—that from the street, Véronique and I must be invisible to passersby. Trespassing in the garden of a stranger, I have just been asked by a woman I have never liked (but must begin to admire) if I will impregnate another.

I start to laugh. I hide it at first as a small cough, but then it is unmistakably laughter. Véronique, who, like me, does not take her eyes off the flowers, says, "I knew this would seem absurd. But reflect and perhaps it is not. You will be intelligent enough to understand that if you will agree to this intention, what is necessary will be accomplished in the doctor's laboratory."

"You think right," I say, failing to control my schoolboy's reaction. And then I think of Lil dancing on that stage, all but naked in her leotard, the fleetingly real desire I had for her body.

Véronique is holding out a blank envelope. "This is a letter for you which Liliane has written which you will please guard from reading until you are alone. You will please tell your decision to her." Yet one more envelope containing a mystery I long for and dread. Curiosity as ever the victor, I wouldn't dream of refusing it.

For the hour it takes me to drive back to Tealing, we are silent. Except that Véronique, under her breath, hums Bach for a while, some solemn renowned air which I cannot quite identify, something funereal that I have heard played on the organ. Mal would know it in a flash— and scold me that I didn't. I am sure she does this unconsciously, that it is an escape valve for her enormous relief at having put this task behind her.

In the driveway, I continue to sit behind the wheel. I listen to the motor pinging as it cools. Efficiently, without asking for my help, Véronique ferries a dozen grocery sacks into the kitchen. David's pickup is absent—and then I remember that he and Lil are not to be present this evening and know that it was by design—but there is an unfamiliar car parked on the road out front. At the thought of sitting down to dinner with anyone, let alone strangers (or, even worse, past familiars), I shrivel with dismay.

When Véronique takes the last two shopping sacks from the car, I restart the motor. When she looks at me with surprise, I tell her that I will return by tomorrow evening. She has no ready reply. I do not wait to make her find one.

At the motorway, I must choose to head north or south. I choose north. I do not need the company of the English. I drive toward Oban, toward cruel, beautiful Glencoe, toward a landscape to scour the mind of confusion. Not till I've left Glasgow behind do I realize that, for the first time since my brothers' birth, I am certainly—rivetingly—the center of my family's attention.

NINE

SOMETIMES I BEGAN to see my life as one of those Joseph Cornell boxes about which I'd done so much plodding research. It was, all of a sudden, highly compartmentalized: private home life/ life at the shop/ relations with my straitlaced family across an ocean/ evenings with Mal/ and—like a dusky passionate snowscape down in a corner— mornings with Tony. Because this part of my life (especially this part) touched none of the others, I did not tell him about my mother. He knew very little about my family and did not ask.

I would leave for Scotland in a week, be absent for another two. I planned to tell him on the day of my departure, to minimize questions. Though we had been meeting nearly every day for over two months, I wanted him as desperately as ever, but I did not want his analysis or his astringent jests.

That morning, Tony was not out on his lawn, nor did he answer the bell. This was not unprecedented. On a few other mornings he had been absent, but when I'd show up the following day, he'd be there. I never asked about his absences; he never explained.

I knew Tony wouldn't be the type to take offense, so after idling by the gate awhile, I took a banking slip from my wallet and wrote a note: *Family emergency abroad. Flying out tonight, return in 2 weeks. Will see you then.* Seeing my words to Tony on paper filled me with panic and excitement. They made real what all our sly fleshy tanglings never quite did. After I wedged the note into the doorjamb, I stood and stared at it. I wondered how I would endure the next fortnight. I resolved that, on my return, I would bring Tony—force him, if need be—fully into my life.

Chronic turncoat that I am, I began to have second thoughts about taking Mal to Tealing. ("I might have known you grew up in a house with a name," he said wryly the night I answered his questions about my family. "Explains your aura of entitlement.") When he called a few days before our departure, I hoped his sudden invitation for dinner meant not just that he was well enough to cook but that he'd planned a good meal as consolation to me for his own cold feet.

The woman who answered Mal's door pulled me in with both hands, grasping my upper arms so tightly that I could feel her long nails through my sleeves. "You! You! I am so glad to meet you!" she cried, and her small oval face, pink and refined as a cameo, spread into a tissue of delicate lines, a human blueprint of joy. Simply because of her air—I could sense that she treated this home as hers—I knew she was Mal's mother. And she looked at me (I saw this later) through his eyes—though in her face their blue was not so frosty. She looked much younger than any mother of her generation I had met; her long beaded earrings, long hair (though gray), and long cotton skirt mirrored with mica all reminded me of Cambridge twenty years before, of girls like Lil.

Mal emerged from his bedroom looking oddly theatrical. Over his trousers he wore an ivory linen tunic so large it was almost clownish. "Well good, that spared me introductions," he said. His mother still held my arms, looking me up and down with pleasure.

She leaned toward me to peer directly into my eyes, then turned to Mal and said, "He's got to be a Pisces. I see the fish struggling upstream and down, the valiant conflicts of a good, hardworking submarine conscience." Then she looked back to me. "Water is the most freeing of the elements. Heavier than air, but once you get the hang of it, deeper and more rewarding, full of hidden surprises. You can't hear so well, but the things you can see!"

Mal came toward us and pulled her off me, folding her against his side. "Mom, cut the astrology crap." To me he said, "This is an image she projects, to test you. I've told her it's sadistic, though she always insists it's sincere."

"Well, *now* I love doing it just to mortify you," she said. "How about that?"

She reached out to shake my hand, as if we were starting over. "I'm Lucinda. I already know who you are."

Who did she know I was? Friend? Occasional errand boy? Neighbor?

Mal broke the silence by saying, "Mom, this is beautiful, it really is, but I'm swimming in it. I look like I belong in Sherwood Forest, with leather breeches and a little dagger in my belt." He turned to me. "Birdlike, isn't that what I'd be called in this garment?"

"Oh, sweets, like a peacock," said Lucinda.

"Thank you for reminding me of my vanity, darling mother."

"I refer to your beauty. You have always been the most beautiful of my children, from the day you were born."

Mal had a smile for her I had never seen on his face, the kind of smile you give a beloved child (the return of the smile his mother had for him). He spread his arms and looked down at the shirt I knew she must have made. "You could take it in, couldn't you?"

"It'll fit you when you flesh out again," she said as he allowed her to tuck the shirt into his trousers. Then she gave him a small shove. "There now. Go sit."

So, on Lucinda's orders, we found ourselves seated in the living room, hands in our laps like obedient, well-mannered boys. Mal flicked his eyebrows at me once, his only admission to the acute self-consciousness we all feel, regardless of age or station in life, when anyone meets our parents. Before I could say anything, Lucinda was back, carrying stemmed drinks. Margaritas, the glasses chilled, the rims unsalted just as I like.

"Sweetheart, yours is lime juice with a splash of Grand Marnier. Would Susan permit that torsion of the rules?"

Mal faked a sigh. "Yes, Mom."

"She wishes she could go with us," he said when she'd left again. "She said she and my father spent a passionate weekend in Edinburgh before we children came along. Kissed on the castle ramparts. Bought Shetland sweaters they still wear, darned-up moth holes and all. Dad golfed at St. Andrews."

So we were going. I could not picture us on a plane together, belted in side by side, let alone eating at my parents' table or discussing current events (traditional silence fodder) with my brothers.

"I wouldn't mind going to one of those islands," he said. "The Shetlands and the Orkneys are too far north, of course."

"There's Arran. Arran's not a bad drive." This proposal echoed in my head with an embarrassing intimacy, but Mal simply nodded and said that sounded fine. Or he could drive himself; he didn't wish to interfere with the family business I'd have.

As I talked about what one could see thereabouts (local sights I'd grown up seeing dozens of times, dragged along by my parents with endless sets of guests), I thought Mal dismayingly agreeable. Was he resigning himself to something, winding down? Or was he on a new drug (he hadn't coughed once since my arrival), another powerful substance which, in altering the chemistry of his immune system, had arbitrarily softened his edge?

When Lucinda joined us with her own margarita, she sat close beside me on the couch. "To your trip," she toasted, touching my glass first.

"To a safe trip," I said. "I've never loved flying."

"That's what I meant about air. You can never quite trust it, can you?" Before I could answer, she said, "You know, you have a lovely brogue. Very subtle."

"It's called a burr, Mom, and if it's subtle, maybe that's because he's been trying like the devil to lose it," said Mal. "Don't make him more self-conscious than he already is."

"A funny word, burr. A burr is a thorny little ball. And isn't it a wood-cutting tool?" she asked me.

"Yes," I said, wishing I had something witty to add.

"Well, boys, the menu," she said, placing her glass on the table. "I am giving Mal a holiday from his brave new diet. I see no harm in a break for one night. So we are having soupe au pistou—and that, let me tell you, is a cure in itself—and sole bonne femme and haricots verts and baba au rhum. Straight, unadulterated Julia."

"Julia?" I inquired.

"Child! *La* Julia," she said. When she added, "My second all-time heroine," Mal chimed in perfectly.

"So go ahead, ask her who's number one," he said.

"Margaret Sanger, no surprise," said Lucinda.

"One the mistress of control, the other a mistress of indulgence," said Mal. "And number three is, let's see, a tie between Ginger Rogers and Cyd Charisse. The tragedy of my mother's life is that Dad has the rhythm of a brick." Again, Mal and Lucinda wore identical, colluding grins. They had the same slender lips, the same uniformly delicate, well-spaced teeth. Standing, she walked over and kissed him on the forehead.

"When I need a sidekick, I'll let you know." She stroked his hair. "Now I'll go be that *bonne femme* and pull things together."

"Set the table in the kitchen," said Mal. "No need to get fussy."

"But I love getting fussy. And I'll be the one washing up."

A few minutes later, as Mal began telling me about a less than stellar review he'd had to write about a pianist he normally revered, Lucinda called from the kitchen, "Where are my dishes? Did you go and pawn them?"

"For drugs. But tremendously fun drugs, I promise!" he called back. He was looking out a window when he added, "I've lent them to a friend who's giving a fancy lunch!"

"The entire set? Platters and all?"

"Platters and all, Mom!" His raised voice made the room around us feel small. He looked at me. "What do you call your mother—'Mum'?"

"Yes. Mum."

"It sounds so different, don't you think? That *o* in Mom evokes so much more longing, so much more Oedipal dependency this side of the ocean. Or do I overanalyze?"

"You're a critic, you can't help it," I said.

Lucinda's meal was old-fashioned—I'd forgotten how rich food could be—but it was, as she promised, splendid. She did most of the talking, as I could see she was accustomed to doing. She told Mal about his father's latest battles over education, tourism, land conservation and development. She asked me about my mother, then told me about a cousin of hers who'd had most of a lung removed ten years ago and still skied the black diamond trails. She quizzed us both about the city's local politics. ("The more local the issues, the more real the fights": clearly a personal motto—no doubt one of many.)

Mal drank a few sips of wine and ate most of his food. When Lucinda was talking and I looked at him, I saw him smiling at her in a distant way, as if at a pleasant memory. Sometimes I wasn't sure he was listening. But after we'd finished dessert, after Lucinda had served us tea (green for Mal, Earl Grey for me, chamomile for herself), he said, "All right, Mother. Bring out your pictures. I know you've been dying to show off all evening."

Happily, as if she had indeed been waiting, she reached out and pulled a Kodak envelope off the counter behind her. "My girls," she said to me, pressing the envelope against her chest before pulling out snapshots.

"This is where she hits you up for money, so beware," said Mal.

Lucinda laid a dozen pictures on the tablecloth, dealing them out like cards. Her long nails were unpainted, and her traditional diamond ring was outnumbered by younger, more rustic rings: silver, jade, and turquoise. Around her neck, on a black silk cord, swung a bluntly fashioned pewter cross whose descender bisected a peace sign. If I had seen that symbol in recent years, I hadn't noticed it; now I recalled the cheap vandalism of my teens, when I and my schoolmates, without the slightest knowledge of anything *but* peace, had impudently scrawled and carved that mark everywhere from our desks to the frosted windscreens of our masters' cars.

"Connie and Debra," said Lucinda, turning a picture in my direction. "They're both due at the end of this month—and can't wait to deliver, let me tell you. To a pregnant woman, *August* is the cruelest month. But they've both been training with a local baker and haven't missed a day. I'm very proud of them. Debra, I'm told, has a real knack, and if everything goes well, I may pull some of your father's strings next year to get her a scholarship at a culinary school in Boston."

The pregnant girls I was looking at—holding hands on the steps of a suburban brick house, flanked by squat green yews that echoed the shape of their bellies—were girls indeed. They looked no older than fifteen or sixteen; eighteen, at a stretch. I realized I had so little contact with people this age that they seemed to hail from another species. But thirteen or nineteen, I thought, these girls ought to have been vandalizing desks, not giving birth.

"So they'll soon have tiny squalling brats and fourteen-hour jobs sweating in front of industrial ovens," said Mal.

"They will," said Lucinda haughtily, "have beautiful healthy babies they thank God they've been blessed with, loving help and wisdom from the experienced mothers at the house, and part-time jobs in an air-conditioned bakery that supplies all the fanciest restaurants and ski resorts from Middlebury north. And they will finish high school."

"Well good for them, Mom. And good for you." Mal reached across the table and squeezed her hand. "And you," he said, turning to me, "get out your checkbook. Make it out to 'The House.' That's what they call this utopian female refuge." He tapped a finger on the brick house behind the two girls.

I laughed nervously.

"Not now," said Lucinda, "but don't you worry, you'll be on my mailing list the minute I get back home."

She went on to tell us about several other girls, the ones who, unlike Connie and Debra, would be giving their babies up for adoption. Lucinda spoke of them all as glowingly as she would of her own daughter (whose news she had relayed to Mal—perhaps more efficiently than fondly—over the soup). I had never mixed with social workers or crusaders for the underprivileged; I now had a concrete image of what it meant to have a "mission." Beside Lucinda, I felt boorishly self-involved, but I was fascinated and would have been happy to stay much later than I knew was proper.

When I could see that Mal was fading (his mother seemed not to notice), I made my excuses. Lucinda saw me to the door, where we exchanged compliments. As I turned to go, she held me back. "You never told me if you *are* a Pisces."

"On the cusp," I said, "though I don't give much credence to the stars."

"Give credence to anything God honors with light," she said, almost sharply, and then, "Which cusp?"

"The Aquarian side."

"Oh my. Oh my." She seemed overjoyed, pressing her hands to her cheeks. She hugged me a second time. "Water, water everywhere."

"And not a spot to dive," said Mal, still sitting at the kitchen table. But Lucinda and I ignored him, saying another round of good-byes. This woman, I thought as I walked downstairs, turning to wave when I could feel her gaze still sheltering me, this woman might become my *adversary?* Wasn't that the word Mal had used?

MY LUNATIC MOMENTUM dwindles as I leave the sooty northern reaches of Glasgow. Signs tell me that I am approaching Loch Lomond and the many smaller serpentine lakes which fill the glacial gullies of central Scotland. I glide to a halt in the middle of a stone bridge over a stream and open the glovebox to look for a map. The glovebox holds an ice scraper, a scatter of petrol receipts, the business card of a mechanic, and a jaundiced white handkerchief, neatly folded, which must have been my father's. No maps.

I stand on the bridge beside the car and watch the trickling water below me, wondering how many lakes it will join before it reaches the coast. Only then is my destination clear. Like a homing pigeon,

I turn back south and, every turn correct as if by instinct, head to Ardrossan. There, I drive without a wait onto the ferry. It casts off within five minutes.

I have not been back to Arran since the brief excursion I took with Mal the first time he came to Tealing. Seen from the bow of the low-slung ferry, it rises like the archetypal island of dreams, green with spring grass all the way to its camelback ridge, its shores salted with patches of humid evening mist. There are more houses on its slopes than I remember, but that is probably an illusion born of my relentlessly romantic expectations.

The inn where Mal and I stayed for a night was part of a working farm near Goat Fell, the island's summit. My father recommended it because a travel writer at the *Yeoman* had just discovered the place, though he had yet to write it up and make it fashionably inaccessible. Half of Mum's malignant lung had been removed two days before, and she told me she was tired of seeing my hangdog face arrive so dutifully at the very first minute of every visiting period. "Go! Take that American bloke to Sweetheart Abbey, somewhere picturesque and mobbed with tourists! Make him listen to bagpipes! I'd rather see you when I'm home, where I can put you to good use instead of watching you simper at the foot of my bed. You're so obviously wondering if I could die right here, right now. So go, and leave your good-boy guilt behind." She said this with her typically brusque cheerfulness, forcing her voice till she was breathless and the nurse had to scold her and make her put on an oxygen mask. (My mother was never soft-spoken, soft of step or opinion. This made her a determined patient but not a good one.)

The road up the hills from Brodick is clear, and the early evening sun shines, still warmly, on fields of grazing sheep. When Mal and I took this road, it was drizzling, and we became mired in a massive flock. A farmer was herding them home with the help of a small avid collie (purchased, for all I knew, as a puppy from my mother). The sides of these roads are closely walled, so there's rarely a way to pass such bucolic comings and goings, and the farmers make no apology. Cars may back up by the dozen and they wouldn't spare you a glance; the best pace a flock of sheep can do is a tortoiselike hurry.

Like a grimy cloudmass, the animals undulated before us. With the windows down, the smell of wet wool was strong. "Charming," said

Mal, "for the simple reason we don't have a curtain to make." As I inched the car forward, keeping a respectful distance, there were long silences in which we could hear only the bleating complaint of the sheep and the clack of our windscreen wipers. The rhythm of the wipers began to seem vaguely sexual to me—as an absurd variety of things did over that fortnight away from New York—and I lapsed into thinking of Tony. Whenever I wasn't with my mother, or talking to Dad or Mal or David or Dennis, I was thinking obsessively about Tony, about his body, its hard, soft, and callused places, summoning up the pale brown hair whorled like tiny nests around his nipples, the single barely audible gasp he uttered when he came, and his voice: flirtatious yet dry, camouflaging too well whatever he felt. (Living inside my tumultuous desire, I would forget that I kept my own emotions concealed.)

Mal startled me when he laughed. "Imagine being in the midst of a terrible love spat when you round a corner and find yourself stuck in this livestock jam. You've been needling and needling away at your lover, and now he's just confessed he's having a passionate affair and is planning to leave you. You're calling him every name in the book, a fucking whore, a faithless traitor, an asswipe, a cunt, you always *knew* his heart was nothing but compost . . . but physically, you have to move by agonizing inches, with nowhere to go, forward or back, while these poor dim-witted creatures make their sad little noises. . . ."

Uneasy, I said nothing.

"You aren't amused."

"I don't think I'd be so articulate. I suppose I'd get out and walk back down to the village."

Mal eyed me coolly. "Sometimes you are so constipatedly humorless."

As it happened, the sheep turned in at the farm where we'd be staying; this farmer's wife was our hostess. The place was a good step up from your average bed-and-breakfast, however, because the family lived in a separate, modern cottage apart from the farmhouse, a place of ingenuous charm.

Now, turning off the road, I see a glossier sign than the one which hung here eight years back. The inn looks freshly whitewashed, its walls bolstered with portly bushes of flowering broom. The roof is lush with new thatch, and there's a pebbled car park off to one side, so that guests no longer pull up by the tractors at the barn. I have a sudden memory of the wonderful porridge (served with good strawberries, cream, and maple syrup imported from my second homeland) and wonder if I'll be laughed out the door for thinking I can book a room on the spot.

In the parlor, two tweedy older couples are sitting on the sofas, sipping sherry and exchanging stories about their day. Where I remember garish paisley carpet, the plank floors have been bared and sanded and laid with tasteful imitations of Persian rugs. I recognize the city hand of a hired designer and feel a little sad; Mal and I both loved the formerly tidy, earnest bad taste of this place, down to the violet tartan lino on the floor of Mal's bedroom ("My kitchen would die and go to heaven!" he cried).

The farmer's wife strides out from a back room and shakes my hand. She's plumper and grayer but, like her establishment, more nattily dressed. "Cheerio, you're a lucky lad tonight! We've a cancellation, and there's even a plate of lamb I could hot you up if you're peckish."

In fact, I am famished, having had (how many lifetimes ago?) a bowl of soup at the Globe with Véronique and then missed my tea altogether. In memory of Mal's mother—though I know, from Christmas cards and charity drives, that she is alive and well—I give a little credence to the stars, accept a cup of tea, hand over my credit card, and take a newspaper into the parlor to wait for my lamb. The two couples nod a civil greeting but do not (thank you again, stars) try to include me.

After supper, Mrs. Munn leads me upstairs, carrying my whisky on a tray. The perfect hostess, she does not say how odd she must find it that I have no bags. Because of the last-minute cancellation, I have one of the biggest rooms, at the front of the house on the second floor. I have a queen-size four-poster tarted up in blue-tulip chintz (Ralph should be here), two matching slipper chairs, my own bathroom, and a southern view of the island as it tumbles to the Firth of Clyde. The water, normally a dowager gray, mirrors the rose-colored sky. I'm a lucky lad indeed, but a lad who's perversely sorry not to have one of the two tiny rooms on the top floor, little more than cupboards under the eaves sharing a common bath and looking up toward the summit of the fell.

I should go out and walk under the beautiful sky, for—again—I will be here only one night. But it's time to read Lil's letter, before I collapse into sleep, and I couldn't do it while sitting on some cold rock already damp with dew. I am no longer a country boy, not even a boy of the suburbs.

My vital organs shrink in unison at the sight of Lil's handwriting: a torrent of it, covering both sides of three pale green pages. At a glance, her soul poured onto paper. What did I expect, a telegram? PLEASE AID PROCREATION STOP DAVEY SAYS OK IF CHILD TURNS OUT POOFTY STOP PLEASE GO FORTH AND LIVE LIFE AS NORMAL STOP. But won't that be the essence? All right then:

Dear Fenno,

Believe me, believe me, neither of us (you or I; David or I) could ever have imagined ourselves in this situation six months ago (or even, really, six days ago!). You should know right up front that it's a situation of my making, not so much David's, and any response you have at all I will accept fully, so long as it doesn't harm your family in any way. Whether you say yes or no or you'll think it over, whether you are flattered or insulted or flat-out embarrassed, that is essential to me.

I am picturing you reading this letter in your old room (which will always be yours when you come to visit), and as I know Véronique or Dennis will have explained, David and I plan to stay elsewhere tonight, because I know you need time and space for a bombshell like this. I wish I could have waited to write to you in New York after your return, but for obvious reasons, that just isn't practical.

You will be asking a hundred questions, and I want to answer some of them here, before we face each other and talk. First, about Véronique: I hope you don't think me a coward, but there is no earthly way David could have approached you, simply because of who he is, and I knew that I would just become a teary mess. All the tension and disappointment and misery I've felt these past few years would break the dam, and there you'd have been, in a doubly awful position for having to console me as well as hear this outlandish proposal. So I hope you understand that part.

Second, David. I will tell you that when I came up with this idea, he looked at me as if I'd gone daft. You know your brother well enough that my telling you this can't hurt. You think of him as conservative, conventional, and you're right, to the extent that's how the world will always see him. Inside himself, and with me, he has other dimensions, both wilder and more tender. That's why we've lasted through this hell together while all our friends make their families, while Dennis and Véronique seem to pop out their wee ones like loaves of bread from an oven (she says they won't have another, and she may believe that but I don't).

Because of how rigid he can be, David would not consider adoption. He gives an enormous amount to Oxfam every Christmas, and free care for the pets at that home for autistic children in Kircudbright, but he will not compromise on his own flesh and blood. Sometimes I think it's the influence of your mother, all that breeding and pedigree talk you grew up with, all that control over bloodlines. (The suggestion of some anonymous donor, which I would never have made but the doctor did, appalls him even more.) When we got news of your father's death last week, one of the first things David said was that he'd never live to see the grandchildren we'd be giving him. I knew then that he was living in absolute delusion. I realized that he'd have us try forever, giving up when I was far too old, and I knew, too, that the doctor was about to tell us he didn't consider it ethical to continue helping us—so I had him tell David face to face. But it was before then— it was the day after we heard about your dad—that I told him this idea. At first he said no, flat-out no (he said it would be unfair to you, and you would never consider it for a minute, and I told him I had a hunch that wasn't quite so).

If I go on too long about us, it's because I want you to have the whole picture. I have been thinking incessantly about you, too, trying to imagine how something like this would change your life forever in ways that I can't influence or prevent. I'm assuming, for instance, that you've never wanted children for yourself; perhaps that's narrow-minded, and if so, forgive me. The legality of it all I couldn't care less about—obviously we wouldn't expect you to sign anything—but there are these cold awkward health matters we'd have to deal with, and I promise to make it all as easy as possible.

I'm not going to say David agreed to this easily. But he told me that he does love you unquestioningly, that he doesn't care about your being gay, that he thinks you're the cleverest of the three of you and that you've made the right life for yourself. I say this because I think, from our awful conversation on the way back from church, that you think he doesn't like

*or respect you. Far from it. If anything, I think you intimidate him and you
are blind to that. That's why I was so cross with you; I'm sorry. I just saw
this horrid gaping gulf between what I hoped I could achieve and what I
had to do to achieve it. Because in the end, this is about my wishes, and I
won't pretend I'm not being selfish. David would be disappointed not to
have children, but it wouldn't be the end of the world for him (and no, to
be honest, of course it wouldn't be for me, at least not literally). His work
still consumes him with a sense of concrete daily accomplishment, and
though I'm a happy apostle to that accomplishment, it doesn't complete
me the way it does David. . . .*

Lil goes on for another page, mostly about those "cold awkward
health matters." Her cringing desperation, which she makes no effort
to contain, makes me resent her at first. It surprises me, though it
shouldn't, as do her momentary lapses of logic (who would excuse an
aversion to adopting with free castration for kittens?).

But haven't I often envied those who are unflinchingly honest?
(Wasn't Lil's dancing, which flickered repeatedly in my mind as I drove
north this evening, enchanting because of its aggressive physical can-
dor?) And I know I will forgive her the benevolent lie—that she
thought first of me, not of Dennis. (How my eavesdropping led me
wrong there!)

When I finish her letter for the second time, I laugh at the cockeyed
notion that *this*—not Mal's death or my poorly timed debauchery—
might finally get me tested. "Life is unpredictable, that's obvious and
not a bad thing," Mal once said. "What's insulting is that it has a Wall
Street sense of humor." Tasteless jokes in abundant supply.

THE AFTERNOON FOLLOWING our arrival on Arran, it had continued to rain on and off, so Mal and I drove the circumference of the island, stopping to smell the sea at a lay-by with a view toward Ireland,
taking tea in Lochranza, where a second ferry shuttles passengers north
to Kintyre. By dinner, the sky began to clear, and the late sunset was
spectacular, rebounding in purples and golds from cloud to departing
cloud.

Having Mal with me at Tealing for the past week had been both a trial and a comfort. It became instantly and unspokenly clear that both of my brothers assumed Mal and I were lovers. That we shared my old room—never mind that we had to, never mind the extra bed—underscored that assumption. I wasn't sure which was worse: my failure to foresee this natural conclusion or the misery I felt at my inability to correct the misunderstanding. I had never come out to my brothers or my father, but I had never actively tried to deceive them and knew they weren't dolts. (My mother, half a dozen Christmases before, had told me quite bluntly that she knew. We were alone in the kitchen, and I was showing her the American method I'd learned for dressing a turkey, applying it to our annual goose. As we merged the ingredients we had prepared—I the mushrooms sautéed with thyme, she the chopped apples, sausage, and sage—she said, "You know, you needn't be ashamed about your being gay. With me anyway. I'm a fairly liberated mother, I think you know that." Mortified but grateful, I agreed fervently; only the most modern of mothers would let her son meddle with the Christmas goose. She laughed, kissed me on the cheek, then gave a stern glance at the bowl of dressing we'd made. "Your grandmum would be scandalized by all these *herbs,*" she said, accentuating the *h*. "'For shame!' she would say. 'Food that is fresh needs na frippery na fuss!'" And then she asked if I'd mind washing the beetroots. The subject never came up again.)

In no way was I ashamed of Mal's companionship. He was (no surprise) the perfect guest, hearing my father out on thorny political topics, quizzing my brothers earnestly and extensively about their ambitions and interests . . . a challenge when it came to Dennis, whose leading ambition of the day seemed to be smoking as much dope—which he affectedly called ganja—as he could fill his lungs with. He had just started pastry school in Paris, and he said there was nothing so mindblowing as constructing a mille-feuille napoleon at dawn while thoroughly stoned. Mal listened to such nonsense graciously, as if he were being enlightened.

The comfort in Mal's presence was the way in which he deflected attention from me, so that I was not held accountable every minute in my family's presence. Drifting in and out of my dire thirst for Tony, I was certain that were it not for Mal, everyone would notice my distracted, inattentive behavior. I fooled myself into thinking that Mal did not know me well at all and so would not notice this behavior himself.

So under that splendid sunset on Arran, we left the inn after dinner and walked out along the footpaths which hugged the stone walls between heathered fields. Mal's energy seemed greater than it had been in a while, and we wanted to prolong our day, since we would be leaving the next afternoon. Mal would drop me at Tealing and take the hired car on to London. After his meeting with Miss Norman, he would fly directly home.

We walked for a good stretch of silence, Mal a few strides ahead, as if to prove his endurance. He said suddenly, "My mother says, such an everymotherly thing, that I need country air. This place may just prove her right."

"She wants you back home?"

"At *her* home. They don't even live in the house where I grew up. But even if they did."

"She just wants to take care of you."

"She wouldn't have the time!" He laughed, and in the pink light he looked unconditionally happy.

"I have a feeling she'd find it."

"Yes," said Mal, "you're right there. She could have raised thirteen children and she'd still have had time for her marches on Washington, her dinner parties for Dad and his cronies, her coed quilting circle, her book group, and her Prime of Life aerobics class. Do you know, she thinks I should take up weights? 'Just little ones, à la Jane Fonda!'" Mal stopped and seated himself on a wall, facing the sunset.

I couldn't help looking at his wrists as they rested on his knees—all those bones so achingly pronounced. I was tempted to say that maybe it wasn't such a bad idea, moving to Vermont. I told myself that if he were another kind of writer, if his work did not depend on a life in the city, I would.

"I don't know how my mother managed always to seem so present when she had to be absent so often, making political waves. I mean, there she was, her picture or her name in the paper every other day, it seemed—to our absolute mortification—when there she was making our sandwiches for school. Mark of a control freak, I suppose."

"That's not very kind," I said, feeling an odd loyalty toward Lucinda.

"No and yes. But that's not my point. My point is that I realized, just recently, that her marriage to my father is probably just like that. I used to think they must have a dismal marriage, because when were they ever together? That their separate busyness was the only kind of peace they could have. But I think it's an illusion, their apartness. Their apartness is only a surface." Mal stood and continued on the path we'd chosen.

I had never given my parents' marriage much thought, perhaps because I never wanted one of my own. I had seen them disagree but rarely really argue, so I took for granted that they were happy and took it for granted themselves. "We haven't been married, so we can't exactly judge, can we?"

"You certainly haven't been, have you," said Mal.

"So, you have?"

He shook his head. "No, but I was courted."

We walked silently again for several paces. We were heading steadily downhill, and I began to worry about our return trip, whether Mal could make it. With a loosened shoelace as an excuse, I stopped and sat to retie it. Mal faced me and said, "You saw the pictures of Armand."

I did not look up from my shoe.

"I found two of them under the rug when I swept the floor that week. Did you know him at all?"

"I went into his shop sometimes. That's all. He seemed pleasant."

"He was sweet." Mal laughed. "Why not, around all that sugar?" I wished he would sit, because I wanted him to rest and because I did not like being face-to-face just then. This was not the sort of conversation we had (not the sort I had with anyone), and I didn't want that to change.

I said, "He made this remarkable coconut cake," and was immediately sorry when Mal frowned at me as if I had told a bad joke or confessed to a lie.

But then his face softened again. "The very first week, Armand told me that he wanted to end his life a married man. I thought it was the stupidest, bravest thing I'd heard anyone say in a long time. I hadn't told him that I was newly plagued as well; in fact, I never told him. I had no symptoms, just a prophylactic drug or two, just the results of that test I so responsibly—so gullibly—let my doctor give me. I did plan to tell him . . . sometime, but then time, as it stretched out and made him the honest one, the fragile one, made a permanent liar of me. Ever seen *Sabrina?* He was almost the Audrey Hepburn to my William

Holden. Except I wasn't so dashing. Or so carefree. And there wasn't a solid square older brother, no Bogart to elope with. . . . You know, he had a stroke, isn't that strange? I've come to envy him that far more than I used to envy him his sweetness."

I wanted to suggest that we start back to the inn, but it would have seemed rude. Mal looked at the sky above us, where stars had begun to prick through the gathering blue, like lights on a city skyline. "So are we roaming in the gloaming—or is that dawn?" he said.

"Aye, the gloaming it is," I said. I rose and started uphill. I was thankful when he followed without comment.

He rested on the wall one more time, and after he'd caught his breath, it was here that Mal got to the point I suppose he had been aiming for all along. "I've decided I do not want to die in a hospital, and I'm sorry if it's a burden, but I'm asking you to take this seriously," he said. "I just went to visit a friend at Saint Anthony's. He was wholly conscious, not even delirious, but every orifice, every *pore,* was grossly distended by a hose of some sort. He looked like a still. And I actually took him flowers. Trivial-minded ass."

From the wall, he picked up a small gray stone and held it for a moment against his cheek, his eyes briefly closed. "My mother is a big fan of hospice. My God, what an awful word! Ah, hospice with the mospice. Come right in, so glad to see you! Help yourself to a Hospice Twinkie! . . . Chatty rounds of gin rummy with people whose breath already reeks of formaldehyde. No. Fuck, no." He threw the stone far off into the field. There was still a red mark on his cheek, his weary blood slow to recede from the smallest threat.

"She brought it up?" I asked. I was surprised, because as clearheaded as Lucinda seemed, how could she foresee her son's death? Why should she be different from any other mother?

"She's known for a long time. I told her after Armand died. It was far too late at night and I had this rare moment of conscience. Maybe she deserved to know, she was my mother, maybe I owed her time to get used to the probability that I could drop dead anytime, just like Armand. I reasoned, Would I go off to war without telling her? My mother's an insomniac, like me—vice versa if it's genetic. That's part of why she gets so much done. I can remember hearing the sound of her sewing machine, when I was little, at three o'clock in the morning. I liked it. It was like the noise of a beehive; it made our house sound like a productive, orderly place. Then, when I was an adolescent, I figured it proved my parents were miserable and, thank God, had no sex life. This must be how she worked out her rage at being oppressed by The Senator.

"I've always had this private joke about my insomnia. What most people call the hour of the wolf I call the hour of the quilt. I love to think of every bed in my parents' enormous house covered with some gorgeous multicolored thing made by my mother while everyone around her slept—probably every bed in her shelter for knocked-up Polyannas, too. Just think: whole houses full of people snoring away beneath my mother's sleeplessness. . . . So the night of my urge to confess, I figured, well of course she'd be up, if not sewing then making signs for a protest or petitions for a county fair. She's never gone in for confronting the clinics, you know. She thinks it's counterproductive, and she's right. . . . Anyway, that night, wouldn't you know it, I woke her. Of course it didn't matter, she was hyperconscious in an instant. She made herself tea while I told her, and she didn't cry, or if she did, she was careful not to let me hear. She just listened for a while. I told her right away that if I had to die, I wasn't planning to be Catholic about it. Because I'd already thought about what I feared most. Dying by inches. I may immerse myself in opera, but intubation, I bet that puts a crimp in your aria."

Mal did not raise his voice during this speech, but it grew hoarse. He began to sound almost like Mum had sounded, just the day before in her hospital bed. "So it was entirely my fault, entirely, that my mother got a head start on her defenses," he said, nearly whispering now. "Did I really think I would overrule her faith? Ah ye of bloated ego. . . . And then, when I had made my case, after she had told me how much she loved me, she started to talk about my *sins,* oh so gently of course, and how she worried about me because she knew I no longer prayed. And I thought, The fucking *nerve* of her. And when I got off the phone, I lost it. I just lost it. I thought I would have a stroke of my own out of sheer rage, join Armand then and there."

At last, Mal stood up. I held out my arm, thinking that he needed my help for the last bit of hill, the steepest part, but he laughed.

"Really," he said, and started ahead of me again. "I hate it when my little tirades make you feel even more guilty about your superior health. Unless that's an illusion and you're keeping another truth close to your chest. Well, smart move if you are. Don't say a thing. I mean it."

When we made it to the top of the hill, Mal said, "You haven't called home about Felicity, not once."

"Wasn't it you who said animals aren't children?" I said, though I was glad for the change in subject.

"I'm thinking, God knows why, about your pal Ralph. It's merely considerate."

So in the foyer, I stopped to use the public telephone. I caught Ralph at the shop. In the background, Felicity sang her jubilant scales.

"So it's raining," I said.

"There too?" said Ralph, missing the joke.

"Oh no, it's clear right now. The stars are incredible."

"Well don't rub it in, darling. Nights here are smoggy as ever. The humidity's astronomical, and our AC tab will follow suit."

Ralph asked about my mother, I told him she was doing well, and then he reassured me that, August doldrums aside, everything was running smoothly. Felicity appeared to have forgotten my existence but would no doubt punish me when I came home. "If you called to confirm you're extraneous, well there you are," said Ralph, sounding old and snippish. I realized he was the closest thing I'd ever had to a spouse and rang off feeling thoroughly depressed.

The parlor was empty. While my back was turned, Mal had made his way quietly up to his room. On the other side of the wall, I lay awake in my narrow bed thinking of Mal's mother next to mine, the two alike in their forcefulness yet otherwise wildly different. Then I remembered the one other thing they shared: a china pattern. And then, just before I drifted, it occurred to me that I now knew just how those plates—Lucinda's—had been smashed.

I PULL INTO THE DRIVE at Tealing two hours past midnight. A wholly conscious coward, I've spent the day ostensibly "thinking"—doing little more than driving numbly about. Mrs. Munn's breakfast, which I was the last to consume, was more satisfying than ever, but my mood had changed overnight from giddy and bemused to restless and testy. My dreams, though I couldn't recall their plotlines, were anxious, leaving an afterimage of David's face at its most disapproving. Irrationally, I let the image niggle away at my mind, like sand in a shoe you're too lazy to stop and remove.

I checked out as late as possible and drove slowly around the island with my windows open. Against a flat sea, the gulls' voices rang out keenly. The sunlight felt mild and buttery, casting few shadows. All this serenity, alas, had little effect on me, and knowing it was time to get back, I took the first afternoon ferry. But leaving Ardrossan, I began to wander again, almost compulsively, taking the most circuitous backroads, feigning an interest in the lakes, unable to keep my mind on the questions at hand. If I thought about them for more than a few minutes, I began to feel indignant, as if I were no more than a pawn in some genealogical scheme. The sky, empathic old fellow, began to bristle with clouds.

For dinner, I stopped in a pub and ordered trout and peas in honor of Dad. While I ate, the rain struck up its clatter; with that as my excuse, I prolonged the meal with a pudding (a trifle which tasted like floral soap). Clearly desperate for further delays, I carried it to the bar and let the barman expound on the O.J. Simpson trial and all the many ways in which it proved that television had ruined America and so, because America couldn't help meddling in every other nation's business, would soon finish off the rest of the world as well. (Behind him, the evil telly itself droned on, rehashing the day's athletic feats.) Before yesterday, I could not have imagined a conversation which would make me much less comfortable than this one, yet I stayed till the barman locked up the till.

"Oh fuck," I say in quiet disgust as I kill the motor. Because, although the front of the house is dark, light spills from the kitchen windows at the back, illuminating the soft insistent rain that's nearly blinded me for the past two hours of driving. I long for the kitchen as it used to be in Mum's time: an almost neglected room, at its most functional when one of the collies was in whelp. A room which, most days, was cool and uneventful as a cloister.

When I open the front door, I can just hear Elton John. "Daniel is travelin' tonight on a plane. I can see the red taillights, headin' for Spayeeyayain . . ." A poignance all too predictable.

I'm surprised, though, to find Dennis stationary: sitting at the kitchen table reading the *Yeoman* (in our father's day, would O.J. have tainted those pages?). Every surface is clear and clean: no pastry makings, no marinating meat. He looks up and doesn't quite smile. "Hello," he says simply, neutrally.

"Hello," I say back. I sit down facing him, dropping the car keys between us as if in surrender. My eyes and my legs, freed from their task of getting me here, are throbbing.

Dennis closes the paper neatly and folds it away to one side. He clicks off Elton John but not the maudlin emotions that gremlin voice always summons from my youth. "Life is looking a little strange in these parts," says Dennis. He seems to have shifted down from his high gear of the past few days, that breakneck emotionality embracing joy in his work, love of his family, grief at losing our father. Sincere but unapproachably frenzied.

Still, I won't give him the satisfaction of a reply. I want to punish him a little for lying in wait. He says, "We might have worried about you, but we didn't. Under the circumstances."

"Good," I say, sounding as hostile as I mean to.

"Are you all right? You look a little put out."

"Put out?" I say with a burst of laughter. "I've never felt in such a bind."

"Some would say they'd never felt so flattered."

"Some would, wouldn't they?" Here we go, I think: Enter the vice ambassador.

I am about to tell him to lay off when he says, "So where did you take Dad?"

"Dad?"

"The ashes. Where did you take them?" Now he does smile, but it's the nervous, crooked smile of someone averse to confrontation.

"Fuck the ashes. The ashes are on the front hall table, and I'd be happy to see them stay there."

"No," Dennis says, as if to a child. "None of us has seen them since two days ago, since the luncheon. Vee noticed they were gone when she went to change the flowers yesterday evening."

I go to the cabinet where my father keeps an extra bottle of whisky. My hands shake as I pour myself a glass. I do not offer one to my brother. I take a gulp and let out an intentionally crude sigh of satisfaction. "Let's see. Today I wear many hats. I am a patiently awaited

refugee, I am a graverobber—no, an ashnapper. Oh, and a sperm bank—
second choice! Any other roles you'd like me to assume? Belated god-
parent to any of your children? But no, that's right, how could I forget,
I don't even *pretend* to worship God."

Dennis blinks a few times, as if I've shined a torch in his eyes. "Why
are you so cross?"

"Why are you so full of assumptions?" I walk out the kitchen door
toward the front of the house. My father's box is not on the table. I take
a gulp of whisky and look again. I return to the kitchen. I sit down
again.

"You're right; he's gone. Any kleptomaniacs on the guest list?"

"You didn't take him?"

"Let's see now. Who suspected me first—you or David?"

"It's just that you're the one who—"

"I, at this point, am the one who couldn't care less. I don't even know
why I expressed an opinion. I don't even know, since Dad's dead, why
any of us would bother to waste any energy over where to dispose of a
fucking plastic box of ashes that were probably scraped up from somebody's fucking barbecue pit because people don't burn down so tidy
and dry." I am both horrified and thrilled to hear myself possessed
by Mal.

"You're right," Dennis says quickly. "I mean, it's Davey who cares
the most about this."

"So let him have his way. I'm sorry I interfered."

"It's just that he . . ." Dennis sighs.

"Oh that's no mystery," I say. "It's just that for some reason he has it
in for Mum!"

Dennis's turn to go for the whisky. "In a way," he says gently, surprising me into silence. I wait for him to fetch a glass and fill it.

When he returns to the table, he says, "Do you remember that little
game I told you about, the one where Davey and I used to steal things
from her handbag? We'd bet each other how long it would take her to
notice the things were missing."

"The medals," I say.

"Well, clearly not the medals, if they weren't Dad's," he says. "In any
case, we didn't play the game for long."

"Mum would've caught on too fast."

"No," says Dennis, "that wasn't it. I don't think she ever did."

He refills my empty glass and says, "Really, what happened might be pretty trivial, but for Davey . . . or I don't know, perhaps I was a little dense about things like that. Not thinking about them spot on, the way Davey does about everything."

"What things?"

"Well this was, I don't know, we were nine or ten, because you were away by then. I think we'd done it half a dozen times, always replacing stuff before she could suspect us or making it turn up somewhere logical. So we'd stolen things like her change purse, a tin of mints, her lipstick . . ." My mind reverts to my father's macabre little bequest, a far stranger theft, so I have to lurch back, disoriented, to Dennis's simple remark. "And then it was my turn and I took this unidentifiable thing which turns out to be a packet of condoms." He pauses, as if expecting me to interrupt, then goes on. "I can't imagine what I thought they were, but when Davey saw them, he knew. And I mean, he even knew—or maybe knew, because things aren't always what they appear, are they?—he was certain of what it meant. That there was somebody other than Dad."

"Than Dad? Oh get on," I say, but Dennis continues, ignoring my protest.

"It's not as if he had to explain the facts of life. I wasn't that simple! I mean, I knew the mechanics of it all, in theory at least! But Davey had a few older friends, he'd begun to avoid me in school when he was with them, blokes a lot faster than we were. He liked lording it over me, the things he suddenly knew that I didn't. But this—this time he was upset, and he yelled at me, as if I ought to have known better, and said I had to put it back in Mum's handbag right away, before she went out again. He wouldn't tell me what it was for days. He hardly spoke to me."

How like our grown selves we are as children, I think, imagining the brooding ten-year-old David, a folk art miniature of his ultraresponsible adult self, wearing the face of my recent dreams. Unfairly, I imagine him as a father, rigid and terse. I do not think how loyal to our own father his instincts were. I certainly do not think about our mother, what instincts might have been leading her.

"He started spying on her then. He didn't tell me that, but I knew what he was doing," says Dennis. "When she'd go out to exercise or feed the dogs, he'd climb to the foxhole—with a book, as if I'd believe he was reading—and watch her from up there. One day, months later I think, when I'd basically forgotten that business, he told me he'd seen her with the foreman from the farm on that big estate, the man who kept sheep for that Colonel Doodah who moved here about the time we did, the foxhunting chap.

"And I challenged him, So? The man worked his collies with Mum, had an interest in the puppies. By now, I was trying the tough act with Davey, to hide how wounded I was he'd snubbed me in school . . ."

"Seen her 'with' him?" I interrupt. "How 'with'?"

"Oh I asked that too, and he said he thought they must have been kissing from the way they came out of the kennel, and I laughed and started calling him Sherlock. After that, he never mentioned it again. Not directly."

What if I'd been the brother David approached? Sometimes I wonder at Dennis's acceptance of the surface, as if the way things appear is enough for him. But I suppose that other, more virtuous mysteries consume him: how cheeses age, how meats roast, why yeast and eggs rise and collapse. I sigh. "So he despises Mum."

"Oh no," says Dennis lightly, as if I've just asked whether rain's been predicted. "But he's sure Dad knew, and *that* he despises."

Simultaneously, we look at the clock above the cooker. It's past three.

"But where is Dad?" says Dennis as he stands and takes his whisky glass to the sink, puts the bottle away. "I mean, who would go and pinch someone's ashes? It's not the sort of thing you misplace."

"No," I agree, though I do remember that my friend Luke's ashes went astray while being shipped to his mother in Florida, turning up, just fine, in New Orleans. Rumor had it that UPS gave her a year's free shipping or some other tasteless benefit meant to console her. "We'll look tomorrow, and I'm sure they'll turn up." Mentally, I push back that tomorrow as you would a day you are scheduled for major surgery—this tomorrow a worse one, because anesthesia will not be an option.

"Don't you ever sleep?" I say as we leave the kitchen.

"I nap," says Dennis. "Little catnaps. That's my secret."

Well there's Dennis, I think, his secrets all harmless and pretty.

MEETING US NOW, learning the superficial facts of our parents' lives, you would assume that David had been the closest to our mother. He's the one who's happiest out of doors, for whom animals are not just objects of fascination but beings who need respect (for what they give us, hard work or affection; for their pain when they suffer; and simply for their various kinds of differentness). It's easy to imagine him, side by side with Mum, learning at her knee about whelping and worming, infections, dysplasia, mites and ticks.

But you would be wrong. David loved the dogs, sure, but no more than any boy would. Sharp at all the sciences, he came to his profession in a roundabout way. As a boy, he'd tell grown-ups he wanted to be a geologist (Dad had told him that this was the closest modern-day work to global exploration).

If anyone worked at Mum's side, it was me. Before I went away to school, I liked to help out with the collies, not their training but their everyday care: feeding them, running them just to wear them out, even mucking their pens. While my brothers' assigned chores were in the house, mine were mostly in the kennel. Mum kept a chart there, on an inside wall of a cupboard holding feed, medicines, and leashes. On the chart, each dog's name stood above a column keeping track of inoculations, mineral supplements, teeth cleanings, wormings. After each small task was finished, she'd have me check it off. I loved that job, loved keeping such visible order. I loved rubbing liniment into a sore limb; loved, once a week, carrying out the can of meat drippings Mum reserved by the cooker and pouring it onto the dogs' kibble, to keep their black coats as glossy as pressed coal. When they saw that can coming, their ears would dart up, their noses prod my hips and legs, their tongues warm my hands.

My mother was an oddball in the world of sheepdogs. She was not a farmer, certainly not a farmer's wife; this was a vocation of pure luxury, and she did nothing to hide it. Among the craggy types at the trials, she might have been shunned but for her open, raucous personality. Two or three times I had accompanied her to trials requiring an overnight stay, so I had seen how she thought nothing of mixing it up with those men at a pub (my father busy elsewhere, of course), and when farmers came by Tealing to buy a puppy or borrow a dog for stud, she'd take a bottle right out to the kennel. Perhaps this talent of hers—the ability, against all odds, to make herself an insider—was one I had an unconscious need to study. It was certainly one I admired.

Once, there was a pup born with a hernia. Mum's vet told her that the hernia could be fixed by hand at so young an age if someone was willing to put in the time. So three times a day, before and after school and then again before bed, I'd sit cross-legged at the whelping box and hold the pup in my lap, stroking her ears and limbs with one hand while holding the hernia in with the other. I still recall the sensation of pushing the lump of flesh back through the muscle wall in that taut little belly, using just the tip of my right middle finger. It felt like forcing a marble into an elastic velvet pouch. To the tiny pup, it was painless; she would gaze up into my face, wagging her tadpole tail and smiling with eager innocence.

Some mornings I went down to the kitchen before even Mum was about. The pups' mother came to trust me completely, hardly woke as I searched the small round bodies by hers for the markings unique to Quint, the puppy I thought of as mine. One morning I was so absorbed in my task that Mum's voice jarred me. "Look at you, Fenno. You're a born parent. The gals'll fight each other off for you when it's babies they start to dream of."

I was brokenhearted (though I'd never have shown it) when Mum let that puppy go to a farmer up north. Not long after, I shipped off to school, and so many other concerns and preoccupations fell upon me—from all sides, like collapsing walls—that when I next returned home, the dogs seemed like distant old friends, friends whom you've never stopped loving but with whom you have surprisingly little to share. All my parental instincts, if that's what they'd been, seemed to have washed away in the tide of puberty. I never stopped to wonder if it hurt my mother to see me gravitate toward other things—like me, she wouldn't have shown it—but I suppose it must have. Even so, we were left, for the rest of her life, with an ease together that I'm not sure she shared with my brothers.

TEN

"HELLO THERE, MAY I HELP YOU?" She reminded me of Lucinda, this woman—barefoot, wearing a loose tie-dyed dress that nearly touched the ground, wiry gray hair springing stubbornly out of a hair clip. She was cutting roses when I came to the gate.

"Tony. Is Tony about?" I said primly.

"Oh Tony? Tony's gone home. We've just been back a few days." She was smiling broadly at me, as if to assure me that any friend of Tony's was a friend of hers.

When I continued to stand there, mute and clearly confused, she laughed. "Isn't that just like Tony, not to let people know his plans. He left the place immaculate, but I imagine I'll be getting his calls for weeks." She asked me if I wanted to use the phone, to ring up Tony at his flat, but I declined. I was stunned, of course, having assumed all along that this was Tony's home . . . but this would have been the assumption of a blind man. None of the trappings here—the fragile teacups, the misty Victorian pictures, all those gentle romantic belongings—had made a suitable backdrop for Tony.

I wandered slowly back to Bank Street, defeated by jet lag and the malodorous heat. When I had walked these streets in spring, they had smelled of new growth and fresh breezes, but now at this hour, at least until the pavements were hosed down, they smelled like an urban low tide.

In front of Ralph's building, I stood about, uncertain, as if I were waiting for my own shop to open. While I was away, the neighbor's rose of Sharon tree had bloomed and dropped its flowers. They lay about the pavement, furled and wilting, some of them flattened. They looked like small cigars, each one the turgid purple of a bruise. I decided to go up to my flat and take a second shower. Surely I was still half asleep, half dreaming.

An hour later, I unlocked the shop. In the phone book, there was one viable listing: a T.B. Best, way uptown. I punched the numbers, bucking my native hesitation. After four rings, I heard, "Hi! Theresa and Joey here. Talk to our beep!" I turned to the stacks of mail Ralph had arranged for me with little adhesive notes of superfluous explanation. I tried to see them as thoughtful.

Felicity sat on my shoulder. Still retaliating, she pecked at my earlobe every so often and made a low trilling sound halfway between a snarl and a purr. I had arrived back the evening before, and she hadn't let me sleep more than four hours. Not that I'd have slept much anyway, thinking of Tony.

As I veered through the day, grateful for all the tasks I had to catch up on, I tried to maintain the odd relief I'd felt at hearing Theresa and Joey's beep. Into what kind of insanity had I allowed myself to sink? But that evening, as I watered the flowers and cleaned out the birdbath which Ralph had allowed to film over with slime, my hands shook on the hose. I needed to call Mal, I reminded myself, ask how London had been. I needed to call all the authors scheduled to read in September, confirm the schedule before printing it out and making copies to set by the door and post at other shops. I needed to call my mother at one in the morning if I was still up, which I knew I would be. She would have been awake for an hour by then—to hell with recuperation—and I'd pretend I was calling to tell her I'd reached home safe and sound, let her make affectionate fun of me. Tony was the last thing I needed.

Time plays like an accordion in the way it can stretch out and compress itself in a thousand melodic ways. Months on end may pass blindingly in a quick series of chords, open-shut, together-apart; and then a single melancholy week may seem like a year's pining, one long unfolding note. That first day back I recall in fuguelike detail, with perfect pitch, but as for the next few months, the autumn and early winter before my mother's death, I remember only snatches of a superficial tune. Mal, just as his doctor had promised, rebounded with a new choreography of drugs—though he slept a great deal, often in the day, to keep himself alert for working at night. I did not visit him much in those months, but he came by the shop every few days. Mum's doctor, on the other hand, proved wrong, even if his optimism was guarded, but I knew about her decline only from Dad. Mum sounded, despite the worsening cough she could not control, as energetic as ever when we spoke.

Ralph had reclaimed many of my evenings and treated me, with an occasional chiding allusion, like a child who had erred but returned to the fold. Against my will, there were times when I actively disliked him. Nevertheless, I found his company easy and distracting.

It was in January, after Mum died, after Mal accompanied me a second time, somehow willing to serve as my social foil, when time changed tempo again, when my life seemed to spin around, a car hitting an icy patch and whipping me in a vicious circle to face the same direction but with a fearful new perspective.

Our readings had hit their stride. We filled the bookshop to capacity every time, no matter how nasty the weather, for chapbook poets and mystery writers alike. I'd given in to Ralph on the T-shirts, and often now our customers would take off their coats to reveal the store's logo: *Plume,* in archaically quilled script, above the *m* a wheeling owl. To this day, the sight of those T-shirts embarrasses me; I do not own or wear one.

That morning, it had snowed enough that I had to shovel the pavement. In the early afternoon, I telephoned my father for the first time since leaving Scotland. We exchanged stiff but agreeable small talk. Everything, everyone, was fine, just fine, as fine as could be expected. A waste of the telephone lines, but a dutiful waste. At my feet, under the desk, lay Rodgie, my newest companion. He had been one of my mother's favorite young dogs, and I had, perhaps rashly, brought him back to New York. Felicity still expressed token offense at his existence every time we returned from a walk, but Rodgie was young enough to accept a large, loud bird as a dominant sibling. Mavis and Druid accepted him, too, on condition that he respect their rights to the shop's one brief stretch of exposed baseboard heater.

That night, we expected to turn people away. It was 1989, and our reader had just published the first aggressively gay novel—a novel of mournful, mock-lyrical rage—to grasp the bottom rungs of the *New York Times* Bestseller List. Ralph cleared my desk to lay out twice the usual quantity of wine. I unfolded the hired chairs an hour earlier than usual; half an hour before the reading, they were spoken for.

Ralph liked greeting people at the door. He was a fixture in the "nabe," as Mal had put it, and loved making strangers feel welcome as well. I preferred playing stagehand, laboring to maximize floor space, fit as many chairs in as I could, move a few freestanding shelves. Not until I stood at the podium to introduce the author did I scan the assembled faces and see how many looked stricken. I saw men much younger than I with dark spots on their faces, thinning hair, canes propped between brittle legs. But everyone looked happily expectant, and the applause which greeted the author (also stricken, also much younger than I) included hardy, militant cheers.

Once the reading began, I moved back among the shelves, but even there listeners had crowded in, sitting on the floor or leaning against the walls of books that blocked any view of the reader, many with their eyes closed. I pushed slowly toward the rear, making whispered apologies, until I could slip into the garden. On a more pleasant evening, I'd have found a few guests out here, gossiping over the free wine, but tonight it was bitterly cold and beginning once again to snow.

The hard white ground reminded me of the churchyard ceremony two weeks before. The earth was frozen solid, so there would be no burying Mum before a thaw. But there we all were, so Dad had her coffin placed on the plot where she would go, and the vicar performed the rites. There had been a large hymn-singing service in the church, but at the grave there was only immediate family; on my mother's side, only a cousin whom my brothers and I had hardly known. Mum had had no siblings, a father who'd died when she was young, and a mother I could barely remember. So we were six: my father, my brothers and I, Lil, and the cousin. The air was so cold, it stung our faces like broken glass.

At the vicar's bidding, we read, all together, the Twenty-third Psalm. Then he gave a brief homily, attempting light humor by remarking how my mother, of all his parishioners, would approve most heartily of the Lord as a shepherd, particularly if His collies' bloodlines came from Tealing. My father did not smile. I don't think he had the energy. He read a poem called "Dog," by Harold Monro. It's about an idle dog, not a working dog, but Mum had loved the lines "Beauty is smell upon primitive smell to you: To you, as to us, it is distant and rarely found." (Dad was the one who discovered the poem, and copied it out for Mum, before I was born. She'd kept it in the kennel, tacked up beside our checklist.) Finally, we spoke the Lord's Prayer. When we returned to the church, to warm our hands and feet before driving home for the reception, I went in last, turning for another look. There was Mum's coffin, defiantly still above ground. In a way, how like her to die before the rest of us, as if to scout the terrain we would all have to cross—and yet, I thought with my last backward glance, how absolutely unlike her ever to be left behind.

I faced the magnolia tree, its branches sparkling with ice, and thought of my mother's body, in cold storage somewhere until spring. The subject of a headstone had never been raised, at least in front of me. Perhaps that was entirely Dad's business. Already I had given him opinions I ought to have kept to myself. Today, I had meant to apologize to him for acting so indignant about the possible sale of the house—as if I were still a child, still lived anywhere even near there. But when we spoke, I hadn't had the courage.

From the shop, I heard occasional rounds of laughter at the gallows wit of the book being read; briefly, the laughter expanded as someone opened the door to the garden. I turned to look as it closed, muffling the laughter again.

It was Tony. He was smiling blandly, the same smile with which he had greeted me nearly every morning the summer before. The anger I felt at that smile joined forces with my grief; I turned away at the onset of tears.

"Well I can't exactly blame you if you're miffed, now can I? But to be fair, your little disappearance surprised me. Isn't that what the French call to 'parteer ah long glaze'?" said Tony, as usual mocking everything beyond his personal culture. "Or should I say, ah la Scotteesh?"

I wiped my eyes and faced him. "No. That means to depart without saying good-bye, without a thank-you or a note or even an apology. I left you a note. My mother was ill and I went to see her. She's just died, in fact. If there was a vanishing act, it was yours."

Tony's smile never faltered. He stepped too close to me, and I stepped back. "I'm sorry," he said. "Sometimes I can't help being elusive. I was also gone for a while. I was in Paris. But I might have called, right? Not like I had to hire a detective to find you."

"You didn't even live there," I said. "In that house."

"Well I did, for several months. I do that. I take care of people's houses. I like the change of scenery. If you'd been around when Madam Professor came back, you'd have found that out. Did I ever say the place was mine?"

I started toward the door. "I'm cold," I said, as coldly as I could. My anger, against my will, was beginning to thaw. "And I have to be inside for the end of the reading." As I passed Tony, he did not touch me, as I had hoped and feared he would. But he followed me, and just before I opened the door to squeeze back into the crowd, he pushed something into a pocket of my jacket. "My phone's on the back," he said. "I'm sorry you didn't have it before. I tend to forget I'm not listed. It isn't on purpose, you know."

Ralph and I and a group of fans took the young author to dinner that night. Once we had ordered, I excused myself to go to the loo. There, I pulled the postcard out of my pocket. It was a reproduction of a picture I had helped Tony create: his distant face in the back of a spoon. The silversmith's markings on the stem of the spoon looked like Chinese characters. Clover studded the surrounding grass. Over Tony's barely discernible head, the edges of a large white cloud were ominously sharp. I turned the card over. There was nothing written there, but printed on the left hand side was *Tony Best, photographe,* below that a New York phone number, then *Maison Pluto,* with a Paris address and phone.

I had intended to rip it up and flush it down the toilet, but I didn't. A week later we met at a Thai restaurant, then went to a club. Stepping into that tide of bodies felt like returning to a glamorous foreign country I had visited, long ago, with disappointing results. (Would I like it this time, the way everyone else did, the way you were supposed to?) We did not dance but drank beer and milled about, watching the other men. Watching me turn down drugs, Tony did the same. We barely spoke; we would not have heard each other anyway. After a stretch of time which might have been one hour or six, I felt calmed by the anonymity. Then Tony led me behind a curtain into an alleylike room. There was no furniture, and the lighting was blue, dim yet harsh. Half a dozen men fucked with abandon, as if each couple occupied a pod of invisibility. I had known about this, but I had never wanted to see it. It was more upsetting than I had imagined.

I walked quickly back through the dancers, the drinkers, out to the street. Tony followed. When I hailed a taxi, he climbed in close behind me. "It's not my thing. I just thought you might like to look," he said when the club was a few blocks behind us.

"How little you know me," I said.

"Like you've made a big effort to let me," he answered, but wisely kept his distance against the opposite door.

It was so late that it was early—hour of the quilt—and I did not bother to turn on the lights when we entered the flat. Two hours later, when the sun rose, Tony got up and dressed. Lying half awake in my bed, looking through the kitchen, I saw him examine the pictures on my mantel before he left.

The following week, he invited himself for dinner. He was all manners, complimenting my simple food, carefully skimming my bookshelves, charming Felicity by scratching the back of her neck; in no time, he had figured out exactly how she liked it. Eventually, he browsed his way to my family pictures. He held out the one of my parents posed in front of Tealing.

"This the place you grew up?"

"Yes," I said.

"Faaan-ceee!"

"Modestly," I said.

"Come with an equally modest trust fund?"

"Yes."

Tony put the picture back. "Well you're very mum tonight. How long are you planning to hold that grudge?"

I was going to object, but then I said, "Until I know precisely what's going on."

Tony did not laugh. "What suits you?"

"I don't know."

"Well, see? Despite appearances, I'm not the cagey one around here."

"Well, you're the one who knows where I live."

"As of last week," he shot back. "Listen. You want something, Sir Gawain, just ask. This is America, land of stake out your lot before someone else does. Land of the squeaky wheel."

"Ask and ye shall receive?"

"May. May receive." Tony leaned on a windowsill now. Directly behind him, Mal's lights went on.

Tony told me that he liked house-sitting not as the means of deception I apparently imagined but for the simple reason that his apartment was very small, essentially a darkroom at the top of six flights in Hell's Kitchen. Not a place to visit, and if he was there, he rarely answered the phone. He'd be there to work or sleep or to pick up messages from the phone he rarely answered.

We saw each other every week or two, always when Tony chose to call. I did not like calling him, because I could see him, all too easily, standing beside the phone with his lopsided smile, listening to my voice spool through his machine. I paid for our dinners, and he led us to clubs, where we roamed and watched. We'd end up at my flat. I relaxed enough to let him make me laugh. On an afternoon when I closed the shop for inventory, he came by with a portfolio of pictures he had made on his recent trip to Paris. They were large black-and-white close-ups of ancient stonework complicated by suggestive but indecipherable shadows. The shadows might have been natural or contrived. When I asked questions, he refused to explain a thing. "Don't act like a tourist," he said. "Just look."

I did not love the pictures, but they fascinated me. Or I told myself they did. I bought four and kept them in a cupboard for months, conveniently forgetting to have them framed.

NOW *THIS* IS DISTURBINGLY AMERICAN, spending so much time in cars, I think. As if they're a refuge, a burrow.

I have been sitting for several minutes in the car park of the clinic. I haven't been here in three or four years, and the place has been enlarged and spruced up. I pretend to myself, pathetically, that that's why I'm still sitting here. I'm admiring it all: new sign, new extension (a charming cottagey barn), and window boxes of morning glories—Lil's touch, of course—just beginning to tuck themselves in for the rest of the day. The hard rain of the night before has stopped, but thin gray clouds, like smoke, still sprint across the sky.

I'd thought that if I got here early, I'd have them to myself, that we'd be on neutral ground (for me), away from prying ears (well who could blame those ears, any ears, in this titillating, vaguely seedy situation?). But there are two cars beside David's pickup, as well as another pickup with a small horse trailer in tow.

I actually consider driving back to Tealing. I sigh and step out of the car.

It's clear the action is in the charming barn. I hear a startled whinny, the protest of hooves on cement. I hear my brother's voice, reassuring the animal it's in sympathetic hands. He sounds like a voice-over in an ad for life insurance. When I reach the open doors, a middle-aged man and a teenage girl look my way. The man nods to greet me. They are watching as David and Lil subdue a small fat pony (the small ones bite quickest and hardest, Mum used to warn us). The pony is cross-tied in the barn's central open space, and Lil stands at the head, stroking its neck while keeping its mouth reined in. Repeatedly, it jerks its nose toward the ceiling, flaring its rosy nostrils. "Easy, boy, gentle boy, calm boy, there's a lad," she murmurs over and over. Gradually, its protests dwindle.

"All right then, the drug is going to work," says David, who's half-crouched beside the pony, holding a flexed foreleg against his thighs. "There you go, right on schedule," he says as the pony's head begins to droop in Lil's arms. "All right then, Nero, a little tailoring and you'll be good as new. The cut is deep but fairly clean." He looks up at the man (nearly as small and plump as the pony) and says, "I do wish you'd called, so I'd come to you. It's dodgy transporting a horse with a wound, even superficial." He's spotted me, behind the pony's owners. He looks at me briefly—on the word *dodgy,* I swear—then back at the plump man.

"'Twas airly I found him, and I thought we could git 'im in before I could ring you. Ye'll sew him up good, will ye?" says the man.

"Nero will be right as rain, you've no worries there, but I'd like to discuss the fencing on your farm. I'm accused of newfangled thinking, but I'm no fan of barbed wire, if it can be avoided. Electric's the thing." As he speaks, David is already stitching up Nero's gash. Nero's head lolls against Lil as she holds him. Now and then, his eyes spring open and he snorts gently, like a sleepy drunk at the wheel of a car.

The girl, who sounds as if she's been schooled a social class or two beyond her dad, lights into him about how a neighboring farmer gave him the same advice. "In case you haven't noticed, it's not the Middle Ages anymore."

"Lass, ye've enlightened your ma and me on this fact I canna say ha many times," her father says gently.

I'll just bet she has, I reply in my head. Standing politely away to the side, I take in the daughter's dark green fingernails, her pierced nostril and eyebrow. Surprisingly, my knee-jerk sympathies lie with the dumpy dad. (Is this an omen? Does the thought of parenthood—custodial or biological—sting?)

Still focused on his handiwork, David says, "Gillian, should we discuss what you're feeding Nero? He's grown a bit . . . rotund, shall I say?" He looks up at the girl with a flash of handsome grin and she laughs, charmed. In her gush of a reply, she manages to implicate her dad in this maltreatment as well. Something about the cheap grain he orders for the cows and goats. He does not begin to object.

"Excuse me," David says to Gillian when she's finished diverting the blame. "Fenno, would you mind waiting in the surgery? There's tea on the hot plate. Introduce yourself to Neal."

Just like that, I'm dismissed. Lillian hasn't looked at me once.

I have the petulant urge to head back to the car and ditch the buggers, David and Lil, Dumpy Dad, the punker and her pony. Excellent riddance to all. But I let myself into the main clinic, through a perky new Dutch door with polished latches. I'm greeted in stereo by a young man in a white smock hunched over a calculator and a woman with a Siamese cat in her lap. The cat purrs contentedly away. A hypochondriacal cat, I suppose. Clearly not an emergency, and I decide that this will be a test. I will make my decision based on whether the cat gets service first or I do. Because, idiotically, I'm here without having decided on a firm reply to the looming question. I was to decide on my drive north. I was to decide while luxuriously housed on Arran. I was to decide on the aimless journey back. I was to decide in the late, sleepless privacy of my childhood room and, finally, during the early-morning drive I made here an hour ago. Each time I failed.

I take a seat next to the perky Dutch door and, before the cat's mistress can mention the weather, pick up the nearest magazine, a veterinary journal. Resolutely, I page through inflamed udders and jaundiced livers and suppurating gums just to remain safely inside my shell and marinate in righteous indignation. Neal, incurious about my petless presence, returns to his calculations, rocking witlessly to and fro as he punches in his numbers. (Now *there's* a contender, I hear my mother whisper tartly in my ear.)

I have actually begun to read about squamous cell carcinoma in short-haired cats when David walks through the Dutch door. Without quite looking at me, he puts a hand on my shoulder and squeezes it briefly as he says, "Hello there, Wally, shall we snip those stitches and hustle you back to your place in the sun?" The woman stands, holding Wally in her arms. I can tell from her bright expression that she's infatuated with my brother, as I suppose all his female clients must be. David strokes Wally (who cringes at his touch), then turns to lead cat and mistress through an inner door. Wally begins to emit a barely audible yowl, like the whine of bad radio reception. My sentiments exactly, I think as David shuts the door behind them.

I stand and fling the magazine onto the table, a parting gesture of disgust witnessed by no one, but then there's a startling buzz. Neal picks up a phone. "Yes, yes . . . oh yeah?" he says, looking straight at me. He sets down the receiver and says, "You the famous Fenno?"

"Famous?" I say (or snort).

He laughs. "The wild brother from New York City."

"I'm hardly wild."

"Well, wild or no, Mrs. McLeod's waiting for you in the barn."

I think of Mum, the only Mrs. McLeod I know: waiting for me in the kennel, in the car, downstairs at Tealing, at the airport before she was ill—and now perhaps, if Lucinda's concept of the universe wins out, waiting for me in life-after-death. Or, if David's wins out, waiting in a Church of Scotland Hell for the equally damned souls of her lovers (to be followed by me) while Dad inhabits an alpine cloud bank, a literally divine Greek isle. There he roams, eternally and happily pensive, expecting his good son Dennis and his bullishly captivating chum Marjorie Guernsey-Jones. Whether David would make it to Heaven I see as a toss-up, though right now I can't be objective.

AS THE WEATHER WARMED toward another summer, I seemed to be living a life of chiaroscuro—or scuroscuro: between one kind of darkness and another. On the surface, Tony and I seemed to have an understanding, but I did not honestly know what it comprised. I never did merge our life with the rest of mine, as I had once determined to do. I never even tried. Sometimes Tony would come to a reading. He might stay, for the wine and cheese, and we might leave together once I cleaned up. Ralph would throw me a furtive leer, but he did not pester me for details since he was now busy, at last, with a courtship all his own: an architect from Princeton whose house, on weekends, welcomed even the dogs.

Mal's health began to slide again, if subtly. In May, along with narcissus and lilacs, the Hungarian dermatologist made his debut. The spots appeared inside Mal's mouth, and Dr. Susan, as I'd come to think of this all-important but faceless figure, recommended another doctor. This doctor would inject the latest potion of hope directly into the lesions.

After returning from his first visit to the new doctor, Mal rang me and asked for a favor, the first in months. Would I stop by a certain Japanese restaurant and pick up miso soup? At his door, he looked several shades paler than he had a few days before. His voice sounded muffled because he was moving his mouth as little as possible.

Mal set the carton of soup on his kitchen counter. He turned and said very slowly, "I've a pact with this devil disease. Get to have the rudest, most damning symptom of all . . . neatly hidden away . . . but twice the pain. Deal of the century." *Rudest* came out "oodest," *century* "thensery." Then he zipped his mouth shut with a finger and led me back to the door.

Abruptly (though this was how most news came from abroad), Dennis called to announce his wedding, less than a month away. I had no idea who the woman could be. They'd met in Paris, he said. She was gorgeous, smart, decisive—and to his delight had decided that he, Dennis, would do. "Do?" I said. "Merely do?" No, no, Dennis assured me, laughing, they were passionately in love. "And will *that* do?" I asked tersely. "Oh Fenny, you've lost your sense of humor. Sometimes you know! You just know! Haven't you ever felt that way?" Of course not, I wanted to snap. Do you see me sending Kodacolor Christmas cards of soul mate plus offspring? But I congratulated him, told him I couldn't wait to meet her. I did imagine she must be angelic, though I had yet to meet anyone French who possessed that virtue.

Did the wedding have to be rushed? He laughed. "Well yes, rather so—if she's to fit into her grandmother's gown, which she's always wanted to wear." He laughed some more, laughed as if drugged, and his bride, in my mind, became a good deal less angelic.

"If you can't make it, I'll certainly understand," he said. "And it won't be a grand business anyway, Mum's death being so recent."

It could have been the grandest affair of the century, planned a year in advance, and Dennis would still have forgiven my absence (I don't think he'd know a grudge if it mugged him). So I was relieved, and not because I didn't want to be there.

In June Mal stayed home, mostly in bed, for a week. For the first time, I entered his bedroom. Like mine, his back windows overlooked a row of gardens, some slovenly, some tidy, but all in some semblance of bloom. The two long walls leading to the windows were lined with records and books, and across his broad dark sleigh bed lay a quilt which I knew Lucinda must have made, a crazy quilt of velvets, velours, jacquards, and satins—greens, blues, and golds with an occasional sliver of black. "Two decades of party dresses I had to *beg* her to with-hold from Goodwill, down on my knees," said Mal when I asked. "I said, 'Well if I can't wear them, Mom, at least let me cocoon inside them.' And who knew? They might just cure my insomnia. That won my case."

Mal never let me cook, but I would pick up dinners from the Gon-dolier's Pantyhose, Le Codpiece de Santa, and a Chinese restaurant newly christened One Fun Yum. He seemed to have become ravenous. Gone was the ascetic diet, and the cancerous lesions in his mouth, he said, had all but vanished. "More like Cindy Crawford beauty marks, not those Carl Sagan black holes just waiting to suck down my brain."

But Mal was tired, bone tired. "Literally," he said. "I can actually feel my femurs from inside out. Sometimes my ribs seem to itch." The pro-fessionally laundered shirts I had picked up the previous week re-mained in their packages, stacked on their shelf in the cupboard. I did not ask about work, about concerts he must be missing. By the Fourth of July, he felt strong enough to visit friends on Fire Island.

Tony and I stood on the barren roof of Ralph's building and watched distant fireworks over the Hudson River. He brought a camera that night and photographed everything, almost randomly: the treetops and rooftops around us, the sky when it lit up, blooming with neon chry-santhemums. Our faces and torsos, our glasses of wine, the sparkling tarpaper under our feet. When the fireworks ended, he left abruptly. "Appearance I have to put in," he said. I did not need to ask to know I wasn't invited. For hours, I comforted poor Rodgie through his first night of bottle rockets and cherry bombs. He slept, shaking when the explosions came, under the sheets against my naked legs. His silky fur was wistful consolation.

I called Mal almost every day; when he felt well, he would bristle at the sound of my voice. "You again? What, you need a cup of kidneys for a pie?" He did not go to Europe for the festivals, but he was still reviewing new recordings and covering the few local concerts that mattered in the off-season. From working, especially from writing, he would gain more energy until he was, if not fully active, able to refuse with predictable arrogance all my offers of help. "Is this the diaper service calling? The baby hasn't been born yet."

When he did need me, he was all business, his gratitude hidden. I did not mind, because I had begun to think of this time, this season, as Mal's Last Days, and my vigilance was selfish. I did not want him to die, and I knew I would miss him, but I planned on looking back and seeing myself as a minor league angel. What might yet be expected of me, I did not care to know, but I would face each task as it came. So far, my tasks were easy.

In September, when Mal's lights were on more evenings than not, I began to wonder about his work. Unsure whether I wanted to reassure myself or brace myself for The End, I would search the paper for his byline, and just as I was sure his continued shoptalk must be delusion or pretense, there it would be, over an interview with Michael Tilson Thomas or a review expressing arch bewilderment at the hackneyed art direction in a new *Swan Lake*. "If we must go through the anguish of expiring on those waters yet again, cathartic though it may be, don't we deserve the justice of a fresh imagination? Don't we deserve to mourn without the black tutus, the crowns of black nylon roses, the forest backdrop that looks like it was lifted from a decorator's dumpster at the Plaza Athénée?" He made less effort now to soften his critical blows.

One evening when I picked up his cleaning, I found two young women in front of his building unloading boxes from a taxi. "Excuse me, excuse me!" one of them called out as I climbed the front steps. "You live here?"

No, I said, I was visiting a friend.

"Not Mal, not Malachy Burns?"

After a bit of scrambling and ferrying, the three of us stood outside Mal's flat with four cardboard boxes, a large framed picture wrapped in paper (plus a newly cleaned tuxedo and a package of pressed bed linens). "Hey, Mal," the girls chorused when he answered the door. "Hope it's all here! Juliette did the packing. She said to say thank you for letting her snag your spot. You can borrow it back anytime, she says."

They helped bring the boxes inside but turned down a drink. Before they left, one of them hugged Mal and kissed him on the cheek, clearly surprising him. "Ciao," he called quietly as they closed the front door below.

"Early Christmas?" I said.

Mal began unwrapping the picture. "The next-to-last good-bye. 'Congratulations: You've earned the prestige of working at home.' Proto-severance." Pulling away the paper, he revealed a poster of a richly colored costume design: a girl or boy, it was unclear which, in a turban and translucent harem pants. He or she held a slim curved sword, testing its point on a fingertip. Mal stared at the picture for a few seconds, then turned it fully toward me. "La Sultane Bleue from *Schéhérazade*."

"It's beautiful," I said.

"Well it's yours if you like. I've looked at it long enough."

"Thank you," I said.

"Say no if you want. I wouldn't be insulted."

"I'd like it. I would."

"Well good." He leaned the picture against the wall and walked into the living room. "Have a drink. To you, that's an order. Though I am relieved those girls didn't stay. Nice girls, but girls, and I don't mean their gender. Funny how twenty-four-year-olds begin to look prepubescent. Remember that age? Remember how indignant you felt when your parents' friends told you how young you were? How maddening it felt when you knew they were married by then, even had a baby or two?"

"Or had gone to war," I said.

"Oh mine got off. Not that he wanted to, or so he claims. His mother smuggled him off to Wisconsin, to her childless brother's farm. He'd never milked a cow in his life, but he acquiesced. The world might be at war, even at worthy war, but to his mother, my father *was* the world."

As Mal was to his.

We ordered out for dinner (Codpiece coq au vin), and we ate in the kitchen, in full view of the unopened, unmentioned boxes. I knew better than to offer to carry them back to his bedroom or help him unpack. I could imagine their containing the dull knickknacks of any office—files, staplers, tape dispensers, a dozen half-used pencils and Biros—but more likely they were filled with artifacts as beautiful and rare as the furnishings in his flat: an autographed toe shoe, a costume tiara, the gold-leafed program to a gala premiere, a pair of antique kid gloves, a collapsible silk top hat.

After we finished our chicken, Mal opened his freezer and offered me a choice of several ice creams and sorbets. I declined; he helped himself. Our conversation had hit a lull, and I listened to the sound of a spoon scooping ice cream methodically into a bowl. When Mal returned to the table, he looked at me steadily and said, "Do you realize that you never ask how I'm feeling?"

"I'm sorry," I said, though I was irritated. How much could he expect of me?

Mal shook his head. "No, no. Don't crumble on me now. I wasn't criticizing, I was . . . marveling?" He spooned ice cream into his mouth, closing his eyes at the pleasure. "I may be needy at present, but I do not need a nurse, a daily taker of my pulse."

Not yet, I couldn't help thinking.

IT'S BEGUN TO RAIN lightly again, and the barn is dim.

The minute I enter, Lil says, "Fenno, this is such a bloody mess." She starts toward me with her honeydew embrace, but I stop inside the doorway and fold my arms. This stops her too.

"I can hardly disagree with that."

Her eyes shimmer. "You are so cross."

"Yes. And I wonder if you even know why."

"I'm so sorry," she says. She covers her face with her hands.

I will myself not to complicate matters by comforting her. I say quietly, "If you could please stop crying for a minute, I could think a bit more clearly."

She swallows her weeping and wipes her face on the sleeves of her white lab coat. Beneath it, I catch sight of her flowered summer dress and the delicate freckles on her chest. "That dreadful letter, so stupid to have dashed it off like that without—"

"It wasn't dreadful," I say. "It overwhelmed me, but it would have knocked me flat in a sentence or two. I was already knocked flat."

"But you're—"

"No, it's my turn here," I say sharply. I sigh and look away from Lil's mournful face. I realize I'm leaning on Nero's stall. The pony is lying in the straw, snoring. (Aren't horses supposed to sleep on their feet? My poor selfish mind craves any distraction.) "I wish people would stop treating me as if I speak a foreign language and can't be spoken with directly about anything whatsoever. Am I that intimidating? Am I that difficult?"

"This is hardly 'anything whatsoever,'" says Lil.

"I'm not talking about 'this' or *just* this. The piper at the luncheon! The hymns at the church! The ridiculous ashes, which of course I do not have."

Lil's breath catches rhythmically in her throat, the aftershock of tears. "Well maybe we wish the same thing. And maybe we're not the *we* you see us as. Not even me and David."

"Well I *am* cross at David, I'm very cross at David. I don't have the faintest idea where Dad's ashes got to. If we'd just gone and buried them—"

"Please don't let's talk about that. Please."

"You mean, can we talk about your agenda please? Well, I will talk about whatever I like," I say. "That's part of my point." (I hear myself lapse into a whine, and then, reflexively, I hear Mal: "Nix the Rodney Dangerfield. No one's dissing you; they've just got lives to live.")

Lil begins to cry again. "Oh David should have—I wanted David to . . ."

"If you wanted David to talk to me about this baby crisis, that would have been an enormous mistake." Giving in, I wrap my arms around her, which makes her cry harder, into my shirt.

"Stop interrupting," she sobs. "I wanted him to *apologize* . . ." On the wall, the intercom sounds. "Oh bloody Christ." She pulls away from me and picks up the receiver. She tells Neal she'll ring someone back. She tells him she's fine, she's just had a sneezing fit. Must be the new straw. Observant Neal will swallow that one.

When Lil hangs up, she takes a deep jagged breath. I hold out my handkerchief. She sits in the chair by the intercom and blows her nose. She leans her head against the wall and closes her eyes. "You're right, you talk. Talk about anything."

From the stall next to Nero's, a large bored-looking Angus cow keeps an eye on me. If I were paranoid, her expression would seem accusing.

"If you and David were to have a child that I—that you'd had because I helped you out—that is, if I could—and if I came back on the occasional holiday, the way I do now, what would that be like?"

Lil opens her eyes. "I don't know." Her breath catches in hiccups. "What would you want it to be like?"

"I don't know either, and that's what worries me." Except that I do know one thing: I'm afraid I would want it to make me very important, from the moment I carried my suitcase into the home I loved as a child to the moment I left, each and every time. In truth, I would want to *reign,* as if primogeniture had come back into fashion. But I tell her an easier truth. "You know, I was quite surprised, and I still am, to discover how much I love being an uncle. It's almost embarrassing. I mean, it's so—well, it makes me so much, as your husband informed me the other day, such a textbook poofter." Lil gasps and starts to speak, but I raise my voice. "Well, I don't want that to stop, and I don't want something . . . something other which I can't possibly predict . . . to interfere with that. I mean, it's a very passive state, isn't it? Who would call me 'doting' or 'involved'? I don't take those girls to the zoo or confide in them about the vagaries of life—well, not yet. . . ." The cow regards me like the sputtering fool I am. Nero snores on.

"David says you could be as involved as you like," says Lil. Her body and her voice are stiff—the paralysis of sudden hope.

"Magnanimous Davey," I can't resist saying.

"He is, you know." She says this with sorrow, not anger. Sorrow, I'm sure, at my inability to *like* this brother as much as she knows he deserves.

The pause that stretches before us feels like a long quiet tunnel, an elastic band with eternal give. Now here, I think, here is the quintessentially pregnant pause. I have not lost sight of where I am and why I'm there. For the length of that pause, I am in power. I do reign.

I say, "I'm torturing you, and that's the last thing I want. Listen. I ran away. The fix I'm in, dear Lil—and it's to your advantage—is that I simply can't imagine saying no to you, not about anything important, and it doesn't seem fair to my sanity. Not a momentous statement and not one I came here planning to make, in fact I came here with my head in a storm of dotty confusion, and I'm sorry if that seems thoughtless. But this is a start, isn't it?"

Serendipitously, the cow passes a large gust of wind, and when I look at her now, she beams with genuine benevolence. All right you idiot, I scold myself. Pull yourself together and live. Live: a command I received explicitly some time ago and try to respect for all the privilege it gives me. Never mind that it often feels like a burden I'd rather stow in an attic with the rash luxury, the true luxury, of saving it for some undetermined season in the future.

ELEVEN

IN OCTOBER, Tony left again. This time he announced his departure. He was returning to Paris, because he could care for the same flat (and the same four Persian cats) he had the year before. He might be back by Christmas. He would let me know.

"Now there," he said. "I'm being a good boy, aren't I?" We were eating at the Thai restaurant that had become our haunt. It was cheap, and it was just enough outside my neighborhood that I could avoid running into regulars from the bookshop. I do not thrive on what Ralph calls "schmoozing."

"You're leaving tomorrow, and you tell me now."

"Plans can change! I wouldn't want to mislead you by letting you know too soon and then, oops, the whole thing falls apart. You might have made plans yourself, you know, that depended on my absence."

"I could do that regardless." I smiled. "Orgies and the like." I knew that what he said was probably true, the first part at least. Tony hated making plans of any sort more than a day in advance. It suited him perfectly to buy those cheap air tickets they call you about the day before there's an open seat.

I had never been to Tony's flat and had surrendered my curiosity. And though I knew that he sold pictures here and there, I did not really know how he made ends meet. From what I knew of his history, I was certain he had no family money. If I were American, I'd have asked outright, and I'd recently realized that one reason Tony liked being with me was that my rigid culture-bound reserve was a perfect match for his childlike secrecy (much of it gratuitous, simply a form of control). For all I knew, he had a job, even a respectable job, but concealed it to keep me wondering (and I, of course, would never express such wondering). Now and then we went to art openings and ran into someone Tony knew. Tony would introduce me, and the acquaintance would give me a swift knowing smile, as if to acknowledge our shared role as happy dupes, willing victims to Tony's slippery charms.

Among those charms was Tony's talent for random gifts. A linen shirt the perfect cobalt blue of hyacinths. A beautiful if battered silver reliquary shaped like a miniature foot (a lid where the ankle would be, a primitive glass window over the metatarsals, because it had once purportedly held such a bone from the foot of a saint). A first edition of William Carlos Williams's *Journey to Love* (its title, I guessed, more a tease than a promise). Each gift presented without fanfare or occasion, wrapped in want ads or not at all, handed over as we walked along the street or sat together in a taxi, stalled in traffic. ("Here. Picked this up for you.")

Sometimes I wondered if the gifts were bribes. Payments to maintain our fundamental aloofness at everything but sex. There we felt an equal fire, meeting each other without words but often face to face, looking each other gravely in the eye before contorting our bodies, unexpectedly tireless, into another configuration. Tony rarely stayed till morning, and when he did, our proximity ended the minute he left my bed. He would begin the day by ridiculing my "old-lady hotpot" (the kettle that switched itself off) or my "tender toes" (I like to wear slippers). Or he would answer Felicity's morning summons with "Polyanna want a dildo?" or some other childish retort. In the end, I preferred his predawn departures.

I did not believe that I wanted anything more. After the initial panic at hearing Tony's news, I felt relief. His absence would give me a productive respite for two or three months. This seemed to prove to my dense, illogical self that I was content with or without him, that I was a free agent. I did not wonder if what his absence would spare me was the exhaustion of a longing so relentless it had become nearly unconscious, as if I had failed to realize that the water I drank was salty, always salty.

Around the same time, Mal announced his retirement. He invited me, formally, for dinner. On my arrival, he opened an expensive bottle of champagne. He allowed himself two sips. "To my languishing liver," he toasted on the first. On the second, "To my golden parachute. May the descent have glorious views." He sat down and began to laugh hysterically. "Sounds incredibly sexual, doesn't it? Like 'golden showers.'"

I couldn't laugh. "They fired you?"

"Oh please, 'they' have a conspicuously liberal reputation to uphold. They'd never dare. No, my pride's the one that gave me the ax." Mal told me that he'd begun to experience blanks while writing. Words he was about to type would vaporize, leaving his mind a hazier gray than the screen before him. After a few moments, like an overtaxed computer, it would hum to attention again and reel out all the words he thought he'd lost. But the more this happened, the more he doubted the words that followed the blank. They felt like the words of a mental intruder, a stowaway, and everything he wrote thereafter felt false, imposed, even insincere. He would lose touch with his convictions: catastrophe for a critic.

"I saw myself handing in a piece that my editors would turn down because what I'd written was delirious or demented or just a stupid bore."

I had no easy reply. Mal had built a fire, and I turned away from him to prod the logs with a serpentine brass poker. Behind me, he said, "Here's where you ask if I plan to use all my free time to travel, jet about with friends and family, take solitary walks on the beach because it's really most posh in the off-season when nobody else is there."

I put the poker in its stand and turned around. "No. Here is where you try to humiliate me by making me believe I would actually have said something so fatuous and daft."

Mal laughed. "I can't play these games anymore?"

"You can do whatever you like."

"Because I'm a free soul?"

"That's one way of putting it."

"And another?"

"That you like to pretend you're not cross or fearful or furious at me for . . ." My heart resounded with fear of my own. What was I saying?

Mal said wearily, "For your health? For your continued obligations? For winning the dumb luck trophy?" He smiled vaguely out the window. I had embarrassed him, an impressive feat that left me feeling ill. He stood. "I'm going to put in the cassoulet. I hope you like fennel. . . . No, no. Sit. Stay here and drink the champagne. It mustn't go to waste."

Over dinner, he said he had yet to tell his mother that he had stopped working, but he would have to, and he knew what it would mean: She would make herself much more present in his life, and yes he loved her, but . . .

"You don't want her to take over."

The skin around Mal's eyes looked gray and brittle. New wrinkles reaching toward his temples resembled the fibers of a sable paintbrush. This accelerated aging made him look more than ever like Lucinda. "I don't want to expend the energy it will take to stop her. Or inflict the pain."

"So give in, just a little."

He sighed. "If just a little were only possible."

Conserving energy became Mal's chief occupation. He would save up precious reserves to spend on a weekend away with friends or a few hours on his feet at a museum. At first, he spent most days in his flat listening methodically to his records, by composer or performer, in chronological order. (He was a defiant turntable purist, using his CD player only to listen to new recordings he had to review; these days, of course, it was useless.)

I would deliver firewood now instead of dry-cleaned dress shirts. Sometimes I would reshelve stacks of records strewn on his bed, wash dishes left in the sink. One evening, when he fell asleep listening to Lotte Lehmann singing Schubert, I found a step stool and refolded the linens kept on high shelves in his bathroom. Not long before, he would never have let a stranger dust his belongings or choose his fruit, but now a Honduran housekeeper came to the flat, and he paid both the grocery store and the Chinese laundry to deliver. He did not yet need anyone to care for his body.

He still crossed the street to see Felicity, once or twice a week. He would sit at my desk in the shop for an hour, sometimes reading an art book, while she patrolled the breadth of his narrowed shoulders and preened his thinning hair. One day in November, he sat paging through a slick new tome on Caravaggio. In the singsong voice he used to address Felicity, he said, "Now there was a short, vivid life, wouldn't you say?" As if in affirmation, the sky released an unexpected downpour. It sounded like a truckload of glass beads spilling on the pavement out front. Felicity answered with a passionate glissando.

We laughed. "She'll be doing that long after I'm gone," said Mal, "and you won't play her a note of opera, will you, you cretin?"

"All right, a little people's Pavarotti now and then," I said without thinking. Increasingly, I forgot to go through the motions of protesting his doom.

Mal continued to page through Caravaggio. "And no Streisand, please, especially not those ghastly duets with that hairy castrato BeeGee. You wouldn't own such a thing, would you?"

The rainstorm had darkened the shop, and I went around turning on the banker's lamps usually reserved for evening hours; Ralph liked what he called their blue-blood glow (I thought them clichéd but not a hill worth dying on). Suddenly, the front door blew open with a bang, sending the bells into a brief cacophonous frenzy. In the blast of cold wet air, I remembered another day just like this one, three years before, the day Mal had brought Felicity to meet me. From his shoulder, she was watching me now, and when I met her eye, she tipped her head askew as if to ask, What next?

AFTER A FAMILY CONFERENCE over a late, argumentative dinner, we conclude that Dad's ashes must have been put in the rubbish by the careless adolescents who cleaned up after the luncheon.

When Véronique makes this suggestion, Dennis laughs loudly. We've all had too much wine—Dennis more than I've ever seen him drink by far.

"You think it's amusing?" says David.

"Well hang on, it's awful, of course it is, Davey, but it *is* rather like some situation on *Fawlty Towers* or that restaurant farce everybody thinks I should like, what's it called, *Have You Served Me?*" Dennis contains a new round of giggles.

"You astound me. You bloody astound me." David has been on edge since returning from work, the last to arrive at Tealing after the long day which began, for me, with watching him stitch up Nero's leg. He's made no effort to get me alone, though he did catch my eye during dinner and tried to give me a significant smile. I couldn't help looking away. Now the wine has set him on edge yet further (while making Dennis just plain silly).

"This is what befalls of not engaging true professionals," says Véronique.

"Thank you for your perspicacious hindsight," David says.

If I have resented being on the sidelines before, tonight I am glad to feel like a bystander as these accusations fly (none directed at me, since everyone feels guilty about having blamed me for Dad's disappearance).

And undeniably, I'm enjoying the sitcom angle on our plight, even as I share David's dismay. Then it occurs to me that all those sacks of rubbish are still in the garage, the luncheon having taken place (unbelievably) just three days ago. David, typically frugal, had said he'd haul it away himself.

"So. Let's roll up our sleeves and have a look," I say.

David takes a moment to see what I'm suggesting. "Well yes, right you are, Fen. Let's have a go." He stands and looks at Dennis.

Dennis makes a face of hilarious disgust and says, "Oh dear. I do have a bit of washing up on my hands . . ." He gestures at the long kitchen table, where three courses' worth of dishes lie about.

"And a bit of sobering up," says David. His twin, noisily stacking plates, ignores him.

As we walk to the garage, I say, "Why do you always come across as the oldest when we're all together?" This is the first time we've been alone since our argument over Mum, and I am petrified of what we must face. (That my sperm may stand in for his? That a blood test might show I'm a corpse-in-waiting, the next family member whose ashes might be misplaced? That life can be cruel in devious ways?)

"The middle child's the squeaky wheel, isn't that what they say?" David pulls open the garage door and reaches for the light. "Or is it because I'm the one who still goes to church?"

"Food for thought," I say absently. We step into the damp concrete chill. There are spaces for three cars, one occupied by Dad's old Volvo. In the second is a cache of miscellaneous objects: a lawn mower, three large metal dog crates, an impressive stack of cardboard cartons (according to meticulous labels, back issues of veterinary journals like the one that held me hostage this morning), and an enormous box which claims to hold components of an x-ray machine.

In the third space, the one where Mum's car once stood, lie the vestiges of Dad's memorial luncheon: three stray folding chairs which were found only after the rental company pickup; a threadbare carpet placed under the bar on the terrace; and five bulging sacks of rubbish, each one the size of a walrus.

David sighs. "Maybe we could feel it, the box," he says as he wrestles one of the sacks aside and frisks it from top to bottom. Struggling with another sack, I follow suit.

This strategy tells us nothing. David sighs again. He crosses the garage, rummages behind Dad's car, and returns with a paint-stained tarpaulin. He spreads it over the concrete floor. "This is going to smell heavenly," he says. "How's your stomach?"

"Surprisingly sturdy." I watch, admiringly, as David unfastens one of the sacks and fearlessly dumps its contents onto the tarp. But then, this is a man who can sink his hands into a cow's intestines.

As if reading my mind, he goes back to the car and returns with what looks like a rag. "I keep them in the boot for breakdowns—for fooling with the motor." He gives me a pair of surgical gloves and deftly slips on another.

We spread out masses of sodden paper napkins, tea leaves, smashed fruit crates, floral clippings, peach stones, broken glass, and slimy vegetable offal. It takes us two minutes to conclude the box isn't in this lot—but then we face the far more challenging task of getting it all back into the sack.

Probably because we're trying not to breathe, we work in silence for the first three lots. But sack number four contains the mother lode of chicken carcasses boned by Dennis for the tajine. I step back and gag.

"Let's go outside a minute," David suggests.

We stand gratefully in the dark and the faint rain, a fine fresh mist like spray blown from the sea. "We're not going to find it," I say.

David says nothing for a minute, then, "This is going to bother me."

"That you can't formally lay him to rest, or that someone was deranged enough to steal him?"

"No one stole him, Fen."

"Mistaking the box for something else?"

David laughs. "Like what, a box of bonbons? That'll be a rude surprise."

"Perhaps it'll come back by post, anonymously."

"That's what Lillian thinks. She even searched out in the garden, as if someone might have taken Dad for a walk and left him out to air! She'll be waiting a year for that parcel. She never gives up, not on anything."

This silences both of us. I'll wonder later if he steered us this way on purpose.

"Do you know," says David, "there was a time when I believed, when I actually feared you were plotting to steal her away from me?"

I make an inarticulate sound, between a grunt and a whimper.

"Remember that Christmas I brought her home and I found out you knew who she was? The way you ogled her throughout that dinner. I mean, if looks could ravish . . ." He's clearly amused, as if the thought of my captivating Lillian, stealing her heart, were pathetic or absurd. "You were always the smartest, the most bookish, and she was like this . . . this budding Virginia Woolf, this brilliant firefly glow and I was just tagging along, pretending to love all those books as much as she did, pretending at all the scholarly passions that made me think of *you*. Right after I met her, do you know, I pored over the books in your bedroom, like some desperate refresher course. You had those passions for real."

"But never mind," I say. "*Then* you found me out. The poofter was unmasked."

David looks deflated. He raises his hands in abdication.

I cut off his apology. "No, no, too late. Other waters are rushing too quickly under the bridge."

"Fenno, I'm so dim, what can I say? What can I possibly say?"

Thank you from the depths of my emasculated heart? To hell with your sperm count? May the fertile force be with you? Several ugly suggestions pop into my head. But I say, "Whatever you think you ought to say, consider it already said. Nothing's definite. We'll see what happens."

He nods solemnly. "Take it one step at a time."

"Yes." I would touch his arm if I didn't think he'd flinch. Which would make me angry all over again when, finally, finally, just for the moment perhaps, I am angry at no one.

And no, even after my allegedly iron gut surrenders most of another four-star meal, Dad's ashes do not show up in the rubbish from this one.

MAL ANNOUNCED JAUNTILY that since this Christmas might be his last, he'd spend it where Christmas would be celebrated as it should be, in London. The *Messiah* would be sung as intended, in a cathedral where monarchs were christened, married, and paraded in coffins laden with lilies as large as trombones. The shops would be filled with Dickensian riot and cheer. And setting aside all expected culinary gaffes, the

Yorkshire pudding would be authentically perfect. "Besides, Christmas isn't Thanksgiving. It's not about food," declared Mal.

When Lucinda heard that he would not be going to Vermont, she did not protest; she simply determined that Vermont would follow Mal and, pulling out The Senator's checkbook and contacts, leased a flat for the family.

"There goes finishing school tuition for a dozen knocked-up waifs," said Mal. "Did I need to *state* that an entourage was not a part of my plan?"

He sounded unusually happy, and I said, "So after Christmas, ditch the entourage and come for New Year's where it's celebrated as it should be—land of Hogmanay, first-footing, tall dark men with lumps of coal." This was a role which David relished playing; for several years now, he'd been the one to carry that black briquette of good fortune over the threshold of Tealing.

"Are we a tourist brochure?" said Mal.

"We are, as you've seen, a family desperate for intelligent distraction."

I was glad when he accepted; at the very least, his presence would keep me from impulsively crossing the Channel. I had received a single postcard from Tony, a flip, cryptic message implying that he might be back a bit later than planned: *Tis a sweet life here & am hoping for more. Maybe another situation till March if I get lucky. Are you lonely? Are you partying hard? Remembrez moi?? Save me one of your bonny Scotch smiles. Back before you know it.* No signature. Fine, I thought. My life had begun to feel safe again, even a little airy. But I did have these pangs of yearning, and when they shot through, they were fierce.

As it turned out, distraction was irrelevant that year. Lillian's marriage to David, I was to reflect, had altered relations at Tealing as quietly as a new stream works a placid path through the woods (though granted, Mum had been a dominant force in those days and would have overshadowed almost any new woman brought into the fold). But now, the small planet I knew as Family had been struck by a comet in the guise of my second sister-in-law, the proudly pregnant Véronique. Expensively perfumed, ostentatiously affectionate (even with Dad), perpetually overdressed in velvets, silks, and garments edged in fur, she declared her arrival without even a stab at humility. And her surprising youth—she seemed not much past twenty—made her style and confidence that much more offensive. I disliked her on impact and felt almost pleased when I became certain the antipathy was mutual.

Dad welcomed Véronique with a festive enthusiasm which not only irked but surprised me. It was Christmas, yes, but it was also the first anniversary of Mum's death. He cut holly from the back fields, as Mum had always done, but instead of tying the branches in a simple sheaf and fixing it to the door, he accepted Véronique's offer to fashion them into a stylish wreath. He ordered the crate of blood oranges Mum had always liked and, as she'd always done, poured them into the grand Chinese bowl which came off its shelf only to fill this function. But he let Véronique take a dozen of the oranges, puncture them with cloves and candied flowers, and hang them from velvet ribbons in all the front windows—a decorative gesture Mum would have deplored. I had to agree with my brothers, however, that Dad's summer holiday in Greece had done him good and that his announcement to retire from the *Yeoman* seemed like a clearing of the decks rather than a fatalist retreat.

That Christmas also marked Dennis's debut as itinerant chef at Tealing. This, too, pleased Dad (no doubt relieved that his son was smoking trout instead of dope). He seemed not a bit offended when Dennis went through the kitchen discarding Mum's old boxes, jars, and biscuit tins, even pots and pans he deemed inferior. "Aluminium leeches into the food and then into your brain—causes dementia!" I heard him explaining to Dad, who'd encountered a pile of pots on the snow outside the back door. Dad laughed and said, "Well carry on. Just leave me a skillet for my bacon and a kettle for my tea. Dementia's already set in."

David and Lil were rarely about. They worked like accountants at tax time and dropped by after dinner when they could, made an effort at conversation, then fell asleep in front of the telly, their heads inclined together. Always the last to turn in, I'd switch off the lights and, when this failed to startle them awake, tuck a blanket up around their shoulders. When I came down in the morning, they would be gone, the blanket folded, the cushions smoothed. Even on Christmas, David spent the morning at work. And Dad was absent a fair amount. He still drove into town, to the paper, every other day or so—weaning himself from a long life's work. Typically, I was left alone with the almost inseparable newlyweds.

One day I went upstairs to get a book and found Véronique in the middle of my room, looking about like a foreclosure agent. She apologized for startling me (not for trespassing), then asked if I didn't think that this room, with the lovely warm sunshine beaming through these windows all afternoon, might make a perfect nursery for her children whenever they came to visit. Wouldn't the room just "blossom" if the trim were painted a very pale shade of lavender? *"Comme ça,"* she said, touching her silk blouse, which echoed the blue of her undeniably pretty eyes. While a part of me had to acknowledge that this room was no longer "mine" (and that grandchildren claim more than hearts), I had a hard time containing my fury. "Personally, I find that color a little vulgar," I said.

"A yellow, then, a very light yellow, do you believe?" was her immediate answer. I could not tell if her intense, maddeningly beautiful gaze was ingenuous or mocking.

"Oh yes yellow, by all means yellow," I said. "A brilliant choice. And on future hols, I'll sleep with you and Dennis across the hall. Sort of like a grand slumber party, what do you think?"

She laughed absently and kissed me on the cheek. "Oh you are humorous," she said.

After that, I went out often to wander through the woods and fields, braving colder air than I would have liked, just to escape her invincible effervescence. The new houses I encountered left me with a childish resentment, and the too-large wellies I had to borrow from David left me with blisters on my heels. I disliked the woman even more for these insults to my comfort.

On New Year's Eve day, I met Mal at the rail station. London had been the right choice, he said, even with Lucinda and his brother tagging along ("No faux fiancée this year, thank God"). His sister had decided it was too much trouble to take her small children across an ocean for the promise of worse cold, worse damp, and the risk of Irish bombs. The Senator had joined them only for Christmas Eve and Christmas.

"Get this, the old man's starting a bid for Washington—now, at the eleventh hour," said Mal. "Strom, old buddy, watch your back."

"Your father's what, midway through his sixties? That's not so old in those circles."

"Well it's Methuselean in mine," said Mal. "But that's not the point.

I bet some shrewd young advisor told him that in the eyes of the constituents he needs—you know, all those back-to-the-woodstove New Yorkers—a son dying of plague should cancel out the pro-life Catholic embarrassment of Mom. Maybe the contrast's even poignant. You know, 'Mom's Love Defies Pope,' that sort of cheesy headline. Just think, my life will get a *spin*."

"I wouldn't flatter yourself," I said.

When I changed the subject and told him about Véronique, he snapped, "You don't like her because she's French. It's one of those cultural conflicts sewn into your genes—congenital envy of inborn style."

"Stylish she is," I said. "But just you wait."

She was, of course, the one to open the door at the sound of our arrival. To my dark delight, she greeted Mal by kissing him on both cheeks, looking him over, and stating cheerfully that he was the most underfed American she had ever met. He must get himself straight to the kitchen and let her husband fatten him up. I suppose this was a compliment grounded in the never-too-thin ideal of her world, but to my ears it was unforgivably stupid. Mal's reaction was to smile and ask if her husband made soufflés; a craving for chocolate soufflé had dogged him for weeks. Promptly, with an arm around his bride, Dennis reeled off his repertoire: mocha, white chocolate, gianduja, and the plain old magnificent classic.

"The plain old magnificent classic," Mal answered. "The image I have of myself a few decades hence."

Dennis laughed brightly and clapped Mal on the back. "As I'm sure you shall be!"

As on his previous visits, when the house had been equally full, Mal slept on a camp bed in my room. His insomnia did not travel, but he muttered in his sleep. This was a habit I hadn't noticed the other times we'd shared this room, or perhaps it was new, the fear he encased in wit by day leaking out at night. Either way, it startled me several times a night, sometimes leaving me awake for an hour or longer, chewing on my anger at Véronique (and at Dennis, for loving her) or missing my mother, who would have kept things as they should be, people in positions they had earned.

———

MAL'S T-CELL COUNT had stopped falling, Dr. Susan said, but she didn't like the look of his liver. She made a list of foods he should avoid and told him to say a final farewell to booze of any kind. I heard all this news on my weekly firewood haul as we listened to a Bach flute sonata.

"You know, I've never heard you play," I said.

"I've given away my flute, so I'm afraid you never will," said Mal. When I said I was sorry, he answered quickly, "I'd begun to stop a long time ago anyway. It's not exactly tragic." He glanced at the record jacket beside him on the couch. "But I did play this piece, and not too badly, that last summer before I went AWOL from a concert career." He stopped to listen for a moment. "Very mannerly music, don't you think? Maybe the influence of the harpsichord, which many people find a superficial, robotic instrument—I can't agree. I'm remembering how much more emotional this felt from the inside—though I suppose that could have been the end of adolescence talking. . . . Now here's that cunning melancholy cello. Listen."

I listened—as much to Mal's reminiscence as to the music. I tried to imagine him, seventeen years old, standing with that slim silver instrument poised across a terse mouth, swaying like a tender sapling in a breeze, as I had seen flutists do in the few concerts I'd ever attended.

"I fell a little in love with that cellist." Mal said this so quietly that I was only half certain of the words, and I thought he meant the cellist on the recording until he said, "She was an extraordinary musician, but she left that life behind as well. Lives become so . . ." He sighed. "Complicated by other lives."

I looked at Mal and saw that he was pulling back, on the verge of crying. I said nothing, unsure whether this rare display of sorrow was a response to the thought of that summer, of his brother's cancer and the trauma that must have been inflicted on his family, or of the path he turned away from because of that trauma. Perhaps he was thinking simply of what it had been like to be so young, to feel that life itself was so languorously long. There were so many reasons for Mal to break down completely that I marveled at his persistent self-control.

We listened together until the end of the record, after which Mal rose, took it off the turntable, carefully slipped it into the jacket, and put on the second disc. Through a long solo passage ("Sarabande," Mal whispered at the beginning of the movement, raising a finger), the only other sounds were the crackling of the fire and the hissing passage of cars on the wet street below. We were in the depths of winter—the branches emptied of birds—and the flute sounded icy and patrician. Mal's eyes were wide open but bore the inverted, rapt expression of someone reading. When we had listened to both sides, he put that record away and carried the jacket toward the kitchen. "Tea?" he said, refusing when I offered to make it.

I followed him anyway and watched with alarm as he dropped the record into a dustbin lined with a plastic bag. In it were several other records. "Don't ask," he said sharply. "I'm just thinning things out. And no, you may not have them. Nobody may."

The next time I came over, I heard a sound I'd never heard at Mal's before: the sound of a television. On one of his early visits to my place, Mal had commended me for not even owning one; he kept his, he said, only to watch videotapes in bed—concerts and the occasional film. Now it had been moved from the bedroom to the living room, where it was blasting out the day's most sensational news.

"Yes, yes, I've succumbed," said Mal when he saw my face. He lay on the green chaise, wrapped in a blanket. "Best over-the-counter anesthetic I know."

"I'm not here to disapprove," I said, though clearly I did.

He kept it on every evening now; if I peered across the street, I could see its epileptic glow clashing with the deco carpet on the wall. Once, I looked across and saw something quite different: bodies moving around, faces laughing, hands raising drinks. I was furious. I had assumed Mal no longer entertained and that if he did, I would be included.

The following night, I made my delivery late, on purpose, and found Mal watching the State of the Union address. When I came in, he barely greeted me. "Close your eyes and listen. Now if you had a voice like that, wouldn't you have shot yourself a long time ago?"

I could easily have agreed, since George Bush sounded to me like Monty Python's take on a nursery school teacher. But I said, "Do you care about the state of the union?"

"Union? Whose?" Mal laughed. "Just think. A year from now, my father might be groveling at the webbed feet of this toad." I took from his lap a plate holding a half-finished chicken breast. He thanked me but did not look away from the telly.

I put another log on the fire and sat down across from him, puzzled. Two tiny presidents pontificated from his retinas. I had never seen Mal look so absent from himself. After a few minutes, he said, "Doesn't that dog of yours need walking?"

"In an hour or two."

"Well. I don't need anything else. I can see this isn't your dram of Glenlivet."

"Nor yours," I said. "Ordinarily."

"Time for a new brand of ordinary. Or haven't you noticed."

I stood. "All right, all right." As I started down the stairs, I heard him yell, "Oh ye who we who miscapeepoo! Up your wrinkled blue ass!" I heard a small crash. It sounded like the remote control bouncing off the telly.

The next night, I ran into Lucinda at the health food store. She unsettled me not just with her presence but by kissing me on the lips. "Hello, hello, has Mal told you we're practically neighbors now?"

I told her he had not.

"Children never lose that teenage reflex, do they? Heaven knows the new tricks a mother might dream up to shame a boy in public! I've been here nearly a week." She sounded bright and happy, full of wholesome determination. She had sublet a tiny studio near Washington Square ("No bigger than a beehive!") where she would be staying for the next few months. The House, she explained, had won a grant which would pay her tuition for a crash-course degree in career counseling; NYU had the perfect program. "And Zeke wants me out of his hair while he 'strategizes' for his campaign—a good thing, since we rarely agree on politics, the kind that starts with a capital P. He's fine with my playing at single girl, so long as I return to play the doting wife in front of all those cameras. *That* I can do in my sleep."

"Well good for you—for your grant," I said.

"I'll be studying like a fiend—the Good Lord willing, I still know how!—but we mustn't be strangers." She took my hands in hers and squeezed so firmly that I could feel her rings marking my skin.

I saw in Lucinda's cart several of the expensive fruit juices Mal now drank in abundance, as well as a medicinal tea I had seen in his kitchen.

"Drop by the shop," I said. "Pleasant company can be scarce."

"Sign me up," she said, and kissed me again. I knew I should wait for her, offer to carry her bags, but she would be heading for Mal's, and I did not want him to see us in tandem like that. I had read somewhere that people who are very ill become susceptible to the notion of conspiracies.

I walked home quickly, so she would not catch me up. In my foyer, I turned to look up at Mal's window and saw, dismayingly, that telltale snowy flicker. But in the next minute, when I opened my mailbox, my attention was utterly hijacked by a large blue envelope bearing foreign stamps and a handwriting I rarely saw but knew on sight.

I set down my groceries and opened the envelope. It held an invitation to Tony's show in Paris. I opened the card quickly. The vernissage would be held in four days. After the date, Tony had penned in parentheses *So be thinking of moi*. Nothing else. I closed the card and looked at the front.

Two pictures were reproduced side by side, both (as always) acute, almost uncomfortable close-ups. On the left, a cropped profile of a man's face. You could see only a corner of his mouth, but you could tell he was laughing. At the top, the image ended just below his eye. I looked at the partial ear and the hair behind it. I kept looking. In the sliver of background, there was a tree at night, illuminated by a phosphorescent glow. The light cast by fireworks. I looked again at the ear. I held the card at arm's length. Strange how I knew that ear, though I never see it from that angle.

The image on the right was another cropped profile of sorts: the outer edge of a man's naked pelvis, waist to thigh. Beyond the pale hip, against a wrinkled paisley cloth, a dog's black and white paw. My bedcover. My dog. My hip, obliviously sleeping. I would never have allowed the camera in my bedroom.

TWELVE

THE TICKET COST ME A FORTUNE. Tony would have found a way to wangle some last-minute bargain, but I was not Tony. Anyone but.

I paid the boy in Mal's building to look after Felicity; Ralph would take Rodgie. I told both Ralph and Mal that I had a family emergency in Scotland; my brother had been in a traffic collision. I have been deceitful, but I had never told such a wild lie (and one which left me superstitiously nervous on behalf of David, the brother I'd fictitiously injured). To tell it twice, vaguely answering their sympathetic questions, felt outrageously cruel.

But I would go for only three days. No one would miss me. Lucinda was here to play valet.

I booked a room at a small expensive hotel on the Ile St. Louis; I chose it because it was the only name that came to mind. My parents had stayed there once and loved it.

What was my plan? Did I have a plan? I had never experienced such a schizophrenic rage before, an anger helplessly pierced by moments of narcissistic satisfaction. Perversely, I was a star.

In the three days between the invitation and my departure, I suffered through ordinary life at the shop and a dinner with Mal and Lucinda at his flat. No telly, thank God, though Mal was testier than usual and did not invite his mother to bring out her pictures. When she did, he told her that while I might have enjoyed her show the first time, once was enough. I started to object (in fact, I'd been hoping for this distraction), but Mal's dark look stopped me. Quietly, Lucinda put the pictures back in their envelope, the envelope back in her handbag, and did not mention The House or her girls again. This time Lucinda did not ignore her son's fatigue, so our evening ended early. When I hailed a cab for her, I could see that she was disappointed I had not asked her over to my place.

"You're just over there, right?" she'd said when we came out onto the street. She pointed to my building.

"Right up there." I pointed. The windows were lit; when I would be out past sundown, I left a lamp on for the animals.

"You still have that gorgeous, charming parrot, don't you?"

"Felicity. Yes."

"I'd love to see her sometime. . . ."

"Come by the shop. I bring her with me every day. She's sort of a mascot by now. That was how Mal convinced me to take her." And then a taxi came our way.

"I'm glad you're right there," said Lucinda as I held the door. "It makes me feel safe."

Though I can sleep decently in the cramped quarters of flight, this time I did not so much as doze. I brooded, trying in vain to see the night sky through the reflections in my plastic porthole, trying in vain to find calm in the soft, regular breathing of those sleeping soundly about me. Well then, I would have the afternoon for sleep.

But when I registered at my hotel, I was shocked at the price I had agreed to pay. It was one thing to hear it on the phone, when I had been in a feverish rage, quite another to see it in print, pushed toward me on an accounting sheet bearing my name. I could pay it, but such extravagance went against my nature, and seeing a figure which might as easily buy me a used car as it would three nights of lodging, I worried about the corruption of that nature. Everything connected with Tony defied my normal impulses; anyone could have diagnosed a case of self-rebellion, as if I were my own adolescent child. But here, having come this far for no clear purpose, my recklessness stood perilously tall, a monument built too hastily to stand. Yes, a folly.

So I went to my room, with its gray velvet furnishings and its complementary view of the gray velvet Seine, and I did not sleep. I paced. What was I doing, what on earth was I doing? After close to an hour of pointless flagellation, I had worked my gut into a small tsunami, so I left the hotel and walked a few blocks to a merrily crowded bistro. Having eaten very little on the plane, I made myself consume a heavy Alsatian dish of potatoes, sausage, and cream, the entire thing, and drank two glasses of an opaque purple wine. This time when I returned to my room, I fell irresistibly onto the dove-colored bed, to awake just as suddenly in the dark, befuddled only for a moment. When I saw the luminous digits of the clock (as plain and ugly here as at any chain motel), I sat up and groaned. The vernissage had been going on for half an hour already. When I looked in the mirror, my cheek was creased, my hair dull, and my teeth were mauve from the wine at lunch. I showered and dressed in a panic. It was too late to have my shirt pressed, and my coat was still covered with Rodgie's white hairs.

Hence I was not, as I had planned to be, one of the first guests, able to walk in and stun Tony, throw him off balance from the start. I stepped through the glass door of Maison Pluto into a room which was scathingly lit and thoroughly packed with people, their faces blurred in a haze of cigarette smoke. (The gallery's name, I learned later, was a sophomoric pun cooked up by the director to convey that his artists were all "far out.")

Forced to slink my way in along the wall, I confronted, too intimately, the pictures. They were not as large as I had imagined, but their intense focus was arresting. The first I saw was of a hand, mine, on the crown of Rodgie's head. This picture, I could see from a round red sticker on the wall, had already sold. I felt a surge of impotent fury.

The next picture showed the back of my head and neck against a sky flowered with distant fireworks; the one after that, my bare legs and feet on my bedspread, from an angle that showed a bookcase and, before it, several stacks of books which did not fit. You could read the title of every book.

I had come upon one of the pictures from the invitation—my naked hip, flanked by three red dots—when (rather than the other way round) Tony surprised me. I felt his hand on my shoulder first, and before I could wheel about, he was saying, "Beeyanvenoo, beeyanvenoo! I had a bet with myself about whether or not you'd make it. I think the larger part of me won."

How could you; what the hell do you; what kind of cruel joke; who the hell do you . . . So many indignant openings did not make it to my lips as I took in his bantering smile, his mock French, and the strange combination of distance and warmth that his hand on my shoulder enforced. Seeing a few people glance our way—at Tony, not me—I realized that no one would ever put the pictures together with me, because my face, in its rare appearances here, was visible only in fractions.

"I don't know why I came," I said coldly.

"Of course you do." Tony laughed and dropped his hand. "You came because you miss me. And you were dying to see the pictures."

"I haven't missed you at all," I lied in a low voice. I could see a woman working her way toward us through the crowd, calling in heavily accented English, "Tony, you escape artist you!"

"You're a petty voyeur," I said.

"I?" said Tony. "I'm the voyeur? *Je suis un artiste, moi!*"

The woman pushed between us and hugged Tony hard, covering his face with pigmented kisses and laying her head on his shoulder. He introduced her as Marie-Ange and wrapped an arm around her. He started to turn away, toward another fan, but said, "Are you coming to the dinner? It's just down the street. Marie-Ange, give him *l'adresse,* see voo play."

I could not make myself leave before seeing all the photographs: all anonymous yet invasive. I felt, if not raped, ridiculed, though I knew this reaction to be absurd. Did I secretly wish that my image were recognizable; that I, the physically present me, were not, to everyone here, just a middle-aged nobody of an uptight *anglais* in a rumpled shirt, squeezing my way around the room as if this event was really about the art on the walls?

I left the gallery with no intention of seeing Tony again, but after wandering the rue du Bac and the boulevard Saint-Germain for a damp chilly hour, I gave in and went to Marie-Ange's flat. I was hungry again and, begrudgingly, enjoyed the food. (Well, I can still ignore him, I thought.) I sat next to an Australian girl who had recently befriended Tony and expressed the gushing wish that he would photograph *her*. "Isn't he the most mysterious bloke you ever met? Even though he never acts like he is? I'm so fascinated," she said. "He's just got this bloody magnetic thing going, don't you think?"

Magnetic as a black hole, I kept to myself.

In the midst of this Tonyfest (Tony himself at the far end of the long crowded table, elbow to elbow with Marie-Ange, who was, I could see from her walls, a patroness if not more), everything she said about Tony made me feel small and banal, a worker ant on the labor line of love. She did not ask how I knew him—she seemed to assume the whole world knew Tony—nor did she ask what I thought of his pictures.

Before dessert, Tony worked his way down the length of the table, taking in congratulations and compliments. It had never occurred to me what a fine politician he might make. Deliberately, I stopped watching him and then, for the second time that evening, felt the shock of his hand on my shoulder. "There's something I want to show you," he said, close to my ear. Reluctantly, I stood. As I did, he kissed the Australian girl. "If it isn't my Miss Koalafruit," he crooned, making her giggle.

He led me down a hallway to a spiral staircase. "What do you think of this place—magnifeek, ness pah?"

"Yes," I said curtly, but I followed.

At the top of the staircase was a large bedroom, exceedingly feminine (even by comparison with Ralph's), all white lace trappings, the walls hung with dozens of black and white photographs. One I recognized as Tony's, a shot from the lawn of the house on Charles and Greenwich. On the bed lay three Persian cats. One of them raised its head to growl, then lost interest.

Tony led me into a bathroom and closed the door behind us. He began to unbutton my shirt. I pulled away and reached for the door.

Tony took back my hand and held it against his waist. "Now is this the guy who flew across an ocean to see me?"

How absurd would it be to lash out that I had flown across an ocean because I wished I had never met him, I wished he would never return, I wished I need never fail at resisting him ever again?

"Don't tell me you're pissed about the pictures," he said, though he did not pause in opening my shirt.

"Who wouldn't be?" I said, not stopping his hands.

"Well I can think of lots of folks. You know, you are strange. Interesting strange, but strange," he said. He touched his tongue to one of my nipples. His back was to the sink, and over his head, in a large mirror lit mercifully well, I saw the blood rise to my face. He pulled back just to say, softly, "Stop taking yourself so seriously," and those were the last words from either of us before we returned to the laughter and champagne below.

I knelt on the white chenille rug, partly to avoid my reflection behind Tony, and as I fumbled at his belt—something new and expensive, a complex gold buckle—my hands stopped trembling.

I stayed not three days but a week. Although I called Ralph and Felicity's young caretaker, I did not call Mal. I did not wish to be grilled—in either sense.

I returned to New York spent, demoralized, satiated. Customs was a nightmare, the drug hounds having sniffed up a frenzy at somebody's unclaimed ski gear; by the time I walked through my door, it was close to midnight. The lamp I switched on woke Felicity, and before I could get off my coat, she had flown across the room and bitten me hard. Moderately kind, she chose my wrist, not my face, for expressing her sense of abandonment. She squawked mightily, flapping her wings, then settled onto my shoulder as I walked about turning on lights, glancing at the post, shedding my clothes. It was Saturday going on Sunday, and Rodgie would be in Princeton, with Mavis and Druid and Ralph. Ralph and I had arrived at a state of benign estrangement—my fault, I knew—while our dogs had become a contented threesome. My mother would have been scandalized, this heir to her diligent champions loitering with a pair of slack-brained spaniels.

I plugged in the kettle and sorted the post on the kitchen table. I had changed into my robe, after which Felicity reclaimed my shoulder, avidly grooming herself against my left ear. When I reached up to scratch her neck, she gave me a cursory nip, a reminder that all was not forgotten, and uttered one of her falsely intelligible phrases: "Braggadocio," she seemed to say, and I laughed. "Yes," I said. "You're not far off, lass." Her taffeta rustlings made me glad to be home.

Sorting bills from catalogues, gym prospectuses, and a pair of postcards from tropical islands, I sighed at the thought of the accounting I had yet to receive, the cost of my transatlantic sprint. I had left Paris no more or less happy with Tony. I knew him no better; the only thing I had learned was that I never would.

In the bedroom, I settled Felicity into her cage by the window and folded back the coverlet, now more familiar to me from Tony's pictures than from its place in my home. By the bed, the answering machine flicked its red light insistently: STOP STOP STOP STOP. Listen listen listen listen. A lighthouse gone berserk. I would have ignored it till morning but for the number of calls: 27. I stared at the number. Surely there was nothing to be alarmed about; once, gone only a few hours, I had come home to find the tape filled entirely with the monotonous beeps of a fax machine groping for contact. I sat on the edge of the bed and punched the button.

The first two were empty air, as if someone were waiting for me to pick up despite the message. The third beep was followed by a voice which, for an instant, sent a panic through my veins: my father's. "Fenno, it's Dad. No emergency . . . well, none that I know of. A mate of yours rang here this morning expecting to find you. Are you on your way, a surprise of some kind? Shall I make up your bed?" He sounded bright and healthy. After a pause, he said, "Didn't say, but I think it was your friend Mal. Sorry I didn't ask."

The next message, a poet I knew from the shop; the man was fishing for a reading, though he pretended he'd like my company for lunch. I sped through his chirping voice. The next, a financial consultant looking for clients. The next, Lucinda. She sounded as desperate as I now felt.

"Fenno? Fenno? Fenno, I don't know where you are, but I'm guessing, I'm hoping you'll have to . . . have to pick up your . . . messages. Mal's at Saint Anthony's, there's no one else nearby to call, I'm waiting for Zeke to get here, I'm just, I just thought . . ." Her voice rose to a fragile falsetto. With forced composure, she gave me the number of her sublet. I stopped the machine and, desperate for a pencil, raked aside the envelopes I'd put on my desk.

According to the inane monotone following her message, she had left it two days after my departure. "Oh Christ," I said. I cursed the machine as the next few irrelevant messages droned on. Then, as I hoped, Lucinda again: "I don't know why I'm trying you, I don't know where you've gone, I hope *you're* all right, but I know you'd call me if you got my last message. Mal's been . . . he's breathing on a machine and they're keeping his blood pressure stable and I don't know how much he's aware of right now, but they're saying he's got a fighting chance of . . . recovering. Will you call us? Please?" She sounded calm but weak. She gave her number again and said she'd be picking up messages there. She was at the hospital nearly all the time, she explained, but you couldn't ring the ICU.

Of the last sixteen messages, fourteen were delayed, clearly hesitant hang-ups, and two were casual calls from people I knew and liked but whose words, at that moment, I simply couldn't hear. I was dressing as

I listened to the tape run its course. It was full. Lucinda had left her second message three days back. If I had returned as scheduled, I would have been in the air approaching Long Island.

I rang the number Lucinda had left. It echoed endlessly into my ear. No answer, no machine. Felicity had already burrowed her head under a wing and fallen asleep. So much for avian telepathy. I went to the living room and peered across the street, as if Mal's dark windows had anything further to tell me. I left a lamp on, hoping Felicity would not have to wake without me again. As I locked the door behind me, I wished I could leave her a note.

The cold was a punishment I needed and deserved. My eyes filled with tears at the shock, and I almost broke down at this easy suggestion of grief. I crossed the street and rang Mal's bell. My only rational reason was that if Mal were not back, and it did not sound as if he could be, someone from his family would be staying here. I rehearsed an introduction in my mind. "You don't know me, or know of me, but . . ." But I've neatly fucked over your brother/your son. If he's still alive to hate me for it.

By the time I got to Saint Anthony's Hospital, it was three in the morning. The emergency room looked empty as I passed its aquarium glow. Entering the hospital's less urgent entrance, I had to wait several minutes at the reception desk before anyone came forth to acknowledge my existence. The guard eyed me blankly, no offers of help.

"Hoo, no visiting hours now, honey," said a large, blessedly cheerful woman, shaking her head emphatically. "You got family upstairs?"

I had lied enough, so I explained that a friend of mine had been admitted while I was out of town, and I was anxious to know at least where I would find him once they did allow me up. The woman sat down at a computer screen, which lit her spectacles with a running pattern of tiny stripes—names, names, names scrolling past—and then she punched a key that stopped the stripes, and then another. She said, "Huh."

Not morgue, not morgue, not morgue, I thought. But would she even be authorized to tell me such bad news? What *could* she tell me?

Body released to the family.

Scheduled for autopsy.

No such person. Not any longer, hon.

She said, "Mr. Burns was moved from ICU yesterday afternoon. Doesn't show a room number here, but if you come back after eight, the system should cough one up. Answer your question?"

"Is he . . . ?" I wanted to ask if he was conscious, able to level at me the full arctic sting of his rage.

"Hon, I don't know from medical know-how," she said, guessing at the nature of my curiosity. "Hon, we just guard the portals and the names hereabouts. You go off and get some sleep, won't you? Coffee machine's busted, ain't no hospitality neither. Your friend seems to be among the living, that much I can tell you."

I did not return home but walked here and there through the brutal cold, hands driven into my pockets because I had left my gloves behind. I looked into warmly lit windows occupied by headless but beautifully dressed mannequins and garish arrays of cosmetics. At five, I went into a coffee shop and ordered eggs. Another loner offered me part of his paper, but I refused. At six, I went back to the hospital and sat in the lounge. There was no sign of the motherly woman who'd helped me three hours ago. At seven, as I had hoped and feared, Lucinda walked through the revolving door. She saw me almost before I saw her. She set a shopping bag on the floor and hugged me.

"I thought you'd fallen off the earth," she said without a trace of scolding.

"I was . . . I was completely out of touch. I'm so sorry."

Her smile drove deep lines into her face. "I think he's going to be all right. I think, if I'm persuasive enough, they'll let him go home this afternoon. They've been very kind to us here."

I wondered about the "us," how large it was. Lucinda went over to the reception desk and had an inaudible conversation with the young man now at the computer. I looked down into the shopping bag: bananas, bagels, a *New York Times,* white tulips. A small paper bag.

Lucinda touched my arm and picked up the bag. "I found a place that makes incredible rice pudding. I don't suppose he'll be eating yet, not solids, but you never know. I'm always optimistic." She smiled warmly at me, as if I'd been here all along, a helping hand in the catastrophe. "That's just how I am," she said, and took my hand as if I were her child.

"I tried to call you last night, when I got in . . ." I stopped, ashamed that I was about to make excuses.

"It's ridiculous, but I'm uptown for now; Zeke insists on hotels. He's used to a staff and a telecommunications center; not me, thank heaven."

When we stepped off the elevator, she walked straight to the nurses' station, beaming. I lagged behind, uncertain what part I had to play. I saw heads shaking, then a smile or two, concessions being made. Lucinda came back to me. "They're letting me peek in, just a five-minute peek. I'll tell him you're here and coming back later. They have to clean him up and take him for some tests. If the tests send him home, I'm all for that."

"I'm not sure he'd want to see me anyway," I said.

"Don't be silly. Besides, he's still quite out of it. He was touch and go for a few days, and while he knows where he is, I don't think he knows *when* he is." She laughed at her small joke. I wanted to share her giddiness, her fragile relief, but I was not so optimistic. I was glad the nurses would let in only Lucinda for now. I was sure he would greet me like a second plague (or would that be a third?).

EVERYONE IS LAUGHING. I can't see them from up here, but their voices carry. My twin brothers and their wives still linger at the long wooden table in the kitchen (we haven't used the dining room once), and I will rejoin them after I've packed. Early tomorrow, I will head back to New York. I need to organize myself before another night of drinking and reminiscing. This one will be long and, I hope, free from recriminations or veiled competition.

I can still taste the white chocolate mousse, worthy of a dinner on Mount Olympus. After a week of this food, I'm hitching my belt a notch farther out. The salad days loom, I think idly. What does that expression really mean? It's an idiom whose definition I can't keep straight, no matter how many times I look it up.

Despite those first gorgeous days, it's rained for most of my time here. The peonies are battened flat against the grass, the petals pummeled off their stems; the lawn, though ecstatically green, is a marsh. Dennis was nevertheless determined to grill the meat outdoors (lamb again, this time drenched in coffee, of all things). Lillian held a golf umbrella over the chef and his fire; afterward, they came in wet, shivering and giggling, but bearing a platter of perfect pink lamb, its thin black crust pungently steaming.

The little girls ate with us, engulfing our attention; only after they were firmly put to bed did we discuss the one thing we'd been avoiding: division of material spoils. It was far easier than I'd expected, perhaps because the children's gaiety left us feeling friendly and generous. There wasn't much I wanted to pay to have shipped across an ocean; David, having claimed the house itself, conceded to Dennis the few pieces of furniture he wanted. Véronique—admirably, I couldn't help thinking—held her tongue about everything but the family silver. We did not mention Dad's ashes; there had been ceremony enough, and that would have to do.

My clothing is packed in a minute. I leave out khaki trousers, a comfortable cotton shirt, a jumper, a jacket with my passport tucked inside. My flight does not leave Prestwick till early afternoon, but Lillian will take me for a detour, one more visit to her doctor's clinic, one more "donation." I wince at the memory of yesterday, not so much all the drawing of blood and the prying questionnaires but the embarrassingly genial nurse who led me to my little room; the chair whose upholstery had clearly been waterproofed; the absurdly small cup with the wrapper so hermetically sealed that I had to open it with my teeth; the magazines and videos, all hilariously wrong. Thank heaven I'm a bloke with a good imagination.

Lil went with me. We were in David's pickup again, as we'd been after Dad's service. This time I insisted on driving. We had more than an hour on the road ahead of us, during which I had no earthly idea how we would manage to converse, so the minute we had both closed our doors, I turned to Lil and said, "Look. We're just going to pretend that this is perfectly routine and dull, what we're doing here, which means that we aren't going to discuss it. I have plenty of American friends who would howl at this approach as pathetically British, but that's what we are, isn't it? That's the fate of our natures."

She didn't laugh. Looking pained, she said, "I'm thinking about all these tests I'm forcing you to have. . . ."

"To get these tests behind me will be a relief. Like going to the dentist after great procrastination."

"That's very kind of you."

"See what I mean?" I laughed. "My dear, everything I'm doing here is very kind of me, it's more than very kind of me. That's not the point."

"No." She looked like she was going to cry. I was tired of seeing her cry. I took hold of her shoulder and shook her just a bit.

"Lillian, Lillian," I said, "you've been depressed for too long, you're in the habit. Where's the girl whose scanty dresses showed off her tits and knickers all over the place, leaving hard-ons right and left, who danced like a rock-star nymph in front of the masses? Where's the lass who sent me that passionate letter, who's determined to buck a few pretty lofty conventions to get what she wants?"

For a moment, I was afraid I had driven her deep into herself, that she would ask me to get out of the pickup, that she would back down. She closed her eyes and sighed loudly. She raised her hand, as if she were one of the schoolgirls she used to teach. "That girl's right here. Right here."

And off we drove.

From my childhood desk, I take my father's envelope. Once more, I empty its contents onto the bed. The lipstick, the drawing, my mother's kennel book, my birth certificate, the letter. I decide not to reread the letter, not now. It will only baffle and disappoint me again.

The medals and the key I found in the vase downstairs, those I leave on the table beside my bed; perhaps they have nothing to do with my parents at all. Perhaps David's right: the vase and its contents were left there by Tealing's previous owners (one of them exceptionally brave and, if he is still alive, missing the material proof, poor chap).

I take Mum's passport out of the desk as well and weigh it in my hand, wondering how serious a felony this theft would be; but who else would want it? Looking at her face, I remember something: all our family pictures. Unlike our father, Mum did not come from a "distinguished" or well-documented family; one of its few legacies—and that one perhaps not entirely authentic—is my name. Fenno, she told me, was the name of a fierce, courageous chieftain who lived in the remote Highlands several centuries back and kept his clan safe from marauders. He was part Viking, my grandmother claimed, explaining our pale hair and skin.

So the family photographs, the old ones, are nearly all of my father's more prosperous kin, and though Mum never spoke ill of these relatives, she kept their pictures—and even most of those taken of us, her sons—in a captain's chest under a paisley rug in the living room. In dividing up the larger, more visible objects, we forgot this slice of our past. I think I will not bring it up.

I slip everything, including Mum's passport, back into the envelope, the envelope into the side pocket of my bag.

I turn out my lamp and start toward the kitchen stairs, but I pause at another wave of laughter. How are we all so merry in the wake of a death? Are we reinforcing the parapets of life? I listen. Dennis's laugh is the loudest, David's the deepest-pitched. Lil's . . . Lil's is altogether new; I hardly heard it this past week. It is, to my ears, full of her new resolve, new gratitude, the sense of moving forward after standing still so long. I worry that circumstances will betray her again, but motion is what she needs right now, even if it's risky.

Véronique's laugh is, again to my biased ears, self-consciously seductive. Yet I find myself succumbing to a gratitude of my own; she has been mercifully discreet since our dreadful conversation in that paradise of a garden. She behaves as if it never happened. Yet the distance between us has acquired a bemused tenderness. At dinner, watching my nieces hold court, I thought of taking their father up on his repeated invitations to visit them in France; for the first time, I could picture myself in their mother's house, under her dictates, possibly even enjoying myself.

Thinking of the girls, I realize that I may not see them again before I leave, that I did not say good-bye. I open the door to the room where they are sleeping, my brothers' old bedroom. The glow of a night-light guides me along the straits between mattresses, suitcases, toys, and shoes. There is a cot set up for the baby: Christine sleeps hunched in a tangle of white wool, nested into a corner. Only her forehead and an eyebrow are showing. I reach into the cot and straighten the blanket over her body, pull it away from her face. Just as I have it perfect, she rolls over and twists it up again.

Théa and Laurie, though they have separate, adjoining mattresses, are sleeping together on one. Théa's body is draped half on the mattress, half on the floor. Laurie, the alpha sleeper, lies splayed on her back, one arm thrown dramatically across her sister's neck. Gently, I move Laurie's arm down by her side and pull a blanket across their bodies as well; they do not stir.

The two sisters sleep so silently, I have to peer carefully to see the motion of their breathing. If I kneel down to bring my ear close, I can hear it; it sounds literally pure, as if their lungs were lined with pristine wedding-gown satin. I wish for an instant that they were mine.

Their mattresses are near the ladder that leads to the foxhole. I look up, into darkness. The window is right there, but the moon and stars are well hidden by clouds. How long has it been since I climbed this ladder—twenty, twenty-five years? The opening at the top is narrow, difficult for all but the most nimble adults to pull themselves through.

Out of curiosity, I open the drawer of the nearest bedside table. After a snowstorm that knocked out power for a week when I was a child, Mum put torches in every room; David and Dennis each kept one at the ready.

So little here has changed, I marvel as my hand closes around the torch; it even works. When I turn the beam upward, it collides with the great fan-shaped window, revealing rivulets of steadily streaming rain that make a tiger pattern on the glass. All right, I think, and I climb. I knock my head against the rim of the opening but, with a little contortion, pull myself up and through. I sit cross-legged before the wide window, as we did when we were small, and switch off the torch. I wait patiently for my eyes to adjust, for the silhouettes of fields and woods to come clear. Now the kitchen voices are out of range; all I hear is the rain, its careless clatter. I begin to discern its differing impact on the leaves of the trees, on the slate terrace, against the windows and the shingles of the roof so close to my head, along the copper gutters shunting it away. These must be the melodies Felicity hears when she sings in return; she could easily outsing these torrents, and though her opera would be an imitation, her joy would be deep and real. I, too, seem to be a connoisseur of rain, but it does not fill me with joy; it allows me to steep myself in a solitude I nurse like a vice I've refused to vanquish.

I hear the burn now, too, its eager rushing. Its banks have filled enough this week that it is unusually noisy. I entertain memories of playing by its banks which have not crossed my mind in years. David, Dennis, and I would dig through the leafy mulch with our hands, carving out miniature rivers that meandered down the slope between the trees. This was a time before they doubted my dominion. I was head engineer and would order them to collect rocks and sticks of very particular dimensions, to fashion embankments and dams, bridges and jetties. When the design was complete, I would make them relay water in pots from the burn to the top of the slope, to pour through the waterways I had masterminded. When the burn was dry, we would bring water from the kitchen. We made boats from birchbark, buoys from conkers that fell from an old chestnut tree in front of the house.

In my memory, this type of play seems to extend over years of my life, but in reality it probably occupied us for a single set of seasons, spring to autumn, then became as dull and outmoded as the last year's fascination.

It is easy to imagine our parents spying on us through a window, sharing a moment of pride in our cooperation, our inventiveness, our diligence; picturing our respective futures as happy, productive, intelligent citizens—or even collectively, our lives plaited quite naturally into a family venture: Fenno McLeod & Brothers.

I felt as if a stone were plummeting from my throat to my groin when a new thought struck me: that soon there might be another child, mine but not mine, who would play among those trees by that burn, would grow up in the very house where I had grown up, perhaps in the very room, sleeping in the very bed, going (though I hoped not) to the very same schools. Which of the places, objects, and recreations surrounding me now had shaped which parts of my grown—or outwardly grown—self? Had they anything to do with my innate loneliness, my strange satisfaction at thinking myself so misunderstood, my reluctance to recognize love where I ought to have seized it?

My eyes have adjusted, and through the blur of rain the sky looks curiously bright. Lights are on in one of the distant houses built in a pasture where sheep used to roam; slender trees sway to and fro, unable to resist the rhythms of the wind. Off to the side, Mum's old kennel is a gnomelike mass—the only bit of our material past that David intends to expunge. Otherwise, I'm quite sure, the torches will remain in their appointed drawers, the dusty vases on their high shelves, the stalwart lilacs where they were planted before we were born. Perhaps my father's cabled jumper will remain on its hook in the kitchen, to sag yet further, toward his wellies on the floor below.

In New York, it is fashionable to dissect one's childhood publicly, to see the most ordinary events as the genesis of later failures, disappointments, betrayals. Dinner parties become roundtable discussions about what our parents' proclivities—how they disciplined or toilet-trained us, taught us to draw or ride a bicycle—"did" to us all. The past is a hall of mirrors, not of statues. I think of my mother's possible infidelities and mine; should I be hunting down some subtle connections there?

I look around me; predictably, the space is much smaller than I remember it. At the back are a few boxes which must contain toys we tired of: archery sets, elfin armies, incomplete packs of playing cards. But to the opposite side of the hatchway is an odd assembly of small shapes. On all fours, I crawl gracelessly around the opening to see it more clearly.

A dolls' tea party, much like the picnic under the lilacs. Of course: Laurie, perhaps even Théa, could climb up here and create a separate world, just as we had done. I am happy to see the parasol I gave Laurie, opened and propped in place by stacks of boyhood books, elegantly sheltering the party. The Chinatown doll and two French companions sit around a makeshift table laid with doll plates and cups (no ashtrays this time). The table, a box of some sort, is draped with an Hermès scarf patterned with poppies, and as I wonder whether Véronique permits such casual use of her overpriced accessories, something about the little table strikes me. I lift a corner of the scarf.

FRONT AND CENTER in Mal's vernal living room, the hospital bed looked like a slug on a gardenia plant. Mal was being released that afternoon, and Lucinda had asked me to shop. "Make the place extra-homey," she added. "Plump up the pillows and all that." I bought food—rice, crackers, soft American bread, plain white foods for the toothless—and various "aids" from the chemist which, though each innocuous (alcohol, cotton, peroxide . . .), unnerved me by their sheer number. At least, I reassured myself, adult nappies were not on the list.

What had happened was this. The night after I left for Paris, Mal had taken Lucinda out to a local restaurant—the Gondolier's Pantyhose, from her description. His appetite had been good, she said, but hers had not been good enough, and for that she did not know how to forgive herself. Happy with bread, Mal had ordered nothing to start, while she had ordered carpaccio. But it wasn't what she had expected, all that bright pink meat. She pushed it over to Mal, who said that suddenly, in fact, he was ravenous. "What the hell," he had said, though she hadn't understood why at the time. The more he could eat, the better, she had reasoned.

They had talked about his father's campaign (she had persuaded Mal to attend a Memorial Day parade in his parents' town) and then argued happily about the meaning of the word *miracle*. Lucinda had criticized her son for overusing it to refer to perfectly ordinary, if nevertheless astonishing, creations of God. "By that definition, *everything* is a miracle, which devalues His most extraordinary feats," she said with sunny indignation.

I indulged her digression; consciously or not, she was nailing down a memory for herself.

They had parted outside the restaurant. At three in the morning, she had been roused by the telephone. (This, I guessed, was when Mal had tried to reach me in Scotland.) Mal had got himself to the emergency room after waking up feverish and vomiting. The doctors were fairly certain that the beef was the source of the salmonella. "I had no idea the meat was *raw* or I never would have let him touch it!" said Lucinda. "I'm such a hick, I thought I was ordering an eggplant thing with capers I had in Boston once."

I had visited Mal the previous day, taking with me as laughably inadequate penance a splashy but scholarly volume on the history of Italian opera; he had seen it in a catalogue on my desk at the shop, so it would come as no grand surprise. I prepared myself for his anger, and for his appearance, which I supposed would be one of greater emaciation and pallor.

In my unflagging self-interest, I somehow assumed I would be his only visitor (other than his archangelic mother). So when I entered his room and saw four complete strangers around his bed, chatting and laughing, I could only stop in the doorway, dumb.

Mal saw me at once, or I might have left. "Fenno," he said smoothly, though he was hoarse, "meet a few of my ex-colleagues." I did not meet Mal's eyes until I had shaken hands with a dance critic, two food writers, and a copy chief. A large terra-cotta pot of moss and orchids posed effetely on a table, next to a telephone, a box of tissues, and a yellow plastic pitcher.

These people were more than old colleagues; they were friends. One of them, a stylish gray-haired woman, sat on the edge of Mal's mattress. A young man in black, the dance critic, poured him a cup of water.

Sometime in our acquaintance, I had forgotten that I was not a part of Mal's mainstream life, that he had chosen to keep me drifting along on my separate, obscure little tributary. I had forgotten that I was hardly his only source of help or companionship. I was a neighbor, a valet, a pet-sitter. I felt humbled and insulted.

When we looked at each other now, over the shoulder of the gray-haired woman, who was serving up some spicy rumor about someone whose name I knew vaguely as a byline somewhere in the paper, I could see no malice or anger in Mal's sunken eyes. It was as though he had no memory of our pact, that I would be there to make sure no one violated his dignity just to keep the electronic graph of his heart rising and falling into oblivion. I pictured him on a ventilator, a frightfully well-preserved man-size parsnip or celery stalk, and thanked whatever fortunes had pulled him out of the ICU.

So we had not yet been alone when I unpacked the provisions for his flat. After putting away the foods, I unwrapped the cut hyacinths I had bought at outrageous expense and arranged them in a purple glass pitcher from Venice. I laid a fire but did not light it, uncertain if smoke of any kind might be forbidden. Mum, in her last winter, could not tolerate a fire.

Outside, the light was failing; I switched on lamps. I sat on the couch against the windows, but this put me face-to-face with the hideous behemoth that had taken the place of the velvet chaise (now exiled to the dining room). As I returned to the kitchen to look for a beer or a bottle of wine, I heard Lucinda's voice in the stairwell.

When I opened the door, I could see Mal, supported between Lucinda and a strange man. I could see how quietly infuriated he was by their help and did not offer to join in. "Oh darling, will you put on some water for tea?" Lucinda called up when she saw me.

"Yes, everyone make their darling selves at home, pretty please," said Mal, his voice a hiss as he willed himself up the stairs.

The strange man was Mal's brother, Jonathan. He had Lucinda's curly auburn hair and slim, compact build, but a very different face, round and well-fed, a face without the character of bone. He seemed in a mild panic, anxious to do whatever was required but helpless without direction. "Oh! Yes!" he would exclaim when his mother asked him to fetch something or help her with the levers on the bed.

Mal sat sideways on the couch, knees drawn up, facing the fireplace.

He asked me to light the wood. "I'm not sleeping there," he told Lucinda as she fussed with the bed, trying to raise the upper half. "So send it back."

"You don't have to, certainly not now," she said, "but eventually you might find . . ."

"That I'm near enough death to do so."

Lucinda stood by the bed looking miserable. Jonathan excused himself to go to the loo. He'd done that just fifteen minutes before.

"I think you've had enough of my company for now," she said quietly. "Am I right?"

"Yes, Mother," said Mal. "Perhaps that's it."

She said to me, "Would you mind if Jonathan and I just . . . if we slipped out for a bite? We'll be back in an hour."

I told her that of course I didn't mind. I was relieved when Mal made no comment. (What made it my business to mind?) I think he just wanted them to leave.

It was hard not to stare. His Adam's apple protruded like a morsel of food trapped in his throat, and even through his T-shirt, the place where his clavicles came together looked too precise, the architecture of his body much too evident. The backs of both his hands were bruised purple and yellow from IVs, and there was a bandage at the base of his throat, probably a sign of intrusions which I had agreed to prevent—or, at the least, to oversee.

Looking at Mal in profile, I thought of the expression "so thin she disappears when she turns sideways," which I had heard someone use to describe one of these malnourished girls now looming above the city on billboards. That this aesthetic should be in fashion now seemed cruel, even sadistic.

I sat on the opposite end of the couch. For a time, we listened to the whipcracks and sizzlings of the fire.

"Thank you for the book. I looked at it before I went to sleep last night," he said.

"You're welcome. I bought a few for the shop."

"Carlo is a friend, you know. Did I mention that? We've been out of touch a year or so, but I've stayed at his house on Lake Como. He's done a very thorough job; I'll have to write him a note."

"The pictures are stunning," I said. "They make even me a little curious at what I may be missing."

Mal continued to focus on the fire. He smiled. "Operas are miracles, you know. How they come together, all those meticulous arts enfolded in one . . . A small miracle, mind you, not one of the big ones, not like babies and whales. I'm convinced of it, but my mother tells me I'm blaspheming."

"I heard about that. She's very dogmatic. She has to be."

"Yes . . . yes," Mal said slowly, "but she doesn't understand what I'm saying. That operas are a *proof* of something divine."

"She means that miracles aren't a proof. Aren't proofs of God, by their very intent, heretical? She means they're a demonstration. An end unto themselves."

"No, a random grace. Something like that." He sighed. The few words he'd uttered so far had chilled me. His voice sounded different, too calm. It felt as if he had gone away on one of those modern retreats which cleanse the brain but shrivel the soul.

After a long silence, he said, quite gaily, "So let me guess. While I was in the clutches of several Dr. Frankensteins—tubes in and out the wazoo—you were off somewhere with the ponytail, yes?"

"The . . . excuse me?" I'd known the pleasantry couldn't last.

"The fetching ponytailed boy—man, definitely man—you entertain from time to time. Though I haven't seen him in a while."

"I . . ."

At last, he looked straight at me. "Why have you taken such pains to hide him? Do you pay him? You're not homely enough to be that desperate." He smiled, as if he felt sorry for me. "Did you forget that my windows look into yours as well? The physics of reciprocity?"

"There's plenty of your life you've kept from me," I said.

"Was there some part of my life you knew about and wanted to know better? My privileged status at countless shallow cocktail parties, all that kissy-kissy closeness with famous and semifamous artists, was that something you wanted to share? I didn't think you cared about such things. I thought better of you. Or did you want in on my late-night crying jags?" He said all this with an almost happy calm, no sarcasm, no sorrow.

"Yes," I said. "I was with the ponytail—Tony. I don't know why I thought I'd fooled you."

"Why fool me to begin with?"

"I don't know."

"Because it's habit. Because hiding things is a habit with you. Even hiding things from yourself, hiding your head in the sand. What kind of a life do you have? Eating and walking and dreaming in a quarter-mile radius, just like a dog on a stake. Hanging out with Ralph Quayle, E.S.Q., Petty Emperor of Bank Street. Going home every Christmas to be with your nice but myopic brothers. People who can never quite love you, I'm sorry to say, because they will never quite understand you."

I did not answer. My power to defend myself had seized up like an ill-used joint. Out of the cerebral blue came my old mantra, my marching orders. Upright, upright, upright. Looking rigorously ahead, never down or to the side, had failed me. Dismally. I had meant it as a way to survive, and maybe I had, but I had not kept an eye on my footing, only on my direction.

"I'm sorry," I said. "You'll never know how sorry I am. I made the mistake of thinking—"

Mal interrupted, but wearily. "Well, I'm still alive, that should be something, shouldn't it? Though I do keep thinking of the drug they gave me to paralyze me, to keep me from fighting the ventilator. I'm not supposed to have any memory of that; I was in too deep a state of trauma, I'm told. Or of those electric smackeroos they applied to my chest . . . Now that, talk about miracles, now that starts you up again, I mean *wham*."

I saw Mal, lying on a table, clinically dead, and I saw Lucinda, pleading "Anything! Do anything, please!" and honestly, would I have overruled her? Or wasn't she there yet? Would I have been there first? Would Mal be dead now and I feel somehow proud, like a soldier who'd followed his orders under heavy fire? Wasn't it best that he was still here, as he admitted, kept among the living no matter what the methods?

"Now. It's time to talk about this thing." I looked up from my lap. Mal was pointing at the hospital bed. "Meet Death," he said to me. "Death," he said to the bed, "meet my dear friend Fenno."

I wanted to laugh but didn't.

"Do you know what my T-cell count is now? One hundred. In school, that's a perfect score, A-plus. But this isn't school. I'm a party of pathogens just waiting to happen. Ever heard of cryptococcal meningitis? Well. Just the sound of the name gives you a notion.

"So Mom, she's nothing if not a planner. She's brought in her lovely hospice people. I had a visit in my hospital room. A girl named Mary— how quaintly perfect—who looks like Candice Bergen times two. After she left, my teeth began to chatter." Mal raised his eyebrows, as if inviting me to comment, but he went on.

"You know, sheets, just bedsheets on my legs can be excruciating. It's sort of like having a sunburn but worse. The hairs on my legs bore down into their follicles like tiny pins. Carlo's book? To read it, I had to set it beside me on pillows. Sometimes I'm certain my eyelids are crushing my eyeballs, and when I climb stairs, every little gismo in my knees puts up an independent protest. There's so much physical *pressure*. I don't want to die, but I would love to trade in my body—for just about anything. Last week, or two weeks ago, I've lost track—anyway, before this crisis, my tiny inner guests who trashed their suite so rudely—I was out at Montauk with friends—yes, real, true-blue friends you've never met, and I'm sorry if somehow this made you feel bad, not meeting them all, I'm sorry. . . . Did it ever occur to you that I kept you from the rest of my life so I could keep you to myself?" He paused to regard me fiercely, angrily, but he clearly did not want me to answer because, just as quickly, he looked away.

"We went to the beach. There was a break in the cold, the sun was heavenly, so we took chairs and blankets and a thermos of cocoa. One of the children had that fabulous idea. The ocean was this incredible blue, a kind of not-quite-black, waves chopping all around, and this one sleek speedboat bouncing along. They waved, we waved. . . . It was so white, so . . . jaunty. It would leap on a wave and hover, for long moments, entirely free of the water. Like a high note held impossibly long. . . ."

He took a drink of water from the glass his mother had set on the table before she went out. "God how I envied that boat. So solid, so buoyant, so jazzy-looking. I just wanted to be that boat. I wanted to swap my body for that fiberglass hull, those polished rails, those racing stripes, that perfectly planed wooden deck. It felt like lust, I wanted it so badly. I'd have given up my brain, no problem. If I hang on much longer, I'll be giving that up anyway, you know."

The telephone, which Lucinda had also set close to Mal, rang. "Hello, Dad," he said. "Yes, I'm home. Yes, I hope so. No, she isn't."

They spoke, about the superficial details, for five minutes or so. Mal promised that his mother would call back when she returned.

He asked me to bring him a couple of pillows from his bed. I helped him arrange them so that he could recline on his back facing the fire. He winced as he rearranged his limbs.

I put another two logs on the fire and prodded them until their bark gave in to the flame.

"I told Susan," said Mal, "I feel like three aspirin would kill me. She told me not to be deceived. The body can be quite resourceful in stopping just short of that final surrender, unwilling to evict its oldest tenants. Not like any landlord I've ever known." He laughed faintly.

I could not have spoken if someone had held the brass poker to my jugular vein. I fussed about in every way I could find that kept my back to Mal, sweeping up ashes, straightening the basket of papers and kindling, examining an amethyst egg on the mantel as if I had never admired it before. But my defense was pointless.

"*Basta,*" he said at last, confirming my fears. "*Basta, basta, basta*—as my old friend Carlo and his compatriots would say. *Basta.*" This time the word sounded gentle, not angry. Almost sentimental.

THIRTEEN

EVER BENT ON AUTONOMY, Mal wanted to be alone in the end, but this did not mean he could do without help. Months before, he had gone to one of his doctors (Dr. Susan, I presumed, but he would not say) and expressed what he saw as his very rational despair. He had been told that doctors cannot ethically give out certain information, but a week or so later the doctor had asked about insomnia and pain, dispensed certain drugs, and warned Mal explicitly how to make sure he did not overdose or combine drugs that should not be combined.

That week he kept mostly to his bed—his own. Contemptuously, he made the hospital bed a waystation for miscellaneous books, magazines, coats and other items of clothing. The gypsy caravan, he called it.

There were visitors every day; from my desk in the shop, I would sometimes see them ring his bell and go up, emerging within the hour. I saw one man step out onto the pavement, cover his face for a moment, look upward at nothing and sigh a voluminous sigh, his breath a visible cloud of there-but-for-the-grace-of-God relief. Lucinda spent as much time with Mal as he would allow; he had strictly forbidden her to miss any classes. Jonathan, whose limp demeanor I excused to fear, returned north the day after Mal came back to his flat. The sister had planned a visit but then was banned because one of her children caught the flu.

On Wednesday, Mal took his parents to a matinee of a Noël Coward play. The Senator (whom I would not meet until Mal's memorial service) flew up from Washington for the day. On Thursday, Mal asked to be left alone until evening. He wrote letters, I suppose, since he gave me several to mail when I came by to fix dinner. Most of them were rich with stamps, addressed to France, Italy, Switzerland; one to Chile. As it turned out, he wasn't hungry, and we watched *An American in Paris,* which happened to be on the telly; Lucinda arrived during the opening titles. I had moved the television back into the bedroom, so the three of us sat on the bed, propped against pillows.

Mal beamed when Gene Kelly and that obscure but quintessential Frenchman stood up from their café chairs to sing "'S Wonderful."

"Is there anything in our culture these days that expresses this much silly joy?" he asked. "Anything like this that we're allowed to say we love without being smirked at?"

"Thank heaven your culture isn't mine!" Lucinda said. "Anyone who'd say they didn't love this I would erase from my address book."

Mal snorted. "Not if they had deep pockets."

Gently, she slapped him on the arm. "You are one mean child." She rested her cheek on his shoulder.

I excused myself and went to the loo. I sat on the closed toilet until I felt calm again.

Friday evening, I put on my grandfather's tuxedo. It had been cleaned but not worn since the night Mal had borrowed the shirt. It was early yet, and I sat in my living room with Rodgie beside me on the couch and Felicity perched on a hand. I did not allow her up on a shoulder, afraid she might soil my suit, though she was rarely so inconsiderate. With my other hand, I stroked Rodgie; glutton for affection, he groaned and pushed his head up against my palm. I stared at the clock; leaning beside it was a postcard I had received that day from Tony. *Thanks for your presence,* it read. *You make me glow. Surprises me every time. I'm selling you by the dozen, you might like to know. See you back there in a month. (Don't ask for royalties, rich boy.)* I surveyed my living room and had a flash of objectivity in which I saw how dull it looked.

I was to go by Mal's flat first, then Lucinda's. We would take a taxi to a restaurant that overlooked the northern reaches of Central Park, to a gala benefit, dinner and dancing, raising money so that disadvantaged children could take music lessons. Mal had received the invitation. He told us (though I was in on the pretense) that the two of us needed a fine night out. Lucinda had passed her midterms; a week of warm wind goaded us toward spring. There were things to celebrate, he said, and so, knowing how much Lucinda loved dancing, he had bought the tickets. We were forbidden to decline.

I said good-bye to the animals and turned off all the lights but one. Halfway down the stairs, I stopped. I returned to my flat. Felicity was settling onto her perch, helping herself to her fruit cup, picking out morsels of banana, her favorite. Grapes would be next, then apples.

I put a banana in the pocket of my overcoat and held out my hand. "Come, lass." She flapped her wings as we left the flat, nervous and eager. Before we went outside, I folded her inside my coat against my chest.

Mal had all his lights on; I wondered if his sight was failing, too. When I let my coat fall open and Felicity saw where she was, she let out a long, loud call and flew. She made a low swift circuit of the living room and shot back toward the bedroom. She flew laps, calling out with obvious delight. Parrots' memories, it's said, are as sharp as their lives are long. Mal was sitting on the couch. He watched her with a smile until she made a landing, at last, on my shoulder. I moved her onto the back of the couch, next to Mal.

"Well, doctor, the transfer is complete," he said. He reached up slowly to scratch Felicity's neck. He moved now as if underwater; even this small motion must have hurt. "Thank you," he said.

We had an hour before I would leave to meet Lucinda. I still had not made up my mind if it would be right to try and dissuade him. But I could not get past imagining the words "Are you sure" or "Don't you think." He would outtalk me, as he always had. And he would be angry.

I could hear Mal's breathing. His lungs, which had not recovered fully from the trauma of his infection (and probably never would), were as terminally tired as his limbs; only his mind seemed agile now. This, Mal had argued, was essential. It was what he called the fulcrum point. You do not wait until your mind goes, too.

"You're staring at me," he said. "As if you're a bystander to a wreck."

"I just don't want to believe . . ."

Mal closed his eyes. A fringe of tears formed on the lashes. He wiped them away. "Shut up," he said quietly. "Shut up and will you for fuck's sake live. I am not going to dwell on you now, though I could say a few things. I am simply going to order you to live. Fucking, pissing, shitting live."

His crying was an awful sound, because he would not accept it. His pride had not tired, either.

I sat beside him. I put a hand on his hands, which were clenched in his lap. He did not pull them away. With a deep harsh breath, he stopped crying.

Felicity had flown across the room and settled on one of the chrome railings of the hospital bed. Mal looked at her and said, "I wish it would rain."

I asked him if he wanted a fire, and he said no. He asked me to help him back to the bedroom, into his bed. Felicity followed us, landing on a chair. She watched us intently for a few seconds; something was odd about the way these flightless creatures moved and spoke today, something was out of the ordinary, but we did not hold her interest for long.

"I want you to tell me everything, so I know you know the script," said Mal. I reviewed it all, as if I were his dutiful son, and then I fetched everything he told me he would need. I counted out the pills—morphine and, as Mal liked to call them, his Klaus Barbitols—and put them in a saucer beside the bed. I poured vodka into the purple glass pitcher from Venice. I pushed the empty vials down into the kitchen rubbish, which I would tie up and take outside when I left.

I peeled the banana I had brought and put it on another saucer, which I set on Mal's desk in the bedroom, next to a ramekin I'd filled with water. His computer was gone—given away, perhaps, like the flute.

"You're leaving her?" said Mal.

"Unless you don't want me to."

"Oh I'd like her to stay. I may hear her sing yet." He looked at me. "You'd never clip her wings, would you?"

"No," I said. "Of course not."

He said quietly, "She was deprived of the jungle and her fellow creatures, and for that I've sometimes felt guilty. I would never—never—take from her the gift of flight."

For so many months, I had believed I was waiting for his death, as if I just wanted to finish a chapter in my personal story. Not like the end of Mum's life, when I had childishly imagined so many scenarios of healing: sudden remission, a diagnostic error; presto, a new magic bullet of a drug!

"I've been a terrible friend," I said as I stood at the foot of Mal's bed.

"No," he said. "You've been an excellent friend. Fallible but excellent. What you have been terrible at is something else, something we're not going to talk about now. There's no more time for you, I'm sorry." He spoke with abrupt strength, and I knew that from the moment I closed his door behind me until my appointed return in the morning, I would play out a thousand of the same wishful scenarios I had for Mum.

"Take this quilt off the bed. I don't want it ruined," he said.

I pulled Lucinda's quilt off his legs. I folded it—the assembly of all those fine dresses, those evenings of dance and festivity—and laid it on a wooden trunk which I knew held clean sheets and blankets and a gold silk dressing gown, a gift from a long-ago fly-by-night lover. Too ludicrous to wear, said Mal, but much too fabulous not to keep. I had come to know this home as well as any I'd ever lived in myself.

He told me to go. Just before I reached the door, I heard him laugh his exhausted laugh. I looked back toward the bedroom. He said, "She's tickling me." He sat on the edge of his bed, Felicity on his shoulder, shoving her beak behind his ear. "Go," he said again, his face a brief illusion of joy.

Lucinda opened her door with a similar expression: the smile of a girl greeting the boy of her dreams. She looked so magnificent, it broke my heart. She spun around and said, "How about *this,* young man?" as she held out the wide shiny skirt of a dress that shimmered both orange and green in the light. "I just learned the name of this fabric. It's called 'doupioni silk'—like something a maharanee would wear. I saw it in the window of this vintage shop around the corner. I hardly came equipped with a ball gown!"

She told me I looked handsome. I helped her on with her coat, and she took my arm in a manner befitting the era of her dress. In the taxi, she began to talk about Mal. I had vowed to find a way to talk of other things—her vocation, her husband, her religion, her politics, her quilting, anything else—but I felt too numb to make the effort.

The restaurant had an extraordinary view. On this cold black night, the park looked like a velvet sea, with patches of phosphorescence where lamps shone up through the skeletal trees. A quartet played all the songs Lucinda loved: Gershwin, Porter, Jerome Kern. When we danced (I was glad for my strict boyhood training), she sometimes sang the lyrics over my shoulder. "You're such a good sport to do this," she said at one point as we looped about the floor. "I'm almost falling in love."

"I'm not a good sport. I'm having a lovely time, too," I said. On any other night, this would have been true.

I ordered champagne with our dinner; Mal had told me that this was the one thing she would drink to excess. He hoped it would make her sleep late. After two glasses, she became teary and said, "Two more months. That's all I'm bargaining for when I pray. His doctor told me that wasn't an unrealistic hope. Just till we've had some real spring."

I gave her my handkerchief. "You've been through a lot. I admire you incredibly."

She blew her nose. "Oh no. I've led a completely charmed life until now. I have been the antithesis of Job."

"I know about Jonathan's cancer," I said. "That must have been an ordeal. I'm sure you still worry about him."

Lucinda set down her glass. "What cancer?"

"His . . . Hodgkin's? The summer before Mal was to go off to Juilliard?"

She looked out the window at the view. Her expression was impossible to read. "Mal told you Jon had Hodgkin's disease?"

"He said that's why he stayed up north instead of . . ."

"That's not . . ." She sipped champagne. "Sometimes Mal tells odd lies, his imagination gets a little out of control. He has such an imagination." She shook her head, looking perplexed.

I felt disoriented at her revelation but wanted, yet again, to flee from discussing Mal—especially, right now, from discussing how honest or dishonest he might be. I told her it was time to dance again.

We closed down the party, as I had been instructed we should do. The last song was "A Hundred Years from Today." Lucinda did not sing the words; I hoped she didn't know them. *Don't save your kisses,* warns the song. *Be happy while you may.*

In the taxi, Lucinda leaned against my coat, crying and reminiscing about her son as a baby. She was saying, "You know, I breast-fed that child," when we stopped in front of her building. "Almost no one did back then, you know. Not in Boston, where we were living while Zeke finished his degree. He did it like a natural, Mal, he just came out knowing what to do, how to survive. He did everything early and well—walk, talk, everything. My other children had to be coached and nurtured along. But that's Malachy: he just knows *how,* he's just so . . . masterful. And a know-it-all. Never stops correcting people. I tried to break that habit when he was little, I told him it would make him lonely, but would he listen? Well, what a silly question, right?"

She refused to let me see her upstairs; the temperature had plummeted, and she was sure I'd never get another taxi. I could not find the right thing to say before we parted; when I saw her again, circumstances would surely have estranged us. In the end, we just held each other like old friends after a reunion.

INCHES AWAY FROM MY SKULL, rain gives the roof a good thrashing. I sit with my boxed-up father in my lap. Mal was packaged the same way, but Lucinda chose a high-end container, cherry with a coffin-like finish, even if it was to serve its purpose for only a few months. It did not take her long to forgive me my complicity—either because she was in fact a saint or because Mal had explicitly asked her to in a letter left beside his bed. Up in Vermont that June, after we dropped the ashes in Lake Champlain, after I brushed the last of them from my clothes, after the mass Lucinda arranged, she showed me the letter. It began, *Dear Mom, Before anything else, I have to demand this one thing: Burn me. Get rid of this body. I don't care what you do by way of rites—have Kenny Rogers call a square dance, I don't care—but burn me.*

After my evening out with Lucinda (my second betrayal to undo my first), I went home and changed into ordinary clothes. Mal did not want me to go to his flat before dawn, but I did not want to sleep. I sat in my living room, Rodgie beside me, and wrote down ideas for making this room a happier, more stylish place. I fell asleep despite myself and woke, my face in Rodgie's fur, to the wail of a car alarm. It was six, the sky an indeterminate gray.

I hurried into shoes and a coat. What must not occur was an early-morning visit from Lucinda. She had, more than once, shown up in Mal's kitchen just after sunrise bearing fresh bread and fruit. He had not liked these visits, but he understood her anxiety. She would have been awake for hours, just waiting for the earliest possible time her arrival might seem acceptable.

I stood for several minutes outside Mal's door, key in lock, before I could let myself in. The first thing I saw was Felicity, her gorgeous red plumage a flame in the strengthening light. She slept on the chrome railing of the gypsy caravan; its circumference must have felt just right for her feet. When I closed the door, she raised her head and called to me. She flew to my shoulder. At moments, she looked so startling in her surroundings that she reminded me of the angel in paintings of the Annunciation. What were the angel's first words? Fear not.

I stood and listened. I heard nothing. I walked through the orderly kitchen past the loo and down the hall. It was still nearly dark in the bedroom, but I could see Mal. He lay face down, his head and one arm hanging over the edge of the bed. I listened again. My greatest fear had been that I would walk in on death throes, unearthly groanings, the kind of breathing I had heard from my mother before she died. My greatest hope had been that I would find an irate insomniac Mal, reading or watching the telly, saucer of pills and pitcher of vodka untouched on the table beside him.

I looked at the table. Empty saucer. Pitcher three-quarters full. The plastic bag unused; something about that consoled me. I did not know if Mal was dead, but he was still. His face lay against the side of the mattress. The bony fingers of his fallen arm rested on the floor. What if he were merely asleep? As I moved closer to the bed, I smelled something awful. The exposed sheets looked wet or stained. Out of terror more than sorrow, I began to cry.

Felicity brushed her head against my ear, knocked her beak on my temple, the signal that she was impatient for food. I reached up and touched her. I pulled myself together.

I pushed Mal's upper body back onto the bed. It was astonishingly light, like the body of a lifeless songbird. His skin felt cool, but it might have been cooled by sweat. I felt no breath; I did not want to try to detect a pulse, and he had not asked this of me.

I went to the file cabinet and pulled out the medical folder he had shown me. It was thick with photocopied prescriptions. I had never paid close attention to the particulars of Mal's medicines, to the cause-and-effect connections of this symptom with that drug, this drug with that life-sustaining cellular process. The names of the drugs were surprisingly few, but their repetition, over sheet after sheet, astounded me. They read like an inventory of the important things in life I refused to know.

If it looked as if Mal had succeeded, I was to find and remove all prescriptions for the pills which Mal had used to kill himself. They were clipped together at the back and had come from three different doctors. Mal did not want to risk incriminating them—or have his mother blame them.

When I had folded the incriminating papers and stuffed them into my coat pocket, I took Felicity into the kitchen. From another pocket, I took a bag of seeds and emptied it into a teacup. I took an apple from a bowl of fruit and cut it up. I left her on the counter, eating.

I felt calmer. I returned to the bedroom and looked around, everywhere but at the bed itself. I did not know what I was looking for. A final memory for deliberate imprinting?

What caught my eye was a red leather box on the floor beside the bed. It was the kind of box used to file photographs. The label inside the small brass frame read CHRISTOPHER.

Christopher? I sat on the floor and, weak-willed as ever, took the lid off the box. Inside was a scant collection of papers and photographs. Fifteen or twenty photographs, mostly of a child, a boy. One of Mal's little nephews? But in a few pictures, the boy was much older, at least sixteen. In the latest, he was graduating from high school. Among the papers were two letters addressed to Mal in a careful feminine script, the return address in New Hampshire. (That far I did not go; I set the letters aside.) There was also a letter, older, postmarked May 2, 1968, from Lucinda. It was addressed to Mal at college.

Close the box, I admonished myself. Close the box. I intended to, but before I did, I pulled from the very bottom a newsletter. It was called *Notes in a Major Chord,* dated Summer 1967. On the front page was a picture of a pretty teenage girl, clasping a cello between her knees, and two boys, one at a harpsichord, the other holding a flute. The story was headlined "Spirited Young Trio Delve Boldly into Baroque." They were posing, not playing, and the flutist, with a homely brush cut but an adorable smile, was Mal. He rested one hand on the nearest shoulder of the cellist.

The cellist—she had to be; of course she was—she would be the one with whom he had fallen "a little in love."

I looked again at the boy in the gown and tasseled cap; I looked at his eyes. Pale and incisive, they were so unmistakably Mal's. And then I did close the box—though how desperately now I wanted to read those letters. How much did Lucinda, mother of mothers, have to do with this boy's life, with his very being? Back then, had there even been a choice for the pretty young cellist, even without Lucinda's persuasive meddling?

Like a fever, a series of feelings that seemed entirely wrong for the moment but which I could not suppress overwhelmed me: envy toward the cellist who had been Mal's lover, if only once perhaps, if only as a misguided tribute toward her talent; irritation toward Lucinda, though I could only guess her place in this drama; and a creeping contempt at the lie Mal had told about Jonathan to cover up what he must have looked back on as a crisis he should never have allowed to change his life the way it did. Or maybe it had freed him. I would never know, because this time, between life and nonlife, there had been no choice, not as Mal had seen it.

And then I thought of the lie I had told about one of my own brothers, to cover up a folly of my own.

Kneeling beside the bed, I rested my cheek in the small of Mal's back. I stayed that way a long time. Then I moved to the living room, where I sat facing the street for another two hours, composed and silent, until the phone rang.

"Hello there, you." Lucinda, hungover and footsore but thrilled to hear my voice. She'd had such a wonderful time that she felt as if she'd been a faithless wife. "But never mind; do you think we could do it again?" was the last happy thing I heard her say until, in May, she called me from Vermont and asked me to help with a memorial party.

I told her right away what I had found, as if I had just dropped by, just to check in. By the time she arrived, she had guessed at my collusion. She said coldly, before her emotions took over, "He wasn't yours to let go."

She wouldn't let me touch her. Through the comings and goings (police, medical examiner, neighbors from below and above), she did not look at me once, but I made myself stay. In the late afternoon, when the light was the same shade of gray it had been when I came over, I tucked Felicity into my coat and crossed the street. Poor, neglected Rodgie had wet the bedroom carpet; he looked at me with shame, not reproach. I cried, for only the second time that day, as I hugged him and put on his leash.

When we returned from a long walk, I played the two messages on my answering machine. One was from Ralph, asking where the devil I'd been all day, why hadn't I opened the shop, and the other was from Dennis, the first part muffled by clinking coins and laughter. ". . . You've got to forgive me I didn't ring the minute she came out,

I've been just insane, dashing every which way, living this incredible dream! She's like this tiny . . . God, this tiny angel, I mean literally, everything but the wings! And Vee's in super shape—she was a force of nature! I'm sending pictures by overseas express. Ring and tell me if she doesn't look just like Dad, I swear. But wait, don't try to reach me, I'll ring you later. I'm the happiest madman who ever lived! I'm going to need weights in my shoes!" Two days before, on the first of March, Laurie had been born.

Within weeks, Ralph broke off with the architect. We resumed our spinsterish dinners, and I listened to him rant about the cruel vanity of our gender (from which Ralph claimed exemption). The architect had harped on him constantly to work out, play tennis, run, do anything to rid himself of his middle-aged gut. This was about his *health,* for heaven's sake, and how, in this day and age, could you turn your back on *that?*

"Well just let him try to captivate some studly young washboard. Good luck to him," seethed Ralph. As a consolation prize, I gave in on souvenir totebags, as I had given in on T-shirts. We had now hired two full-time workers, and Ralph's latest notion was that we should open a branch in the Hamptons ("Brookhaven's yet to do in the birdlife!"). As further succor to his maimed ego, Ralph began shopping for a house in Amagansett or Montauk, already fantasizing about retirement. When I told him that another shop would stretch us too thin, he said teasingly, "And there'd always be a room for you, my dear." I would wait to give in on this one.

Tony returned to New York in June, not long after I returned from Vermont. He surprised me uncomfortably, of course, showing up at the shop right before a reading, and when I saw him—the sheen of his tanned skin and his hair, now trimmed to a sort of Brideshead Revisited swing—my knee-jerk desire was dampened by a mixture of anguish and boredom. Boredom at the thought of our certain routines, our certain distance. During the reading, we kissed furtively in the garden, but I made excuses and did not invite him upstairs. For two weeks, I kept him at arm's length, until I felt sure enough to say that I wasn't in the mood anymore. I wanted something else, or maybe nothing, for a while. He was angry but (yes, Ralph) too vain to reveal it. A few months later he called, and we began to meet again, just once in a while, at our Thai restaurant. We make each other laugh, share the bill, then go our separate ways. Sometimes I feel an itch, but I remind myself that I like him better this way. He still gives memorable gifts, if only on conventional occasions, and his pictures still sit unframed in my cupboard. He doesn't ask.

By Christmas, I had let two men lure me out of my cave. They didn't stick, but they did not leave me hopeless. I began to accept, even seek, invitations to leave the city; I let the assistants run the shop for entire weekends. I bought a new couch, a new table and chairs, hired the boy across the street to paint my living room persimmon red. When I saw the room finished and empty, I wanted to weep—"Don't they call this color 'bordello'?" said Ralph—but then I got the idea of repossessing Audubon's flamingo from the shop. Around this great picture, which commandeered a wall, the color found a purpose. And at night, like lipstick, it flattered my occasional guests and made them feel festive.

As I made these changes, Felicity watched with consternation and yodeled an alarm at the arrival of each new object in her domain. I soothed her with papaya, fresh coconut, and frequent visits to the birdbath in the garden. Rodgie was happy; the new couch was deeper and softer. Such plain pleasures, I thought as my animals adjusted.

These are the events I replay, five years later, as I crouch in the attic of the wonderful house which I can never quite believe is no longer my home. Just as I can never quite believe, though now I think I must, that to love me, my family does not need to understand me. There, Mal was wrong.

Perhaps I have been talking to myself, or perhaps the laughter downstairs has become even louder; something, over the rain, must have woken Laurie, because suddenly this small ghostly creature stands at the top of the ladder. *"Onco? Onco, tu es triste?"* she whispers. She climbs up and sits down beside me. She touches my damp cheek.

I put an arm around her. "No, sweetheart, not sad. Not exactly. But . . . *mon coeur est fatigué."* It is the simplest explanation I can find; how could I tell her that my heart is in fact imploding?

Laurie looks into my face, her eyes wide. "I will get Davi's *écouteur!"* she exclaims.

I smile at her sweet logic. "No, no," I say, patting my chest, "my heart is going to be perfectly fine, it just needs a little rest."

She looks at my lap, at the box, and I know from her expression that her mother asked her about it, if she'd seen it anywhere. I lay a hand on top of the box. "You know what this is?"

She nods. "Grand-père," she says quickly, then sets her jaw.

"You know that we've been looking for Grand-père."

She nods again. Now she is the tearful one.

I stroke her hair. "I promise you won't be in trouble." A brave promise. "Not in big trouble," I amend.

"Please don't throw Grand-père in the ocean," she pleads. "I heard that! I heard they want to throw him in the ocean. But not you!"

I set the box aside and pull Laurie into my lap. "Oh lass, is that why you've brought him up here?"

Another fast nod.

I look out into the night and ponder how to explain this to a five-year-old. I rock her a little as I think; strange how the motion comes so naturally to my arms. "You miss Grand-père."

"*Oui,*" she breathes, in this one word a sliver of a glimpse of the Frenchwoman she will become, voice as much a seduction as hips or legs. "He said he was going to take me to a castle, he said there's a big huge castle on a hill, with soldiers and cannons, and he was going to show me."

Out of all our castles (barbaric Scotland mercifully in ruins), I wonder which one Dad promised and realize, of course: Edinburgh Castle, quite unlike any in France, so thoroughly male (even if the soldiers do wear skirts). I will take her at Christmas, but now is not the time to say so. I say, "He would have loved that."

We sit quietly for a moment. "I had a friend who died," I say, "and we, his friends, we put him in a beautiful lake. It's a place where he liked to play when he was a small boy. In the summer, he used to go to a house beside that lake and swim, and sail in boats, and catch fish. He loved that lake. So we thought he would like to go back to that lake."

"Was he a small boy when he died?" Laurie asks.

"No," I say. "Much, much, much older."

"Why couldn't they keep him in the house, or bury him in the garden?"

"He liked the house and the garden, but he loved the lake. He loved swimming in the water." I do not even know if this was true; Mal never spoke to me about the cabin on Lake Champlain, but Lucinda showed me albums of pictures: summer after summer of Mal on the dock with his father and brother and sister, Mal diving, Mal in a canoe. Mal, arms and legs akimbo, midair between a tire swing and his own impending splash.

I remember those pictures well, if I want to, but when I think of Mal, I think of Mal in a tuxedo, Mal on his green chaise, Mal bent over an oven to inspect a flan, Mal with Felicity prodding his neck as he reaches up to poke her back and say, respectfully, "That's enough, sweets."

Laurie's hair against my chin reminds me of Felicity's softness. Suddenly, I miss her terribly. I wish for her wing on my cheek, her nonsense in my ear. Here is a longing I can safely admit.

Once Mal's ashes were in that lake, I began to miss him, to grieve for him, in earnest. These rites do somehow make a difference, take you round a corner. With Lucinda's permission (even blessing), I took three things that belonged to Mal: the quilt made from dresses Lucinda had danced in, their surfaces slippery and rich; Mal's passport, a patchwork of the world he had known; the Guatemalan birthing chair. The picture of "La Sultane Bleue" still hangs on my kitchen wall.

In Vermont, among the hundreds of faces in that flowered meadow beside the lake, I searched in vain for Mal's secret son, those ice-blue eyes, listened for someone to call out the name Christopher, so that I might have another kind of keepsake. I could not believe I would never meet the boy, but why should I deserve such a grand stroke of fate? What did I think my life was—an opera?

If I look out my front windows, straight across the street, I sometimes see a young woman. I think she works long hours, as she is rarely there, coming home after dark in conservative, mannish suits. When she turns on her lights, I see a poster of orchids where Mal put his Chinese carpet. That carpet through that window, on that night of sleeplessness we shared before we even met, was my first glimpse of an entire life I might have shared, a love I managed to lose without knowing it was mine.

Laurie is asking me if her grandfather loved the ocean the way my friend loved his lake, and someone is calling my name, in a loud whisper, from the hall outside the room below. I tell Laurie we have to go down; I let her go first. When I recognize the voice as Véronique's, I decide to leave Dad up in the foxhole for now.

By the time I reach the bottom of the ladder, she is standing in the middle of the room holding Laurie in her arms, quietly scolding her. She smiles at me. She whispers, "Well! What schemes are you creating? We came to believe you had fled!" She does not sound the least bit cross.

"We were playing, Maman," whispers Laurie. She looks at me desperately. I give her a reassuring nod.

"But you are to be sleeping, *chérie.*" Véronique lays Laurie down on her mattress, next to Théa, straightening sheets and blankets, making everything smooth and secure. She kisses her two older daughters; Théa sleeps on.

I kiss Laurie and wink. I tell her I will be leaving too early to say good-bye, that I will see her at Christmas. She smiles up at me, then reaches out to hug me tight before she closes her eyes.

In the hall, Véronique says, "Are you meaning to escape?"

"No," I say. We start downstairs to the kitchen. "I was wandering about, and I was waylaid—by memories and then by your daughter."

"Denis is this way, too, when we are here—what you say about memories." She sighs, resigned to the tidal pull of our family.

At the bottom of the stairs, I squint at the brightness, even though the light is cast mostly by candles. I am met with a fond, tipsy explosion of voices.

"*There* he is!" David and Dennis, in unison.

"Thought you could go to ground?" David again.

"We'd begun to think you'd slipped out for a tryst," says Lil.

Dennis laughs theatrically. "In the bloody monsoon!"

I raise my eyebrows, trying for coy. "Well I did, in a way."

Kind-hearted jeers, even from Véronique. Someone pulls out the chair where I sat for dinner. Someone fills my wineglass, which no one removed. I prepare myself, but happily, for more memories, more drink—too many, too much—and think of the moment when I will open the door to my true, my chosen home, to that laughably daring red room, throw down my baggage, greet my bird and my dog, and unplug my phone. Not because I won't be glad to hear my friends' voices but because I will need to sleep for hours and hours before waking to look again at the life I am learning, just learning to live.

Boys

1999

FOURTEEN

"Bats," Tony says when mosquitoes drive them inside from the porch. "What we need here is bats." He crowds their dishes and glasses onto a tray, refusing to let her carry so much as the peppermill.

Fern holds the door open. "You could install one of those bat condominiums, a thank-you gift to your host."

Tony looks indignant. "Let's keep straight who's doing who the favor."

"That's right; you never owe anyone anything, do you?"

Pointedly ignoring her jab, he muses, "Though bats might be too rude. Bet they'd offend the face-lift brigade down below. Bet those old-money types repel mosquitoes all on their own. Blood too blue for sucking, veins too leathery to puncture."

In the kitchen, he realigns their dinner plates and lights a pair of candles. He even refolds their napkins. Tony has grilled salmon fillet and plum tomatoes, serving them with rice into which he stirred lemon juice and a handful of herbs chosen haphazardly from the garden behind the house. Fern detects lavender, which she's sure he wouldn't know from thyme or sage: it's odd but compelling and happens to work out fine—like a lot of things in Tony's mostly fortunate life.

This house—a shingle cottage on a mapled lane in Amagansett, the latest coup of Tony's ruthless charm—is nearly on the water. The "face-lift brigade" are the neighbors who own the larger, grander house that stands downhill between this one and the ocean, an older couple whom Tony seems to have befriended in less than two weeks. That afternoon, they waved from their porch as Tony led Fern around their tennis court and down the steps from their magnanimous, well-nurtured lawn onto the sand.

Fern has known Tony for more than ten years. In that time she's seen him in twice as many temporary settings, houses borrowed from professors on sabbatical, divorcees on consolation leave, grown children re-

269

cently orphaned and waiting for a spike in the Manhattan real-estate market. An apartment on West End Avenue with four colossal bedrooms and wedding-cake ceilings, an elfin clapboard house in the Village, a Gropius glass box in Litchfield—those were her favorites. This one is almost too pretty for comfort, as spotlessly lavish, as bright and docile, as a house in a magazine. It comes with an aged Volvo, an aged spaniel (now snoring beside Tony's chair), and a well-established gardener's garden, the kind that demands as much work as it gives beauty. But such responsibilities are perfect for Tony, who has a knack for plants and pets alike. Especially dogs; Tony loves dogs with a tender, democratic affection he rarely if ever shows people. Whenever he meets a new dog, he kneels, opens his arms, and eagerly whispers, "Hi puppy hi puppy hiya puppy." Fern has witnessed this greeting on countless occasions—with, depending on the occasion, amusement, sorrow, or furtive rage.

She refills his wineglass. "So who *is* your host—your grateful, eternally indebted host?"

"English professor, semiretired. Owns a couple of bookstores."

"And you know him because . . . ?"

"Friend of a friend."

"A friend I know?"

"Nope."

Tony is always cryptic about the owners of his homes, but Fern likes to needle his miserly nature. She used to think he guarded his connections because he did not want to share them, but over many years she's realized that this isn't his primary motive. What he wants to guard is the identity of people who might give you, if you met them by happenstance out of his presence, some piece of intelligence that, however insignificant to you, would feel to Tony like a violation of privacy. Something as trivial as his hometown (Milwaukee), the name of his childhood dog, the name of his dentist (he is vain about his teeth), his shoe size, or his age (which no one's supposed to know, though once, while he slept, Fern sneaked a look at his driver's license; he is forty-nine). Beneath his open Dairyland accent, Tony is a privacy junkie.

Equally ironic is the work he depends on for regular income between erratic sales of the photographs he takes and sometimes shows. He teaches Braille to children whose parents want them to have this access to the world around them. Like most details of his life outside his art, it's something Tony rarely talks about, and Fern has no idea if he likes or hates the work. He couldn't love it, she figures, or something would have to escape from him, some whiff of passion. He has known Braille for most of his life because his mother was blind—one of the rare personal facts he will disclose.

Someone would have a theory, she's sure, that this is why Tony makes pictures that look so uncomfortably close at things (and maybe this is why he's so private, too—because blindness means never knowing if someone is staring at you). But Fern rejects such simple-minded analysis. Art grows from much more than family drama.

"Show me what you're working on," she says as they finish their meal.

"Sure," he says, because this is one thing he is open about—at least with people he likes. Admirably, thinks Fern, he never spins anxieties around his life as an artist. Ask him how his work is going and he does not recoil. He might say, "Very well, very well," in a carefree tone, or "There's one I'm pretty pleased with at the moment." At worst, "In a rough spot, a rough spot right now." No hand-wringing, no complaints of not enough time, not enough discipline, not enough recognition. In fact, Fern thinks as she watches him head upstairs with a slight serene smile on his face, Tony's attitude toward his pictures is much like the attitude of young parents she knows toward their children: always proud, always willing to look for the good; disappointed and vexed only with justification.

While he is gone, she wanders the downstairs rooms. The first floor is a virtual library: every room, even half the kitchen, lined with books—literature, history, art, cuisine. In the living room there is, strikingly, no couch; five armchairs convene at a low round table. Ample and white as cumulus clouds, they are banked with lace pillows and pale soft shawls. The one wall deprived of books is papered with blue morning glories.

Framed photographs shine on every level surface, all populated by men. The man who appears most often is short and self-consciously groomed, with an unconcealable belly (in his sixties, Fern judges from the pictures in which he looks oldest). Infallibly, he has a dark reckless tan, fine background to a silver mustache, and his dog leans fondly against his legs. In pictures where he looks a bit younger, there is a second dog as well, a twin to the one now asleep on the kitchen floor. Next to one of these pictures lies a round slab of polished pink marble, like an oversize coaster, bearing the engraved impression of a paw and the name MAVIS, along with her life span, 1984–1996, nearly epic in canine time.

As she passes a window, Fern is caught by her own reflection. Even in the timid lamp glow, it's obvious now: the extrusion that startled her a month ago, that makes her fold inward with a solitary thrill, that she cannot stop marveling at in every light and from every conceivable angle. Other people have started to look as well.

Though she hasn't said so to Tony, she's here because of this baby. She's fled the city because she cannot face the baby's father, who returns from a long trip tonight. Right about now, his plane could be passing over this very house, the pilots descending carefully toward New York, toward its nightly jewelbox splendor.

For three months Stavros has been in Greece, where he helped his mother care for her dying mother, then saw the old woman into her grave. A dutiful oldest son, he stayed in his grandmother's village, in a house without a phone or a shower on some minuscule island Fern had never heard of, all this time without complaint. Fern knows this because he sent her ten cheerful postcards, which are taped in a long straight row on her kitchen wall. She sent back four letters, all loving but shallow, each time intending to tell him the news, each time failing. Because of this glaring omission, she found that she could not tell him anything significant, could not express how much she missed him because it would seem deceitful to tell him one thing but not the other. By muting her feelings for so long, she has almost succeeded in erasing them altogether. At the very least, she has confused them, so that now, though she cannot wait to see him, she has run away, buying herself two or three days of . . . what? Prolonging the cover-up? Indulging her irrational sense of dread? She justifies her cowardice by telling herself that you could know a man far better than she knows Stavros and still fail to predict his reaction—his reaction, before she can even explain, just to the altered sight of her.

But if she knows one thing, she knows that Stavros will not be angry; he might even welcome this particular surprise. So what could she fear? That he might think she trapped him? (If he did, he would never let on; unlike Fern, he does not fret about the past.) That he will insist they marry at once? (She has been married before and no longer yearns toward a wedding as if toward transcendance or beatitude.) That he will bind her heart too tightly? (Won't this child, all by itself, do that?) This much is sure: there are too many questions.

Above her, she hears Tony's laugh, a murmur of conversation. He must be on the phone. In a moment he calls out, "Be down soon!" She calls back, "Take your time!"

Cautiously, she unlocks the French doors leading outside, but she triggers no alarms: just silence, or the kind of silence shaped by the sea. Her footsteps on the hollow floor of the porch sound impolite. The backyard, as concise as the house, is enclosed by a scrim of privet hedge and monopolized by flowerbeds: peonies in late, tempestuous bloom, trellised veils of clematis and rugosa roses, gladiolas hinting at the colors sheathed in their spearlike buds. Well beyond the hedge stands the larger house, shingled like this one but far more ambitious and astute in its angles—the only interruption to a broad horizon of sea. The mosquitoes seem to have retired, but the air is cold. Even perfection is never perfect, she thinks, and she goes back inside.

Now she hears the upstairs shower. Sighing (she knows what this means), Fern glances again at the snapshots in the living room. The man who clearly owns this house looks kind but also pretentious, and she hopes he is not Tony's lover, then wonders why she should care. Because, she answers herself, it's important to her image of Tony that he can do better, much better than this. She rarely knows with any certainty if Tony is sleeping with someone, but she can imagine, and anytime she meets him with another man, she does—now with hardly a trace of envy or pain.

"There you are!" says Tony, as if he were the one kept waiting. He's changed from shorts and T-shirt to jeans and a conservative white shirt (long sleeves, tiny buttons) that makes his newly shaven face look burnished, distracts from the gray in his wet dark hair.

He makes her stand aside at the edge of the room as he clears the round table and places four photographs there. He pulls back the chairs, turns lights on and off till he likes their effect. "Okay, okay!" he announces.

At first, they look like test patterns of some sort, little more than fields of texture. "You've gone abstract," she says.

"Me, abstract?" he says. "Now you know me better than that!"

Sand. Sand as a seagull might see it, walking along in search of washed-up crabs and mussels. Wet sand, sparkling sand, marbled sand, sand as smooth as sky. "Sand," she says.

"Yes, yes. But what do you think?"

"Honestly? They're a little remote for me. I guess you'd call them . . . sensual. But me . . ."

"Sensual," he says. "Hmm. Sensual's not for you?"

"I didn't say that," she says, before he can toss out a sexual quip about her pregnancy. "I mean I think of your work as more formal."

"Ah, the F word."

"Tony, this exhausts me, when you make a joke of it all. I have to think out loud."

He apologizes. "I need to try them bigger. I have to rent an outside darkroom to do it, but I'm thinking, I want them on the scale of windows."

"Glass-bottom boats," she says.

"Yes." He nods, looking pleased. "Just so, Miss Veritas."

"There you go again." She starts for the kitchen. "I'll do dishes."

"No you won't," he says. "You'll put your feet up. Go upstairs and smell the air. There's a balcony outside my room. That air, just that air, makes you wish you were rich. Forget fancy cars and the Orient Express."

As she expected, he tells her he's going out, no invitation implied. Fern thanks him for dinner.

"Sweet dreams." He glances down. "Sleep late for Binky. I'll make French toast." Unlike some of the men Fern encounters these days (including some she's barely met), Tony never touches the growing planet her belly has become, and she tries to stop wishing he would.

Upstairs, there are three bedrooms. Tony has the master bedroom, with the back view of the garden and, secondhand, the ocean. In the center stands a four-poster bed draped in florid gauze; unmade, it looks offended by its surroundings. Tossed about on the floor are jeans, shorts, T-shirts, a tripod, a light meter, magazines. On the antique washstand sit two coffee mugs and a beer bottle; on the windowseat, a half-eaten bagel on the edge of a plate. Despite open windows, there is the faint feral smell of sneakers worn barefoot all summer long. This is how Tony lives once he's burrowed into the homes he borrows, but even so, Fern would put him in charge of a castle filled with treasures, because he always leaves a place neater, crisper, more loved than it was when he moved in. He makes a point of it. The owners return to find flowers on the table, champagne in the fridge, pressed sheets on every bed.

He seems to live quite happily with other people's furniture and pictures, other people's closets full of other people's clothes. He has an apartment in the city, but it's little more than a darkroom and a bed. He stores photographic paper in the disconnected oven; the tiny refrigerator holds film, beer, and milk for cornflakes. Dreary as a bunker, Fern thinks when she sees it—never more than fleetingly, just to meet Tony and go somewhere else.

She makes her way through the clutter, past a lace curtain to a balcony just large enough to hold a single chair. The sky is starry, the topmost tendrils of the privet still. She smells the clean smell of open sea and, for an instant, the scent of Scotch broom. The surf sounds contentedly tame.

A door below her opens. Tony whistles softly to the dog. They head across the lawn. The old dog moves slowly, and Tony is patient. He turns around briefly, walking backward, and waves up at Fern. And then his silhouette—defined not by the moon or stars but by the security floodlight in the neighbors' driveway—merges with the hedge. The baby rolls gently inside her, like the shifting of wet sand under a wave. She first felt it, or knew it for what it was, a few weeks ago. Quickening, they call the first tangible movements; every time since, her heart does the same.

THERE IS A CHANCE that Fern will raise this baby on her own; sometimes, perversely, this is the fantasy that gives her the greatest pleasure. Not because she does not want Stavros around but because it feels as if it would be cleaner, less complicated, as if she would not run the risk, once more, of failing at being a wife. Being a mother seems challenge enough. But money: that would be hard.

Fern works at home as a book designer. Just now, at last, after designing publicity brochures and then plain, text-filled books like novels and self-help sermons, she has begun to work on large glossy books: trophy cookbooks; books on fashion and travel; books with page spreads luxurious as that lawn beyond the hedge, photographs of villas and feasts and nymphets atop the Eiffel Tower. Such books may lack intellectual substance, but design is more than white noise to trundle the reader along. Fern attends meetings where everyone looks to her, where what she does might make or break the appeal of a book as an object to be held, coveted, above all *bought*. But the work does not make her wealthy, and she knows she must find some kind of upward momentum: at worst, a job in a corporate office. Two-tone graphs of stock performance, footnotes in four-point italic, portraits of bankers at their desks. Annual reports: a very special circle in hell.

Fern did not set out to be a graphic designer (did anyone?); through childhood and beyond, she painted. In college, she devoured Bronzino and Beckmann, John Singer Sargent and Lucian Freud. Among classmates revering Nam June Paik and Baldessari, she was shamelessly outdated in her tastes. On her best days, she believed she would single-handedly put portrait painting back on the map. When she graduated, she won a fellowship to go to Europe for a year, look at the art in museums and make her own. For all the conventional reasons, she lived in Paris, and that is where she met Tony.

She was sitting on a bench in the Parc Montsouris, drawing a young woman who lay on a blanket, curled around a baby. It was one of those last warm days, September's nostalgia for August, and under the spell of the sun, they slept. As Fern drew, she began to notice a man circling the sleepers, closing in. He moved the way she imagined a tiger would move, creeping. That he held a camera rather than a weapon made him no less disturbing. Fern put down her paper and pencils.

Clever, the man watched his shadow. He was careful not to block the sun from the mother's face, as the sudden shade might wake her. When he leaned across her body and began to photograph the baby, Fern astonished herself by saying, "What are you—*qu'est-ce que vous faîtes?*" She spoke quietly but clearly, as if it were still important not to wake the sleepers.

The man faced her. He walked toward her, smiling. He looked at her drawing. "Apparently, the same as you."

If she was irritated at the comparison (she was making a respectful study of innocence; he was invading it), somehow she was even more irritated that he was American. "I don't think so," she said.

To her dismay, he sat down and examined her drawing, which lay on the bench between them. "Not bad," he said.

She could find no answer to that. She felt invaded as well.

"Let me guess," he said. "Junior year abroad?"

Instead of walking away, she said sharply, "I've graduated from Harvard. I have a grant. And you?"

He whistled. "Yikes. Sorry if I was rude. I'm Tony. No Harvard boy here, but I'm not the pervert you think I am. I'm just doing my job."

His smile, intense in its warmth, made it impossible not to want to know him. How could guile be so attractive? Months later, she would often wish she had gathered up her things, said good-bye (or nothing), and left him behind to do as he wished. But she hadn't. "Which is?"

His smile relaxed. "Which is . . . to take the very, very small and make it large. Make it get some attention. Give stature to the details. Where the devil lurks, you know?" Close to eleven years later, she still owns one of the few photographs he took of that baby, before she interrupted him. A tiny fist, enlarged to the size of a melon. At first glance, it resembles an eccentric bulbous mushroom discovered on a tree trunk deep in a forest. Fern has always hung it in a prominent place. These days she stops to look at it often, this literal vision of a baby's hand, two of which are growing, sprouting digits, beginning to grasp about blindly inside her.

If Tony seduced her, she met him halfway. If she is truthful, she knows that he was attracted more to a concept she formed in his mind than to Fern herself. It was the same concept she once felt she embodied for her parents: good girl, fine student, earnest thinker, winner of everything parents want their children to win (and disdainer of most things parents wish their children to disdain). Tony, she knew within minutes of their meeting, was her obverse, her negative: insolent dropout, tireless comic, bluff opportunist. Proud pilot of an improvised life. Equation for a true artist, if such a thing existed; this was what she feared and what she envied. He had mentioned the devil, and that's what any woman, even so recently a girl, ought to have seen. But if he was a devil of one kind, he was an angel of another. As she was to learn, he seems to break hearts without circumspection but also without any true deceit—and then, for reasons she has never plumbed, insists on holding them fast.

FERN WAKES when Tony comes in. Two-thirty, the green digits tell her in the dark. She listens intently. She hears the locks secured on the three doors downstairs, footsteps in between. The rush of the kitchen faucet: water for the dog, which noisily slurps from its bowl. The metallic jostle of the dog's tags as it labors up the carpeted stairs and into the master bedroom.

Tony does not follow. The world is so still that she can hear the hushed thump of the refrigerator door, brief clank of a drawer holding flatware. Vanilla ice cream is Tony's favorite nightcap. Chair legs scrape the floor, a newspaper rustles.

She has never understood when Tony really sleeps. In Paris, he lived in a rich woman's duplex loft, but when Fern was with him, he preferred to share the bed in her rented room. There, he was free to leave when he chose. Dawn, he said, was the best time to use the darkroom he borrowed. But even when they did end up at the loft, he'd abandon her in the woman's great, soft bed as soon as he thought she'd fallen asleep. He would pace about downstairs and then, often, leave the place altogether. Anxiously, she would hear him cross the expensive rugs: footsteps, then a blank, footsteps, another blank. She would will him to return upstairs (once in a while he would) yet, at the same time, wish he would just open the door and go, so the torture would end. After a while, she no longer believed he went to a darkroom: not because there were no pictures to show (there were plenty) but because, more than once, she ran into him by day with young French men—boys, really— who barely spoke English. Later, neither of them would mention the encounter, but Fern would notice that Tony had cooled a few degrees. In bed, he would turn his back and cocoon himself in the sheet, untouchable.

If for months she said nothing, if she let her misery bloom in passive silence, it was because of the way he loved her when he did: so intently, so quietly, she felt almost holy. He rarely kissed her mouth, and he never quite looked her in the eye, but he'd examine every inch of her body, wide-eyed, and in the cobalt dark she loved to watch his fingers roam her skin. Romantically, she thought of Tony's blind mother and imagined that this hardship must make him different from other men, more sensitive. She closed her own eyes and felt he must be *reading* her, pore by pore.

But then one day—it was May, a day of true spring—she came around a corner to see him with yet another boy, whispering something, Tony's lips touching the boy's sunlit ear. The kind of pleasure on the boy's face was unmistakable. Fern slipped into a side street rather than let Tony see her, but that night when he entered her room, she said, first thing, "Why don't you just come right out and *tell* me you like fucking boys?"

He reacted with a smile, but he was also blushing. He said, "Out of what blue have we launched this missile?"

"You know what I mean."

"Well let's see. No, in fact I don't, so help me out," he cajoled.

She shouted, documenting every one of the five times she had seen him with boys she never saw again, recalling all the street names and times of day. She shouted that *this* was why he never introduced her to friends, because everyone but *her* must know he was gay! Perhaps she was naive to expect fidelity, but was he using her? Was he trying her on like a new pair of pants, to see if this—if *girls*—might somehow fit after all? Was she a lab rat with tits and a cunt? In a flash, she saw his tactile exploration of her body as experiment rather than adoration.

Tony's smile had vanished, but he let the silence seep around them before he said, "So let's get logical here: if I should see you on the street with some other girl, that makes you a dyke?"

"You know what I mean! You can't keep on lying!"

"I'm lost," he said calmly. "I've lied . . . about what?"

Of course, he never had lied, not literally, but she couldn't believe he would feign such innocence. Then she wondered if there were other women as well as men, if she was just one of a small but literal crowd. "Leave," she said quietly.

"Just like that. Because you saw me on the street with a friend."

"Leave." She held the door open. "Get out of my life."

She cried through the next afternoon. Perhaps two thirds of that crying was over her broken heart; another third raged at her own stupidity.

A day later she boarded a train and traveled through Italy and Greece for a month. She'd been told it was lunacy to travel alone through these countries, especially because she was fair and would stand out in all the wrong ways. But to be noticed like that—whistled at, praised, even followed through crowds—was what she wanted right then.

The dense sunlight turned her hair the pure crocus yellow it had been when she was a child; everywhere she went, she felt like a firefly. In the Boboli Gardens, she was approached with extreme courtesy by a plain young man who spoke a charmingly imperious English, fluent but with a strong Italian accent. She let him show her around the palace and take her to lunch. He was visiting from Lucca, he told her, and had to return on the next train, but would she come see him there on her way to Greece? He wrote his address in her sketchbook and, as he handed it back to her, beamed with such ardor that she felt compelled to say, "You're so kind, but I don't know if I can." His face darkened, and he took back the sketchbook. He scribbled so fiercely over his address that the ink bled through five pages.

His wrath unsettled Fern. "But I might—"

"No, no!" he said, shaking his fists in front of his face, "I must know with veritabulla certainty. I cannota bear to sit by my house and think, Willa she come? Willa she not come? Willa she come? Willa she not come?" After he stalked away, Fern was sorry to have hurt him, yet she felt as well an insidious pleasure. For though you could hardly break a heart on such little acquaintance, you could have a taste of that power.

At the postcard stand in Delphi, a dark man with eyes both soulful and wolfish told her that he had rushed to this very site when told by the oracle that he would find there "the woman of my destitute." Fern laughed, knowing it would not daunt him; how nice, if vaguely perilous, it felt to be the object of such comic intensity. She let several such flirtations unfold, but only to a safe degree.

On Paros, toward the end of her trip, Fern let a flirtation unfold into something else. The man was not a parodically passionate Greek but a cocky Englishman, with whom she spent a single sleepless night. The night itself became a memory that she still enjoys, but when it was over and the man made his glib departure, he left her with the very sorrow she had been trying to shed. She went back to Paris with a sense of defeat. Tony had returned to New York but wrote her long letters—as if he had never wronged her, as if she had never expelled him from her life. He did not apologize or voice regrets. He simply told her everything about his life (or everything *but*), describing the tin aesthetic eye of New York next to Paris, the new turn his work had taken, the extraordinary heat . . . His letters teetered on the brink of romance but never quite fell; he might end by saying, *I miss your Miss Veritas wisdoms, your crispy roast chicken, your refined oboe of a voice, your fresh-from-the-garden face* . . . as if he'd forgotten which of their hearts had broken. She did not reply, but she did not throw his letters away.

Fern returned to the States after a summer's worth of these letters, all unanswered, and she called him. They never slept together again and never mentioned that they had. Some people, she knows, are destined to get off scot-free.

She moved to Brooklyn. For five more years, she turned out vividly expressive pictures, thick with impasto and energy, each one filling a wall of the room she used as a studio in her apartment. She painted everyone she knew. Two of these paintings appeared in splashy group shows, but the dealers who came to her studio would say, at some point, the same thing: "They're so . . . *large*." They said this with the same bewilderment Fern felt at hearing it, because by the standards of most work in galleries back then, the paintings were almost diminutive. She could only conclude that she was somehow outpainting herself, exaggerating her stature; apparently, the pictures were too large for *her,* and though she tried to dismiss the implications (did she have a small spirit? was she simply not destined for largeness herself?), she switched abruptly to painting small. She dragged a big sheet of masonite back from the lumberyard, sawed it into squares the size of dinner plates, and painted her friends all over again, each face defiantly filling its frame (I'll show you *large*). The expressions on these faces were always fiercer than Fern intended, and though she placed half a dozen in shows, even sold a few to strangers, she felt weary, as if she were working by rote. She was a waitress, and she had turned thirty. That was when she married.

She was first attracted to Jonah by what she perceived to be his serene decisiveness, his fidelity of focus. Here was a man who ate only one type of cereal, watched one newscaster, owned just one pair of shoes and one jacket to fit each of four social occasions (Fern thought of them as Workaday, Saturday, Glenn Miller, and Sporty). All winter long he wore the same hat, a gray Sherlockian cap with retractable earflaps.

"His closet is a poem," Fern told Anna the first time she stayed over. Fern had known Anna since college; Anna was never short on opinions and, consciously or not, Fern often needed to hear them.

"Well and good," said Anna, "but who's the poet? Gregory Corso? Robert Frost? I hate to say it, but Alfred, Lord Tennyson, that's my hunch." Lord Tenny, Anna called him behind his back, or Mr. Singularity. Fern would laugh, but something else had dawned on her: Mr. Singularity would take one wife and one wife only, till death (one apiece) did they part.

Fern had always been determined to marry an artist, and Jonah, a newly minted art historian, allowed her to have the art without the incurable adolescence she had suffered in the men she had loved before: real or counterfeit iconoclasts, proudly allergic to neckties, loafers, and alarm clocks, to allegiance of any stripe.

And then there were Jonah's surprising loves. When she gave his eulogy, in Jonah's mother's church in Far Hills, from a lofty Episcopal dais, she catalogued them: Rubens, Spanish food, John Belushi, Hawaiian shirts, and vintage comics (he owned the first nine of the original Superman series)—ribald antonyms to his cool, parsimonious nature. What Fern did not say was that though she shared none of these leanings, she had once been certain they were proof of stored-up passions, promises that one day she would wake to find herself beside a hot-blooded ukelele-playing muscleman bent on saving the world through laughter. Gone would be the man who winced at the sound of his tie sliding through its knot, wore dark shin-high socks even with shorts, ate (slightly open-mouthed) the same small bowl of peanuts each night when he gazed into the eyes of Tom Brokaw. Gone the man who answered her keen "I love you" with a whispered utterance that sounded like "A few."

When she'd met him, he'd looked angular, slim, even bold (he wore a red Hawaiian shirt; she didn't see the socks because the party was so crowded), and he had been full of celebratory relief at having finished his thesis (on Rubens). When he spoke about paintings, he was lively; their first conversation was an argument about Balthus, and Fern liked how good-natured he seemed even in the midst of disagreement (he thought Balthus a poseur with little feel for paint or anything human, but he was careful not to make his contempt an attack on Fern). And she liked, back then, that they had been so pointedly introduced, deliberately matched by their host.

Like any delicate creature, love depends upon an ecosystem, a context. Hemmed in at that party by a crush of thirty-year-old frat boys with charm-bracelet wives, there they stood, Fern and Jonah, storks among chimps. She remembers the kinship she felt with him when, over his shoulder, she watched four men climb up on a couch and, waving beer cans and rolling their eyes, perform a tasteless vaudeville of Stevie Wonder singing about his newborn daughter Aisha. Of course, she now knows, this was why their host saw them as soul mates: their otherness among his friends.

"I met the guy playing tennis last week, and listen, you were made for each other," said Aaron when he called to invite her. "You both love art and you both have all these arty friends, and you've both got this great conservative streak—like the best of our parents without their Republican intolerance. I bet you both know how to foxtrot. And listen—I think there's a little money there. You could quit your waitressing job!"

Fern had known Aaron Byrd since grade school; their mothers, together, ran a garden club. All her life, Aaron had seemed to alternate between charming and exasperating Fern. He was the one man outside her family who'd known her forever; the one for whom she was never quite right; the one who would have been her prearranged spouse had they lived in another place or time. So when he told her he'd found her the perfect match, for a moment she was hurt. Here was the man who'd known her longest, known her best in certain ways, and this was how casually, how eagerly he'd hand her off to someone else. But then she thought, He's known me so long, so well, he has to be right.

Jonah's friends expressed delight and amazement: "We never thought Jonah would marry!" Flush with premarital hubris, Fern mistook this remark as a personal compliment ("We never thought he'd find so remarkable a woman!"), not the commentary it clearly was on his die-hard bachelor ways ("We never thought he'd live anything but monkishly alone!").

She moved to Jonah's apartment in the Village and put her painting

supplies in a basement locker, telling herself that after the nuptial fes-
tivities ended, she would look for studio space. She never did; she found
herself, instead, mooning over Jonah's exhaustive collection of art books.
When, within a year of their wedding, he stopped wanting sex, Fern
would take a different book to bed each night and scrutinize its pages
until he had fallen asleep. A habit born of pride, but it led to her fascination with fonts and layouts and margins. She didn't like looking too
long at the art, because art was what she ought to be doing but wasn't.
(She would choose, increasingly, books about dead artists so that she
did not have to agonize over the possibility that they were, at that very
moment, doggedly producing more work.)

Then she took to choosing from Jonah's shelves the artists' biogra-
phies, because they had fewer pictures to envy. Sometimes, at the end of
one of these books, she would read—at first with skeptical curiosity,
then with creeping eagerness—the postscript titled "A Note About the
Type." Here she became familiar with names like William Goudy,
Pierre Simon Fournier, Rudolph Ruzicka, and above all, Claude Garamond, the sixteenth-century type cutter who came to resemble in
Fern's imagination a celebrity with the public stature, simultaneously,
of a Bill Gates and a Richard Gere. According to one book, Garamond
won the patronage of a king for something as droningly obscure as the
"elegance and lively sense of movement" in fifty-two letters, ten nu-
merals, and a scattering of punctuation marks.

These tiny texts were filled with fanlike praise for such attributes as
"a daring homage to all things ancient"; "a trim grace and vigor"; "a
rare beauty and muscular balance"—in alphabets! And there were snip-
pets of history that would tug at her mind—like the unjust obscurity
of one Jean Jannon, a Protestant designer, because he happened to live
in a time of Catholic oppression. A man in the wrong place at the
wrong time, whose tragedy of circumstance would be commemorated
most publicly through an endnote, centuries later, to a biography of the
architect Frank Lloyd Wright.

Over a period of months, compulsively distracting herself from
work, from love, and from the tension of Jonah's fruitless, increasingly
lethargic search for a job, Fern came to discern type the way she had
once discerned color: she knew Granjon from Fairfield, Bembo from
Janson, Electra from Caledonia. Finally, and in the nick of time as
events played out, Jonah's trust fund helped her buy the degree she

needed to refine her fascination. For that, she would always be grateful, but by the end of those two years, her marriage, like her painting, was a thing of the past.

Now, nearly another two years gone by, she lives in the apartment she shared with her husband, but without the man, his books, or the resolutely solitary ways she mistook in him for prudence and stability. Her life in fact contains, thanks to his bitterly grieving mother and sister, not one significant memento of Jonah. They even insisted she give back her ring, which held a stone from a family brooch. In a moment of irrational shame, she acquiesced, for in the year before he died she had sometimes fantasized Jonah dead, not so much out of anger but because she was lonely and exhausted. She did not imagine him dead by violent or torturous means; she simply imagined him suddenly, vaguely gone—as it turned out he *was* to die, in an accident so freakish she found it embarrassing to recount, even to her friends.

IT'S TIME TO TELL HER PARENTS. She fears not their censure but their perfectly realistic concern if she is to raise a child alone. Besides Tony and Anna, Fern has told Heather, her older sister. Others have certainly guessed.

"Oh my dear, what a pickle," said Heather, though Fern had not presented the news as bad. "Who in the world is the father?"

"Well you are in for an adventure!" were Anna's first words. When Fern told her Stavros was the father, Anna said, "Now there's the first real *man* of all the boys you've been with." Though Fern has been seeing Stavros for over a year, few of her friends have met him; she tells herself that this is simply because of the anemic social life she's had since Jonah's death, not because of any reticence about Stavros himself or his place in her heart. Anna managed to meet him, however, when she was visiting from Texas for just a few days. She met him because, not five minutes after walking into Fern's apartment, she found a note on the kitchen table ("And who, pray tell, is 'A thousand kisses'?"). She met him because she insisted.

Fern laughed. "You mean he has the most body hair."

"I mean, he has the most mature occupation, the most mature attitude."

"Well, mature . . . you couldn't get much more 'mature' than Jonah."

"Oh no," scoffed Anna. "Sure, his cerebral cortex went gray when he turned twelve, but that was the man, you remember, who collected comic books and ate Lucky Charms for breakfast every day."

"Cap'n Crunch."

"As we used to say, same diff." Anna sighed. "I met your Stavros just once, but I could tell this: He seemed accessible. No crooked angles. And he was paying attention to you. To *you*."

Anna's positive judgment was a relief, but then, when it came to love, she was hardly in a position to be critical of anything impulsive or haphazard. In the midst of getting her Ph.D. in archaeology at Columbia, she had fallen for a professor she met on a dig in Turkey. He left his wife, married Anna, and moved her into a hacienda on the San Antonio River, where she promptly conceived twins. In Fern's memory, these events took place in about six months. When Anna knew something was right, it happened. She expressed not a qualm about leaving her beloved New York for Texas (a place she had always loudly deplored) or suspending her studies. The twins were now four, and Anna was writing a novel, a thriller melding Biblical archaeology with Arab politics and human rights activism. Fern had no doubt it would sell like highbrow hotcakes.

"I hate it when people talk about twists of fate," Anna liked to say. "When it comes to life, we spin our own yarn, and where we end up is really, in fact, where we always intended to be."

FIFTEEN

FERN WAKES TO THE COMPETING SOUNDS of birdsong and tennis. The play is prolonged and aggressive, interspersed with male
gasps and curses. "Andrew you dickhead!" she hears as the rally halts—
a seventeen-year-old boy, she'd guess, condemning himself for his fal-
tering skill. A world of absolutes.

She puts on her bathing suit and a loose yellow dress. Tony will make
some crack about Little Mary Sunshine, sing a few bars from "Good
Day Sunshine" or "Here Comes the Sun."

But when she finds him, Tony does not immediately see her. He sits
on the back porch, leaning over the railing, binoculars to his eyes.

"Birdwatching?"

He jumps, looks at her and smiles, then returns to his surveillance.
"Taking in a bit of the local wildlife, yes."

Fern stands behind him, squinting to see the tennis court through
the hedge. Four men—barely men, all in white, two shirtless—are
playing vigorously. Tony hands her the binoculars. "See for yourself."

Yes, all worth looking at, each for his own physical assets. All in perfect shape, all on the cusp of their prime.

Tony sighs. "Boys, boys, you are breaking my heart."

Fern continues to look but says nothing. This isn't what she had in
mind, boy-watching with Tony. She wonders if he sees her new state as
an invitation to a kind of closeness she doesn't want, the way her becoming a married woman made her mother begin to offer up details
about her sex life with Fern's father (Fern put a stop to this at once).

One of the men is dark, with black hair and vehemently bushy eyebrows. Stavros, she thinks with a twinge of guilt and longing. Not the
kind of man to whom she had ever been attracted in the past, but she
had proved her own convictions wrong. Or she had changed. She did
not know which.

"Hello, darlings. Isn't the morning just sublime?"

Fern pulls the binoculars from her eyes. The voice belongs to a woman who crosses the lawn with a picnic hamper over her arm. It's the neighbor who waved from her seaside porch yesterday afternoon. She wears green rubber clogs and pink gardening gloves that flare out toward her elbows like medieval gauntlets and match the lipstick on her sun-crinkled lips.

"Gorgeous!" Tony answers, standing. He goes to the steps and offers an arm to help the woman up the stairs, though she hardly needs his assistance.

"Aren't you the rare courtly fellow," she rasps. She has one of those bawdy upper-crust voices that makes her sound as if she's swallowed a handful of gravel. "Speaking of courts, you must play with us again, you gave these old girls quite the workout! And please"—she casts a disapproving look toward the tennis players they were so recently ogling—"please excuse my grandson and his entourage. They play with the manners of Attila. I'm resigned to meeting my end in decapitation by Frisbee."

She looks down at Fern and slips off a gauntlet to shake her hand. "Hello there, lady friend. Let's not bother with intros. I'm just delivering a few goodies—my June harvest's a windfall this year."

Tony takes the basket and lifts the lid. "My, my. We don't deserve such bounty."

"Neither Andrew nor his boorish grandfather will abide rhubarb, though I do make a superb galette."

"Oh but we love it, don't we?" says Tony, grinning at Fern.

She agrees and peers into the hamper. Alongside the rhubarb, there are strawberries, asparagus, and a small bouquet of marigolds tied with a red silk ribbon.

"Will Fenno be coming out?" the neighbor asks, looking hopeful.

Tony shrugs. "Can't say."

"Oh but how thoughtless of me, the place is *yours* for the moment."

"Not a-tall, not a-tall," Tony drawls. Fern all but stares at him now.

The neighbor raises her hands, as if she's being arrested. "Well that's it then! I never, never overstay! Enjoy the day, my dears." She trots down the stairs and back across the lawn. Once on her side of the hedge, she calls toward the tennis court, "Decibels, young men, decibels!"

Fern turns to Tony. "'Gorgeous'? 'Bounty'? Are you morphing into Nathan Lane or what?"

"When on Gold Coast, poor man speak with gilded tongue."

"What was that about 'giving the girls a workout'?"

Tony laughs into a hand. "My third morning here, right here, just sittin' and drinkin' my coffee, I hear someone yodeling, 'Yoohoo, yoohoo there, young sir!' I look around, and there's milady in her matching little tennis dress and visor, waving her racquet through the hedge. She honks out in her best Bacall, 'Do you by any chahnce pullay? Our fawth's apparently ay-wohl.' I tell her I do, but not very well, and she goes, 'Well pullease, pullease, come fill our hole!'"

"You don't play tennis," says Fern.

Tony pretends indignation. "Well, sort of, sort of—how would you know? Anyhow, who would say no? I felt like an anthropologist invited by headhunters to lend a hand at the actual shrinking."

Tony tells her how he pulled a T-shirt over his bathing suit and put on his tattered old sneakers; in the mudroom, he found a racquet. Once on the court, he felt like the savage. Three pewter-haired women in pleated white skirts greeted him with panicky delight. "Pretty good players, the old girls, but I spread a little testosterone on my serve and gave 'em a few passing shots. Ooh, but they squealed like rock-star groupies. It was a riot. And then, as they're wiping their grips with their plush little towels, they insist I join them to 'be refreshed.' But for the mention of iced tea, I might have tucked tail and run."

Fern pictures Tony, bright with exertion, hair damp with sweat. A rare sight, as Tony (or the Tony she knows) avoids all extreme behaviors, emotional or physical. But he looks fit, and for all she knows, he could be an ace at tennis or baseball or hockey or anything traditionally male.

"I kept expecting a taxidermist to show up and mount me on a wall. These women are the type who have an orgasm putting on panty hose. 'Dahling, that backhand of yaws is a pip!'" Theatrically, he shudders.

"You shouldn't be so cruel. She clearly likes you."

Tony laughs. "Who says I don't like her?"

Fern looks into the hamper again. "I'll make a pie," she says.

"I'm for that." Tony heads for the door and holds it open for the dog. "Impress our third," she hears him say before the door shuts behind them.

"Third what?" Fern calls into the house as she follows.

"Dinner guest," he calls back. In the kitchen, he sits at the table. "Here, guy!" Eagerly, the dog pushes himself between Tony's legs.

Tony will have met someone, last night, last week, on one of his nocturnal roamings. The beach, a club, a parking lot; so she imagines. The someone will be in his twenties, good-looking, funny or intelligent or charming. Something besides seductive. Fern will meet him tonight and then, she'd bet the moon, never again.

"Who's Fenno?" she says. "Funny name."

"Just one of the hangers-on to this little estate. Believe me, the professor has about ten best friends once the birds start heading north again. I had to give up and let the machine take calls for my first week here."

Fern looks through the cupboards for things she'll need to make a pie. She finds them all with surprising ease. There's even a large marble board for rolling pastry, which she slides into the freezer. "Lard," she says, pulling out a bricklike package. "God. I haven't used lard since Paris."

At her own mention of their past, she turns to look at Tony. He is bent over the dog, whispering; it takes her a moment to realize he is fingering those long shaggy ears in search of ticks. The dog's face is turned up, smiling, as if he's a guest at a spa. Fern watches Tony pull out a beige tick the size of a shirt button—the dog hardly flinches—and drop it into a jar of soapy liquid on the table.

He strokes the dog's head firmly several times and coaxes him off toward his bed. When Tony finally turns his attention back to Fern, he says, "So, is superdaddy back? Did you tell him the news?"

Fern sets the lard on the counter. "I wish you'd stop making that lame joke. He's not the super. He's my landlord's son. My landlord is a very clever guy, as is Stavros, and they only happen to own about a third of the West Village, so don't act so uppity."

"But did you? Isn't it getting a little late in the game not to spread the joy, get him to make you an honest woman? Just think: real estate this time around. Oh reevoir, Old Masters. Salloo, Trump Tower. No fretting over rent control for you."

Besides Anna, only Tony would make a joke alluding to her life with Jonah. This is a relief, even if the jokes are annoying. At the funeral, nearly everyone began their condolence with "Such a tragedy!" But the real tragedy is that Jonah's death was not a tragedy. It was a farce. And this, secretly, is what now makes discussion of Jonah taboo in most people's minds. If we do not speak ill of the dead, we do not so much as mention the absurdly dead. Sometimes Fern wishes they had gone through a messy, weepy divorce; then she could talk freely about her ambivalent memories, about the things she *did* love about him as well as the things she stopped loving and the things that drove her nuts. But now the entire topic of her misshapen marriage, along with Jonah himself, seems consigned to oblivion. Poor Jonah: a decent man with rotten luck.

"Your French sounds as offensive as ever, and I never said I wanted to marry the guy," she says to Tony.

"Zeus Junior sweeps down from Olympus with a holster full of thunderbolts and what, Miss Veritas refuses his attentions?"

"I haven't exactly refused them, have I?"

"Well you've refused to let them go public."

"That's not true," she says, though perhaps it is. She might make excuses about how busy she and Stavros have been in their respective lives, how the rest of their time they spend alone in each other's company, but they would still be excuses. With her fingertips, she mills flour, sugar, butter, and lard into a golden loam.

After a moment Tony says, sounding subdued, "You do *love* the boy?"

"Oh yes. But then I'm not sure I can remember what love is. Or I can remember what I've always thought it was, but now I'm constantly suspicious."

Tony comes up beside her with a carton of milk. He knows her pastry routine. After he sets the milk on the counter and she thanks him, he touches her belly from the side, a fleeting pat. "Love is about to become something else entirely," he says.

Fern looks at him, surprised. He smiles, but seriously.

"Well, yes." She leaves it at that.

He watches her press the dough into a ball and wrap it in waxed paper. "Come to the beach while it's chilling," he says.

"You go. I'll find you later. I have to sleep, or I won't have much energy tonight."

"Disco nap for Binky."

Fern laughs. "Precisely."

———

JONAH HAD BEEN DEAD FOR HOURS, but Fern did not know it. No one did. She was making dinner in their kitchen, expecting him back any minute. Back from where, she had no idea and did not care, but he liked to eat dinner at seven and always called if he would be late. Courteous and dependable: that was Jonah. But she was angry at him as she chopped onions and garlic, peeled tendons from chicken breasts. As she turned the rice down to simmer, she imagined leaving him: finding a place back in Brooklyn, buying florid thrift-shop curtains, taking her paints out of storage. Because if Jonah could deceive himself that joblessness was a force which kept their marriage a strained, platonic alliance, Fern could deceive herself that passionlessness was a force which kept her from painting.

Her brooding fantasy that evening included Aaron Byrd, the childhood friend who had fixed her up with Jonah (and gloated at their wedding). Recently, he had made partner at his architecture firm; because of the new demands this made on his life, Fern and Jonah had not seen Aaron in months. Suddenly, two days before, Fern had been stunned to walk out the door of their building and see his name in blue Brooks Brothers cursive, directly across the street where a small but fancy faux-antique building was starting to rise. Lovejoy, Rushing, Stein & Byrd: The fleet of names dismayed her. Why hadn't Aaron called to tell her about this project? How many times had he been to dinner here, looked out the window, and eyed that vacant lot with lust? That night, and the next night, she had dreamed of Aaron: Both times he asked her to marry him, both times she accepted with joy, and she awoke with a stirring of erotic nostalgia, which quickly turned to sadness and then to irritation.

It was his fault, in part, that she was married to Jonah. Once, she had thought it charming that they were fixed up and liked each other right away. But in truth, wasn't it pathetic, as if neither of them had been capable of doing this one, colossally important thing without guidance? Fern thought of her parents, who ran an immensely successful nursery, having joined her mother's love of nature with her father's business sense. Joseph and Helen Olitsky loved to repeat the story of their meeting: sole bidders for an orchid plant at an auction raising money for Helen's sorority's scholarship fund. Now if that wasn't destiny, what the heck was?

The wine Fern was drinking revived the wishfulness of her dreams. As she heated oil in a skillet, she saw herself newly settled, alone but relieved, inviting Aaron to dinner, just as she had invited him to countless dinners before and after he introduced her to Jonah, before and after they married.

As she imagined the details of such an evening—what she would wear, what she would cook—her kitchen timer rang to remind her of this actual meal: that the rice was done, the chicken stewed with the tomato, tarragon, and cream. It was ten past seven when she mixed the salad dressing in a jar, and Jonah had not called. Feeling too spiteful to wait, Fern served herself and sat down to eat. That morning, waking from Aaron's second proposal, she had confronted Jonah while he dressed. She told him yet again how lonely she was, how much she wanted things to work out, how much she wanted them to get to a place where they were happy enough, content enough, to think about having a child. Jonah gazed at her from across the room, looking concerned. He said that once he had a job—he was sure this would happen soon, he just had a feeling—everything would improve. He would relax. They would move somewhere they could have a house, a house they could fill with her paintings. He would be dying for a baby. No, they did not need counseling. No, he did not need therapy. Fern needed a little patience, he said, and that was when she lost it. How dare he turn the tables and say that she was the one wanting! *She* was not the one who had no work, not the one who had idle hours to fill, not the one who was frigid in bed!

Jonah merely stared at her, his expression typically, infuriatingly retentive but also defeated. She apologized, hating the echo of her cruel words. She hugged Jonah and wished him luck (he was seeing some dean in Queens about adjunct work). But as soon as he left, she found his wet towel on the couch and was angry all over again. She spent the day at the magazine where she freelanced, and then she went to Gay Men's Health Crisis, where she volunteered on Tuesday nights (phoning strangers and brightly pleading for money, which always left her drained of cheer), and then she shopped at the local market (overpriced, which did not improve her mood), and then she came home, and then she made dinner, cooking for Jonah but dreaming of somebody else.

At eight o'clock, she picked up a novel. Jonah would have been watching TV (a new habit, a symptom of depression—though Jonah said that was hogwash), and she was glad for once not to have her attention compelled by the noise. So much for Jonah's dependability; now that was eroding, too. She felt self-righteous, not worried.

Sometime after nine, the doorbell rang. Standing at her door was Stavros, behind him two policemen.

Fern saw Stavros once a month, when she dropped off the rent at his father's office. They spoke about weather, politics, neighborhood buzz. Now and then, she would see him on a nearby street; they would smile and nod.

Looking up at these three grim faces, her first, illogical fear was of eviction. Next, evacuation (a gas leak or fire, an impending explosion). Her third fear (because the halls were too silent for a public catastrophe) was that a felon on the run must be hiding out in their building.

All these thoughts crossed her mind in the time it took her to say yes, of course they could come in. They went no farther than the cramped kitchen, where the sallow light made the three men look even more despondent.

"Fern," said Stavros in his deep, mossy voice, "something tragic has happened." Without pausing for merciless effect, without touching her—though she could see his hand begin to rise toward her shoulder, then fall—he told her that Jonah was dead, that his body had been found by the super in the narrow courtyard out back, that it looked like an accident, that he appeared to have fallen from their apartment. This very apartment, where Fern had spent the past few hours acting as if he was still alive to enrage her.

She said, "But he's in Queens. And I've been here all evening."

The three men stared at her like a trio of worried fathers, giving her time to catch up. Standing by the kitchen window, she became aware of voices in the courtyard. All right, she felt herself reason, let's just say this is true. Let's not be contrary here. "Can I . . . should I go down and . . . ?"

This time his hand did meet her shoulder, tentatively. She willed it to stay there, hold her in place. "You don't need to see him, I think." Stavros looked to one of the officers, who said, "You can if you want, ma'am, but I wouldn't. Not right now I wouldn't."

"But we'll need you to come to the station," his partner said. "You might call somebody to come in with you, I'd do that if I were you."

The first person Fern thought of was Aaron. This made her burst into tears, tears at the treachery even of her imagination, grief at having effectively wished Jonah dead.

Stavros put both of his arms around her. She leaned her head on his shoulder; he seemed to be just the right stature for comfort. His shirt was light blue, a fine cotton, and her tears instantly darkened the fabric. The hair at the side of his neck, which was damp, touched her cheek. He smelled lovely and clean, like rich expensive soap, linden or vetiver. Fern had a flash memory of Stavros in a neighborhood playground, playing handball on a stretch of tarmac. (She had slowed, transfixed for a moment by his ardor for the game.) He must have played this evening, then showered, and then, somehow, received a call about a body in the courtyard of one of his family's buildings. Did he carry a pager? Who had called him—the super?

Fern needed to stop this wasteful train of thought. She needed to stop crying. Though Stavros did not seem to mind; patiently, he continued to hold her. One of the officers gave short answers to incomprehensible questions that crackled out of his radio. Perhaps they had nothing to do with Jonah. The other officer was writing on a pad of paper.

She pulled away from Stavros's fragrant blue shoulder. She noticed that below his neat, short haircut, more dark curly hair grew down the back of his neck past his collar. The hairs were finer, no longer pure black but a reddish brown. She had never liked so much hair on a man, but that was where her cheek had been and would gladly have settled again.

Stavros was frowning at her, somehow both gravely and sweetly. "I'll go with you, if you like. Or I could call someone for you."

"Thank you," she said simply. "Thank you." He would be the one to go with her; she could think no further. A near stranger had never seemed so significant in her life.

"Ma'am, can we have a look at your back windows?" asked the officer with the pad.

Fern stepped away from the kitchen window; there were also two in the living room. All three were open, as they had been when she came home. It was early September, still summer by day, but the air cooled fast after dark. This was about the hour she would have closed those windows, happy to feel the sly chill. Stavros saw her shiver.

"You need to sit down." As he steered her into the living room, he said, "I'm a useful guy by training, so let me be useful however I can." He guided her, as you might guide a tiny elderly woman with porcelain bones, to the couch. She told him he could make himself useful by sitting there with her, anywhere was fine, while she made the phone calls she had to make.

As she listened to the futile ring of Jonah's mother's phone (it was bridge night; even Fern knew that by now), she examined the green damask on the cushions beneath her and remembered how she'd admired this sofa in Jonah's mother's house and how, to her surprise, it had become abruptly hers, a disconcerting gift—just as Jonah had become on a night when she drank one too many margaritas and joked that they were both so hopelessly square they ought to be married.

SLEEP ELUDES HER, but she likes having the silent house to herself, lying naked under crisp expensive sheets in this pretty bedroom, watching clouds blow listlessly, one by one, across six panes of blue. She spreads her hands on either side of her taut stomach, waiting for movement. There, and there again. When she lies down, the baby goes to work, limbering up, rehearsing for life. She is like a greenroom.

Fern had known that, given the chance, she would find out the sex of the fetus (in her life, there were plenty of mysteries already), but when the sonographer asked, her yes came out like a panicked yelp, a surge of superstitious doubt. The sonographer said, "Ordinarily, I don't like to say unless we're doing an amnio, but seeing what I'm seeing, I'd say there's very little chance it's not a boy." He pointed to something inscrutable on the screen.

It took her several seconds to understand. Then all she heard was *boy,* a formerly short unremarkable word that seemed to burst above her body like a volley of fireworks, that suddenly seemed as bright and complex as a pomegranate or a coral reef. When she left the hospital, she looked at her male counterparts walking the streets as you might consider a swarm of migrating butterflies, one eye empirically curious, the other plainly awed. My *son,* my *son,* she kept thinking, unable to move her hands away from her center. She hailed a cab; inside, she began to laugh. How in the world would she do this thing—not give birth to a baby but raise a boy? A boy. Seedling of a man.

Carrying that otherness inside her, everywhere and all the time, she thinks of Stavros and his features, so different from hers. Will her baby be dark, outwardly defying her genes? Could he inherit that small appealing mole on his father's left eyelid? Before she even slept next to Stavros, when she would examine it at leisure, Fern asked him to close his eyes for a moment so she could see what caused that strange flash of color whenever he blinked. The mole was honestly blue—cerulean, she thought. "It's so beautiful," she said, and was immediately embarrassed. They had not even kissed.

Stavros spared her by laughing quietly. "My father thinks I should have it removed. He says it looks like cancer."

"What a terrible thing to say."

Stavros shrugged. "He's my father. Fathers say what they like."

"You approve of that?"

"Of course not," he said. "But I accept it. It isn't something I'd waste the energy trying to change. Not in my own father."

His last postcard from Greece came enclosed in a small package. On the card, he told her that his grandmother had finally died, in her sleep as everyone had prayed she would, and that all sorts of ancient ceremonies were unfolding. There would be the dividing of her few possessions, he said, and he and his mother would spend a few days in Athens, where she liked to shop. He told her when they would return. He ended by saying how much he missed her and signing off with his usual thousand kisses. But along with the card was a small flat present wrapped in Greek newsprint and tied with black yarn. Inside was a beaded change purse with a zippered closure. The primitive image made by the beads was the figure of a naked woman. Her body wrapped around the purse so that she appeared waist-up on one side, waist-down on the other. Because of the limited medium, she had owlish black-and-white eyes and large pink breasts that stood out left and right, a single red bead for each nipple. Her ample yellow hair hung down her back; on the flat black ground, it looked as if she were lying on a beach towel on volcanic sand. Fern knew enough Greek letters to be able to read the word that ran, like a banner, beside the body: AΦP on the side with her torso, OΔITH alongside her legs. Aphrodite.

The object reminded Fern of crafts she had practiced in camp (gimp necklaces, macaroni bracelets, paperweights made with tiny pinecones and plastic goop in an ice cube tray). Yet it was wonderful, too—crude yet classical, made with earnest labor and a respect for tradition. It would be empty, of course, but she opened it by reflex. Inside was a slip of paper on which Stavros had written three words in Greek. And then, in parentheses, *For my goddess.*

SHE WAKES TO THE SAME SKY, so ardently blue, but to a different set of sounds: voices, outside but nearby, and a steadier, rhythmic sound, not tennis this time but . . . digging. A shovel assaulting the earth. Two voices—men's voices, subdued and private. She cannot hear the words, but she can tell that neither one is Tony's. The conversation stops. Soon after, the digging stops.

Fern rises onto her knees and looks out the window beside the bed. Clasping the sheet to her chest, she unhooks the screen. With her head outside, she hears more distant sounds: lawn mowers, seagulls, children shrieking on the beach. She scans the entire lawn. There: at a back corner, in an elbow of privet, a hole in the ground, a spade on the grass. Just as she spots it, she hears the door to her room open behind her.

"Oh I'm—God I'm sorry." The door closes again, but she saw the man briefly. His arms, face, and clothing were streaked with dirt, but he looked genteel despite the grime. Irrationally—defenseless, naked in a bedsheet, alone in a stranger's house—she isn't afraid. Embarrassed, but not afraid. She assumes this must be Tony's "third," however peculiar his entrance.

From outside the door, he explains himself. "I know Tony's here, I saw the car, I didn't stop to think there'd be anyone else. I'm so sorry."

"It's all right, just wait a sec, Tony's at the beach," says Fern as she pulls on her dress. She opens the door. "Hi."

He continues to apologize: for walking in without knocking, for frightening her, for failing to call ahead. Fern takes in the details she missed: He is dressed, impractically for digging, in khaki pants and a white button-down shirt, sleeves rolled back. He is slender, well-kept but unmuscled, neither short nor tall. His hair, a reddish blond, is fading to the color of desert sand, refusing to gray. Tony's age, but without the insistence on youth—and certainly without the sylvan boyishness of Tony's usual consorts. His face is intelligent, even attractively lined.

Etched in the gray film on his cheeks are threads of pink skin, pathways left by tears. Only his bare feet are clean.

"I'm a friend of Ralph's—Fenno McLeod. I'll just go wash up downstairs and then I'll explain," he says. So this is the hanger-on with the funny name. Fern recognizes his alluring accent as Scottish; this, she supposes, is why he did not alarm her (as if Scotland doesn't have its share of psychos).

After brushing her hair and putting on sandals, she goes down as well. She pours two glasses of lemonade. She finds him on the front porch, rapping his sneakers against a stair to dislodge clumps of soil.

He glances up. His hands and face are clean. "I'm not behaving logically. I'm sorry. I'm used to making myself at home."

"Oh go ahead. I'm like a guest twice removed. I don't even know your friend Ralph, so please. Save the explanations." She hands him a glass.

He thanks her. "Well, not for Tony I won't."

Fern laughs. She sits on a white director's chair (too much of the furniture here is white, she decides; it feels like a test of some kind). She would ask this man how he knows Tony—through Ralph? and just who is this Ralph?—but he does not laugh along with her. He sits on the top step and stares at his hands on the glass of lemonade, then toward the driveway, at an old Volkswagen bus. Sky blue and white, it looks remarkably new.

Fern hasn't seen one of those cars in ages; it's like a postcard from her childhood. There's a silk sunflower wired to the antenna and, on the driver's door, a large reflective Celtic cross. Scattered along the side are several bumper stickers. Three are bold enough to read from the porch:

IF YOU WANT PEACE, WORK FOR JUSTICE.

PERPETRATE PHOTOSYNTHESIS.

LIFE. WHAT A BEAUTIFUL CHOICE. (This one twice, front and rear.)

She looks again at Fenno McLeod, the man who drives this highly declarative vehicle. Seeing her amusement, he says, "I'm not—it's not mine."

How quickly, Fern thinks, we can fear we've been politically typed: by a word, a pair of shoes, a haircut, a bumper sticker on a borrowed car. "Well, whoever owns it has to be a character of some kind. Someone who doesn't mind about the zeitgeist."

Now he does laugh. "Yes. That's absolutely true."

"A woman," says Fern. "Your mother?"

"Not mine, but mother to a horde of people who desperately need a mother. Or need a good one."

"Including you?"

Fenno McLeod smiles at the bus as if at an irrepressible secret. "To me, she's more like a well-intentioned mother-in-law. She acts as if I'm hers, but she treats me well." He drains his glass and sets it down.

Silently, both of them look at the glass. The moisture on its surface is gray with dirt that must have remained in the fissures of his palms. He says, "I came here to bury my dog. If you don't mind, I'm afraid I'd better finish. The heat . . ." He looks again at the bus.

"I'm sorry," says Fern. Then the screen door slams behind her.

"Well what a surprise!" Tony stands above them in his bathing suit and T-shirt. He looks ruddy, as if he's had too much sun. "Fern, meet Fenno. Fenno, Fern. Hey, I sound like Letterman botching the Oscars."

"We've met," says Fern.

"I've just driven out from the vet's," Fenno says. "Rodgie's kidneys failed." He pauses, as if to give Tony a chance at another bad joke. But Tony looks suddenly attentive, even sad.

"Poor Rodge," he says.

"Ralph always said I could bury him here, next to Mavis. Absurdly sentimental, but I couldn't just consign him to the surgery rubbish."

"Poor old Rodge." Tony sighs, but he moves no closer to Fenno.

"Yes, very old. The last of my mother's collies. The last of Mum, I kept thinking in the midst of all that traffic. Well." He stands.

The men exchange warmer smiles. Fern feels a stale, tiresome envy stir. Fenno goes to the bus, opens the back, and lifts out a bulk wrapped in a blanket. He heads around the back of the house.

"Need anything?" calls Tony.

Fenno calls back, "In about fifteen minutes, Ralph's Glenfiddich. I'm sure you know where it's kept by now."

"Well," Tony says to Fern, "good thing I bought two dozen ears and the family-size barbecue pack. . . . And hey, now the party's complete."

A small, nondescript car pulls in behind the bus, and out springs (there is no other word) the boy Fern has been dreading.

"Look at you, look at you, all shiny from the beach!" the boy calls to

Tony. "Hello hello," he says melodically to Fern. He bounds up the stairs and holds out his hand. "I'm Richard. And I love your shade of yellow."

Fern looks down at her dress. "Sun," she says idiotically. Looking up, she sees the kiss planted on Tony's cheek and the sharp flicker of Tony's eyebrows, as if a protocol's been breached. But he does not pull back.

"Which we all worship, don't we?" Richard replies to Fern with a genuine smile. He is immediately likable, never mind his nubile glow and exhibitionist energy. He has that riveting saffron-haired, blue-eyed coloring, freckles like shrapnel but muted by a careful tan, teeth incandescent, chest too perfectly smooth and shapely. He might be twenty-four. (Didn't these boys make Tony feel old? This one makes even Fern feel stiff in the joints.)

When she stands, Richard exclaims, "Oh, and expecting too! Wowie! Congratulations!"

"Thank you." Fern picks up the empty glasses and takes them into the house. She runs water to rinse them, to drown out any insinuating words between Tony and Richard.

But like a puppy, Richard has followed her into the kitchen. "I'm ready to chop or whatever. Put me to work!" Tony stands behind him, looking amused and annoyed.

"It's five-thirty," he says. "This isn't Nebraska."

"Oh I can wait. Just want to be sure I'm helpful!" says Richard. His tank top (tight) advertises a dog walk to fund cancer research. He wears tiny gold crosses in both ears and, on one wrist, a band of braided rope. When he sees Ralph's dog (looking woozily up from his bed), he cries out, "There he is!" and rushes over to kneel and fuss. "What's his name?"

"Druid," Tony says with a smirk. "Like whatever happened to Spot and Rex? Good old doggy-dog names."

"Oh but that's a cool name! Druids were wise and mysterious. They built Stonehenge," says Richard as he strokes the happy spaniel. "Hello, you're a handsome boy! . . . And what a beautiful coat you have, Druid. Someone takes good care of you, oh yes!"

Fern cannot read Tony's face. He seems to be tolerating these effusions as you would a younger sibling's naive behavior.

"Now *this* is a *nice* springer, you can tell. Don't see that often these days," says Richard. "Sudden rage syndrome just about ruined the breed, you know. All because of one stud back in the seventies, an AKC champion bred entirely for looks." He shakes his head. "I'm no fan of the AKC, I can tell you that." He stands and looks brightly toward Fern, apparently unperturbed that no one's acknowledged his statement.

"Shall I take it out?" says Fern as she sees Tony take a glass and a bottle from a cupboard. She is afraid of being left alone with this eager guest, afraid he's the type who will lose no time at probing, in all his burly innocence, toward some murky corner of her heart.

"You'll make a better graveside companion," says Tony. He fills the glass with Scotch.

As she approaches the hedge, Fern sees Fenno stamping down the surface of the grave. Somehow, she's disappointed not to have seen the dog before he was buried.

For the second time, he accepts a glass from her and thanks her. "I should plant something," he says, looking down. He splashes Scotch on the dark naked soil. "My father, right now, would recite a bit of Burns. Disgracefully, I've forgotten every line I ever learned. Proof that I am thoroughly and finally an exile." He raises the glass toward the grave and drains it.

"You're staying for dinner," says Fern, hoping he'll take it as fact.

"I'm not doing any more driving today, that's certain."

"Stay over," she says. "Tony won't mind."

"I hardly need Tony's permission. He has the place because of me."

"And I get the feeling the room I'm in is yours."

"Nothing here is mine; Ralph's just a very old friend. We work together—practically live together, too. We walk in and out of each other's lives like a pair of old unmarried sisters."

Fern is about to comment that he hardly looks like a spinster when Richard's voice interrupts her.

"Hello down there!" he calls out from the porch. "I am so sorry about your dog, about Rodgie! I hear he was truly a fine old soul!"

Fenno shades his eyes. "Who's that?" he says quietly.

Richard is crossing the lawn at a clip, right hand outstretched, face set in a look of almost tearful sympathy. Fern turns aside because she is about to start laughing. As she turns, a tall man comes through the hedge. He looks at her with expectant pleasure. Another member of the

face-lift brigade, she assumes (here to borrow a cup of . . . brandy? dinner mints? dried porcini?), until he says, "I hope you're taking good
care of my brother. He needs it!"

Richard stands beside Fern, speechless for the first time since his arrival.

"I thought I'd have to come fish you out of the surf," says Fenno.
Fern recalls now that she heard two voices outside when she woke up.

"I got a bit carried away and lost track of time. My God but it's
bloody lovely here!" He picks up the shovel with one hand and strokes
Fenno's back with the other. He looks at Fern and Richard again. "Oh
dear, do introduce me," he says, and as Fenno does, there is something
about his tone, his expression, that makes Fern wonder if this brother—
Dennis (younger, taller, more handsome and joyful)—has somehow de-
posed or outpaced him.

"My, my, a real swah-ray." As one, they look up toward the house.
Tony leans over the porch rail, grinning. He looks like a monarch or the
Pope, taking for granted that they will applaud.

SIXTEEN

SOMETIMES FERN THINKS that she thinks too much about family. She lives, it's true, in a time and place of rampant psychotherapy (in which she spent several years herself), but even so, she cannot help looking at people in a perpetual context of mothers, fathers, brothers, sisters. Especially brothers and sisters.

Often, she imagines herself as wearing several leashes, each quite long but held by another member of her far-flung family. She senses various pulls and tugs at various times, never feeling altogether free.

Though Fern has always been a perfect daughter in her parents' eyes—they tell her so too often—this status costs her something in the eyes of her siblings. She isn't the youngest, yet they sometimes make her feel like the least sensible, the least sure, the least anchored. The one who's squandered her talents, ill used her opportunities.

Arcadia, the Olitskys' nursery, still thrives in the pretty town where Fern grew up, tucked back in the Connecticut Berkshires. Her parents are the rare couple living a mutual dream, even if it's one that made their children subtly resentful: resentful at being crowded into a charming but tiny house in a town where all their schoolmates were richer; where, every summer, they had to work in the family business and wait on those schoolmates' parents, loading coiled hose and fertilizer into their trunks, digging holes in their lawns for new trees. Fern's mother, in addition to helping her husband nurture saplings, rosebushes, and hothouse succulents, makes exquisitely tasteful dried wreaths, keeps bees and sells their honey. An almost pagan disciple of Mother Nature, Helen Olitsky named her offspring Heather, Fern, Forest, and Garland. Saying grace at every dinner of their childhood, she would thank God for various minute blessings of the day, then look up briefly, smile at each of them, bow her head again and say to her lap, "Thank you, most of all, for the garden of my heart."

Gar, the baby, is the one who has stayed to take over the nursery. It's easy to see that he loves it, that he inherited every green gene his parents possessed, has an inborn feel for the elemental (he will taste soil readily, as if it were wine, and tell you its composition). But he tends to lord it over the rest of them, to wield his old-fashioned fealty like a deed—preparing them, Fern is sure, for getting the most when their parents die. The year Fern went to Europe was the nursery's worst—drought, gypsy moths, and a random IRS audit. Gar was barely in high school, but even now, he never lets Fern forget that she basically jumped ship. She has long since stopped defending herself.

As if letting his name set his course, Forest moved to Montana, where he preaches a love of nature that requires no cultivation, only protection. He lives in a sparsely furnished cabin at the end of a long dirt road, without neighbors or, to Fern's knowledge, a lover. The managing editor of a struggling left-wing newspaper, he is a perfectionistic wordsmith. Forest would never refer to Lyme's disease, Canadian geese, or the Klu Klux Klan—and he would have a hard time not correcting those who do. When Fern and Jonah took a week of vacation to visit him, she was amused to find on his refrigerator an article called "The Endangered Semicolon" (held there by a magnet shaped like the also-endangered red wolf). "Has it made the government's list?" she asked merrily.

Not that he was humorless or stingy. He took Fern and Jonah on a number of wonderful expeditions, each planned with care. But when she stayed up with Forest one night and tried to discuss the work they suddenly had in common, he said, "Yes, design is very important, but in the end you have to remember: There's style, and then there's substance."

The night before they left, he drove them an hour into Bozeman, to treat them to dinner at a restaurant regarded as Montana's finest. Coming from New York, Fern and Jonah knew this effort to impress them might be overblown, but they said nothing. Their silence felt to Fern like sweet collusion—when they had had no union of any kind for weeks. In fact the food was very nice, and Fern was thrilled to see her favorite dessert on the menu. "Tiramisu at the Continental Divide!" She touched Jonah's knee under the table, the wine having filled her with a warmth she longed to share. "Do you know what it means? 'Hold me tight.' Isn't that romantic?" she said to Forest.

To which he replied, with a reticent smile, "Actually, it means 'pick-me-up.' I suppose because it contains espresso."

Embarrassed, Fern removed her hand from Jonah's knee. She told the waiter she was too full for dessert. She and her husband slept that night, as they did back home, on opposite sides of Forest's extra futon. Unfairly, she knew, Fern blamed Forest for dousing in her, on purpose, a rare, precious spark of conciliation toward her husband.

With Heather, Fern is the closest and also the most contentious. For their entire childhood, they shared a room. Heather was the athlete: swam, played field hockey, fenced. At schoolwork, she was comfortably mediocre. After high school, she went to a small vocational college where she majored in "leisure studies." Fern used to look down on her for this—but does not feel so smug since her sister has become the chief U.S. commerce and tourism rep for Tuscany, shepherding elite groups of journalists and merchants to Italy six times a year. Her kitchen is always stocked with extraordinary sweets and cheeses, her closet with sophisticated shoes. She lives on Lake Shore Drive with her husband, a financial analyst, and their two athletic, well-mannered sons. Heather met Eli at her first job, in a travel agency, and likes to say that he gave her a "head start on life." If Eli is there, he'll shoot back, like a soaring badminton birdie, "And this lady booked me on the Concorde to Love."

For the odd weekend, Fern likes to visit, almost more than her sister, her sister's wondrous life. It's a small, happy planet on a speedy orbit around its own benevolent sun. Heather is also generous, if myopically so; she always insists on taking her little sister shopping on that Moneybags Mile or whatever it's called. Fern, who stopped resisting long ago, will return to New York with a silk dress or cashmere jacket, an item she may wear once a year to the rare dress-up lunch with a client.

The problem with Heather is that she's made herself a junior mother to Fern, though Fern is only two years younger. Ever since Fern's move to New York, Heather has kept up a constant critique of her sister's love life (not even sparing Jonah): "Honestly, honey, the boys you pick, they're all so . . . ingrown or something. Is it that city? Does it just turn everyone into a narcissist or what? I don't mean you, of course. . . . But look at Eli. Hardworking, civic-minded, wakes up happy every day. Now, Fern, can you tell me that a single one of those broody guys I've met wakes up to greet the day with a smile?"

"So introduce me to one of Eli's happy pals," Fern has replied, not entirely joking. But Eli's friends, like Eli, are married, perpetually necktied, and have a small round area at the dome of their skulls where their hair has been subtly, permanently flattened by the yarmulkes they wear so often—like medals for their responsibility and goodness—to all the right occasions.

Had Heather seized on the secret of their parents' translucently peaceful marriage? Fern feels a wrenching envy at this thought, a sense of having been left behind. Who is the smarter sister now?

"OH MAIZE—BRILLIANT!—OR CORN, yes, that's what you call it," says Dennis. Fern shows him how to peel away the husk and silk, twist them off in a single motion. "I'm having an authentically American experience—shucking corn! And here I am in need of tutoring; wouldn't my students have a laugh?"

Fern asks him what he teaches. They are sitting on the back porch stairs with a bag of corn between them, another for the husks at their feet.

"Cooking, as a matter of fact. I'm a guest instructor at this culinary institute place. Teaching a class titled—not my title!—Trends in Culinary Cross-Pollination. And am I ever the impostor!"

"You aren't a chef?" asks Fern.

"Indeed I am. I have a little mongrel of a restaurant in France—have you ever been to Aix? These American food blokes—not really critics, more like collectors—happened in last summer when I was having a bang-on day. What do athletes call it—the zone? I was in the zone. So the food blokes stayed till closing time and chatted me up and invited me over for a month. I'm crashing on my brother's couch and having a fine time pulling the wool over everyone's eyes. I cook almost strictly French, I'm hardly a basher of traditions, but these chaps heard my accent and imagined haggis provençal or mouton Marmite or some such concoction. Though I do have a 'trifle française' using eau de vie in place of sherry, with apricots and fromage blanc."

She tells him it sounds delicious; he answers that indeed it is. Like Richard, this man has a luster that in itself must make him popular—besides which he's very good-looking: tall, with straightforward rectangular features (face, torso, hands) and the kind of expressive physicality that women find reassuring. His cheeks are perpetually rosy, suggestive, authentically or not, of modesty and sweetness.

"Are we missing out on a four-star meal?" says Fern. "You ought to have told Tony what you do."

"Oh no. Nothing a chef likes better than being fed, and I've been fed quite nicely hereabouts. Though I will confess, I do not begin to comprehend your dairy products. We Brits are backwards in the cow department, except for clotted cream and double Gloucester, but bloody hell, these bricks of yellow rubber! My students force-fed me a thing called Philadelphia, more like a nursery paste . . ."

Fern has settled contentedly into nodding at this banter when Richard comes out of the house bearing a platter. "Hello! I'm here to collect the ears!"

"Hear, hear," says Dennis.

Fern transfers a dozen from her lap. The corn is yellow and white, the kernels opalescent and well aligned. "It's so early, but it looks wonderful."

"Oh this'll be from way down south, nowhere close by," says Richard.

"Ah, what the jet plane's done for the human tastebud," says Dennis.

Leaving the two men to share their pleasantries, Fern goes inside.

Fenno is setting the dining room table with gold-rimmed plates. She watches him from behind; he moves slowly and deliberately, as if it's a ceremony worthy of contemplation. She realizes he must be slowed by his grief, by weariness. When she asks if he'd like help, he looks up, startled.

"Napkins." He nods at the sideboard. "Top left. The purple ones."

Half the drawer contains antique silver napkin rings, long cellophaned candles, and a stack of the delicate glass cuffs that Jonah's mother taught her to call bobeches. The other half is filled with fabric napkins, flowered and plain in a dozen colors. "This is someone's second home?" says Fern.

"Not quite. Ralph's auditioning for retirement. Next winter will be a dry run."

"To see if he goes nuts from the isolation."

"More likely from the cozy, communal drunkenness."

"Not exactly a dry run then."

Fenno's laugh is polite but distracted. He points her toward wine-glasses and candlesticks. They circle the table in tandem, taking turns at different places. Across the bowl that Tony filled with roses from the garden, Fern steals glances at Fenno. His face at rest has a mournful set, his nose long and narrow, mouth a downcast crescent. For a gay man on Long Island at the end of June, he is oddly, perhaps defiantly pale. She suspects, approvingly, that he is not part of this scene, of boy-watching with binoculars from Victorian porches, of bringing home charming strangers for candlelit dinners.

Tony leans into the room. "How are we doing, dears? The chicken's all done and sucking up its juices. Water's boiling and aching to get at that corn."

Fenno looks at Tony with pointed indifference as he twists the last candle into its pedestal. "And plates are pining to be licked."

They have been lovers, she's certain now, and not in the transient, calculating way that Tony and Richard are lovers. When Tony retreats, she says, "How long have you been here—in the States?"

"Twenty years. More."

"Here to stay."

He smiles. "Sometimes I still pretend otherwise."

The speakers on top of the sideboard emit a faint hum.

"The new Van Morrison, the one who's seen the light of God," says Fern after just a few notes. "Tony's current favorite."

Fenno raises his eyebrows. "Curious, some of his tastes." In the look he gives Fern, she sees him guess her history, too. They are even.

Through the doorway dances Richard, holding aloft the platter of steaming corn. Dennis follows, carrying, with equal flamboyance, the chicken and grilled asparagus. They set the platters at opposite ends of the table. Tony comes in last, with two bottles of wine and a loaf of gar-lic bread swaddled in a linen towel. Fenno lights the candles. The five of them stand back, somewhat shyly, regarding the table like an altar. Tony says, "Little mother at the head."

"All right, but I refuse to serve," Fern says.

"Don't worry, don't worry. It's every man for himself, in utero or out."

To Fern's left sit Dennis and Fenno, to her right Tony and Richard.

The table curves out in such a grand way that it's hard not to feel like a hostess, like someone in charge of the conversational tides. The men's faces are orange, their eyes gleaming as they lean in, helping themselves and deferring politely all at once, filling their plates only after Fern's been coaxed into taking far more than she should eat.

"*A notre santé,*" says Dennis, lifting his glass.

"Chinny chin chin," says Tony.

After a round of appreciative murmurs, Richard looks up from his food. "Is this summer or what?" he says, his lips glistening with butter. His plate is heaped with vegetables and bread, no chicken, and he's drinking only water. Of course, thinks Fern as she bites directly into her meat, such obstreperous health does not come free.

"Well heaven bless the jet plane if this isn't local fare. And your chicken marinade is *magnifique,*" Dennis says to Tony.

"So, Fenno's brother with the fine French accent, where've *you* been hiding?" says Tony.

"He lives in France," Fenno says primly.

"He hides the lot of us over there, on the other side of the pond. I'm the brave pioneer, the first one to sally forth and visit."

"I've always made it clear you're welcome, all of you." Fenno looks uneasy at Tony's attention to his brother, though it's not clear whom he wants to protect. Fern remembers, long ago, introducing Anna to Tony, not sure if she wanted them to like or despise each other, seeing safety on both sides.

"After your fashion, yes," says Dennis.

Tony says wryly, "Oh, I know that fashion. More Helsinki than Milan."

"Excuse me, but . . . anyone?" Richard's holding a small object aloft between his fingers. "It's the real, Rastafarian thing."

Tony doesn't answer; Fenno shakes his head. When Richard glances at Fern, she says, "Oh no," and he grins. "Good girl," he says.

But Dennis is positively beaming. "My wife would macerate me, but oh yes, I'll try a bit of that. And my children aren't around to see how foolish I'll be." His hand meets Richard's over the roses. Fern catches the first whiff of dope. She can count on one hand the number of times she's tried it—not because she disapproves but because it always scorched her throat and perhaps because she doesn't like the idea of losing control in some unpredictable way. So the fragrance of marijuana brings her no specific memories, only the general sense that she is refusing a certain kind of intimacy. She feels reluctant, apprehensive, stodgy; she feels flashes of an old indeterminate sadness.

She is contemplating this feeling, even as she tells herself that for once she is in a dissenting majority, when Fenno startles, as if stung or kicked, and reaches into his shirt pocket. He pulls out a compact cell phone and opens it, turns its face toward the candles. He scowls at it, then tucks it back in his pocket.

"Now will you look at that," says Tony. "Rob Roy girds up for the twenty-first century."

"Just checking the thing's on. It's new; I haven't actually used it."

"But you're on the alert, just in case an order of coffee table books goes astray? Or what? This guy," Tony says to Richard, "doesn't even have e-mail."

"I'm sort of on call, for one of the girls."

Tony laughs and shakes his head, as if he's caught his friend at some unsavory scheme. "You mean, at that Lulu's place?"

"That's right," Fenno says agreeably.

Tony turns to Fern. "Now you will love this. Ask the guy what he does with his spare time—I mean, practically does for a living. Go on. Ask him."

"Oh yes, this is stellar," says Dennis. He hands the joint to Richard and sits back in his chair.

Fenno leans toward Fern. "What Tony finds so titillating, because he's never got past his pubescent squeamishness about the birds and bees, is that I volunteer at a drop-in center on the Lower East Side for single girls who are pregnant and waiting to have their babies. It makes him squirm to think of me mixing it up with all that conspicuous fertility."

"No, I love this, I really do," says Tony. "I don't think I know anyone who does anything this Good Samaritan and really enjoys it, does it for the fun, not the do-gooder brownie points. I'm being serious here."

"Wow. Like you're a midwife?" Richard giggles. "A mid-husband?"

"Vocational training. I teach a class on composition skills and another on desktop publishing. We produce a small newspaper."

Tony cuts in. "*Girl Talk.* Soon-to-be-welfare-moms give their opinions on the Mideast peace talks."

Richard says, "Don't be catty, I think it's cool," but he drapes an arm around Tony's shoulders. Fern sees Tony pull slightly away.

"*Girlspeak,*" Fenno says, "and they give advice to other teenage girls on things like health and diet and love. They research subjects like city services for mothers. Some of it's a little absurd, I agree, but they're proud of it. We're up to six pages, biweekly. If we get a grant I've gone out for, we can introduce color and distribute to other school districts." He seems unruffled by Tony's goading; he loves describing this part of his life, even if that's what brings it out into the open.

"So what's with the phone? Breaking stories on birth control?"

"What's with the phone is that one of the girls I teach asked me to be her Lamaze coach. She's due a week from today."

"La-mahz." Tony's laugh is high-pitched, the way it gets when he's drinking too much wine. "So you, what, took those classes and practiced positions and all that? Chanted 'Push!' with all the hubbies?"

"I took the classes, yes," says Fenno.

"And I bet you loved it."

"*I'd* love it," says Dennis. "Entrée into the mysteries of another tribe. I have four children, but my wife's a bit old-fashioned there. She let me in that room only for the final moments of truth."

"Your wife's not old-fashioned," says Fenno. "She's what's known in these parts as a major control freak." He shakes his head with amusement. "And it's not mystical, what I learned. It's a lot of very practical stuff, like why a woman gets heartburn so much when she's pregnant, why babies are born with conical heads. I know about the best brands of breast pumps, where to lease them, and how to massage a blocked milk duct—a skill I hope I'll never use. I know all about the pros and cons of *circumcision.*" He leans in for effect, knowing, as Fern does, that under the table all the men's thighs are tensing.

A wave of loud male laughter follows, and everyone glances at Fern. Richard covers his mouth dramatically, as if to apologize for their boyish reaction.

"All that and runs a bookstore too," Tony tells her. "Right around the corner from you. Plume!" He says the name with fanfare, and of course she knows it: a watch pocket of a place that catches you off-guard with its cool, Green Mansions interior; not a hole in the wall but a garden in the wall, the kind of shop where you are compelled by its very perfection to buy something, anything, and feel forlorn if you walk out empty-handed.

"That's a dangerous place, I've spent a lot of money there," says Fern, though in truth it was Jonah who bought so many books there, so many expensive books, for which she would scold him. Books on Giotto, Caravaggio, Goya, Vermeer. Jonah's mother owns most of them now.

"Thank you," says Fenno.

They pass the platters back and forth for seconds. Richard and Dennis exchange another round of tokes. Dennis exhales audibly and says, "You've got to wonder, what kind of mums could these young girls possibly make?"

"First off," says Fenno, "a good number give their babies up for adoption. And with those who keep them, the social workers at the center follow up for years. Some of them make very decent mums. Some of them even marry the fathers, though I often wonder if that's so wise."

"Oh, my mom had me when she was seventeen," says Richard. "I hardly know the guy I'm supposed to call Dad. But she's been just fantastic, I still can't bear to live too far away from her. We talk on the phone like every other day. Go ahead and laugh, but she's my best friend." He looks at Tony, knowing full well who'd laugh first. But Tony just smiles, no comment.

"Well, against all modern logic," says Dennis, "maybe starting out young isn't such a bad idea. Maybe you don't have enough time to take your selfishness for granted. Vee was twenty-four when we had Laurie, and I worried about that. I thought, you know, she should enjoy her freedom longer and rubbish like that, but she was certain. She's quite the devoted mum."

"Twenty-four is ten years and a world away from fourteen," says Fenno.

"Yes, yes, point taken—but think of our mum, getting on to her thirties when she had you. She had all these *routines* that had nothing to do with children, and then she got the dogs. I tell you, I can't think of a time when I didn't almost wish I was a puppy; the *pups* were the ones who got that unconditional love we're all supposed to give our offspring."

Fenno frowns. "She loved the dogs as you're supposed to love dogs: consistently."

"Yes, but also more intimately, with more real attention, don't you think?" Dennis seems unaware of the corn kernels stuck to his chin. "Like dear old Roger, may he rest in peace. Do you remember the way she kept him close while she was dying? She'd whisper in his ear and nuzzle up with that dog as if he were human. She talked more to him than to Dad!"

Richard laughs. "Well *dogs*. When it comes to love, dogs make pretty steep competition for us people. And rightly so."

Fern looks at Tony, who hasn't spoken in a while. His arms are folded, his expression no longer wry as he watches the brothers debate.

"What was your mother like?" she asks him.

"Above reproach." Typically, his tone discourages any sort of reply.

Looking around the table, Fern pictures these men as sons, little boys adoring and resenting their mothers by turns. She tries to picture the mothers themselves. Richard's would be pretty in an ordinary way, and flaky, but warm and loyal; perhaps a drinker (the caution inspiring Richard's near-purity), living in one of those flimsy little houses shaped just like the houses in a Monopoly game. The Scottish mother she envisions as an artistocratic, dog-besotted Brit, a tumble of Jack Russells under her long tweed skirts; her voice loud and trilling but holding the children (when not with a nanny) to quieter standards. Tony's mother remains a cipher, a generic Madonna behind dark glasses and a long white cane. (How does a blind mother negotiate city streets with a baby? How does she push its carriage, aim a spoon at its bobbing and weaving mouth?)

"So, boys, what makes the perfect mother?" says Fern. "Tony?" She nudges his elbow. "Since yours sounds as if she was."

He hesitates but says, "Stands up to any bullshit your father deals out."

Before Fern can ask, *Like, for instance, what kind of bullshit?* Dennis says emphatically, "Just being there when you turn around. That is the cardinal virtue of the perfect mum."

"Amen to that!" says Richard.

"But that could hardly describe the mother of your children," Fenno says to Dennis. "Véronique with her ambitious career."

"You forget that Vee works at home!" Dennis says. "Oh yes, she's out and about to meet with clients, but she totes the wee'uns along, especially now that she's in demand, and when she's in the garden or the office, she'll drop just about anything at a moment's notice."

"As you don't think our own mum did."

Fern wonders if it's because he's stoned that Dennis seems to take this subject so lightly, that he seems not to notice the stern expression on his older brother's face. "You know how there were wife-swapping parties way back when?" he says now. "I remember reading about them in some tabloid when I was away at school and thinking, well, what a curious thing it might've been if we'd had a chance to mum-swap now and then. You know, see, just see, what it was like to have one of those domestic mums, about the house and baking biscuits, plumping your pillows . . ."

"You'd have been suffocated," says Fenno.

"Yes well perhaps, perhaps. But didn't you feel like she ought to have been a bit more regretful, shed just a single tear perhaps, about sending us off to school, to ice-cold washings and canings and all that militaristic rubbish?"

"For God's sake, they stopped caning by the time you and Davey were there. And everyone we knew got sent away to school, some a lot sooner."

Dennis pauses, looking at his brother with an odd smile. "You know, she was off on this jaunt to New Zealand when Davey had that awful fever and had to go in hospital because she couldn't take him home."

Fenno looks confused and annoyed. "We all got fevers now and then."

"No, no, this was the mumps or some other pox you're not supposed to get when you're twelve. I've never asked Davey since, for obvious reasons."

"You are high as a fucking kite. What are you talking about?"

Van Morrison's wheedling voice forces itself on the room for a long moment before Dennis lets out a mulish, snorting laugh. "You don't know that's what did in his sperm?" He tries to stop laughing but fails. "Oh crikes."

Fenno says, "You blame Mum for Davey's getting sick at school?"

Dennis shrugs dramatically. "Silly, isn't it? And Mum did plenty of things just right. I mean look at us. We love what we do, and isn't that a rare thing? I think she taught us to hold out for that, I mean by example, don't you think? All three of us. No coincidence there. And we're *mates,* I think she made sure of that. . . ."

Fenno appears to be rearranging his napkin in his lap.

"That's incredibly important, loving what you do," says Richard. "I love what I do, too."

There's a slight pause before Fern says, "What do you do?"

"I groom dogs right now, which is also a fabulous way to meet interesting people, but I'm training to be a veterinary technician."

Another pause follows, but imperturbable Richard plunges on: "I do housecalls and charge a top rate. I groom Ross Bleckner's dogs and Kim Basinger's and once I did Mike Nichols's, too. He has the most beautiful Gordon setter."

"Roth Bletchner, is that someone famous?" says Dennis.

"Society painter," says Tony. "Party animal, mainly. Hangs out at fund-raisers for charity cases like unemployed interior decorators or lifeguards who just came out of the closet. Gets his picture taken with liposucted debutantes."

"I think you're jealous," says Richard. "Ross is a great guy. Not a snob at all. He even asked my advice about the Lyme's disease vaccine. He has this standard poodle that's one of the smartest dogs I've ever met. She likes to listen to opera while we work. Isn't that fabulous?"

Tony snorts. "A poodle. Well need you say more."

"No, no. You're confusing standards with miniatures and toys. Standard poodles are the real thing, a dog bred for hunting. Steady and smart."

"The real thing. Well, I stand corrected." Tony's hands are poised over his plate, his fingers splayed like talons and blackened by char from the chicken skin. Fern has never seen him so persistently edgy; she doubts he would behave this way if he and Richard were alone. He must be embarrassed before the others that his date (his gigolo?) is this happy-go-lucky dog groomer. But that's no excuse. What did he think, that the boy would show up for dinner and debate the fallout of Clinton's impeachment or deconstruct Don DeLillo?

Van Morrison is done spreading the Word, and the wake of silence feels morose. In it, Fern becomes aware of her reluctant clarity, of remaining sober while others do not, of watching temperaments shift in ways she would not otherwise perceive.

Richard stands. "My turn! Where's the music stashed?" He sprints into the living room before he gets an answer.

In his gaping absence, Fern says, "Shall I cut the pie?"

"What a fine idea," says Tony, sounding genuinely grateful. "Miss Fern here makes the world's most outrageous pies," he says to Fenno.

Fenno nods. He looks ten years older than the man Fern met upstairs that afternoon. "I'll clear," he says.

From the kitchen, as she searches for a broad-bladed knife, Fern recognizes the opening notes of Beethoven's Pastoral Symphony. Should it surprise her that Richard would choose something so old-fashioned? No. Gigolo or not (and wouldn't the money go toward his vet-tech tuition?), the boy has a long, likable streak of cornball sweetness.

Pausing to appreciate the pie before she cuts it, Fern lets the music—joy distilled—invade her. Long ago, before Jonah, she had wished that a neat fragment of this symphony's ecstatic panorama could be extracted for a wedding procession. When she hears it now, its joy is painful. She is listening to a recording of her lost, outmoded certainty of what love would be: how uplifting, even in its storms.

TWO MONTHS AFTER JONAH'S DEATH, she ran into Stavros at a neighborhood toy store. They were shopping for nephews with adjacent birthdays. Fern walked in at the exact moment Stavros was startled by a velvet devil exploding from a jack-in-the-box. The instant of irrational terror on his face—on the face of such a conventionally masculine man—made her laugh. He looked happy to see her.

The manager of the toy store said, "And it's a collector's item, too."

Stavros regarded him as if he were nuts. "After being played with by a three-year-old?" Fern laughed again.

They looked at trucks, trains, gyroscopes, rubbery bath toys. They didn't buy a thing. As they left the store, Stavros said, "A drink, a cup of tea?"

"Tea," she said, charmed by so quaint an offer. She expected him to choose a coffee shop, but he led her to a large sooty building one block from hers, to the ground floor rear apartment. When he turned on the light, she must have betrayed her amazement, because he laughed and said, "My parents' place. I have to water my mother's plants. She's in Greece, and Dad doesn't do domestic things. If I had sisters, he wouldn't let me do them, either."

The living room was large but claustrophobically filled with dark weighty furniture, brocades and velvet in colors and muted patterns that reminded Fern of minerals: agate, granite, bloodstone. Icons hung on the wall, but they were equally dark and poorly lit. The air smelled heavy as well, of meat and spices. She sat on a voluminous blood-colored couch and watched Stavros make himself at home in a kitchen not much larger than hers. After putting a kettle on the stove, he walked through the living room and pulled back brown velvet drapes. "Come have a look," he called to Fern as he opened a pair of French doors and stepped outside.

Someone with talent and patience tended the garden before her. At the center was a tiled fountain (now dry), at the back a geometrically plotted planting bed. On three sides, the brick walls were nearly obscured by tall, well-established poplars and yews, beneath them sturdy bushes of box, hydrangea, mock orange, and lilac. From her childhood, Fern knew all these plants in an instant, even without their flowers. Stavros made the rounds with a hose. "Not much to look at now, but you should see this place in June." She admired the moss on the stones, a rose still in bloom, chrysanthemums of a bluish purple she had never seen before. Herbs grew in the mazelike bed at the back. Most were shriveled or cut back, but sage and rosemary, waist-high, still flourished in the sharp November air. She bent to smell them.

"Here." Stavros plucked leaves from three different plants. "All oregano. Varieties my mother swears you cannot find here anywhere." One by one, he rubbed them between his fingers and held them under Fern's nose.

She sighed, shocked at how their distinct but harmonious scents called up the Greece she had seen, nearly ten years ago, for only two weeks.

"I'll cut you some to carry home," he said.

As he surveyed the garden, his breath rose in prominent plumes. "My mother's left me complicated directions for mulching, in case she has to stay away much longer. You can't imagine *what* she'd do to me if anything died."

"Oh but I can." Fern told him about Arcadia, her summers of horticultural labor, the price of trial and error (your pay docked by the price of any plant you'd clearly killed—which only exacerbated finger-pointing among the Olitsky siblings).

In the living room, under a gaudy chandelier, they both drank tea, something dark and strong with a hint of cinnamon. Stavros told her about the courses he was taking when he wasn't helping his father run the neighborhood empire: real estate law and Homeric Greek.

"Your father must be pleased—about the Greek."

"Oh no. He thinks it's pointless and sentimental. His parents are dead, his brothers all came to this country, and he hasn't been back to the island where he grew up for ages. He left for good reason, he says! So Mom takes one or two of us over each summer, for a few weeks. She jokes that he won't let her take all three of her sons because then she might never return."

"She's not happy here?"

Stavros shrugged. "You know, I've asked her that. She never answers directly. I don't think she thinks in those terms."

Fern looked around at the saints, the pottery displayed on trays, a large black cross hanging like a list of commandments beside the kitchen door.

"This is where I grew up," said Stavros. "I know what you're thinking. My father owns this building; why not the penthouse? Well, my mother would never leave that garden. That—that I know makes her happy."

"But this is a huge place . . ."

"Two bedrooms. My brothers and I shared one."

Three boys in one room. Fern recalled her childhood gripes about shared bedrooms and bathrooms. But she had had yards and orchards and fields, a basement playroom. "How did you get any privacy?"

Stavros smiled at her for a moment before he said, "In Greek, you know, there's no word for privacy."

She laughed.

"I'm serious." He crossed the room and sat next to her on the couch, uncomfortably close. She stopped laughing.

He said, "Where you are sitting, that's where the only telephone was when we were growing up. Whenever I talked on the phone, my mother would come and sit right here. She was almost never out of the apartment, and she might be knitting or sewing on buttons or peeling potatoes, but whatever she was doing, she would come and sit this close while I talked to my friends. I especially hated it when she brought onions to cut up beside me. And when I hung up, she would say, 'So who flunked that history test? So who broke up with this girl Mary? So it is what movie you are going to see?'" Stavros put on a thick accent and held his face aggressively close to Fern's. Nervously, she laughed again. She could smell that same rich soap she had smelled two months ago, when she had cried on his shoulder.

He stood up, taking their cups to the kitchen. "She'd even stand outside the bathroom and wait while we took our showers."

"I'd have killed her," said Fern.

"Well yes, we could see our friends didn't live like that, but there was no complaining without consequences from our father. So when I was thirteen, I decided I could live like this by imagining that I was a very famous child, like what's-his-name, Grace Kelly's son the junior prince of Monaco, and had to have a bodyguard no matter where I went."

Fern stood in the doorway of the kitchen while Stavros washed their cups and laid them in a rack to dry. "Only problem was, I developed a celebrity complex and had to be brought back to earth."

"How did that happen?"

"That," he said, "is much too private to tell."

They laughed together. He told her his Greek class started in half an hour, but before they left the apartment, he took a pair of scissors and a ball of string from a drawer and went back into the garden. When he returned, he handed her three small bouquets of his mother's oregano. "If you like," he said, "hang them upside down for two weeks to dry them. But keep them in separate jars, so their flavors stay separate too." (In a dark place, in glass, away from the stove. From her own mother, Fern knew the routine.)

As Stavros locked the apartment door behind them, she asked, "Where do you live?"—half dreading he still lived here.

"I'm almost embarrassed to tell you." He looked at the ceiling. "Six floors up. But my mother doesn't have keys. When I go out of town, the super waters my plants."

"You're a gardener, too?"

"I am not," he said, though he sounded regretful. "I have a cutting of my mother's philodendron that all the mythical heroes I'm reading about couldn't begin to kill, and I made the mistake of starting an avocado pit last year. It won't stand up anymore without the support of an exercise bike I never ride, but somehow I can't bear to put it out of its misery."

On the sidewalk, she was about to say good-bye when Stavros said, "I haven't asked how you're doing. How are you doing?"

"I'm doing fine," she said. "Except . . ."

He waited. She sighed. "Except that my mother-in-law is coming this weekend to take away half the furniture."

Stavros frowned. "Because . . . ?"

"She thinks Jonah's death is my fault."

"Excuse me?" he said loudly.

"I can't explain, it's too complicated. The worst of it is, she used to like me, so the thought of seeing her this way . . ."

He said, "Would you like me to meet her and let her in?"

She thought about this for a moment. "You know, if you could just . . . be around. It's a huge favor, but she's so angry and I'm afraid she might . . ."

He looked at his watch. He touched Fern's shoulder. "I'm late for my class. I'll call you tomorrow and figure it out."

That was exactly what she needed: someone to figure things out. Even just the superficial things. And that was how it began.

"I'M NO DOCTOR, but this is what I prescribe." A glass of white wine and a stack of antique dessert plates seem to glide in from nowhere, landing on the counter beside her pie. A silver pie spade, its handle engraved with pansies.

Fern looks at the wine with longing. "Maybe three ears of corn will cancel it out." She hasn't touched alcohol in months and wonders if this one dose will send her, like a slingshot, into a state of abrupt, extreme inebriation. She takes a sip and turns around to smile at Fenno.

He is looking straight at her belly. "Five months?"

"You'd be an expert, wouldn't you."

"Unwitting amateur."

She cuts the pie in quarters, the quarters in half.

"That looks lovely," says Fenno.

"I like hearing men use that word. It sounds so sweet."

"Well sweetness, that's not a virtue of mine."

Fern looks at him. "I don't know. Look at what you've agreed to do for this girl . . . what's her name?"

"Oneeka." His expression betrays that it's taken him time to say this name without risking laughter.

"You could easily have refused her; it sounds like 'labor coach' wasn't a part of your job description."

"No, but I have to admit to a prurient interest—though I'm touched by her trust, and I like her. Childbirth is hardly something I'd otherwise witness. And then of course, I'll have no responsibility for the baby."

Fern pries the first slice free and cradles it onto a plate. "I wouldn't count on that. I bet she makes you godfather. Or names it Fenno, if it's a boy."

"God, I hadn't thought of that."

"I hope you like children," she teases.

"In fact I do. It shocks me sometimes."

"Are you one of those men whom everyone clamors to have as a godfather for their kids? I've noticed it's sort of the rage nowadays: the bachelor goddaddy who gives the most money and the most imaginative presents."

"The godfaggot, you mean. The fairy godfather." He laughs. "Well, nieces, I have plenty of those—as you may have gathered from my extremely stoned brother. I do love his daughters, all four of them. He likes to joke that he doesn't have to feel politically guilty because he and his wife simply co-opted my reproductive allotment. I told him that would be *one* baby, not two, and he told me that though it might be hard for me to face, my abstinence was depriving some poor woman somewhere of having *her* baby."

Fern spoons whipped cream onto five neat slices of pie, then leans against the counter and sips her wine. The sensation is extraordinary, like testing the ocean in May, feeling the icy cold rush up your legs and thrill its way into your bloodstream. She feels as if she's just waking up, glad to be in this kitchen with this man—and not looking forward to joining the others again. "But how often do you get to France?"

"I see them in Scotland, at Christmas, sometimes in the summer. And my brother back home, he and his wife have twins. A boy and a girl."

Fern is amused and touched by his obvious pride in these other people's children. Would she look this way if she mentioned Heather's sons? "How old?" she asks.

"Wonderful ages—three, six, seven, and nine. Or maybe, when

they're not yours, all the ages are wonderful. I have this idiotic fantasy that some of them, someday, might come over and stay with me, maybe to study." He picks up three plates. "Let's taste your creation, shall we?"

As they enter the dining room, Richard is saying, "The great news is that viral counts are down, but Y2K fears are through the roof. On the beach, it's like, all these people who last summer thought they were going to die are now just worried their stockbroker's system is going to crash. Like suddenly everyone's getting so healthy and paranoid all at once. It's sort of funny."

"Hardly everyone," says Fenno as he sets a plate in front of Richard.

"Pardon me?" Richard says brightly.

"Not everyone is getting so suddenly healthy."

"But everyone's on that new cocktail now . . ."

Fern has always been appalled by that infelicitous term; before AIDS, didn't drugs come in protocols and regimens, with appropriately military connotations? Fern the ex-waitress sees that old bar tray of twists and wedges, olives and onions, cherries more livid than neon. A tray of frivolous options, which these men don't have.

"Everyone isn't. And on it or not, people are still dying all over the place. Perhaps fewer people we know, but they are." Fenno says this wearily and not unkindly, as if it's something he's obligated to say.

"Tell you what," says Tony. "Let's talk about Y2K. Now *there's* a fresh subject." He digs his fork into his pie and takes a large bite, closes his eyes and murmurs loudly, "Mm, mm, *yes*."

Richard laughs, relieved. "Well the really scary thing I've heard is that, you know those rusty old missile silos in Russia? They're going to blow because they've been totally neglected. Like, *because* the cold war's over we're going to be nuked by those guys."

Dennis says, "Oh I seriously doubt that."

"Why? All the genius geeks are too busy fixing stuff on Wall Street. I'm telling you, that's all my clients talk about: like what if their stocks go poof?"

"Poof!" Tony echoes mischieveously.

"You should take this stuff more seriously," says Richard.

Tony touches him for the first time that Fern has noticed, clamping a hand on his shoulder. "Well I am glad you do. But if *we're* all going to go poof, what's the point of preparing for the future, taking all your courses?"

"Well the truth is, you never know, do you?"

"Now that *is* the truth," says Tony.

Dennis looks down the table at Fern. "Lass, this is a heavenly tart you've made us. Just brilliant." As Fern thanks him, he peers across at Richard and points at his plate. "But you, you've hardly touched yours!"

Richard looks at Fern and makes a despairing face. "I'm sorry, I know it must be scrumptious, but did I taste lard in here?"

"God, *I'm* sorry," says Fern, though she knows she shouldn't feel bad. No one told her she'd be feeding a vegetarian. No one told her a thing about what to expect of this evening; no one could have.

"A dab of pig fat won't make or break your karma," says Dennis. "And if it will, *I'll* jolly well eat your portion."

"Stop behaving like an ass," Fenno says, so quietly he might almost be addressing himself. But it's clear to Fern that he regards Dennis and his giddy indiscretions through the eyes of a father, not a brother. She thinks for a moment of her own brother Forest and his incessant judgments.

Richard has just slid his plate across the table to Dennis. Dennis freezes for a moment, the plate between his hands. "Sorry," he says, but defiantly. He stands and carries the pie into the living room, closing the door behind him.

Fern excuses herself to go to the bathroom. When she comes out, she hears her name, whispered loudly several times. Dennis sits in the dark of the living room, half-submerged in one of Ralph's plush white chairs. "I feel just rotten," he says.

Fern isn't sure how to reply.

His face is unclear in the gloom. "You know, all that insensitive AIDS talk—my brother's lover died of that. And he was one of those chaps who held on for years, way before these new drugs . . . I ought to have stood up there somehow. . . . Ohhhhh." With a mawkish sigh, Dennis rubs his face. "Oh dear but I *am* out of practice at this state of being." He giggles abruptly, reminding her how stoned he is. "Better get a little sea air. Ventilate my wonky brain." He isn't quite looking at her, and she wouldn't be surprised if he'd forgotten her presence as he stands unsteadily and goes out to the porch.

The dining room has emptied. On the table remain the bowl of roses, already beginning to droop, and four discarded napkins. A fifth lies on the floor. Crumbs wait to be brushed up, a tendril of smoke drifts from an extinguished candle. The front door bangs shut.

Fenno is at the sink, rinsing dishes. Without a word, Fern opens the dishwasher and reaches to take the first glass.

"Here we are again," he says. "Like survivors of a shipwreck."

"Did Richard leave in a huff? I would have."

"Richard? That boy gets the gold medal for imperturbability. Or simple obtuseness. No, they went for a walk; Richard said it's essential to 'fully metabolize the food, jazz up those antioxidants!' And you know Tony."

"Habitual prowler."

They smile at each other, relaying dessert plates; the dinner plates, with their gold rims, will have to be washed by hand.

"When I'm with Tony, sometimes I feel like part of a collection," says Fern.

Fenno nods.

"He holds onto everyone he's ever loved. Or who ever loved him. He never lets you go."

"No he doesn't," Fenno admits. "Tenacious—in a backhanded way."

It occurs to Fern that Tony cares for lovers the way he cares for other people's bedrooms: undependably while he is there but then, once he leaves, making sure to tidy up, polish the dresser and press the linens. She remembers what Dennis told her about Fenno and wonders if Tony's ever watched a lover die. No; that would never befall the fortunate Tony.

Fern and Fenno are quiet now as they work. She sponges down the counter and the stove. He washes the fancy plates, the massive corn pot, the wooden-handled knives. She pours soap into the little boxes in the dishwasher door. He takes the wine bottles to the mudroom, to their appointed recycling bin. She locks and turns on the dishwasher, regretting the way its rumble drowns out the soothing whispers of night. The symphony ended some time ago; once the kitchen was clean, the house fell silent.

"Where's my brother got to?" says Fenno when he returns.

"He went to the beach. To clear his head. He's a little mortified."

"Bloody hell," says Fenno. He walks quickly back out through the mudroom. Fern follows. The moon is bright, and a glint of gold attracts her eye to the abandoned plate, not a crumb left on it, balanced on the porch rail. Fenno stands amid the white chairs, frowning out at the view. "Bloody, bloody hell."

"He won't drown," she says. "He's too alert for that."

"That's not what worries me," says Fenno. "I haven't seen him like this—like some teenage pothead—for years, but he's been acting absurdly juvenile ever since he got here last week. Twenty years ago when he acted like this, he'd go out and make a very public fool of himself."

Down across the lawn, through the hedge, along the emerald tennis court, she can still hear that damned dishwasher grinding away, louder than the ocean, like a conscience that refuses to quit.

SEVENTEEN

FERN IS CERTAIN THAT JONAH did not kill himself. First among those who are certain that he did is his mother, who finally came right out and accused Fern of driving him to it by ignoring all the warning signs. How could any wife be so blind to such perilous despair, such hopelessness?

And how could any mother accept that her son might die by such a ludicrous mishap? This was how Fern excused Jonah's mother's behavior.

It did not help that the police reached no clear conclusion. Or that Jonah had no life insurance to force a conclusion. His keys were on his dresser in the apartment. His wallet, with money and cards, was in a pocket on his pulverized body. Leaning out their kitchen window the day after the fall, Fern showed the police a fairly broad ledge (structurally pointless, she thought, except to the birds) that ran at floor level along the courtyard wall. By their living room windows, it met the back fire escape.

Soon after moving in, Fern had accidentally locked herself out of the apartment in her nightgown. Their newspaper had been left on a neighbor's mat, and as she went to retrieve it, their door blew shut. Two hours later, Jonah found her sitting there, perusing, out of desperate boredom, the Automobiles section. He annoyed her by laughing, but he told her that, aside from never leaving without her keys, she might want to know about a backup scheme the previous tenant had used: Climb out the hall window, take the ledge past their kitchen to the fire escape, open a living room window. Fern looked at the ledge. "Are you nuts? Have you done this?"

"No," said Jonah. "But it's good to know about."

"Right," she said. "I think I'd rather read car classifieds."

Jonah was not daring by nature, but in their last months together, Fern thought his judgment seemed poor or inattentive. She no longer let him shop, because more than once he came home with bruised or wilting produce. He gave money to the infamous beggar who claimed, year after year, all around town, that he needed busfare to make it upstate to his big break in repertory theater. And he lost an essay he'd been working on for two months when a thunderstorm stunned his computer. He hadn't made a backup. "Are you nuts?" Fern heard herself say too often, too meanly. Perhaps this was what Jonah's mother meant when she said Fern was heartless, but this did not drive him to suicide. Jonah might have been dismayed, and dismay might have made him absentminded, but he wasn't hopeless, not yet.

Stavros sat quietly on her couch that night while she talked to Jonah's sister, then to Heather, Anna, and her parents. He went with her to the police station and sat quietly on benches in two dreary hallways while she looked at Jonah's body and then answered questions. He did not read or talk on the phone or pace. He simply sat. How respectful, Fern thought when he rose to take her home.

Unlike the police and Jonah's mother and her friends and siblings and parents, Stavros asked no questions—except, more than once, whether she would be all right. She asked him to come by and look at the ledge. Yes, he had heard about the previous tenant's balancing act (the man had a wife who sometimes bolted him out). "The guy was a lunatic." Stavros made Fern lean out the window beside him. He laid a hand on her back, as if she might need to be anchored. "See all that pigeon shit? Slick as oil, I promise you that." Starting the next day, of course, the window was nailed shut; often now, the hall smells stale, of garbage and the neighbors' cooking.

When Jonah's mother came to take his things, she came with Jonah's sister. Fern had always liked Jonah's mother, mainly for her strong, outspoken persona; she wasn't a woman you'd want to offend. The mother, once so fond of Fern, now embraced her with clear reluctance; the sister—whom Fern had never liked—barely said hello. She carried a stack of flattened cardboard boxes and a bag of moving supplies. As he had promised, Stavros came over; when the women arrived, an hour late because of Saturday traffic in the Lincoln Tunnel, Stavros was reading the newspaper on Fern's kitchen counter. As it was morning, Fern realized this gave the wrong impression entirely, but there was no room for explaining. Stavros said how sorry he was. He said he'd thought they might like some assistance. Jonah's sister gave him a long steely look, but Jonah's mother put on a conspicuously brave smile and thanked him. Fern remembered Jonah's perfect manners and felt a shiver of sorrow. She did not miss him, but she felt the loss of something irreplaceable in her life, even in her heart.

Stavros packed Jonah's clothes in a suitcase (they fit into one), and he helped Jonah's mother pack the books and the contents of his desk. Frequently, she excused herself and went into the bathroom; in vain, Fern tried not to hear her modulated weeping. Jonah's sister, who spoke perhaps seven words to Fern in the three hours she was there, wrapped pieces of furniture for the movers. Fern said nothing when she wrapped the green damask sofa.

The four of them worked mostly in silence; Stavros, the outsider, spoke the most often because he needed instruction. Fern was terrified when he offered to go out for sandwiches; relieved when Jonah's mother wondered aloud how anyone could think of eating at a time like this. Nevertheless, when Fern was in the bedroom alone, having remembered the drawers in Jonah's nightstand, his mother came in and closed the door. Dramatically, she even stood against it.

"I suppose we should be allies in grief," she said. Her pause did not call for an answer. "But there are certain things a woman owes her husband in a time of need, things he can't get anywhere else. I don't believe you gave Jonah those things! You left him all alone! And after you told him you wouldn't consider a move to half the places where he might gladly have worked!"

Fern sighed. She had never forbidden Jonah to apply for jobs in Wisconsin or Nebraska; she merely told him she couldn't picture herself in such places. He had laughed: *Same here.* But defending herself now would be unseemly. "I loved Jonah," she said. "I gave him everything he let me give him."

"*Let* you give? He was crying out for compassion! And look at you— you've hardly shed a tear."

It was true that she had hardly cried in front of Jonah's mother. If this was a crime, so be it. She said, "There's nothing I can say to make you feel better. I wish you could understand how much I wish I could."

"No one can make me feel better, no one will ever make me feel better! That's obvious!" cried Jonah's mother. "But do you even wish that my son were still alive? I'm not sure you do!"

"Of course I do, of course I do!" And then Stavros knocked on the door, probably because he had heard their raised voices. Did Fern have any shipping tape? Jonah's sister had used up the roll she brought.

THE BEACH IS ASTONISHINGLY WHITE. At the waterline, the sand glitters like new snow every time a wave retreats. The waves break quietly, filling the air with restful murmuring. It's close to midnight; in the distance, in each direction, a solitary figure moves along the water.

"I wish you'd go back to the house," says Fenno.

"I don't feel like being alone there. Really. You go left, I'll go right."

"Better look in the dune grasses, too," he says with a sigh.

They set off, each turning now and then to check the progress of the other, zigzagging to and from the tideline. Sometimes she rises above the verge of a dune to find herself smack on a forced green lawn; once, she surprises a teenage couple, entwined and naked on a chaise. "Yo, lost your dog?" says the boy, grinning. He is a smooth one. Giggling, the girl hides her face against his chest.

When she next looks back, Fern can see that Fenno has already passed the figure she spotted in that direction. In her direction now, there isn't a soul in sight; whoever she saw must have turned inland. Finally, she sees Fenno waving his arms and shaking his head.

He waits for her by the big house. The floodlight is off, and most of the great lawn is blackened by the shadow the house casts in the light from the moon and the ocean. Just beyond the shadow, the tennis court seems to phosphoresce. But for this optical deceit, Fern might not have noticed the large dark shape on the pavement. As she points at the shape, it begins to sing:

"And if I were like lightnin', I wouldn't need no sneakers,
I would come and go whenever I would pleeeease . . .
Oh I'd scare 'em by the shade trees and I'd scare 'em by the light poles
But I would not scare my pony on my boat upon the seeeea!"

Fenno walks swiftly toward the tennis court saying his brother's name in a low, stern voice.

Fern follows him but hangs back a bit. Dennis lies splayed face up in the part of the court called no-man's-land, between service line and baseline. The few times she and Jonah played tennis, he told her repeatedly that this is precisely where you never want to strand yourself.

Stand back or advance to the net. Somehow, she couldn't seem to learn that lesson.

"Get up." Fenno stands over his brother.

Dennis laughs and waves up at Fenno, as if from a great distance. "Halloo, my Amoorican brother. I'll bet you're not keen on Lyle Lovett."

"Get up now."

Dennis puts both hands over his mouth but makes no effort to rise. When he takes them away, he says, "I deserve your wrath, I know; just please do not deport me!" He lifts his head from the court and catches sight of Fern. "Oh—hello!" He waves at her, beckoning.

When she stands just behind Fenno, Dennis winks at her. "Am I not in Amoorica? Land of the bravely free? Land of the free-to-be-me?"

Fenno reaches down and grasps his brother's wrists, trying to pull him up. His silence is the kind that anyone sober would read as ingrown rage, a fear of what he'd say if he did speak, but Dennis is far from sober.

"No—wait. Look! Look up! Oh!" Dennis has pulled his hands free and lies back, pointing toward the sky. Fern and Fenno look up.

"Oh my, it's the . . . what are they called? The myriads? The neriads? You know—that summer meteor shower. Oh my." An awed smile shines on his handsome face.

Fern scans the sky but sees nothing, nothing more than the few murky stars that manage to penetrate the afterhaze of the day's humidity. She sneaks a look at Fenno's face. He is still scowling.

"Oh my that was brilliant, wasn't it?" says Dennis after a moment. He rises to a sitting position.

"Hallucinations tend to be brilliant," says Fenno.

Suddenly they are blinded by the floodlight. The gravelly voice of milady calls out, "Darlings, won't you please go to bed? Thank you ever so much!" And mercifully, the light expires.

Fenno's shadow engulfs his brother. "Up. Right now."

Dennis scrambles to his feet. He seems not the slightest bit off balance as he starts up the slope toward the hedge. Once they are through, Fern sees Fenno glance at the corner of the lawn where he buried his dog. For her part, she glances at the windows of the master bedroom. A light is on, and shadows bruise the lace behind the balcony. Standing back to let Fern into the house before him, Dennis touches her belly. "You are going to have a smashing time. You are going to be a smashing mum." Fern smiles awkwardly.

Fenno puts a hand on Dennis's back to steer him in and toward the stairs. "My brother, my warder," jokes Dennis as they head up, single file.

"My brother, master of the facile compliment," says Fenno.

Unsure of her place, Fern stands in the doorway of the second guest room. Fenno directs Dennis firmly toward one of the twin beds, but there is no resistance. As he sits, Dennis says to Fern, "My final request before execution is another piece of that luscious tart. Somehow I'm still famished!"

"She'll fetch you a glass of water, and that's it," says Fenno. He glances apologetically at Fern.

By the time she returns from the kitchen, Fenno has removed his brother's shirt and maneuvered him between the sheets. He's already sleeping.

She and Fenno meet each other's eyes and then, automatically, look together at Dennis as if he were their child, a baby who's had a rough night and is finally out for the count. She lifts the glass of water she brought and drinks it down without stopping.

THE NIGHT AFTER Jonah's mother packed his belongings, Fern made dinner for Stavros, to show her gratitude for his covert protection. They talked about the mayor's "cleanup" of Times Square and the prostitutes it had displaced to, of all neighborhoods, theirs. They talked about the water catastrophe sure to be caused by overdevelopment of the southwestern states. They talked about the brain conference in Washington and laughed about the new neurosis it had created for all their friends with children. ("The whole thing funded by a Hollywood director; what does that tell you?" said Stavros. "Of course, wait until *we* have children," said Fern.) So when she carried their tea into the living room, she stopped short, alarmed for an instant. She let out a short bitter laugh. "Oh. Right."

She walked around a cluster of boxes and set the mugs down on the coffee table. Resolutely, she sat on the foreclosed sofa, now shrouded in a sheet. Across from her, the bookcases stood three-quarters empty. Jonah's mother had thoroughly dusted the empty shelves, so they looked more expectant than abandoned. "Oh God, how will I stay here?" said Fern.

Stavros seemed to inspect her for a few moments before speaking. "I could find you another place, though it wouldn't be . . . such a deal. But . . ." He shrugged and sipped his tea.

"But what?"

"But I think you could just as easily rearrange your things and be glad to have your own place. In the long run. I don't mean to sound callous."

"My own place. You mean, my own albatross of memories."

"You'll be sad wherever you are. But"—Stavros shrugged again—"people overestimate the power of the past."

"Now *there's* callous!"

He smiled apologetically. "I come from a culture of hand wringers, vengeance seekers, people who name children after ancestors by rote— first child, paternal grandfather; second child, maternal, on and on and on. Drives me nuts. The trouble is, if you convince yourself the past's more glorious or worthy of attention than the future, your imagination's sunk."

Briefly, Fern just stared at Stavros. "So what about the lessons of history?"

"Well that's obvious. That goes without saying," he said impatiently.

"And how come you're so busy learning a dead language?"

"Because I like the stories it has to tell." He leaned forward, elbows on his knees. "Know what I like about real estate? I mean, okay, it's a business with a sleazy aura, and it's nouveau, and I'm working for my dad, but it's all about the present and the future. Keeping people under a roof."

"For money!" said Fern. "Here, for an *obscene* amount of money. Don't tell me real estate's not about money." Why was she so indignant? She had no reason to think Stavros and his father were greedy or unkind; she'd even heard they had two buildings where they kept the rents absurdly low.

"You do these practical, constructive things all day, and then," said Stavros, ignoring her insult, "you go home and you have a shower or a beer and you sit down . . ." His voice softened. "And you read about Penelope and her loom."

Fern saw him stepping in the door of his apartment, just floors above his parents but unconcerned about the implications, kicking off his sneakers and sitting down to read *The Odyssey* in the ornately cryptic words of another millennium.

"You can't be Greek without respecting archaeology, I promise you that," he said, "but building museums to your culture—institutions that open every morning and close before dinner—is not the same as building a museum to your life, putting all your grievances in glass cases wired with alarms. You know, my mother has this cousin back on her island—he's not especially bright, this guy, but he makes these funny beaded wallets and sells them down at the one taverna that carries a few pathetic souvenirs. He used to do them with images of nothing but the classical stuff: the Parthenon, the Argo, portraits of the gods—he did this really funky Medusa—but a couple of years ago he became obsessed with the space shuttle, of all things. So now he does these beaded wallets with red, white, and blue space shuttles. It's absolutely wild. I love it." He laughed. "How did I get here? Am I being insensitive or what?"

Fern shook her head. "No—and I think I want one of those wallets. Does he export them?" They both laughed then, having recovered from what Fern would come to think of as their first disagreement. Almost together, they glanced at the clock on the wall (Fern's, and hence spared from packing). As she saw him out the door, Fern said, "So, off to Penelope and her loom."

He looked pleased. "Yes. And Penelope is nothing if not patient."

Later that month, she did not go to Connecticut for Thanksgiving but joined Stavros, along with his family, at his uncle's house in Queens.

For the next year, they saw each other often, if less than they might have liked. Stavros took both his job and his courses seriously, and he played handball three times a week, sometimes even when the temperature fell below freezing. Most Saturdays, he checked up on certain elderly tenants or helped his mother around her apartment; perhaps every other Sunday, he went with his father to the tiny Greek Orthodox Church that sat in the middle of a parking lot downtown, and if the afternoon was sunny, they would play chess in Washington Square. He had a few close friends, all of them canny New Yorkers (not unlike Anna) whom he had known since high school. With or without Fern, he had a full life.

Fern threw herself into work as well. She rearranged her apartment radically, as Stavros had suggested, and she took a few of her paintings out of storage and hung them where Jonah's Old World landscapes had hung. She found a deep, comfortable antique couch, a bargain because it had been six inches too long to fit into the elevator of the owner's high-rise building. It was covered in a tasseled red velvet that Stavros said had unavoidably seamy associations; Fern argued that it was a noble prop, the sort of piece you'd see in a royal portrait by Ingres or Géricault. "Oh royal, sure," said Stavros. "Like, Cleopatra died here— and a good deal else besides." Ever the landlord, he insisted on pulling away the fabric underneath to check for roaches. "Absolutely vacant," he proclaimed. "Unheard of in this market."

When they spent time at her place, they came to live on that couch, as if it were a small room unto itself or a punt drifting on a river. Reading or talking or eating Mexican takeout from tinfoil trays, they could lean against opposite ends, their feet nestled against each other's thighs. More than once, as Stavros read his law books, Fern sketched him surreptitiously in the pages of the graph paper notebook she used to work out ideas for design and proportion. The couch was so plush with down that when they stood up to go to bed (and sometimes they did not bother), the impression of their two bodies—entangled elbows, knees, heels, and buttocks—might remain there to greet them in the morning.

Last summer, Stavros reintroduced her to badminton—a swift-footed, competitive sport as played with his brothers and their small sons when they turned the entirety of a tiny Astoria backyard into a court. The brothers seemed startled when Fern asked to play—their wives thought the game absurd—but it took her back to Connecticut lawns on summer nights, when you played fast and furious if just to elude the mosquitoes, played till your parents yelled, three or four times, that you would go blind if you didn't quit (never mind that the birdies glowed in the dark, descending like tiny brave paratroopers only to be smashed aloft again). Fern and Stavros played no more than six or seven times, but the sweaty pleasure of it, the dizzy laughter and the lasting elation after winning, assumed the very texture of that summer in her mind.

At the end of the following January, a year after they had become involved, Fern became pregnant not by accident (not quite) and certainly not by cunning, but by impulse. They had spent nearly the entire weekend in her apartment, it was snowing hard, and he ran out of condoms. Nestled in that couch, neither of them wanted to leave, and they believed themselves too lazy and worn out for passion—until the middle of Sunday night. In the dark, he asked her if it would be all right (not if it would be safe), and she said it would be fine. She had always been so careful that what would this one time . . . But then, as he began to kiss her shoulders, the insides of her arms, she thought about time in a different way and knew there was a chance she would conceive. She thought about a baby she had held on her lap at Christmastime: Stavros's fourth nephew. ("On my father's island, they only give birth to boys," he explained. "Look out at the clotheslines there and you notice at once: in every direction, pants and more pants, nothing but pants! The wives they have to import from my mother's island, just a short row across a channel. My poor mother, she thought that by coming to America, my father might give her a daughter. No, I am not kidding!")

She thought about Tony's picture of the baby's fist, hanging in her bedroom a block away. She thought, perhaps, too much about herself and not enough about Stavros. And then, carried somewhere quite distant in his arms, she stopped thinking altogether.

A month later, she knew she was pregnant. But Stavros had told her that in March he would be going to Greece to help his mother out. He wasn't sure how long he would stay—a few weeks, a month at most. So, thought Fern, now would be a cruel time to tell him this news. He would be back by the end of her first trimester. She had never thought in such terms, but she had heard Heather and Anna use them.

As weeks turned to months, she began to wonder how much this baby really had to do with Stavros at all. One night when she struggled toward sleep (such nights were increasingly frequent), Fern lay in her bed, miserably alert, and asked herself if she had allowed the baby to be conceived because she hoped it would create so vast a love that every other love, every foolish memory of love, even this new love, would be eclipsed. Was she so weary of endings that she was determined to make her own, far less fragile beginning, one she would share with no one so that no one could take it away?

FERN LIES ON HER LEFT SIDE (best for the baby, her books instruct), exhausted but wakeful yet again. The lights of a car move maple branches across the wall, across a painting of boats at sea. It doesn't help that, through the wall, Dennis snores like a truck idling without a muffler. At least it obliterates any noise from the other bedroom. Tony, she knows, makes love silent as a stone—but Richard she'd take for a man of vocal, jubilant lust.

She goes downstairs for water. Returning from the kitchen, she hears Fenno's voice: "Midnight cravings?" She looks into the living room, where the voluptuous white chairs, all vacant, cast off a neon blue.

"Out here." His voice carries through an open window.

She steps onto the porch. He lies on a hammock that wasn't there before. Well, he knows this place and its hidden possessions; she can guess, from what she's seen, that the absent Ralph deems a hammock too scruffy or even third-worldly to suit his aesthetic. Probably a gift from a houseguest, it is not even white but as garishly colored as a macaw, even in the moonlight.

"You couldn't sleep?" says Fern.

"Next to the human chainsaw?" He laughs quietly. "I never knew, before this visit, just what my sister-in-law endures—what she keeps in line."

"Is he like that often?"

"I doubt it. I think he's inebriated with his temporary freedom—not that he doesn't love his life, God knows—and he's regressed to the benignly delinquent habits he had before he met his wife." Fenno must notice that she is shivering. He holds out a blanket. "Join me for a moment?"

Fern looks around at the uninviting Adirondack chairs, collecting dew on their slick veneer.

"Here." Fenno folds up his legs, and Fern pulls herself into the opposite end of the hammock. He's smiling at her kindly. He says, "So, can I ask where your husband is this weekend?"

"Husband?" Caught off balance, she answers, "My husband—the husband I had—is dead."

"Oh Lord," says Fenno. He sits forward, and the hammock sways, threatening to spill them both.

She seizes the ropy mesh. "No no. I'm sorry. That happened nearly two years ago. You mean the father of the baby, and he . . . well, we're together but we're not married, and I haven't told him yet, and I"—she stops and shakes her head—"well this sounds like a version of what you hear every day, isn't it? From those girls you work with."

"Less than two years a widow, five months pregnant with a man you love—though wait, you didn't say that, did you?—and you haven't told him. That's not a story I hear."

She hears the word *widow* and holds back laughter. From the first time, at the funeral, someone used that word to mean *her*, the notion has struck Fern, callously, as funny, not sad. For months she had lain awake at night beside Jonah wondering what it would mean, what it would feel like, to become a *divorcée*, and then, joke of fate, she became a *widow*. But she does not tell this to Fenno. She tells him how Stavros has been away for months, how there's no phone, how it doesn't seem fair to spring such a surprise on a person in writing. And yes, a person she loves.

"When does he return?"

She hesitates, ashamed. "Anytime."

"Will you marry?"

"I don't know."

"Now why should I ask you such a question?" says Fenno. "We hardly live in our parents' world."

"Hardly," she agrees. Their feet collide as they shift to stay comfortable. They look at each other and murmur apologies. "The thing is," she says, "I keep having doubts. And you are not supposed to have doubts, not about this. But then, I have doubts about everything now."

"You miss your husband. It hasn't been two years."

"Well it's . . . complicated. A cliché, but true." Though she isn't sure why, she feels oddly relaxed. She recalls her years of therapy, after Paris and before Jonah, how surprised she was to feel her stories flow so easily forth, like a long straight stream in a smooth granite bed. Almost that easily now, she tells Fenno about her marriage. His eyes never stray from hers, as if this tale of a commonplace marital breakdown is positively riveting.

Some way through, Fern remembers what the brother told her: that Fenno had a lover who died of AIDS. She hasn't witnessed such a death up close, but she thinks of the ailing men at the office where she once worked (and, sheepishly, how this is part of why she was glad to start working at home, because what could you ever say to these men as they literally dwindled away yet worked fiercely on?). Perhaps it's this detail—knowing something tragic about Fenno—that spurs Fern to tell him a small secret of her own, a detail about her last morning with Jonah that she has told no one.

After she had leveled her accusations (the most cruel, that he was frigid in bed), her fury had seemed to rise, not abate. She had crossed the room to where he stood by the closet and clapped her hands sharply three times in front of his face, the way you might summon a disobedient dog. She shouted, "Wake up! Wake up! You are in an emotional coma, you're like a mummy in a tomb!"

Jonah's eyes filled, and in his defeated silence she heard the echo of her hands more than her words. She could not imagine which of them felt more humiliated; she might as well have slapped him. Only then did her rage dissolve and did she, pathetically and too late, apologize.

When she saw his body that night, the police explained that he had fallen on his back. On the steel table, he did look strangely flat, as if he were floating, the back of his skull underwater; but there was the face she knew, if paler, the only signs of death the darkness of his lips and the black clotting in his nostrils. His eyes were closed no differently than in sleep. Her first thought, both trivial and selfish, was that she hoped someone, anyone, had been very kind to him that afternoon, because no one could have been meaner than she was that morning. That was when she'd cried the hardest.

Fenno says, "That's a terrible story."

"I never knew I could be so cruel," she says.

"Oh no. Oh my *dear*," he says, "what an ingenue you are in the cosmos of cruelty."

Fern wants to ask what makes his cruelties so much crueller, but she says simply, "Well, you've been through a lot more than I have."

"Oh?" he says lightly. "According to whom?"

She hesitates, but then she thinks, How could it be a secret? "Dennis told me about your lover . . . who died. It wasn't like he was gossiping, he just—"

Fenno leans toward her, and the hammock quakes again. "He wasn't my lover . . . though he ought to have been." He laughs at the morbid absurdity in his statement. "My dear, dense brother, so exuberantly ignorant of so much . . . I used to think of him as lighthearted—and he is that; in fact, I think he's the rare creature who has no secrets, nothing to weigh him down that way—but now I've begun to think of him as a touch light in the brain. Yet look at how much he's got right in his life. And love—though once I didn't think so, he seems to have got that right above all."

He shifts again, grimacing, and stretches his legs out straight, along one edge of the hammock. One of his feet settles lightly, unavoidably, against Fern's hip. "Before you came out, I was finishing off the wine and looking at this view. I know this view well, yet I've never seen it quite like this. I was thinking how some of us live up here and some of us live down there"—he gestures grandly toward the house on the beach—"some of us have the infinity of the ocean at our doorstep, others the platitude of a nicely groomed hedgerow. Ah yes and some of us, lucky dogs, see cascading stars while the rest of us see none and think, disdainfully, that they must be an hallucination.

"Some of us get love just . . . exactly . . . right—as right as it can be—and others get everything else right *but*." He smiles flatly. "Not a bad view from here, is it? But we're always looking over somebody's shoulder."

"Well, but they'll be the first ones flooded in a hurricane," she says, realizing immediately that the joke is all wrong.

"And so bloody *what*." Having spoken so harshly, Fenno nudges her hip with his foot. The gesture feels affectionate, and she is reminded of sitting on her red velvet couch across from Stavros. "Listen, I am hardly bemoaning my existence. Oh no. I've come to see just how rich it is. Prudent or no"—he reaches down with one arm and holds aloft an empty wine bottle—"let me barter a secret of mine."

Fern braces herself; now he will talk about the lover's—the not-lover's—death.

He says, "You asked me if I liked children and I told you that I do. In fact I have children of my own—two. Though they aren't *my* children. Do you remember how Dennis mentioned our brother David, how he nattered on about David's not being able to have children? Actually, I'd never known why . . . but there's a tangent I won't follow." He sighs.

He tells her a remarkable story about giving sperm to his sister-in-law because her husband couldn't conceive. He tells her plainly, in just those words. He tells her he knows he was second choice (who wouldn't prefer the straight brother, the twin you loved before you even learned what love might be?). He tells her about going to a clinic stocked with blue-ribbon porn—straight porn—and then, on his way out, passing a wall papered solid with snapshots of tiny babies, all fragile, ugly, bewildered by new life and flashbulbs—but priceless beyond words to people he would never meet.

"Months later, I get a call that here they are, these messianic twins, and I'm happy for the parents, pleased with my good deed, but not until I get the birth announcement in the post—the photograph, a boy and a girl, both just as splotchy-faced and dumbfounded-looking as the babies on that clinic wall—do I realize how instantly priceless they are to *me*. On the back of the snapshot, their mum wrote, 'Oh Fenno, you will never know!' Just that.

"I knew," he says, looking out at the ocean, "that she was too exhausted and overwhelmed to write me the letter of momentous gratitude I expected as my due, and I knew that what she meant to convey was that I would never know how deep her gratitude was, how much she will always love me for what I gave her . . . but when I read it again, running my fingers over those little faces too many times, like one of Tony's students learning how to read, when I read it again I thought, Or does she mean that I will never know this particular joy, the joy of those little lives entwined in mine? Though of course she didn't mean that. Of course not."

He pulls his legs back into his chest, tightens the blanket around his shoulders. "You know, I am precisely that fabulous godfaggot you described. I take them those imaginative presents, add faithfully to a fund for their future, but there is no way I can be in their lives as I sometimes dream. When I first lay eyes on them every time, put my arms about them if they're not too shy, I think, This is *my* daughter, this is *my* son, and I have this addled fantasy of whisking them off like that evil dwarf in the fairy tale. . . ."

"Rumpelstiltskin," murmurs Fern.

"Yes. That's the sort of character I'm always in danger of becoming." He looks back at her. "I see my secret babies only once or twice a year, but I've got this fantasy that one day, like every child, they'll need to run away from home, and here I'll be, the reputedly—and only reputedly—wild uncle across the ocean. . . . And whether or not they ever seek refuge that way, I have plans to take each of them on an eccentric holiday—to the jungle, the North Pole, the Indian ruins out west . . . whatever strikes their fancies when they're old enough to fancy such things." Whether they would ever know that he was their biological father—that was something about which his brother and sister-in-law could not yet agree. "I understand my brother's insecurity, even perhaps his prudishness. That's just who he is," says Fenno. "And maybe it's for the best, keeping matters simple."

He tells her that for a while he was sorry he hadn't insisted on being at the birth; he'd like to have held his babies then. But there are certain intrusions to which he isn't entitled. And this, he confesses, is part of what he looks forward to in helping Oneeka, learning what it might have been like. "You're right about that," he says to Fern. "Of course I expect to be given some sliver of responsibility, if just for a day or two. I crave it." He pats his shirt pocket, as if it contains an engagement ring.

Fern looks at the sky, trying to determine the hour. It is not yet brightening, but the clouds, just a few, look a bit more vivid. This is the time of night when, absent a storm, the wind seems to rest and the clouds stand so still that they look as if they are painted on a ceiling, like the sharp dwarfish clouds in pictures by Henri Rousseau. Fern thinks of her favorite: *Carnival Evening,* in which two costumed lovers —small, ethereal dark-faced figures—stand in a wood of leafless trees. How she misses painting.

Fenno follows her gaze and murmurs something that sounds like "Hour of the quilt."

"What?" Fern says gently.

"Private nonsense," Fenno says. "You should be in bed, both of you."

He stands and helps her to her feet. Her legs are stiff and numb, so she leans against him for a moment, and perhaps he interprets her physical dependence as a plea of some kind. "Never talk yourself out of knowing you're in love," he says, "or into thinking that you are."

"Mind what you love," says Fern. "That's what my mother preaches."

From the living room, after saying good night, she spies on him through the window as he resettles himself in the hammock, wraps himself close in both blankets and closes his eyes. He's smiling.

"WHIPPED CREAM. What we need here is that whipped cream from last night." Tony is leaning into the refrigerator, clanking jars from side to side, searching.

"Gone. Used up," says Fern as she enters the kitchen, still in her nightgown.

Fenno looks up from the table. Tony closes the refrigerator door. Both men look thrilled to see her, and she wonders if they have a hard time being alone with each other. Tony says, "How did we dream?"

"We didn't. And we are praying there's still coffee." She looks out the front window: Richard's car is gone. Dennis is still audibly asleep upstairs.

"Abso-loo-maw, petite mare." He pours her a cup and pulls out a chair. It's ten-thirty. On the table is a plate of muffins and a Sunday paper; hours ago, Tony will have been into the village and back. Fenno's hair is wet. The *Book Review* sits by his plate. In a wall socket beside the toaster, his phone (his reliability, she thinks) is busy recharging itself.

"Now don't stuff your faces, because milady has invited us down to the manor for brunch." Tony looks at the clock and then at Fern. "Right this minute, as a matter of fact. So time to gussy up."

Fern shakes her head. "Believe me, she wants you all to herself. But I'll be expecting an invitation when you house-sit next summer while they're off to the Serengeti. Or isn't that the proper safari season?"

"Hard for you to believe that I merely like the woman."

"In fact, though she seems perfectly likable, you're right."

Tony just smiles; he radiates the afterglow of good adventurous sex. Fern looks at his captivating face and remembers the agony of loving him. But she remembers as well the last thing he said to her that night, almost exactly ten years ago now, as she held open the door to her room in Paris. She had just told him to get out of her life, and he said, sounding almost casual, "You think everybody wants some one person, everybody's looking for that singular, whatever-you-do-don't-die-before-me soul mate. Well, everybody isn't. I'm not. You just won't pay attention to that."

"Well maybe I am looking for that. And maybe you were never in the running," she said, the sharpest insult she could grope for in an instant.

He had shrugged, unscathed. "To each his own," he'd said.

Fenno is telling Tony that he has to get back to the city, that some-one named Felicity will bite off his head if he doesn't get back soon.

"Would you mind taking me? I should get back, too," says Fern.

Tony pretends shock. "You are both abandoning me? And that cute wastrel brother of yours?"

"You have Druid," says Fenno, "and that's what a sadist like you de-serves. The company of a loyal, aging mute."

"Me, a sadist?"

Fern folds her arms. "The way you treated that poor guy Richard?"

"Oh please. 'Poor guy'? He's one of the charmed."

"And you—you're one of the damned?"

Fenno opens the *Book Review*. He smirks, as if this dialogue is all too familiar.

Fern stands and touches Tony's shoulder. "Mustn't be late for your first date." She walks with him out the back door.

On the porch, Tony kisses her cheek. "When you get back, tell that nice boy he's going to be a father, will you?"

"I will, but how do you know he's nice? You haven't met him."

"Hey, sometimes you know these things." He pauses, then looks her in the eye. "I predict you're engaged by next week. He's no fool—you've never loved a fool, have you?—and you, Miss Veritas, you are a catch. You are sublime." He kisses her again, this time at the edge of her mouth, and she says nothing, letting his rare but honest affection sink in.

She watches him sidle through a flowerbed, pulling up the tiny weeds that sprouted overnight. Three gladiolas have opened: two red, one white. With a pocket knife, he severs them carefully near the base of their stalks. As he walks down the lawn, the flowers mimic perfectly his slim, alert posture and shameless, colorful outlook on life. Fern feels a deep pull of tenderness and forgiveness. Just your motherly hor-mones, Tony would say.

IN THE POLITICALLY FESTOONED BUS, they start for the city with the windows wide open; the car is much too old for conditioned air. Dennis groans as he climbs in back. Yet he sounds indomitably cheerful as he exclaims, "Wearing my favorite hairshirt!" Having been coaxed out of bed to leave, he falls asleep again almost at once.

Fern loves how high up they are, seated on the puffy old seats with their blue and silver upholstery (a plaid you'd expect on Bermuda shorts). A rosary swings from the rearview mirror, and Fern's sun visor bears yet another slogan: HAPPY IN HIS HANDS.

"Someone is definitely Catholic," she says as they leave the shelter of Ralph's mapled lane. She clicks tight the old-fashioned lap belt.

"She founded the center where I volunteer. It's called Aunt Lucie's Place. She's the Aunt Lucie—though she doesn't live there. She orders us around from Vermont and Washington, if you can believe it."

"Could I visit sometime? Are visitors allowed?"

"On one condition. They have to be Aunt Lucie's guests. And let me warn you: If she meets you and likes you—and in your case she will— she will own a piece of your soul."

"Well, good luck to her if she can find it."

"We could use help on the paper's design . . ."

Fern laughs. "Yes, and I've still got four months just yawning with free time." She wonders what he remembers of their confessional hours on the hammock. She'd like to think she will see him again, yet even the talk of her visiting this Aunt Lucie's Place does not convince her; it may be nothing more than idle chat to tide them over until they part for good.

Ten years ago, she'd have been falling in love with this man by now, and while it would have been an obvious mistake, and while her heart might have been bruised if not broken, her reasons for loving him would not have been wrongheaded. Like her, he is an agonizer. Like her, he feels the atmosphere about him too acutely: the stealthiest shifts in wind direction, ozone level, barometric pressure. Sometimes it's almost too much to bear.

Only when it was too late had she examined the similarities she was drawn to in the men she loved: in Tony, her passion for looking at things, turning them round in the eye and trying to give them meaning; in Jonah, her shameless love of old-fashioned pastimes and objects. (The moment she'd fallen for Jonah she remembers all too well: under a pink tent at someone else's wedding, a turn in a dance when he smiled and pulled her assuredly, graciously toward him.) She believed that what Tony offered her was a life of constant surprise, quite unlike her parents' life; Jonah, in the ruins of those hopes, offered a life of constant safety, quite like her parents' life. And Stavros?

When Stavros had criticized building a museum to your past, Fern had felt instantly fingered, though he had hardly known her then. Because there it stood sometimes, against her will, an edifice as solid to her as the Met. A great wing, she's afraid, is devoted to the botched loves of her life, a wing filled with the oldest but most damaged things. Yet her museum contains not just the grievances Stavros railed against, Vesuvian artifacts chipped from treacherous lava and silt, but objects, like silver heirloom ladles, shiny with domestic joy, objects in which you could clearly see your own face. Fern does not think of herself as someone who dwells in the past, yet it does preoccupy her, and no one leaves her more uneasy about that preoccupation than Stavros. She feels as if he has perceived this tendency in her and will be determined to root it out. This is what he offers, and what he threatens.

When it comes to love, there is the timeworn caution that the very qualities you fall for hardest may be those you grow to despise. With Stavros, she wonders if the opposite might hold true: that this quality she nearly fears—his aversion to sanctifying the past—is something for which she will one day be grateful.

When Fenno asked about her husband, she was stunned to realize that she feels as if she is still married to Jonah. It's guilt, that much is clear, which keeps her from laying the marriage to rest, but perhaps it's not the guilt she suspected: not guilt because she stopped loving him but guilt at a grandiose doubt that she has so far refused to admit. When she told Fenno how ruthlessly she attacked Jonah, wasn't she admitting that perhaps he did kill himself after all? That perhaps she dealt the decisive blow to his hope?

By Riverhead, the warm wind and the loud engine of the old bus begin to sedate her. At first she struggles to stay awake, but she realizes there's little reason she shouldn't sleep. Fenno doesn't seem to want much conversation; he's tired and, he admitted earlier, he has to concentrate when behind the wheel of an American car.

Once she surrenders, she is instantly dreaming, back at last night's dinner, sitting at the head of the table. But at the far end, beyond the Scottish brothers, Tony, and Richard, sit her own two brothers. Tony is giving a detailed account of how his father was a raging drunk and used to beat his blind, defenseless mother. Sometimes she'd hide in the linen closet when she heard him coming in, Tony is telling them, nearly crying. Fern is stunned and riveted—she's never heard him talk like this, so openly, with such emotion!—but no one else seems to be paying close attention. She is especially angry at her brothers: Gar is examining the roses, foraging among the petals, rubbing pollen between his fingers and sniffing it; Forest is fidgeting, his boredom too dramatic. "Midwesterners can't pronounce *nuclear* or *milk*," he says at one point, and she glares at him; she didn't hear Tony say either of these words. Adding to her agitation, she knows that, though she can't see him, Jonah is sitting in the living room, just listening in the dark, and she's terrified someone at the table will mention that she's pregnant. As she is about to scold Forest and Gar for their bad manners, Fenno whispers that he has something to show her; could she come out to the kitchen? She wants to hear all of Tony's story, but Fenno insists. "It's a matter of months," he says. But then he leads her to the front porch, not the kitchen. "Look." He points at the VW bus in the driveway. All the stickers and emblems have been removed, and it's a different color—a springtime green. It's unmistakably brand-new, just delivered from the manufacturer. But how is this possible, she's thinking, when they don't make this model anymore? She is also surprised that Fenno doesn't notice he's been ripped off, that someone's stolen the bus he borrowed and left this one instead. She's about to tell him when she spots someone in the driver's seat, waving. It's Stavros, but because of reflections on the window, she can't see his face and has no idea if he's happy or angry to see her. "How bloody predictable," she hears Fenno mutter and opens her eyes to realize that these are the words of the real Fenno, not the Fenno in her dream.

A moment after she wakes, so does Dennis. Both of them must have sensed a loss of momentum, for having sped this far without delays, they are nearly in sight of the city when the Long Island Expressway exerts its particular torture: a rude halt stretching for miles without apparent cause.

As Fenno stops the bus, they lose what little relief they had from the heat. Fern notices, down to her right, that the driver of the adjacent car is giving her a thumbs-up. She's baffled for a moment, then guesses that he's read the bumper stickers on her side of the bus—but whether he agrees with the notorious Aunt Lucie on her support of greenery,

God, or pregnancies carried to full term, Fern has no idea. She gives the man a hasty smile.

Dennis groans. "Oh crikey, the chervil. Your mate Tony told me I could nick a bit of that lovely chervil. I was going to do a chervil-asparagus soup for my class."

"I can take you to a market where you'll find it in town," says Fenno.

"Oh but the freshest stuff—"

"Go back to sleep, Dennis, would you?" says Fenno, but gently. "We could be stuck here an hour and I will not permit you to fray one more nerve than necessary."

Dennis laughs. "My brother, admiral of the fleet."

"My brother, the ne'er-do-well stowaway," Fenno retorts.

Surprisingly, Dennis follows his brother's orders. Within minutes, he's snoring in small bursts like a backfiring moped.

Fern regards the sea of traffic before them. "Can I ask a favor? Can I use your phone?"

"Of course," says Fenno.

It takes Fern a moment to figure out how to turn the thing on; she doesn't own one of these objects because she hates the notion of becoming a slave to convenience. Maybe this is just another fear she needs to shed.

Her machine picks up at once. The first message is Heather, Friday night: She's won some Alitalia sweepstakes and is bringing Eli for a romantic Fourth of July weekend at the Plaza. She can't wait to see Fern, and will she finally get to meet the father of her first nephew? Is there a nursery in the works? She just *loves* decorating. Fern rolls her eyes. Certainly Heather's known about this trip awhile, as it's only a week away; what is she, a pregnancy health inspector, to give so little notice? But Fern can't help feeling a surge of excitement. Not all of Heather's advice will be unwelcome.

The next message, left an hour later, is the one she'd hoped for. His voice is still a shock. "Where are you? Are you asleep? We're just through customs, Mom's getting the car with Dad while I sit with this mountain of luggage—mostly my poor old grandmother's dishes and linens Mom can't bear to part with—and I have to see you now. The way Dad drives, we'll be there in about ten minutes. Expect me, whether you're sleeping or not."

Sweat clings to Fern's cheek where she's pressing the phone to her ear. The next message was left yesterday morning at nine. "Either you are out like a rock, your phone is off the hook, or you are away. But where could that be? Like, what—you have a life that takes you away from home? What can you be thinking when here I am!" The message ends in laughter, but he is hurt; he'd written her the details of his return.

Silently, Fern begins to cry; where does she stand in the cosmos of cruelty now?

"Are you all right?" Fenno says sharply. Fern realizes that she has one hand at her waist, as if to make amends to the baby inside her. It must look to Fenno as if she's in physical pain.

She tells him she's fine as she hears the third message, left just three hours ago. "So I am doing something here that is at least slightly against the law, assuming you won't prosecute. I am at the office, and I am taking the key to your apartment off the board, and I am going there now to ransack the place and figure out just where you are. Or wait. Or fill the place with flowers. I'm not sure what." This Stavros sounds no longer playful but determined, on the verge of grim, re-signed to news he hadn't expected but plans to face at once. News there will be, of course. Whatever his reaction, he will not despair or brood. He is, it occurs to her, a man who wakes up happy each day, or gives each day the benefit of the doubt (does it matter if, for a change, Heather approves?). All of a sudden Fern longs to pull Stavros up into her life the way a tornado can pull up a house.

"End, of, messages," stutters the robot voice she wishes she could evict from her machine. She hands the phone back to Fenno and curses the cars that stretch with such astonishing meekness before them.

She's not sure how far they've crept when Fenno says brightly, "Well here we are." As if there'd been a break in the traffic, he's smiling with relief.

"Here we are where?"

On both sides of the dismal highway stand rows of tiny dismal houses, interspersed with a beer outlet, a Dominican travel agency, a pizza parlor without a customer in sight. Fenno points to a sign:

LITTER REMOVAL NEXT 1 MILE
BETTE MIDLER

"The Bette Midler Mile," says Fenno. "I had a friend who loved this sign and never ceased to find it hugely cheering. And he wasn't a naturally cheery sort of chap. He was very arch, very critical of just about everything under the sun. But he loved Bette Midler—not her music, he always had to remind you of that, but her spirit, her whole persona. He just loved picturing her right here, with all her ambition, her energy, bent over, bottom in the air, picking up polystyrene cups and wadded napkins and used condoms and takeaway Chinese cartons . . ."

When Fern looks over at Fenno, his eyes shine. It's easy to guess that the friend is dead, that this is one of many memories of the friend, passed on to her, to anyone, as a way of assuring that Fenno will not lose it.

"I'm sorry, but can I borrow that thing again?" she says.

She fusses with the tiny buttons, gets the number right on the second try. His machine still says, as it has for months, to direct all calls to the office, to his father or their assistant. But it beeps receptively nonetheless. "Stavros? Stavros, it's Sunday afternoon and I'm stuck in a car at the Bette Midler Mile on the L.I.E. and I'm coming straight back to find you, wherever you are." She pauses and adds, absurdly, "It's Fern." Then she calls herself again and talks pleadingly to her apartment, to Stavros if he's there. Last, she calls his office.

She sits silently with Fenno's phone in her lap. He does not reach for it or comment on what he overheard. As inexplicably as it stopped, the traffic moves. Fenno accelerates, and a hot breeze, better than none, blows across their faces.

Fern tries to believe that Stavros has not given up on her and orders herself to be calm. Leaving the last message when he did means that he did not go to church with his father. (Was that rebellious, his first Sunday back, and if so, does it signify the depth of his feelings for her? But no; he will have gone to church every single Sunday on his mother's island, sure to have a devout population.) Where will she find him? The playground on Horatio Street? Will he be back at his apartment or the office—or is he so hurt that he did not pick up at the sound of her voice? She wilts at the thought of searching for him in this heat.

The city comes into view, both near and distant, haughty as Oz. It looks so sharp—exceptional for summer—that you can see the eyebrows of gleaming sun at the top of the Chrysler Building. A mile closer and they will see the reflections of passing clouds in the Citicorp tower—its only redeeming feature, according to Aaron Byrd. Every time Fern catches sight of the city like this, she feels the same disbelief. That is my *home*. Her spirits rise and sink at once. It is not an easy place to call home, but she is impatient to be there.

Once, over dinner with Stavros, she asked him to describe the islands of his parents' childhood. He told her they weren't nearly so glamorous or picturesquely tended as the Greek islands she had seen; the houses were cramped, the beaches were stony, the air often stank of goat. In tiny yards, old cars rusted into not very classical ruins. "On some streets, you'd think you're in some tacky part of Queens, but that's not to say they don't have their beauty," said Stavros, "and all that sea. I don't really understand my father's contempt. But I didn't grow up there, thinking that's where I'd live forever. I go there and it's a novelty. The place is so small that everyone knows who I am and I'm treated like a prince. Who wouldn't like that?"

Fern nodded and said, "I've always wished I could live on an island."

Stavros looked up from his food and stared at her with bemusement.

"What?" she said, sensing a hint of mockery in his expression.

"You know, it's always amazed me how many perfectly intelligent people wish for things they already have."

"What do you mean?"

He touched her hand across the table. "You do live on an island."

She thought about that for a moment. She wanted to argue that it had no beaches, that the water wasn't swimmable, that there were too many people, that this wasn't the kind of island she meant. But then she thought of the Hudson River in fall and spring, the way it could smell like the open sea, splay the light so generously across the city's upturned face. The sound of gulls; the sense you had, like it or not, of proud isolation.

Mind what you love. For that matter, mind how you are loved.

As they clear the tollbooth to the Midtown Tunnel, there is a bout of breathless, aggressive snoring from the backseat. Fern and Fenno laugh. He says, "Listen: would you come over for dinner one night—after the chainsaw departs? With or without this Greek chap whose name I've forgotten."

"Stavros. He's American," she says. She feels herself blushing. "Yes, I'd love to—with or without him. We'll see about that part."

"That would be lovely," says Fenno, his eyes on the road as they enter the tunnel, swooping down into the dark, defying the weight of a river.

Splinters in the heart, invisibly and erratically painful: this is how Fern has thought of her accumulating sorrows. Impossible to expel or withdraw; if you're lucky, they slip out on their own. But perhaps they are more like the seeds inside a brightly patterned gourd, beyond germination but essential to the wholeness of the gourd itself. Without breaking its durable, ossified skin, you cannot remove them; sometimes they will clatter about and make themselves known. It's just the nature of things.

She closes her eyes: she is so tired yet so inflamed—with expectation, anxiety, with an impatient kind of thrill. Unexpectedly, she thinks of her favorite picture of Jonah, taken the day of their wedding: ducking confetti as they leave Helen Olitsky's exquisite garden, he wears a silky loose Hawaiian shirt (green waves crowded with surfers) and the dimpled boyish smile she never did stop loving. That day, she looked at that smile and meant every word of the promises she made. Despite the disillusionment that followed, she might have kept them for the rest of her life—at least in deed—but she will never know this for certain and cannot help wondering how she could possibly make such vows again without remorse. A clean slate, a fresh start: what erroneous notions. Yet why should they stop her from making other, equally risky pacts?

So here then is Stavros. She envisions him holding the hand of a very small boy as they walk along a modest, crooked lane hemmed in by plain lime-washed houses. Here are the clotheslines, just as he described them (pants, pants, nothing but pants) and the rusting cars and the goats, but all these homely sights are trumped by the primordial whites and piercing blues of Greece, the magnificent sea and sky she remembers from Paros and Delos, Delphi and the temple at Sounion.

That's when she recalls exactly where she will find him: in Washington Square, at a chess table across from his father. Afterward, he will almost certainly go to his parents' apartment, perhaps help his mother with her long-neglected garden. It would be harder to show up there. So then, their reunion will be anything but private; that will be an appropriate penance. Stavros may have been the one to travel abroad, but he is also the one who's been waiting, like his heroine Penelope, for Fern to come into port. Let the passing dog-walkers overhear her confession, let the chess geeks stare as she makes it clear how sorry she is, how ridiculous she was not to be certain. Let the curmudgeonly father look up from his bishop and his queen to appraise her body in disapproving wonder.

The Midtown Tunnel is a funny place, Fern has always thought. Approach the city by any other route—the lofty bridges, even the Holland and Lincoln Tunnels—and you will emerge knowing precisely where you are. But this route takes you in obliquely. You come up not into the city's tarnished brilliance but onto a road beneath a shabby underpass, gray shadows broken only by weedy trees of heaven and billboards promoting airline shuttles. You emerge onto a nondescript sidestreet—one that, every time, leaves you confused. The needle on your compass spins, because you are no longer able to see the city's outlines or even to see that you are on an island, a glamorous place in many eyes, but to yours—to Fern's and, she suspects, to those of the man beside her—a hard yet reassuring place to live.

When they stop at the first traffic light, she looks to either side and is suffused with a sense of comfort when she spots the sunlit avenues, the taller, more permanent trees. As they wait for the light to change, Fern and Fenno look at each other briefly. In this exchange, there is a kind of security, like the settling of an anchor on a harbor floor, and she reads on his face what she imagines to be the same recognition and pleasure she feels: *Here* we are—despite the delays, the confusion, and the shadows en route—at last, or for the moment, where we always intended to be.

ACKNOWLEDGMENTS

FOR THEIR SPONSORSHIP of prizes and grants that helped support and encourage my work, I thank the New York Foundation for the Arts, the *Chicago Tribune,* the *Bellingham Review, Literal Latté,* and the Pirate's Alley Faulkner Society (especially Joe DeSalvo, Rosemary James, and H. Paul and Michael X. St. Martin). For giving generously of their time and expertise to answer various research questions, I thank Dr. John Andrilli of Saint Vincents Medical Center in New York City and John and Christine Southern of C&J Medals in Reading, England. And for sharing with me their wee bit of Scotland (which I have embellished), I am happily indebted to my McKerrow cousins across the ocean, most of all Matthew, Gordon, and Allan.

For support of a more intimate kind, I thank my longtime companion, Dennis Cowley, and my parents, as well as Bette Slayton. Thanks must also go to the readers whose thoughtful responses helped me persevere: Lindsay Boyer, Shelley Henderson, Alec Lobrano, Daniel Menaker, Katherine Mosby, Nick Pappas, Tim and Jessalyn Peters, Mark Pothier, Lory Skwerer, Lisa Wederquist, James Wilcox . . . and the late Robert Trent, unforgettable and deeply missed.

Finally, for the enthusiasm, trust, and know-how that turned this story into a book, I am profoundly grateful to Dan Frank and, above all, to three remarkable women: my agent, Gail Hochman; my editor, Deborah Garrison; and Laura Mathews, loyal friend and muse.

ABOUT THE AUTHOR

JULIA GLASS was awarded a 2000 New York Foundation for the Arts fellowship in fiction writing and has won several prizes for her short stories, including three Nelson Algren Awards and the Tobias Wolff Award. "Collies," the first part of *Three Junes,* won the 1999 Pirate's Alley Faulkner Society Medal for Best Novella. She lives with her family in New York City, where she works as a freelance journalist and editor.

A NOTE ON THE TYPE

The text of this book was set in Garamond No. 3. It is not a true copy of any of the designs of Claude Garamond (ca. 1480–1561) but an adaptation of his types, which set the European standard for two centuries. It probably owes as much to the designs of Jean Jannon, a Protestant printer working in Sedan in the early seventeenth century, who had worked with Garamond's romans earlier, in Paris, but who was denied their use because of Catholic censorship. Jannon's matrices came into the possession of the Imprimerie Nationale, where they were thought to be by Garamond himself, and were so described when the Imprimerie revived the type in 1900. This particular version is based on an adaptation by Morris Fuller Benton.

Composed by MD Linocomp, Westminster, Maryland

Printed and bound by R. R. Donnelley & Sons, Harrisonburg, Virginia

Book design by M. Kristen Bearse